Outstanding praise for the novels of Holly Chamberlin!

## THE SEASON OF US

"A warm and witty tale. This heartfelt and emotional story will appeal to members of the Sandwich Generation or anyone who has had to set aside long-buried childhood resentments for the well-being of an aging parent. Fans of Elin Hilderbrand and Wendy Wax will adore this genuine exploration of family bonds, personal growth, and acceptance."
—*Booklist*

"Chamberlin successfully portrays a family at their best and worst as they struggle through their first holiday without a beloved husband and father and have to redefine their relationships."
—*Library Journal*

## THE BEACH QUILT

"Particularly compelling." —*The Pilot*

## SUMMER FRIENDS

"A thoughtful novel." —*ShelfAwareness*

"A great summer read." —*Fresh Fiction*

"A novel rich in drama and insights into what factors bring people together and, just as fatefully, tear them apart."
—*Portland Press Herald*

## THE FAMILY BEACH HOUSE

"Explores questions about the meaning of home, family dynamics and tolerance."
—*Bangor Daily News*

"An enjoyable summer read, but it's more. It is a novel for all seasons that adds to the enduring excitement of Ogunquit."
—*Maine Sunday Telegram*

"It does the trick as a beach book and provides a touristy taste of Maine's seasonal attractions."
—*Publishers Weekly*

Books by Holly Chamberlin

LIVING SINGLE

THE SUMMER OF US

BABYLAND

BACK IN THE GAME

THE FRIENDS WE KEEP

TUSCAN HOLIDAY

ONE WEEK IN DECEMBER

THE FAMILY BEACH HOUSE

SUMMER FRIENDS

LAST SUMMER

THE SUMMER EVERYTHING CHANGED

THE BEACH QUILT

SUMMER WITH MY SISTERS

SEASHELL SEASON

THE SEASON OF US

HOME FOR THE SUMMER

Published by Kensington Publishing Corporation

# Home for the Summer

## Holly Chamberlin

KENSINGTON BOOKS
www.kensingtonbooks.com

KENSINGTON BOOKS are published by

Kensington Publishing Corp.
119 West 40th Street
New York, NY 10018

All Kensington titles, imprints, and distributed lines are available at special quantity discounts for bulk purchases for sales promotion, premiums, fund-raising, educational, or institutional use.

Special book excerpts or customized printings can also be created to fit specific needs. For details, write or phone the office of the Kensington Sales Manager: Kensington Publishing Corp., 119 West 40th Street, New York, NY 10018. Attn. Sales Department. Phone: 1-800-221-2647.

Kensington and the K logo Reg. U.S. Pat. & TM Off.

eISBN-13: 978-1-4967-0155-8
eISBN-10: 1-4967-0155-0
First Kensington Electronic Edition: July 2017

ISBN-13: 978-1-4967-0154-1
ISBN-10: 1-4967-0154-2
First Kensington Trade Paperback Printing: July 2017

10 9 8 7 6 5 4 3 2 1

Printed in the United States of America

*As always, for Stephen.*
*And this time also for Françoise.*

# Acknowledgments

There would be no Holly without my incredible editor, John Scognamiglio, so all thanks and appreciation. I would also like to thank Deborah Eve Freedman for her inspiration. Her work with storytelling provides an enormously important service to those healing from trauma and loss. Plus she's really funny.

In memory of Douglas A. Mendini and Ann LaFarge, good friends and wonderful colleagues.

What we have once deeply loved we can never lose.
For all that we love deeply becomes a part of us.
—Helen Keller

# Prologue

"I can't believe we have to go home already. It's so unfair."

Frieda Braithwaite smiled at her older daughter across the breakfast table in the resort's main dining room. Bella's brownish-blond hair was pulled away from her face into a ponytail, emphasizing her high cheekbones and large blue eyes. "Bella," she said, "we've had seven days of fun in the sun. We've eaten fantastic food and danced until dawn. Well, almost. I don't think there's anything unfair about that. The only unfair thing is that your grandmother couldn't come with us."

"Poor Grandma." Ariel, Frieda's soon to be fifteen-year-old daughter, pushed a stray curl of hair from her face. It was a futile effort. Ariel's long red curls obeyed no one. "It would have been so great to be here with her. She was so excited about the trip. But I guess it's not easy to travel with a broken leg."

"And when you're confined to a wheelchair." Aaron Braithwaite shook his head. "If your grandmother were less of a heroic sort . . . But that's Ruby Hitchens for you."

Bella sighed dramatically. "It stinks about Grandma's accident, but I still wish we could stay here for a few more days. I mean, it could be forever before we get the chance to come back!"

"That doesn't make sense," Ariel pointed out. "But I know

what you mean. This really was an awesome vacation. Thanks, Mom and Dad."

Frieda looked to her husband with fondness. "It's your father who deserves the thanks. He was the one who moved heaven and earth to get this week away from the firm."

Aaron put his hand over his heart and bowed his head. "I'll happily accept praise and adulation, but don't forget it was your mother's idea to make Bella's sixteenth birthday into something really special. And next year," he said, turning to Ariel, "we'll do something really special for your sixteenth birthday."

But Ariel didn't seem to have heard her father; she had her nose in the guidebook she had started studying weeks before the vacation. "Oh, wow," she said suddenly. "I don't know how I missed this! There's a museum of Jamaican culture in the next town. It says they've got pieces dating back to pre-Columbian days. OMG, they even have stuff from the 'Redware people.' That's before the Taino tribes settled here. And they've got artifacts from the Spanish invasion and the English invasion and pieces from the Maroon culture, too. Please can we go?" she asked, looking up from the guidebook.

Bella laughed and rolled her eyes. "Ariel, you are such a dork. How can anyone possibly be interested in looking at a bunch of dusty old clay pots?"

"I doubt the pots are dusty," Ariel said matter-of-factly. "They're probably kept in glass cases to prevent people touching them. And the cases probably have a specially controlled atmosphere to help with preservation. And I'm sure there are lots of other things on display besides pots."

Bella rolled her eyes again and reached for her juice. "Yeah," she said. "Like broken pots."

Frieda looked at her watch. "I don't know, Ariel," she said. "We have to be at the airport by noon to return the rental car and catch our flight. It's already almost nine thirty."

"Wait a minute. There might be time," Aaron said, checking his own watch. "When does the museum open?"

Ariel glanced at her guidebook. "Nine."

"And the airport is only about forty minutes from here. Frieda?"

Frieda shook her head. "We'd be calling it pretty tight, Aaron."

"Nonsense," Aaron argued. "Look, clearly Bella has no interest—"

"Uh, yeah!"

"So why don't you two stay here, catch some last rays, and I'll take Ariel to the museum. The luggage is in the trunk and I've already checked us out, so that's no worry. I'll text you when we're on our way back and then we'll head right out to the airport."

Frieda looked at Ariel's face, shining with excitement. She had been such a good sport about coming to Jamaica even though Ariel and the sun didn't play well together and, with her keen interest in history and art, she was more suited to galleries stuffed with antiquities than to sunbathing and surfing. And Aaron was a responsible man; if he thought they could make it to the museum and back in plenty of time for the family to catch their flight home to Massachusetts, then why object any further?

"Sure," Frieda said. "Sounds like a plan. You two have fun."

"We will!" Ariel jumped up from her seat. "Thanks, Mom. I'm so psyched."

"Then we'll be on our way," Aaron said, rising from his own chair.

"Be careful and don't forget to drive on the left side of the road."

"You worry too much, Frieda." Aaron smiled and leaned down to give his wife a kiss on the lips.

Frieda, who had just taken a bite of toast, gave him her cheek instead. *I am so lucky,* she thought as she watched her husband and daughter walk out of the dining room hand in hand. *I am so lucky to have this beautiful family.*

"Sometimes I don't know how Ariel and I are related," Bella said when they were alone. "Pots? Seriously? What's interesting about a pot?"

"You know," Frieda said, "we'll probably be going to Paris next year for Ariel's sixteenth. I'm thinking you might want to get used to the idea of looking at old pots and oil paintings and religious statuary and historic buildings."

"Blah." Bella shuddered. "At least that's a whole year away."

When they had finally finished breakfast—Bella decided to

have another helping of scrambled eggs from the buffet—Frieda and her daughter left the dining room and settled in the comfortable open-air lounge not far from the resort's reception area. Potted palm trees stood between prettily cushioned chaises and low tables made of glossy rattan. Bella put on her sunglasses and buried herself in her iPhone. Knowing Bella's obsession with the Internet, Frieda had made sure that the resort was equipped with Wi-Fi before booking a reservation. An unplugged Bella was not something either of her parents wanted to be around for more than a few hours. As for Frieda, she turned to reading Iris Murdoch's *The Sea, the Sea* on her Kindle.

Absorbed in the novel, lulled by the warm breeze and the sound of the gently swaying palms, Frieda was oblivious to the passing of time until a child's gleeful shout brought her to the moment. She checked her watch. It was almost eleven. *Aaron and Ariel really should have returned by now,* she thought with just a trace of annoyance. *If they missed their flight . . .* Frieda took her phone from her bag and sent Aaron a text. *Where r u?* He didn't reply. Well, Frieda thought, maybe the museum was a dead zone, and she knew that Aaron refused to text while driving, so if they were on the way back to the hotel . . .

Rapidly Frieda typed Ariel's cell phone number and sent the same message she had sent to her husband. But Ariel didn't reply, either.

"Who are you texting?"

Frieda looked up from her phone to find Bella watching her.

"Your sister," she said. "But she isn't answering."

Bella snorted. "Ariel is such an airhead. You know how she's always losing her phone. She probably dropped it somewhere and doesn't even know it's gone."

"Be fair," Frieda said. "She doesn't lose her phone. She just misplaces it."

"Whatevs. Try Dad."

"I did," Frieda told her. "But you know he won't answer if he's driving." *But why wouldn't he ask Ariel to reply?* Frieda wondered. A sharp sliver of worry stabbed at her belly.

"Well, they'd better be on the way back," Bella said. "I want to be home in time to watch *The Bachelor* tonight. If we miss our flight because of some boring old museum I will so kill Ariel."

"We won't miss our flight," Frieda said. "Don't be dramatic."

Bella looked back to her phone, but Frieda couldn't resume her reading. In spite of the fact that Aaron thought she worried too much, she wasn't a person prone to panic. Still, she didn't like that neither Aaron nor Ariel had responded to her message. Their silence didn't feel right.

"I'll be back in a minute," she said, rising from the comfortable chair and moving out of her daughter's hearing. She called Aaron's cell phone; when he didn't pick up she left a message on his voice mail. "Hey, it's me. Where are you guys? It's getting late. Call me." She then called Ariel's cell phone; when Ariel didn't pick up, Frieda left a message on her voice mail, this one delivered in a voice that was just a little tense. "It's Mom. Please call me, okay?"

Frieda could feel her face constricting in a frown as she walked back to where Bella was waiting.

"You called them, didn't you?" Bella asked, removing her sunglasses.

"Yes," Frieda admitted. "But the calls went to voice mail."

"We are so going to miss our flight!" her daughter complained loudly. "It's after eleven! Why don't we just meet them at the airport? Send Dad another text and tell him we've gone ahead."

"They'll be here," Frieda said firmly. Of course they will, she thought. Of course they will. There's the potluck dinner at the Andersons' tomorrow night. They'll want to see the pictures of our vacation. And Aaron's got that big presentation on Friday and Ariel has a violin solo in the school's concert on Wednesday. Of course they'll be back. They have to be.

"It's eleven fifteen, Mom." Bella was pacing now, her purple flip-flops slapping the floor.

Maybe, Frieda thought, they should leave for the airport. She could give a message to the clerk at the reception desk for Aaron and Ariel and entrust their plane tickets to her as well. She could leave another voice-mail message telling Aaron she and Bella had gone ahead. But what then? She couldn't get on the plane not knowing what had become of her husband and daughter. *What can I do?* she asked herself. *What is there I can do?*

"Mom," Bella moaned. "Come on. We could get a cab or maybe the resort bus could take us. If we don't leave now . . ."

Frieda shook her head and stared down at her phone as if willing it to ring.

"You don't think anything could have, you know, happened to them?"

Frieda looked up at her daughter, whose expression had suddenly and drastically morphed from one of annoyance to one of concern. "Of course not," she said with a lame attempt at a smile. "They probably just got caught in traffic."

But by eleven thirty Frieda was sick to her stomach with fear. It was now too late to get to the airport in time for their flight. She fought back the panic she was afraid might overwhelm her. She had to keep a clear head for Bella's sake.

"I'm going to talk to the clerk," she said, her throat dry. Bella followed her to the reception desk, where Frieda briefly explained the situation.

"I'm not sure what I can do," the clerk replied kindly. "I'm sorry."

A burst of loud laughter followed by voices speaking in the local patois caused Frieda to flinch. She just wanted to be back home, safe and sound in their house on Maple Drive. The Braithwaite family. All four of them. She wanted them to be home.

"Can you call the museum?" Frieda pleaded. "Maybe they're still there. Maybe my husband just lost track of time."

"I'm scared, Mom," Bella said, her voice trembling. "Dad never loses track of time. He's the most punctual guy ever."

Frieda said nothing. She couldn't. She stared at the young woman as she placed a call to the museum. She listened to the clerk's questions and to her maddeningly uninformative replies. After a moment, the clerk hung up.

"Yes," she said. "An American man wearing a blue shirt and glasses and a girl with red hair were there, but they left about a half hour ago. Would that be your husband and daughter?"

Frieda nodded and swallowed hard. "How long would it take to drive back to the resort?" she asked.

The clerk shrugged. "At this time of the day, ten minutes?"

Bella grabbed her mother's arm. "Mom, what are we going to do? Something's happened to them; I know it!"

Mindlessly, Frieda shook her head. Something has happened. Something has happened. And then the glass doors of the reception area slid open and two uniformed police officers walked into the lobby.

"Oh no," Frieda murmured, grabbing Bella's hand. "Please God, no."

"Mom!" Bella cried as the officers walked toward them, their faces set. "Mom! What's going on?"

"Mrs. Braithwaite?" the taller of the two police officers asked.

Frieda could only nod. She was aware of little whimpering sounds coming from Bella and of a roaring in her own ears. She was vaguely aware that the clerk had come out from behind the desk to stand just behind them.

"Mrs. Braithwaite," the officer went on, his voice gentle and low. "I'm afraid I have some bad news for you. Perhaps you would like to sit down."

# Chapter 1

Ruby Hitchens stood at the living room window of her house on Kinders Lane, awaiting the arrival of her daughter and grand-daughter. She glanced down at her watch, a serviceable Timex she had had for more years than she could remember. It was almost two o'clock. They should be arriving soon.

And for the first time ever Frieda and Bella would be staying with Ruby for the entire summer. It was imperative that they did because just before the one-year anniversary of the car accident that had killed Aaron and Ariel, Bella had suffered a serious set-back. Every advance she had made toward happiness had stalled. She suddenly refused to see her grief counselor. She suddenly stopped confiding in her mother. Her interest in the world around her had waned alarmingly. Frieda was at her wit's end. Ruby was not. She had summoned her family home.

"We can't let this situation go on," Ruby had told her daughter. "Bella is slipping away from us and we're allowing it. Maybe to-gether we can prevent a disaster. We have to believe that we can."

Ruby shifted and her right leg protested. "Stupid leg," she mut-tered. Well, it wasn't the leg that was stupid; in fact, there was nothing stupid about the incident that had resulted in her right tibia being smashed to bits a little over a year ago. It had happened very early one morning. A fifteen-year-old patient had suddenly gone wild, flying from his bed, tearing out his IV drip and monitor attachments, and thrashing angrily at whoever got in his path. Ruby had joined two other nurses trying to subdue the boy before he could hurt himself, but he managed to break free. Ruby and her colleagues pursued him and Ruby managed to catch the boy just as he tore open a door at the end of the hall. And that's when it happened. The boy, his eyes wide with fear, roughly pushed her away and she had fallen through the doorway and down that never-ending staircase.

It wasn't the patient's fault. A bad reaction to one of the medications he had been given had caused the brief but terrifying event. He had little recollection of the episode afterward and had been released a few days later. Ruby hadn't been so lucky. Two surgeries; three months of putting absolutely no weight on the leg, which meant getting around in a wheelchair and with generous and uncomplaining assistance from her beau, George Hastings; a slow graduation to a walker and then crutches; and, finally, a cane. Now, sixteen months later, Ruby walked unaided but with a slight limp that she suspected would be hers for life.

A limp she could live with. What Ruby sometimes felt she couldn't live with was the unreasonable but no less painful guilt she felt about having missed that fateful vacation in Jamaica the previous April. If she hadn't intervened with that disturbed patient she wouldn't have broken her leg. If she hadn't broken her leg she wouldn't have had to stay home while Frieda, Aaron and the girls went off to celebrate Bella's sixteenth birthday in style. If she had been in Jamaica with them maybe she could have . . . Could have what, Ruby thought for the thousandth, the millionth time. Could have prevented the car accident that had taken Aaron's and her sweet Ariel's lives?

"The little cricket on the hearth has stopped chirping," Ruby whispered aloud, "and the sweet sunshiny presence has vanished, leaving silence and shadow." It was a paraphrase of a few lines from *Little Women*, one of her favorite books. Like Beth, Ariel had been one of those special people whose enormous influence was only fully realized in her absence.

And indeed Ariel's favorite place to be in her grandmother's home had been curled up in one of the armchairs in front of the living room fireplace, a big stone structure with a wide mantel and deep hearth. The house surrounding this magnificent fireplace had been built in three stages, starting in 1834. From what scant records there were at the town hall, Ruby had managed to estimate that around 1872 an addition had been added and then, around thirty years later, a new kitchen and, for the first time, a bathroom. There had been a barn on the property at one point but that was long gone; in the mid-1980s the then owners had replaced it with a two-car garage.

After so many years of living in cramped spaces, whether it was an apartment over a store in town or a cottage behind a landlord's spacious three-story home, Ruby gloried in wandering the many rooms of the farmhouse—nine in all if you counted the mudroom off the kitchen and Ruby did. She gloried in knowing that it all belonged to her and her alone. If there was little cash to leave to her family at the end of what would hopefully be a long life (she was only sixty-four and gunning for another twenty years) then at least there was this structure, solid and tangible, to gift to the future.

There were hooked or braided rugs in every room, many made locally. The aforementioned stone fireplace kept the house heated during the autumn and winter months. The kitchen was painted a cheery yellow and there were lacy white curtains on the window over the sink. There were four bedrooms on the second floor. Ruby's bedroom was decorated in shades of soothing blues and greens. The second bedroom was a bit smaller; the center of attention there was a beautiful white coverlet with matching white curtains. The third bedroom was painted a rosy pink. In the smallest bedroom, the one with a pullout couch, an enormous wreath of pinecones hung over the bed, a gift from the grateful mother of one of Ruby's patients.

Ruby had found most of the furniture at antique shops and yard sales. Phil Morse, her best and oldest friend and a master of home decoration, had advised her in the art of haggling so that even after the purchase of major items like the pine table for the kitchen Ruby's budget hadn't suffered unduly. Even though there was nothing the house really needed in the way of essentials, Ruby still enjoyed cruising flea markets and antique malls for the odd "must have" item, like the bright orange Fiesta Ware vase she used as a container for wild flowers and the milk glass salt and pepper shakers just like the ones Ruby's mother had owned.

In short, Ruby felt she couldn't be happier or more content living where she did, in this lovely house in Yorktide, Maine. Well, one thing might make her happier she thought, looking again at her watch. It was ten minutes past two. She hoped there hadn't been an accident—*Stop it*, Ruby told herself. *Don't let that happen. Don't let fear take over, not after all you've been through.* Not, she thought, when there were so many challenges to face, like the matter of George, that wonderful man who had presented her with a dilemma she wasn't sure she had the strength to solve.

Just then Ruby spied her daughter's car as it turned onto Kinders Lane and breathed a sigh of relief. She hadn't been seriously worried; she hadn't really thought there had been an accident. Still, the sight of Frieda's serviceable Subaru pulling into the driveway was very, very welcome.

There was a lot riding on this summer, Ruby thought, hurrying to the front door, most important, her granddaughter Bella's future. And that meant the future of the entire family. What was left of it.

# Chapter 2

"Bella, aren't you hungry?" Frieda asked. Her daughter's voracious appetite was well known; even in the weeks after the accident she had shown interest in eating while Frieda had barely been able to tolerate the cups of strong, hot tea people seemed to keep forcing on her. But since the anniversary of Aaron's and Ariel's deaths in April, Bella's progress toward a place of peace seemed to have come to a halt. No, Frieda thought. What had happened was more like a reversal, not simply a halt.

"Not really," Bella said, pushing another bit of her dinner around the plate.

"Eat something," Ruby said. "No wasting away allowed in my house. Besides, I'll take it as an insult to my cooking if you don't eat."

Bella gave a ghost of a smile and took a bite of the pasta and calamari Frieda's mother had prepared.

"So," Ruby announced suddenly. "Now is as good a time as any to discuss house rules."

Frieda was surprised. "You've never set house rules before," she said. "I mean, besides the obvious like 'don't forget to turn off the burners on the stove when you're done using them.'"

"True," her mother told her. "But you've never spent more than two weeks at a time under this roof. You've always been more my guests than my roomies. This summer it's different. If the three of us are going to cohabitate peacefully for the next few months we each need to help out around the house. We'll take turns making dinner as well as cleaning up after it, and that means not only loading the dishwasher and washing the pots and pans and knives but also wiping the table and sweeping the floor. Oh, and scrubbing the cutting board. We can't have one of us coming down with salmonella poisoning."

Bella, who had never shown the least bit of interest in housekeeping, didn't protest her grandmother's directions, as Frieda might have expected her to. But things were different now. Bella was different. They all were.

"And Frieda," Ruby went on, "you can share the grocery shopping with me and running whatever odd errand needs to be run. George has been handling most of the yard work since my accident—stupid leg—but he might need assistance at some point. He's got a home of his own, after all."

"Sure, Mom," Frieda said. "Whatever I can do to help." After all, she thought, her mother had offered a lifeline to her daughter and granddaughter this summer. Without Ruby's assistance Frieda wasn't sure she could help Bella in the way she needed to be helped—whatever way that was. "Whatever either of us can do," she added.

Her mother nodded. "Good. Bella, you'll need to keep your room clean and tidy, which means changing your sheets once a week and vacuuming the rug and dusting the furniture. And we can each do our own laundry so there won't be any mix-ups resulting in shrunken clothes, et cetera. I'm partial to my cotton sweaters staying in one piece."

Bella still didn't protest these additional chores, but Frieda thought her expression betrayed the slightest bit of rebellion. If that was true, it was a good thing. Bella once again showing some spirit.

"And as for Bella's paying job—" Ruby began.

"A job?" Bella's voice held an undeniable note of annoyance. "Why do I have to get a job?"

At last, Frieda thought gratefully. A bit of resistance! "Mom," Frieda said, "I'm not sure that's really necessary. Bella needs time to—"

"It will be good for her to get out of the house and interact with people," Ruby said firmly. Then she turned to Bella. "I've arranged for you to work at Phil's shop twenty hours a week, more if you want the hours. He'll set your schedule."

Bella laid her fork on the table. "But I know nothing about curtains and rugs and stuff like that," she said.

"You'll learn. Phil's a good teacher and he's more patient than most people."

Frieda watched her daughter's face closely as the brief spirit of protest faded.

"All right," Bella said quietly. "May I be excused?"

"Yes," Frieda said before her mother could usurp her authority.

Bella got up from the table and a moment later Frieda heard her climbing the stairs to her room. She had barely touched her meal.

"Mom," Frieda said, "don't you think you're being too tough on Bella?"

"No, I don't. Don't bite my head off, Frieda, but I think you might be indulging Bella's grief by not urging her into more activity. Have you encouraged her to start studying for her driver's license again?"

"No. Back in March she said she was thinking about it, but then she told me she was still too scared to get behind the wheel. She said that if her own father—"

"I know what she said," Ruby interrupted. "But she's going to have to get past the fear sometime if she's to be independent."

"She's doing all right on her bike," Frieda protested, but she knew her mother was right. The crushing fear of driving that had come over Bella since the accident had to be conquered. At least Bella found riding in a car tolerable. That was something, wasn't it?

"And when she wants to go somewhere too far away for her to cycle there, what then? Is she going to rely on you forever? Are you going to allow that?"

"Mom," Frieda protested. "Don't be dramatic. It's only been a little over a year."

"And what about Colleen, her grief counselor?" Frieda's mother pressed on. "They were doing good work together from what I could see. Have you told Bella she needs to go back to seeing Colleen?"

"I've encouraged her to go back, yes."

"But have you forced the issue?"

"No," Frieda admitted.

"You can, you know. You're her mother; you're allowed to tell her what to do." Ruby sighed. "I know you don't want to hurt her, but I'm afraid you might not be doing what's ultimately in her best interest by, well, by letting her off the hook. It's not okay that she not engage."

There was truth in what Ruby said; Frieda couldn't deny that. Still . . . "It's just that I'm so afraid of pushing her too hard or of alienating her to the extent that she'll never come back to me. To us."

"I know." Her mother reached across the table and took her hand. "I do. And I'm sorry if I came across as a bit heavy-handed just now. I'm not opposed to coddling. We all need to be protected from the misery of life at times. But only at times, or else we become quivering masses of uselessness."

Frieda managed a smile. "Charlie, my grief counselor, says that avoidance has its place in healing, but it's a very small place. It's sometimes hard to remember that."

"Smart man." Ruby released Frieda's hand and sat back.

Frieda sighed and rubbed her forehead. "Bella and I were a comfort to each other after the accident, Mom. What happened to make it all go wrong? I'm so afraid Bella's setback isn't only about the feelings the anniversary of the accident brought on. I'm so afraid that I relied too heavily on her this past year and didn't give her enough of the care she needed. Maybe she just can't bear the burden of my grief any longer. And if that's the case, how can I change things? What if I've caused irreparable damage to my child by being so selfish?"

Ruby shook her head. "No. I saw how well Bella was doing. She was making real progress. Whatever happened to send Bella slinking back into the darkness had nothing to do with you; I'm sure of it."

Frieda smiled ruefully. "How can you be?"

"All right then, I'm as sure of your innocence as I can be."

"Thanks," Frieda said. "I guess. By the way, where's George? I thought he'd be here."

"I asked him not to join us for dinner," her mother told her. "I thought it would be better for the three of us to be alone this first night."

"Was he okay with that?"

Her mother smiled. "George is okay with everything. Sometimes I think he's too good for me."

"Mom, you completely deserve someone who treats you with the respect and love George shows you. Believe it."

Her mother didn't reply but pushed back her chair and stood. "I'll clear away the dishes tonight. You had a long drive. Why don't you just relax this evening?"

"Thanks, Mom," Frieda said gratefully. "I am tired. And Mom? Thanks for asking us to spend the summer with you. I know our being here might cause some disruption to your life."

Ruby smiled. "You're my family. I wouldn't have it any other way."

# Chapter 3

It was after eleven and Bella had been up since seven that morning, but as tired as she was, she just couldn't sleep. At the moment she was sitting on the edge of her bed, lights off, staring at the closed door of the room with the rosy pink walls. She knew this room so well. The whole house, really. It was welcoming, almost like a friend.

Unlike the new house back in Warden where she and her mother had lived since the previous August. There was a sense of anonymity about the place; it almost felt as if they were living in a hotel room, that the house wasn't really theirs and might never be. Her mother had sold some of their furniture; other pieces were in storage. Only a few photos of Bella's father and sister were on display in the living room. In Bella's room there were no photos at all. And nowhere were there signs of the Braithwaites as they had been: no scuff marks from the times Bella would forget to take off her soccer cleats before going into the house; no horizontal pencil marks on the wall next to the fridge where her father had charted Bella's and Ariel's growth; no bit of kitchen counter stained yellow, evidence of the time her mother had spilled a jar of curry sauce; no strands of Ariel's long red hair in the brush on the bathroom sink. The odd thing was that Bella found some comfort in the anonymity of the new house. At least, she found it more tolerable than she had found living in their old house, where the memories were loud and painful and constant.

It was odd, Bella thought, but here, at another house so full of the past, she was okay with staying in the room she had once shared with Ariel. She could easily have moved into the smallest bedroom. There was a couch there that folded out to a bed and a closet where she could hang her clothes when she remembered to hang them.

Bella glanced over her shoulder at the empty bed by the window and then turned back to face the door. Maybe she could ask her grandmother if Phil or George could move the bed out of the room. Or maybe she could just do it herself. There was a screwdriver in the junk drawer in the kitchen. She could take apart the frame and . . . Then what? How was she supposed to get the mattress and box spring down the stairs without disaster?

Whatever. The bed could stay. She would try not to look at it. Maybe she would just pile all of her clothes and stuff on top of it. That might prevent her from seeing in her mind's eye Ariel's gorgeous red hair spread out on the pillow, her knees tucked up against her chest, her hands folded under her cheek in her sleep.

Bella sighed. It had been so much fun sharing this room with her sister. Sometimes at night, with the rest of the house asleep, they would sneak out to the Jernigans' property, on which there was a natural spring. Ariel had liked the sound of the spring bubbling in the dark. Bella remembered her sister telling her how the early Christians often built shrines to saints on sites that had been sacred to the pagans, so that the sites—like natural springs—remained incredible sources of spiritual power and belief through the centuries.

"You really find this interesting?" Bella would ask when Ariel went on about old stuff, which she often did.

"Yeah," Ariel would say. "It's fascinating. It's our history."

"Whose history?"

"Ours. Human beings."

Sometimes Bella had wondered how Ariel had put up with her

sister being so stupid. But the answer to that question was easy. It was love, pure and simple. The love shared by siblings, which could be far stronger than even the greatest love between friends. On some level Bella had always known that, but it had taken Ariel's dying to fully open her eyes to the depth of the bond they had shared. You don't know what you have till it's gone. Whoever had first said that was so very right. Bella had lost not only a sister. She had lost the other half of herself.

Bella got up from her bed and went to the window. There was little to see by the one small light near the door to the mudroom and the sky was moonless. She leaned her head against the cool glass, closed her eyes, and remembered those final days with her sister. Even though Ariel hadn't gone with Bella to the resort's disco or to play beach volleyball—Ariel hadn't liked dance music and she was hopelessly bad at sports—they had had such a good time together. One night they tried curried goat. "Could use more Scotch bonnets," Ariel calmly noted as Bella wiped sweat from her face and reached for her water. They went shopping together. They went to a reggae concert one afternoon. They took long walks on the beach during which they talked about all sorts of stuff.

In short, they had been as they always had, the very best of friends. Then, Bella thought for possibly the millionth time, I had to go and ruin everything at the last minute by calling Ariel a dork for wanting to poke around in a dusty old museum. It was only a joke, but words hurt, no matter how innocent the intention behind them. So why had she said it? What was wrong with her?

And worse, even though Ariel hadn't been there to hear it, Bella had told her mother she would kill her sister if she was the cause of the family having to take a later flight home. It was a horrible thing to have said, even in jest—you would kill someone because they made you miss a television show?—and the words haunted Bella. Since the anniversary of the accident those damning words had never been far from her mind.

Bella turned from the window. Wearily, she lay down on her bed and pulled the fresh cotton sheet over her legs. Her mother seemed to think it would be helpful in some way if they lived with her mother for the summer, but in what way it would be helpful Bella had no idea. What was going to happen or not happen here at her grandmother's house in Yorktide that could or could not happen back in Warden? Bella turned on her side and tucked her hands under her cheek as Ariel used to do. She guessed that only time would reveal the answer to that question.

# Chapter 4

The house was profoundly quiet, but through the open window Frieda could hear the mournful hooting of an owl. She hadn't turned off the light yet. It was comforting somehow to look at the colorful bits of sea glass arranged on the windowsill. It was one of the simple pleasures of being at home with her mother. And some feeling deep down made Frieda believe that if healing and happiness were ever to be found again it would be at the house on Kinders Lane.

Frieda would never forget the housewarming party her mother had given not long after she had settled in. Ruby had been downright jubilant that afternoon, leading tours of the house, bragging about the bargains she had gotten on various bits of furniture, offering endless platters of appetizers to her guests. After all the years of hard work, self-sacrifice, and sometimes frighteningly real financial struggle, Ruby Hitchens had heroically achieved her goal of owning her own home.

And it wasn't the first time that home was acting as a refuge for family, Frieda thought. Last Christmas without Aaron and Ariel back in Warden had been awful; around every metaphorical corner there was a memory of happy holidays spent as a family of four. And being in the new, much smaller house had added to the sense of loss and desolation.

"Let's get out of here, Mom," Bella had said fiercely one afternoon. "I can't stand it in this place."

*Neither,* Frieda had thought, *can I.* So on Christmas Eve they had packed up the car and made their escape to Yorktide for the remainder of the school break. If the days under Ruby Hitchens's roof hadn't been joyful, they had at least offered some degree of peace. And if memories of past Christmases had followed Frieda to Maine, at least they were happy memories.

Unlike other memories that were tinged with regret. Frieda turned from the window and walked over to her bed. How oblivious we are to the potential tragedies just around the corner, she thought as she lay down. How blithely we waste our lives. What haunted Frieda most about that last morning of her husband's life was the missed opportunity for a last real kiss with the person she loved best in the world. Why had she given Aaron her cheek? He wouldn't have minded if there was a crumb on her lip. But it was too late now.

There would be no more kisses. There would be no more shared meals. Aaron would never again bring his wife a cup of coffee in bed. Who knew that after the death of a loved one, simple daily activities such as making coffee could cause such confusion and disorientation? That first morning back in Warden after the accident Frieda had found herself staring at the jar of coffee beans and the grinder, momentarily stymied. How to begin? How many ground beans made how many cups of coffee?

It had taken real strength of will to brew that pot of coffee, the first of many reminders that focusing on real-world tasks was a very important part of dealing with death. You might want to retreat to your bed and pull the covers over your head, but you couldn't, not for long, not when there were decisions to be made, bills to be paid, a child to comfort, and your own health to maintain. All on your own.

Frieda shifted under the cool cotton sheets. She never thought she would be a single parent as her mother had been. Frieda was well aware of all Ruby had sacrificed to raise a child with virtually no financial support from the child's father. Steve Hitchens. The man who defined ne'er-do-well more precisely than anyone else Frieda had ever known.

Ironically, the situation in which Frieda found herself, raising a child on her own, was all her fault. She had been the one to push for the idea of a big family vacation during spring break. Aaron had been reluctant to take the time off from the architecture firm where he had recently become a junior partner, but he had good-naturedly given in to Frieda's persuasions. "Sure," he had said. "Let's do it."

And that had been that. Decision made. Lives irrevocably altered.

Frieda yawned and turned out the light on her bedside table. She was so very tired. Though she knew it was a futile gesture, she patted the empty space next to her in the crazy hope that she would find her husband by her side.

# Chapter 5

"I took one look at Bella this afternoon," Ruby told George over the phone that evening, "at her sad eyes and wan complexion, and I felt furious all over again with my ex-husband for failing our family. Not once has he been there for us when we needed him, like now, when his daughter and his granddaughter are suffering. Where is he now? Who knows! He's never even met either of his granddaughters! And it isn't because Frieda's withheld the girls from him. It's his choice to be absent."

"And his loss in the end," George reminded her.

Ruby sighed. *And yet,* she thought, *I continue to take Steve's calls. And I continue to love him somewhere deep down inside.* "George," she said, "thank you for listening."

"You're in mourning and grief is hard work. I'm glad I can be here for you. Still, I don't have to remind you that dredging up old hurts doesn't accomplish anything of value."

"I know. All it does is wear me out."

"Try to get some sleep," George advised. "I'll pick you up at eight o'clock tomorrow morning. Your appointment with the eye doctor is at eight thirty, right?"

"Yes. He said it would take about twenty minutes for the pupils to dilate. Bring a book to read."

George laughed. "I'll have my iPhone. I'll keep plenty occupied."

"You and that iPhone! You're an addict, George. Good night."

"Good night, Ruby," he said. "Sleep tight."

Ruby changed into her pajamas, brushed out her thick shoulder-length hair, only sparsely threaded with gray, and crawled into bed. She was very lucky to have George Hastings in her life. For years after Steve had left Ruby and their eleven-year-old daughter she had been totally focused on raising Frieda, getting her nursing degree, and building a career. There had been no time for men—at least, that's what Ruby had told herself. In reality her heart had been so badly broken by Steve's infidelities and eventual defection that she simply refused to risk having it broken again. Mostly she was fine being on her own and when periods of loneliness arose, like, for example, when Frieda became a teen and began to spend more time with her friends and then when Frieda married and moved to Massachusetts, Ruby had managed to do a very good job of quashing the loneliness with extra shifts at the hospital and a renewed dedication to her beloved book group, The Page Turners.

Then, not long after Ruby had turned sixty, along came George Hastings. They met one afternoon in the hospital cafeteria shortly after George had started working in administration; he had moved from New Hampshire to Yorktide to take care of his ageing widowed father. Being divorced with no children, George was perfectly placed to be Walter's caregiver. "I'm just returning the favor," George had explained. "Dad's been a good father to me and now it's my turn to be a good son to him."

What began as a chatty companionship over weak coffee and uninspired sandwiches slowly became something more, a friendship Ruby came to cherish. After about six months, George invited Ruby to dinner. "Someplace other than this cafeteria," he said. "Someplace where the food doesn't come wrapped in plastic and the coffee actually has a kick." Ruby said no. George said, "Why not?" Ruby realized she had no good answer. She liked George. And what was the harm in going to dinner? Everyone had to eat. So she said yes.

To Ruby's immense surprise, a romantic relationship blossomed, one strong enough to override the fear of having her heart trampled on again. George loved Ruby and she loved him. He had been a rock when she broke her leg and then, only weeks later, when Aaron and Ariel were killed. Through the dismal days after the double funeral George had been there not only for Ruby but also for Frieda and Bella, who both considered him family. And Phil had long ago given George his seal of approval, something not lightly bestowed.

Ruby sighed. Everything had been just perfect until Walter died back in early May and George had dropped the proverbial bombshell. "I want us to be together all the time, Ruby," he said one evening when they were sitting on the front porch after dinner. "For the rest of our lives. Will you do me the honor of becoming my wife? Will you have me as your husband?"

The proposal was endearingly old-fashioned and completely unexpected. People their age didn't need to get married. She and George weren't going to be having babies and raising families. Neither had parents left to disappoint or to anger. They were each economically independent. As a couple they were perfectly fine the way they were, not legally bound but emotionally committed.

"It might be best to wait until after the summer to . . ." Ruby had replied quickly. "To talk about our future. Frieda and Bella will be here soon and they plan on staying until the end of August when Bella needs to be back for the start of the new semester."

"Oh," George had said, sitting back in his chair. "I didn't know that."

Ruby felt a rush of shame when she remembered how she had lied to George. She hadn't yet approached Frieda with her idea, one she did indeed feel strongly about. "We just decided earlier today," she said. Another lie. "You know that Bella's been having difficulties since the anniversary of the accident and I thought that it would be best if we were all together this summer."

"Yes, of course," George said promptly. "It's a good idea. And I wouldn't have mentioned our getting married just now if I had known. I'm sorry, Ruby. But since the idea is out there, will you promise to give it some thought when you can?"

Ruby had promised, but she hadn't yet given George's proposal the respect it deserved. And yet George continued to love and support her. *While I use my daughter and granddaughter as an excuse for not confronting my fear of marriage . . .*

Well, Ruby thought, she might have bought herself some time by having her family under her roof for the next few months, but the matter couldn't be avoided forever, not if she cared for George, and she did. Ruby turned off the lamp on the nightstand and settled gratefully against the pillows. She had always felt that if there was an intelligence orchestrating the lives of humans, sleep was one of its greatest gifts.

# Chapter 6

"You know you don't have to ring," Frieda said as she let George into the house at five minutes to eight the next morning. "Just because Bella and I are here doesn't mean you're ostracized."

George smiled and gave Frieda a warm hug. "Just being polite. Where's Bella this fine morning?"

"She's not up yet," Frieda told him as she led him to the kitchen. "She's been sleeping late these days, but that's going to have to change once she starts working at Phil's."

"Maybe he'll give her afternoon hours," George suggested.

"Nope." Ruby turned from the sink, where she had been rinsing out her coffee cup. "Her hours will be at his convenience. Bella needs to be pushed. It's the only way she'll come back to us."

Frieda fervently wanted to believe her mother. For as long as she could remember Ruby Hitchens had seemed so sure of herself, so convinced in her beliefs, so settled in her determination. There had to be things that worried or puzzled her. There had to be, but Frieda didn't know what those things were.

"Frieda," George said. "I almost forgot. Jack Tennant asked for you the other day."

Frieda smiled. She had gone through grammar and high school a year behind Jack Tennant. He had been one of the nicest boys in

Yorktide and was probably now one of the nicest men. "How is he?" Frieda asked. "I haven't seen him in quite a while."

"He seems good. For a while there after Veronica died we were all pretty worried about him, but . . ." George smiled sympathetically. "Well, you know better than anyone what he went through."

Frieda nodded. Though Jack had lost his wife to cancer and she had lost her husband in a car accident, the result was crushingly the same. Emotional devastation. "Is he still working at the community college?" she asked.

"Yeah. He's head of admissions now." George looked down at his iPhone. "Come on, Ruby. We'll be late if we don't get a move on."

"Right. Oh, Frieda, I thought we'd grill some fish for dinner. Would you mind stopping into Gascoyne Fish Market? Whatever catches your fancy will be fine. Did I say 'catches'? Get it? Catches. Fish."

"Yes, Mom," Frieda said with a smile. "I get it."

"Very amusing, Ruby." George grabbed Ruby's hand and hurried them out of the kitchen.

Alone, Frieda leaned against the sink and rubbed her forehead. The tiniest mention of a seemingly insignificant thing like the buying of fish for dinner could open the proverbial floodgates of poignant memory. She remembered as if it were yesterday the evening she and Aaron had gotten into a friendly conversation with a local Jamaican fisherman. He had generously given them two of the largest of his day's catch for the resort's kitchen to cook specially for the family.

Everything about that last week together had been special, most of all the fact that it had turned out to be so unexpectedly romantic. The girls had been mostly busy on their own, leaving Frieda and Aaron to themselves a good deal of the time. One afternoon they had taken a guided hike into the hills. Another evening they had gone into the town for an authentic meal of Escoveitch fish. Afterward they had stopped in a café and caught a fantastic performance by a local band. Best of all, they had made love three times in that one week. By the last day of the holiday they had felt rejuvenated as lovers as well as partners in raising two children.

And then . . . Losing Aaron at just that point in the evolution of their relationship had felt like a massively cruel trick of the universe, an enormous slap in the face Frieda could barely comprehend. Correction. A slap in the face she couldn't at all comprehend.

Frieda straightened her shoulders. She would put the past aside at least for the moment. She had work to do, new jobs to find, and a budget to balance. Bills didn't pay themselves, as her mother used to say when Frieda was growing up and they were struggling to make ends meet. Now Frieda knew all too well what her mother had meant. A career as a freelance marketing writer and copy editor was all well and good when there was a second heftier and steady salary coming in, but when it served as the family's sole means of support making ends meet could be difficult.

Before fetching her laptop Frieda wondered if she should wake Bella. She was halfway to the stairs when she changed her mind. Bella didn't start work at Phil's shop until the following day; there was no need to rouse her from what Frieda hoped was a sweet and dreamless sleep. She knew all too well how rare a gift that was.

# Chapter 7

Bella locked her bike to the old-fashioned hitching post outside Phil's shop in downtown Yorktide and pushed open the door of Wainscoting and Windowseats. Here goes nothing, she thought. For the life of her she couldn't see how working in a store that sold stuff like candlesticks and chandeliers was going to make her feel less guilty for being a jerk to Ariel about wanting to go to the museum the morning they were scheduled to leave Jamaica, or less guilty about not having thanked her father enough for giving her a birthday present that had made all her friends jealous—before the accident, that is. But Bella had long ago realized that there was pretty much no saying no to her grandmother.

Phil was waiting to greet her, a dust cloth in hand. "Good morning, Bella," he said. "It's nice to see you again."

Phil Morse was a handsome, tall, broad-shouldered man about her grandmother's age. Phil always wore really nice clothes; Bella was no fashionista, but she could recognize people who were. His dark hair, short on the sides and a little longer on top, always looked perfect, as if he had just come out of the hairstylist's salon. But the most attractive thing about Phil was his personality. He was seriously nice and witty and smart. He had to be smart to be able to afford his beautiful house, which he had had specially built by a Boston-based architect he had known since their undergraduate days at the Rhode Island School of Design. Why Phil wasn't in a relationship had always puzzled Bella. She knew he had lost his partner to cancer, but that was a bazillion years ago, long before Bella was even born. Well, Phil might be alone, but he didn't seem to be unhappy, so . . .

"Hi, Phil," she said. "I guess I should thank you for giving me a job."

"Yes, you should thank me, even though I know you didn't ask for it."

Bella managed a smile. "You know Grandma."

"I do. Now, come here." Phil gave her a hug; his familiar scent was comforting and it almost brought tears to her eyes. Bella was surprised. She hadn't been able to cry in months.

"Come to the office," he said when he released her, "and I'll fill you in on your duties and how things are done around here."

The first thing that caught Bella's eye when she walked into the office at the back of the shop was a plaque on the wall over the larger of two desks. *If you're going through hell*, it said, *keep going.* Underneath those words was the name *Winston Churchill.*

"One of my all-time favorite mottos," Phil said, "though it's now agreed he never actually said those exact words. Do you know who Winston Churchill was?"

Bella looked away from the plaque. "I think so. I mean, I think he had something to do with history."

Phil sighed and looked heavenwards. "What do they teach young people in school these days? Yes, Bella. He had something to do with history. He was England's Prime Minister from 1940 to 1945 and then again from 1951 to 1955. Trust me, he knew a bit about hell."

*I do, too*, Bella thought. *But I'm not always sure about the keep going part.*

"You can put your bag in here," Phil said briskly, pointing to a deep drawer in the larger desk. "It locks. You'll get a fifteen-minute break every two hours. If you work a full day, you'll have an hour for lunch. If you want to bring your lunch you can eat it here at this smaller desk. And I'd recommend bringing lunch from home; you know how pricey everything is here and the crowds lining up at the sandwich shops and clam shacks for food will be long." Phil pointed to a small fridge under a counter on which sat what looked to Bella like something from an old black-and-white movie about the space age. "The fridge is yours to use, but stay away from the Bezzera Strega. That's the espresso machine to you and me. It's highly temperamental. If you want a cup of coffee, just ask."

"I don't drink coffee," Bella said. "But thanks."

"Are you ready to roll up your sleeves? And yes, I know that you're wearing a sleeveless top."

"I guess."

Phil smiled kindly; Bella had never seen him smile anything but kindly. "Look, Bella," he said, "if you want to be miserable, fine, that's your decision. As long as you do your job well I won't complain. I can't have you overcharging the customers for drawer pulls or doorknobs."

"Sorry. I mean, I'll pay attention."

"Good. Now, let me show you around." Bella followed Phil out of the office and back into the shop itself. "It's pretty simple, really. Over here is the fabric for sale by the yard. Belgian linen, velvet, textured linen weave, et cetera. Everything is clearly marked, and if a customer has a question about what fabric is best for what purpose come and get me." Phil pointed across the shop. "The area rugs are over there next to the ottomans and footstools and benches."

"Benches?" Bella said.

"Yes, the kind you place at the foot of your bed. Sometimes they include a storage unit for extra blankets and whatnot. This center table as you can see is where we display the candlesticks and vases and such. Table linens are over there and window hardware—curtain rods—and drapery are against the wall over there."

"Who buys this stuff?" Bella asked, looking from a pile of pillows on a small couch, many decorated with fringe, to three fancy chandeliers hanging overhead. "I don't even know what some of this is. What's wainscoting, anyway?"

"The simple way to put it is that it's a lining of an interior wall. Most often done in wood, oak if you're lucky, but it can consist of other materials."

"So, do you sell wainscoting?"

"No."

"Then why is the shop called Wainscoting and Windowseats? What about window seats? Do you sell them?"

Phil sighed. "Alliteration, Bella. A catchy phrase. An evocation of a comfortable domestic life. And plenty of people buy this 'stuff,'" he went on. "I've got a loyal clientele of year-round residents from as far away as Kennebunkport and Cape Elizabeth. They're people who redecorate their homes regularly and don't want to buy everything online. I provide good old-fashioned face-to-face service."

"What about summer people?" Bella asked, running her finger along a small wooden box inlaid with some shiny material. "Do they buy anything?"

"The ones with vacation homes do," Phil told her. "And on occasion I get a tourist who's been on the hunt for a particular item and he finds it here in my shop. You'd be surprised how many people travel to the ends of the earth, so to speak, in search of the perfect bowl for the perfect potpourri."

Bella shrugged.

"Bella," Phil said, "a shrug is the least eloquent means of communication."

"Sorry."

Phil waved his hand dismissively. "Oh, I don't really care. Just don't do it in front of the customers. They like to think you're interested in them, even a little. Now, let me show you how to use the computer and then I'll open the doors. It's usually busiest after lunch, but some mornings can be hectic. You never know. What is certain is that if we get rain we get customers, so try not to call in sick on a rainy day."

"I won't," Bella said. "I like rain. I'm not afraid of gloom."

Phil put a hand gently on Bella's shoulder. "Don't forget," he said, "that sunshine is pretty good, too."

Bella swallowed hard and nodded. She wanted to thank Phil again—for what exactly she couldn't say—but this time she knew that if she risked a word the tears would begin to flow.

# Chapter 8

F rieda lifted her long blond hair off her neck in a vain attempt at cooling down. It was a real scorcher of a day, the kind of day that made you want to be holed up in an air-conditioned room. And Roy's Garden Center was not an air-conditioned room.

"Frieda."

At the sound of her name, spoken by a familiar voice, albeit one she hadn't heard in years, Frieda turned around. "Jack," she said with a smile. "Hi."

Jack Tennant had hardly changed at all since high school. His skin was remarkably smooth and the ubiquitous middle-aged sagging chin hadn't yet manifested. There was not a trace of gray in his hair and Frieda bet he could still fit into his old basketball uniform. The thought made her flush with embarrassment.

"How are you?" she said briskly, extending her hand. "I can't believe we've seen so little of each other these past years. It seems every time I'm in town you're in Chicago for a conference or Colorado for a hike!"

Jack laughed and shook Frieda's hand. "I think my wandering days are coming to an end. Travel doesn't hold the same interest for me it once did and I've scaled back on the number of conferences I attend. Every once in a while I'm pretty much compelled to go and listen to a bunch of other college administrators as bored as I am go on about changing admissions policies or new software aimed at making my life infinitely easier—once I figure it out."

"Hmmm, that doesn't sound very appealing."

"It isn't," Jack said. "So, what brings you to Roy's on this insanely hot day?"

"My mother asked me to pick up a few potted plants. Anything colorful, she said. I don't know if you've heard, but Bella and I are spending the summer with her. Things have been . . . Well, they've been difficult, especially for Bella."

Jack nodded. "I understand, Frieda. I really do, and I'm sorry."

"Thanks," she said. "Are you doing well? It's been four years now, hasn't it?"

"Four years this past February that Veronica passed, yes," Jack affirmed. "And I am doing well. It took some time and there are still some painful moments, but with every passing day there comes a little more peace of mind." Jack smiled. "Listen to me! I sound like one of those posters printed with slogans supposed to encourage you to keep on keeping on. A kitten clinging with his front paws to the branch of a tree."

"But you're right, Jack," Frieda said. "Time does help the healing process. I mean, it's only been fifteen months since the accident, but I do feel better than I did. Mostly. Of course, then I feel guilty for moving on, as if by healing I'm allowing myself to forget Aaron and Ariel."

"I know all about that cycle, too," Jack said. "Survivor Guilt they call it, right? Getting Better Guilt. It's a nasty business whatever form it takes."

Frieda nodded. "It is. But on matters less gloomy and complicated, what are you doing at Roy's?"

"I needed a new spade," Jack said, indicating the small plastic bag in his hand. "The handle broke off mine. Well, I'd only had it about twenty years, so I got my money's worth. Hey, would you like to go for coffee or get lunch sometime? I'm sure there's plenty to catch up on, and not all of it sad."

Frieda smiled. "Sure. That would be nice. I don't have a lot of work at the moment—summers can be slow in the world of free-lance—which means I've got plenty of free time. I guess that's both a good and a bad thing."

They exchanged cell phone numbers and Jack headed in the direction of the parking lot, new spade in tow, while Frieda went in search of the plants her mother wanted her to buy. Jack Tennant. Her memories of him didn't seem to have a marked beginning. Well, why should they? She had known Jack almost her entire life. In third grade they had been in the school's Christmas play together. In middle school they had both been members of the glee club. Later, she had watched him play on the high school's varsity basketball team and perform trumpet solos with the orchestra. It would be good to exchange memories of the old days, back when life was relatively simple. Back when they had both been so innocent of true sorrow. Sure, Frieda thought, her father leaving when she was eleven had been upsetting, but it was nothing to having lost her husband and child, or to Jack's having lost his wife.

Nothing.

# Chapter 9

"I hope everyone likes garlic," Ruby murmured as she tasted the basil and parsley pesto sauce she had just made. *And if they don't,* she added silently, *then it's more for me.*

Ruby spooned the pesto into a large pan and then regarded the old-fashioned crank-handled ice-cream maker sitting by the toaster. She had bought the machine earlier that afternoon at a flea market in South Berwick. Aaron had had one just like it. He and the girls had loved to make a big production of churning their own ice cream. And if the results weren't always perfect, the fun of the process more than made up for poor results.

You would be hard-pressed to find a more wonderful father than Aaron Braithwaite, Ruby thought with a sigh. No matter how demanding his work schedule, he always made time to take Bella to Boston Breakers games at Jordan Field or to take Ariel to see a play at the Huntington Theatre. Each summer Aaron and Bella went on a camping trip to the Lake St. Catherine region in Vermont, and when there was a special exhibit at the Yale University Art Gallery in New Haven that Ariel was just dying to see Aaron would happily escort his younger daughter. Whether it was watching old horror movies with Bella or *Downton Abbey* with Ariel, Aaron Braithwaite had proved his love for his children time and time again.

Ruby began to grate a pile of Parmesan for their meal and glanced again at the ice-cream maker. What she was going to suggest to Frieda and Bella at dinner was perhaps a risk, but it was a risk Ruby was willing to take in an effort to encourage Bella to remember the simple pleasures of family life. To encourage Bella to come home.

At exactly six thirty Ruby heard a car pull into the drive and she smiled. It was George, of course. Call me what you like, but never call me late for dinner was his motto. He joined Ruby a moment later and after kissing her cheek he began to set the table.

"Busy day at the office?" Ruby asked, stirring the pot of boiling pasta.

"No more than usual," George told her. "Though I was stuck in an interminable meeting with the budget people. Seriously, I almost laughed out loud when one of them started to compare the cost of our using mechanical pencils to the cost of our using the old-fashioned wooden kind. Really? In this day and age this is an issue?"

Before Ruby could reply, Frieda and Bella joined them.

"Hello, George," Frieda said. "Mmm, what smells so good?"

"Your mother's been hitting the garlic again. Hello, Bella."

"Hi," Bella said, taking a seat at the table.

After mixing the boiled pasta with the pesto sauce, Ruby brought the meal to the table. "Sit and enjoy," she said. "It's better when it's hot."

Frieda and George each took a healthy serving of pasta and began to eat. Bella put a small helping on her plate and began to move it around with her fork. "It tastes even better when it's in your mouth," Ruby told her granddaughter.

Dutifully, Bella took a bite.

Ruby hesitated for a moment and then said, "Guess what I found in a flea market this morning?"

"A flea?" George quipped.

"Ha. No. Take a look at the counter. I found an old-fashioned ice-cream maker, just like Aaron's."

Frieda glanced over her shoulder and then looked down at her plate. Ruby couldn't read her expression. Bella showed no sign of having heard her grandmother.

Ruby soldiered on. "I was thinking we could make our own blueberry ice cream. Lord knows there are plenty of blueberries around this time of the year."

"I'll be your taster if you like," George said. "I know it's a tough job, but somebody's got to do it."

Ruby smiled at him gratefully. Bella shrugged and coiled a few strands of fettucine around her fork.

"I think it's a great idea, Mom," Frieda said, finally looking up. "Really. We haven't . . . We haven't used our machine since . . ."

"Good," Ruby said briskly. "Then it's settled. I'll get the machine cleaned up and ready to go."

"If you need help, just let me know," George offered. "That's not being entirely altruistic. I want ice cream."

"At least you're honest!" Ruby turned to her granddaughter. "How's it going at Phil's, Bella?" she asked.

Bella looked up briefly. "Okay."

"Just okay?"

"Yeah."

"Are you learning anything interesting?" Ruby pressed.

"Not really." Bella put her fork on the table next to her plate. "Can I be excused?"

Ruby held back a sigh of frustration. "You've hardly touched your dinner."

Bella shrugged. "I guess I'm just not hungry. Sorry."

"Of course you're excused," Frieda said. "I'll clean up the kitchen for you tonight. You can take my next turn."

"Thanks." Bella got up from the table and left the room.

"She's going to waste away at this rate."

George shook his head. "Poor kid. I wish I knew what I could say or do to help."

"Thanks, George," Frieda said. "I know you'd do anything for Bella, but I'm not sure what can be done. And yes, Mom, I know I let her off the hook again."

"Your heart is in the right place. Look, are you sure you're okay with this ice-cream thing?"

"Yes," her daughter told her. "I think it's a good idea. Bella used to love concocting different flavors with her father. Remember the chocolate with coconut and almonds?"

"Yes, but I'd like to forget the chocolate with bubble gum and gummy bears." Suddenly Ruby was flooded with doubt. "Maybe this is a bad idea after all," she said. "Maybe we should let the past alone. It's the past for a reason, right?"

"No, Mom," Frieda said. "We'll go ahead with your plan."

George got up from the table and brought his plate and glass to the sink. "Thanks for dinner, Ruby," he said. "Sorry to eat and run, but I've got a pile of paperwork to do tonight. Those mean budget people gave me homework. Take care, Frieda."

"I'll walk out with you," Ruby told him. "Are you sure I'm not making a big mistake with this ice-cream thing?" she said when they reached the front hall.

"No," he said, "I'm not sure, but I wouldn't waste another minute worrying about it. Remember—"

Ruby smiled. "Worry is interest paid on a debt that might never come due."

"You were listening! Good night, Ruby."

Ruby watched him drive off and then returned to the kitchen, where she found her daughter still at the table.

"The pesto really was excellent, Mom," Frieda said with a smile. "Though I don't plan on breathing on anybody for quite some time."

"Garlic is supposed to thin the blood, you know."

"Heart-healthy?"

Ruby nodded. "Not to mention handy if you happen to find yourself in the presence of a vampire. Here," she said, reaching for an empty glass, "let me help you clean up."

# Chapter 10

Frieda had lied to her mother. She wasn't at all sure it was a good idea for the family—what was left of it—to make their own ice cream like they had in the old days. The memories might prove too poignant to bear. That was one of the frustrating things about memories. Sometimes they were as welcome as a warm embrace. And sometimes they were as unwelcome as a pinprick.

Frieda turned onto her side and adjusted the light cover around her. Well, the memories of the fun times the family had shared might be hard to bear, but for Bella's sake she would attempt to make the experience a positive one. Correction. For Bella's sake she would succeed in making the experience a positive one. There was no choice but to succeed. There was no choice but to accept the new reality and face the new future.

A future without Ariel. Frieda turned onto her back again and stared at the ceiling. How she missed every little thing about her daughter! She missed the scent of her skin. She missed the pattern of freckles across Ariel's nose and the way she crossed her long legs at both the knees and ankles. She missed the sound of her giggle. At times she found the loss of Ariel's physical presence almost harder to bear than the loss of the person inside the so tenderly familiar body.

And the person inside that body had been so very special. Ariel had always been different from the other kids, even her two closest friends. While girls in her class were experimenting with makeup, Ariel was teaching herself about ancient Egyptian hieroglyphics. When most kids were obsessing about the latest boy band or female pop star, Ariel was discovering Mozart. She hadn't set out to be different from the majority of her peers; she just was and her being different hadn't bothered her in the least. So what if her eighth-grade classmates' greatest desire was to spend spring break in Disneyland? Ariel had shrugged at the idea of a theme park and had instead asked for permission to enroll in a week's intensive course at the community college in the identification of local flora.

But Ariel's biggest desire, bigger even than her desire to make first violin in the school orchestra, had been to visit the great cities of Europe. She hadn't known it when she died, but her mother had already begun to plan a week in Paris in celebration of Ariel's sixteenth birthday. Frieda had sent for brochures and city maps; she had spent time online discovering places to stay and sights to visit. They would journey down the Seine on a *bateaux mouche*. They would climb to Sacré-Cœur in Montmartre. They would spend an afternoon at the Musée national du Moyen Âge. They would eat croissants for breakfast and crepes for lunch. And on July 6, Ariel's birthday, they would . . .

Frieda rubbed her temples with the tips of her fingers. They would do none of those things. Not one of them. But . . . Why not? she thought with a sudden clarity. Why not celebrate what would have been Ariel's sixteenth birthday? Why not honor the day with a private, formal gesture of remembrance? Last year the wound had been too great, but time had passed and recognition should be paid to what would have been a landmark in Ariel's young life. Frieda was sure it was an idea of which her grief counselor would approve.

Yes. A small celebration in honor of Ariel's birthday was a good idea. It would benefit them all, Frieda's mother, her daughter, and herself. She didn't know why she hadn't thought of it sooner.

# Chapter 11

Bella turned onto Clove Street and stopped her bike in front of what had been Ariel's favorite store in Yorktide, The Bookworm. She stared at the window display, at the large selection of books by Maine authors, at the colorful poster of the famous Andre the seal, at the row of *New York Times* best sellers. She hadn't been inside the store since the Christmas vacation before the accident. The owners of The Bookworm had hosted an open house one afternoon, with free hot chocolate and homemade cookies and two local musicians playing holiday music on a guitar and fiddle. There was a raffle, too, on a first edition of some book Bella had never heard of and Ariel had won.

Where was that book now? Bella wondered. Was it packed away with the other books Ariel had left behind? She felt her throat tighten as she continued to stare at the shop window. They had had so much fun that afternoon. . . .

Abruptly Bella turned her bike around and rode on to Wainscoting and Windowseats. As she came through the door Phil emerged from the back of the shop. "You're late," he said.

"Am I? Sorry."

Phil smiled. "Well, only by a few minutes."

"I went by The Bookworm."

Phil looked at his watch. "I shouldn't have thought it was open yet."

"It wasn't. I . . . Never mind."

Phil outlined Bella's duties for the day and returned to the office to handle some paperwork. "Running a shop isn't all fun and games," he intoned. "There are a whole lot of nasty financial matters that need constant attention."

The first few customers were what Bella had already come to think of as "the usuals," by which she meant women somewhere between her mother's and her grandmother's age, very well dressed and wearing either sophisticated jewelry like delicate gold bracelets and diamond rings or arty jewelry like big, chunky necklaces and dangling earrings. But the fourth customer of the morning was not "a usual." Bella thought she was probably younger than her mother, maybe thirty-five or so, and she was wearing a pair of cut-off jeans, a T-shirt, Crocs, and no jewelry whatsoever.

"Hi," the woman said brightly.

It was only then that Bella saw she had a companion, a girl about six or seven with wild curly red hair. The girl stared at Bella with big, solemn green eyes.

Bella barely managed a nod in reply to the woman's greeting. The girl . . . She didn't really look like Ariel except for the hair, but that one strong resemblance struck Bella as forcefully as a physical blow.

"What . . ." Bella cleared her throat. "Can I help you?" she asked, uncomfortably aware that she felt slightly sick to her stomach. She tried to look away from the child but just couldn't seem to.

The woman smiled. "I know," she said. "It's the hair. People are always kind of amazed by it. This is my goddaughter, Cindy."

The child, Cindy, gave Bella a little wave. Bella opened her mouth to say something, anything, but not a word would come out.

"Good morning!"

Bella startled at the sound of Phil's voice just behind her. "Can I help you find anything?" he asked the woman. "Bella, would you be a dear and reply to the e-mail on my screen. Thanks."

Gratefully Bella hurried to the office and sank into the chair at the smaller desk. That little girl . . . Bella took a few deep, slow breaths and gradually her stomach calmed. *It was just because I was remembering the party at The Bookworm,* she thought. *It was just because Ariel was on my mind that I reacted so badly.*

A few minutes later she heard the door to the shop open and shut. Then Phil was standing before her. "You okay?" he asked. "She bought some candles, by the way."

"Yeah," Bella said. "I'm okay. Thanks. I'm sorry I—"

"No apologies." Phil perched on the desk and smiled kindly at her. "So many things can call up the memories. Resemblances. An overheard word. A song. A chill in the air. Sometimes it feels there's no escaping the past and all it meant to us, even for a moment."

Bella nodded. "Yeah." She thought of her grandmother wanting them to make ice cream like she and Ariel used to do with their father. Bella didn't see the point. Her father and sister weren't coming back, no matter how many pints of ice cream they made.

"You know," Phil said brightly, "I'm throwing a Fourth of July party again this year. I'm going all out. I'm renting glassware and plates and utensils so I don't have to spend days cleaning up afterward. There'll be the usual feast and I found colored sparklers in addition to the traditional white. It might all be a bit showy, but everyone should be allowed one showy display in a lifetime. Maybe two."

Bella tried her best to feign enthusiasm. After all, Phil had rescued her from having to deal with that woman and the red-haired girl. And he had been sensitive enough to cancel last year's party out of respect for her father and sister. "I'm sure it will be great," she said. "Your best party yet."

Phil laughed. "It had better be, what with all it's costing! Now, let's get back to work. I spotted a tour bus on my way in this morning and I'm betting we'll be inundated with browsers before long."

"Not buyers?" Bella asked.

Phil sighed. "I'm afraid we're a little pricey for the tour bus crowd. Still, we have to be pleasant."

*Pleasant,* Bella thought, getting up and following Phil out front. It used to be so easy to be bright and pleasant. But not so much anymore.

# Chapter 12

Frieda had made eggplant stuffed with lamb and Mediterranean spices for dinner; Ruby's contribution was a Caprese salad and a loaf of fresh sourdough bread. Ruby's appetite was hearty, as was her daughter's, but once again Bella seemed more interested in playing with her food than eating it.

"How was work today?" Ruby asked her, though she didn't expect much more than the usual one-word answer.

"It was okay," Bella said, glancing up briefly. "Busy."

"Being busy helps the time pass," Ruby pointed out.

Bella shrugged. "I guess."

"Well," Frieda announced, "I've been busy thinking. I'd like to celebrate what would have been Ariel's sixteenth birthday with a small party."

Ruby darted a look at her granddaughter. Bella had to have heard her mother's words, but her expression remained unengaged. As for Ruby's own expression, she hoped it didn't reveal the extent of her discomfort. Her gut told her this was a bad idea, not the acknowledgment of Ariel's birthday but the way in which Ruby's daughter wanted to do it, with a party. "Are you sure that's a good idea, Frieda?" she asked carefully.

"Why wouldn't it be?"

Ruby thought hard about how to answer without sounding critical, but before she could speak Frieda had turned to her daughter.

"Bella?" Frieda said. "What do you think?"

"I think it's macabre to have a birthday party for someone who's dead," Bella said flatly.

Ruby was struck by her granddaughter's use of the word macabre. It was a strong word, far stronger than silly or stupid or pointless.

"Then let's call it a celebration," Frieda suggested. "A celebration of Ariel's life. We didn't mark the occasion last year."

"We couldn't," Ruby pointed out. "It was too soon, no matter what those grief counselors told us."

"All the more reason we need to do it now," her daughter insisted.

"Why, Mom?" Bella demanded. "Why do we need to do this? Why do we need to keep remembering out loud? You didn't make me go to the memorial for Ariel at school back in April."

"I thought that would be too difficult for you, too public," Frieda explained. "This will be just you, me, and Grandma. We'll have a cake and we'll make a toast to Ariel and we'll share our most special memories of her. It will be a way of honoring her life. Of keeping her memory alive and with us."

"Maybe we could talk about this some other time," Ruby said diplomatically. "Let the idea sink in."

Frieda opened her mouth to protest (Ruby assumed), but Bella spoke before she could.

"Phil told me he's doing the Fourth of July party again. He said it's going to be better than ever."

Ruby nodded. "Yes. He mentioned it to me."

"I'm not really in the mood for parties." Bella looked steadily at her mother. "Big or little."

"Well, we have to attend Phil's party," Ruby said firmly. "No two ways about it. He'd be hurt if one of us didn't show up for any reason other than a bad case of the flu or . . ." *Or a death*, Ruby added silently. Phil had canceled last year's party, only a few short months after Aaron's and Ariel's passing; the only other time he had canceled was soon after Tony's dying, and that had been over thirty years ago. Death had a way of distorting everything, of interrupting and harassing the everyday. Yes, Ruby thought, she could understand Bella's aversion to celebration all too well. There were times when celebration was cathartic. And there were times when it was . . . Well, when it was macabre.

"You guys don't have to do anything for Ariel's celebration," Frieda said into the silence. "I'll handle it all."

"I'm not hungry," Bella announced suddenly. "May I be excused?"

Ruby bit her tongue.

"All right," Frieda said.

Bella took her plate to the sink and then left the kitchen.

When she had gone, Ruby turned to her daughter. "This party for Ariel. Just think about it a bit longer, okay?"

Her daughter sighed. "I don't know why you're objecting so strongly to this idea, Mom."

"Bella clearly isn't happy about it and—"

"And you're the one who keeps telling me not to coddle her, to push her out of her shell." Frieda laughed. "Now you're saying I should abandon the idea of marking my child's birthday because Bella isn't in the mood?"

"I'm sorry, Frieda," Ruby said. "I'm not telling you to do or not to do anything. I'm just asking you to reconsider. Frankly, the idea of a party doesn't sit well with me, either."

Frieda frowned down at her plate. "All right," she said after a moment. "I'll reconsider."

"Thank you," Ruby said. "And thank you for cooking tonight. The meal is delicious."

Frieda nodded. Together the women finished their dinner in silence.

# Chapter 13

It was a gloomy day, blustery, cold, and rainy. Bella wasn't surprised she had met no one along the Marginal Way. She remembered what she had said to Phil the other day about liking gloom and what he had said about the sunshine being good as well. The problem with sunshine was that it made everything all so obvious and public and right in your face. It was way easier to hide and feel safe in gloom.

Bella adjusted her baseball-style cap so that it sat lower over her eyes and shoved her hands into the pocket of her sweatshirt. The Marginal Way, located along the cliffs between Perkins Cove and Main Beach, was a dramatic spot in all weathers. Ariel had loved it here. She thought the gnarled pine trees were romantic; the colorful dragonflies in high summer exotic; the blue-green ocean expanding to the horizon inspiring. Ariel had been one of those people who could always find the exciting in the most mundane; she could transform every little detail of life into something spectacular. Frankly, sometimes it had gotten on Bella's nerves. "What's the big deal with a stupid piece of fruit?" she would ask when Ariel went into raptures about an apple at the farmers' market. "Just look at its color!" Ariel would exclaim. "It's the most intense red I've ever seen! Isn't it gorgeous?" Well, Ariel's enthusiasm for beauty was probably due to all that reading she used to do about art history. Her room had been plastered with postcards of famous paintings and statues and buildings.

Bella sank onto one of the benches overlooking the sea and hunched her shoulders against a gust of wind that drove raindrops against her face. Why, she wondered, did people used to say you could "catch your death of cold" in wet, chilly weather? You couldn't get sick from air, but maybe in the old days people didn't understand that. Ariel had loved cold weather, maybe because she suffered so much on really hot days. "Ariel is a delicate flower," their father used to say. *Not like me,* Bella thought, frowning. *I'm tough. I'm a freakin' cactus. I can handle anything. Ha!* If it had been she who had died in the crash, Ariel would already have gotten past the sadness and depression. She would probably have set up a scholarship fund or something in her sister's memory. Ariel had been tough in the ways that mattered.

"Mind if I sit here?"

Startled by the interruption, Bella looked up to see a girl about her own age. She was wearing jeans and a red rain slicker with the hood up. Her hair—what Bella could see of it—was brown. She was pretty, but her face looked haggard. It wasn't a look you usually saw on young people, Bella thought, except when they had gone through something really bad. She remembered catching sight of her own face in the bathroom mirror a few months after her father and sister died and being thoroughly shocked at what she saw, Bella but not Bella, a much older, sadder, and no wiser version of herself. Since then she tried to avoid looking at her reflection; you could wash your face and brush your teeth without the help of a mirror, and as for makeup, well, she had stopped wearing makeup shortly after the funeral. No amount of makeup could disguise the look of grief.

"Sure," she said. She wasn't in the mood for company, but a stranger probably wouldn't want to talk too much. Besides, she thought, she could always get up and walk away.

The girl smiled and sat next to Bella on the wet bench. "Looks like you and I are the only two people in town who don't mind a little rain," she said. "I like the rain, actually. Rain fits my mood these days."

"Mine, too," Bella said. "I was pretty much just saying that to someone."

"I'm Clara by the way. I'm working at The Flipper until the end of August. Then I'm off to college."

"I'm Bella. My mother and I are staying at my grandmother's in Yorktide for the summer."

"You have a job?" Clara asked.

"Yeah," Bella said. "At Wainscoting and Windowseats. My grandmother's friend Phil owns it."

"Lucky! You can't get fired. My boss can be a bear."

Bella shrugged. "Phil's cool. I've known him all my life."

They sat in silence for a long moment, Bella almost forgetting she wasn't alone, lulled by the rhythm of the silvery waves out at sea and the pattering of raindrops on the rocky ground at their feet. Finally, the girl spoke again. "So, where are you from?" she asked.

"My mother and I live in Massachusetts," Bella told her.

"Are your parents divorced?"

Bella winced. "No," she said, staring resolutely at the water. "My dad's dead. He and my sister died in a car accident a little over a year ago."

Clara shook her head. "I'm so sorry. Really, I'm sorry. I guess I just assumed when you said you and your mother . . ."

"It's okay," Bella told her. "Where are you from?"

"A little town in upstate New York. Bet you've never heard of it. Whimsey Corner."

"You're right," Bella said. "Never heard of it. How'd you wind up in Maine?"

"A friend of my parents used to work here in Ogunquit during the summers a million years ago," Clara explained. "She thought it might be a good thing for me to do this year. She said I'd have fun. My parents agreed. They kept reminding me how much I'd always wanted to see the ocean. So my parents' friend called the guy who owns The Flipper—she used to work with him—and got me a job." Clara laughed. "I'm eighteen, legally an adult, but I didn't have much say in the decision."

Bella knew all about adults thinking they knew what was best for you. There was the vice principal of her high school who had argued that Bella should attend the school's memorial service for Ariel back in April. There was her former grief counselor, Colleen Milton, always pushing her to face challenges like going through the photos the family had taken on that fateful final vacation. And her mother and grandmother could be bossy and know-it-all, too. Her mother was trying to convince her that a celebration of Ariel's birthday was a good thing and her grandmother was insisting they make ice cream like they had in the old days with her father and that Bella go to Phil's Fourth of July party even though she didn't want to.

"Why?" Bella asked. "Why did your parents and their friend think it would be a good idea for you to come to Ogunquit?"

Clara sighed. "You really want to know?"

"Yeah," Bella said. Why not? she thought. Maybe hearing someone else's story would get her mind off her own, even for a few minutes.

"Okay, I'll tell you the short version. The guy I was seeing for the past four years broke up with me a few weeks before graduation. He didn't give me a real reason. He just said he'd decided to go to California for college and that it was best if we see other people. I had no idea anything was wrong. We were supposed to go to the same college. We were supposed to get married. But . . ." Clara cleared her throat.

"Sorry," Bella said. "Sounds tough."

"It was," Clara said, her voice catching. "It is. I loved him with all my heart. I still do. I think about him every minute of every day."

"But why go so far from home? I mean, why not stay in Whimsey Corner to be close to your friends? They must all feel for you, no?"

"No," Clara said flatly. "I'm on my own. I mean, I had friends, but once I met Marc I stopped seeing them. My mom told me that I was making a mistake giving up my girlfriends for a boy. She just didn't understand that with Marc in my life I didn't need anyone else."

"But now?" Bella asked. "Do you need those friends now?"

Clara shrugged. "I'm fine. I don't need any of my old friends. Not that they'd want me around after all this time."

"Do you know that for sure?" Bella asked. "Maybe they'd be happy if you reached out."

"Trust me. They wouldn't be. They were all madly jealous when Marc picked me and not one of them."

Bella hesitated for a moment and then the words just came flowing from her mouth. "I have no friends anymore, either. When Ariel, my sister, died I just couldn't stand to be around them, even my best friend, Kerri. Everyone wanted to help. Everyone thought they knew what I was going through. Everyone wanted me to talk about losing my dad and my sister, but I didn't want to talk about it. So I pretty much rejected them all. Even Kerri, and I'd been friends with her since fourth grade."

Clara didn't reply, but Bella realized she didn't much care. It had been enough to say what she had said; it had been enough to finally make the choice to talk to someone about her life. Once again the two girls sat in silence before the gray sea under a leaden sky, and Bella thought more about Kerri. It had been about two months since they had last talked. Well, since they had argued. Clearly, Kerri no longer needed Bella in her life. But do I need her? Bella wondered. Of course not, she thought. No.

"Look at the two of us," Clara said suddenly. "Sitting on a bench getting soaked by the rain! We must be nuts!"

Bella smiled. "Maybe it's time to go. The wind is picking up, too. Welcome to summer in Maine."

"I'll walk back into town with you," Clara said, "if you're heading that way. My car is parked off Main Street."

"Yeah," Bella said. "Sure."

The girls rose and silently walked back along the graveled path that led into town, past a row of beautiful resorts, their green lawns and blue pools now empty of guests. When they reached the end of the path, Clara briefly put a hand on Bella's arm.

"Hey," she said. "You want to get together sometime? Hang out?"

Bella didn't hesitate. "Yeah," she said. "That might be okay."

They took out their phones and exchanged numbers. "I've got to get going," Clara said then, tucking her phone into the pocket of her rain jacket. "My shift starts in about fifteen minutes."

"Okay," Bella said. "See you." She watched as Clara walked off, her head bowed against the pelting rain. Bella didn't know quite what to make of the encounter. Meeting Clara the way she had felt somehow serendipitous, as if it was meant to happen. Since when had she ever shared so much personal information with a total stranger who wasn't being paid to tell her that what she was doing was wrong and what she should be doing instead?

But maybe, Bella thought, she and Clara weren't total strangers after all. Okay, a boyfriend breaking up with you wasn't half as devastating as your father and sister dying in a car crash in a foreign country, but still, it was loss and Clara and Bella had that in common. They each had lost so very much.

Loss. It might be a bond on which to form a friendship. Bella shoved her hands deeper into the pockets of her sweatshirt and headed toward the lot behind the pharmacy where she had locked her bike.

# Chapter 14

"What did you do with yourself on your day off?" Ruby asked her granddaughter at dinner that evening. "I mean after this morning when we concocted what will be the world's greatest blueberry ice cream." It was true that Bella had been more of a witness than a participant in the process, but at least she had taken her turn at the crank.

"Hung around."

"I assumed that," Ruby replied patiently; it took some effort. "Teenagers do it so well. Where did you hang around?"

"Mostly on Marginal Way," Bella said without looking up from her plate. "I met someone there. She's working at The Flipper for the summer."

"Oh? What's her name?" Frieda asked.

"Clara," Bella said. "I didn't ask her last name. She's from some little town in upstate New York. Whimsey Corner."

"How old is she?" Frieda asked.

"About my age," Bella replied, again without looking up. "She just graduated from high school."

Frieda frowned. "She's a long way from home for someone so young."

"She said it was her parents' idea she come here. They have a friend who used to work in Ogunquit."

Ruby spooned another helping of carrot salad onto her plate. "Well, to each his own. Are you going to see her again?"

Bella shrugged. "We might hang out."

"And how was your day?" Ruby asked her daughter.

"Not bad at all," Frieda said. "I landed another copyediting gig. It's with a new and very talked about academic journal. The money is decent enough and the job scope is reasonable."

"Good for you," Ruby said warmly.

"Oh, and Jack Tennant called. We're having lunch tomorrow."

Bella finally looked up from her dinner and frowned. "The guy whose wife died? Why are you having lunch with him?" she asked.

"Why not?" Frieda said. "We grew up together. I mean, we weren't close friends, but we did go to the same schools for twelve years. That's a connection."

Ruby nodded. "It's comforting to be with people who knew you back when. It becomes more comforting the older we get."

"I don't miss being with Kerri," Bella stated.

"You might someday," Ruby said, getting up from the table. "If everyone is finished I'll get the ice cream. Frieda, would you clear away the dinner things? Bella, would you grab some bowls and spoons?" Ruby opened the freezer and removed a large plastic container. "Ah, there's George's car now!"

Frieda laughed. "The man has a sixth sense for food, doesn't he?"

A moment or two later George joined them in the kitchen. "I'm prepared to be amazed," he said. Ruby smiled at him and scooped some of the ice cream—which was a really gorgeous blue/purple color—into one of the bowls Bella had lined up on the table and handed it to George. "Here goes," he said.

Ruby watched as George put a heaping spoonful of ice cream into his mouth. "Well," she said, "what do you think?"

George said nothing. With a grimace, he swallowed.

"What?" Ruby demanded. "What's wrong?"

"I need a glass of water," George croaked. "Pronto."

Frieda hurriedly fetched him a glass and he drank it in one gulp. "It tastes like salt," he rasped. "And a lot of it."

"What? No, it doesn't. Here, let me try." Ruby dipped her spoon into George's abandoned bowl. A second later she turned to the sink and spit out the small bit she had taken. "Oh my God," she cried, "that's awful! What did we do wrong?" She turned around to see Bella smiling slightly.

"You were the one who did the measuring, Grandma," Bella said.

"Oh. Was I?"

"Mom," Frieda said. "Could you have mistaken salt for sugar?"

"Maybe," Ruby admitted. "Obviously."

George coughed and sank into a chair. "I can't believe you actually swallowed it," Bella said to him, and Ruby saw that her granddaughter's smile had strengthened.

"I didn't want to be rude," he said miserably.

"Poor George." Frieda put a sympathetic hand on his shoulder.

"Let me get you some good, strong coffee," Ruby offered. "It will get rid of the taste of salt. I hope."

"If I didn't have to get up early for work tomorrow, I'd ask for some good, strong whiskey. But coffee will do." George smiled at Bella. "I guess it's back to the drawing board, eh?"

Bella shrugged. "I'm going to my room," she said. "Bye, George."

"I'm off, too," Frieda added. "I want to get a bit more work done before bed."

When her daughter and granddaughter had gone upstairs, Ruby turned back to George. "Thanks for being such a good sport," she said. "I'm sorry I almost killed you."

George laughed and finished his coffee. "It'll take a lot more than a surfeit of salt to knock me over. Just promise me that next time you do a taste test before you measure out white grainy stuff."

Ruby promised and walked with George to the front door, where he kissed her warmly. She watched as he got into his car and drove off. And she thought, *What woman in her right mind wouldn't leap to accept his proposal of marriage?*

Maybe, Ruby thought, turning away from the door, the problem was that she wasn't in her right mind.

# Chapter 15

Frieda hit send and the e-mail with its attachment flew off. Until she heard back from the head of the marketing department at the well-funded historical society back in Warden about her next assignment she had only the one new copyediting job lined up. And though money was always welcome and indeed necessary, she would be lying if she said she wouldn't appreciate a few moments of downtime. The last months had taken their toll and there were days when Frieda thought she could very easily sleep right through breakfast, lunch, and dinner.

Still, there was light on the horizon. Bella had found what might turn out to be a friend here in Yorktide and that made Frieda happy. Poor Bella. She had gone through so many pronounced stages of grief since the accident. At Frieda's initial one-on-one meeting with Bella's grief counselor only weeks after the tragedy, Colleen Milton had explained that it was common for teen survivors of a trauma to need to know every little detail of what had happened in an attempt to make sense of it all. Indeed, not long after that meeting Bella had become obsessed with asking questions. Had Ariel been wearing a seat belt? How fast had their dad been driving? Had he stuck to the left side of the road or had he forgotten and veered into the wrong lane? It didn't matter that the accident was not a result of driver error; Bella still wanted to know. Had her father and sister realized they were about to die? Had they been scared or had things happened so fast they didn't have time to be scared? Had they suffered or had both died right away? Some of the questions Frieda could answer and some of them she simply could not. Nobody could and that had made Bella near mad with frustration.

Finally, that phase of fevered inquisitiveness had passed, to be replaced by—Frieda's thoughts were interrupted by the ringing of her mother's landline. She got up from the kitchen table and reached for the receiver of the old-fashioned wall unit.

"Hello," she said. "Ruby Hitchens's residence."

"Frieda?"

Frieda froze. She recognized the voice immediately though it had been approximately thirty years since she had last heard it. Her father. Her ne'er-do-well father.

"Ruby isn't here," she blurted, already moving the receiver away from her ear.

"Wait, Frieda. It's you I want to talk to."

Frieda hesitated and then put the receiver back to her ear. "How did you know I was here?" she demanded. "Did Mom tell you?"

"Yeah," her father said, "she did, but believe me, she had no idea I'd be calling to talk to you."

Frieda wasn't sure she believed that. But why would her mother not warn her if she knew he would be calling? Then an unpleasant thought occurred to Frieda. Maybe her father was in Yorktide; maybe he intended to do more than just talk to his daughter on the phone, like show up at the house uninvited. That would be an unmitigated disaster. She didn't know what she might do if she came face-to-face with the man after all these years. Something unpleasant, of that she was sure.

"Where are you calling from?" Frieda asked.

"A diner. One of those old-fashioned ones with a pyramid of doughnuts under a glass dome on the counter and decades of grease on the grill."

Frieda tried and failed to keep the annoyance out of her voice. "I mean, where in the country are you calling from?"

Her father laughed. "I never tell your mother where I am. She never asks."

*Mom knows better,* Frieda thought darkly. Her mother knew she would only hear a lie or a prevarication if she did ask. Frieda stared at one of the old photos of Ruby and Frieda stuck to the door of the fridge with a magnet; it had been taken at a birthday party when Frieda was about twelve. Not long after her father had left them without a backward glance.

Frieda looked away from the picture. "Why contact me now, Dad?" she asked. "This is not a good time for me. I thought maybe you'd get that."

"Let's just say the spirit moved me."

Frieda rolled her eyes. "Why didn't the spirit move you fifteen months ago when my husband and child were killed? Oh, sure, you sent a card, but let's be real, Dad; a card was pretty inadequate given the situation."

"You're right," he said. "It was pretty inadequate and I'm sorry for that."

Frieda didn't reply; she didn't want to accept an apology offered so easily. It was probably a lie.

"Is Phil hosting his famous Fourth of July party this year?" her father went on, as casually, Frieda thought, as if they were in the habit of chatting on a daily basis.

"Yes," she said. "He canceled last year's because of . . . Out of respect for Mom and me and Bella."

"That's like him. I remember the first Fourth of July party your mother and I went to at his place," Steve said. "It was back before Tony got sick. I admire Phil's keeping up the tradition."

"I didn't think you were the type to admire constancy," Frieda snapped.

"I have my moments," her father responded mildly. "So, are you working?"

"Of course I'm working. Someone has to pay the bills now that . . . Anyway, I've always worked. Ever since I was twelve and started to babysit."

"You have your mother's work ethic, that's for sure. What about Bella? How is she spending her time in Yorktide this summer?"

"She's working for Phil at the shop," Frieda said. Steve Hitchens didn't have the right to know more about his only surviving grand-child, a grandchild he had never cared enough about to visit.

"I hope she finds the time to have some fun," her father said. "You're only young once."

"Bella is not much in the mood for fun these days," Frieda blurted. "I need to go."

"Okay. Can I talk with you again?"

Frieda felt her entire face contract in a frown. All sense told her to deny her father the privilege of her time and conversation. But what she said was, "Yeah."

"Can I call on your cell phone?" he asked. "It would give you more privacy than you must have now on your mother's landline."

"No. Use this number." Privacy? She didn't want or need to have a cozy private chat with a man who was virtually a stranger.

"All right," he said. "Thanks, Frieda."

And then he was gone.

Frieda replaced the receiver. For a moment she wondered if she had imagined what had just transpired. Why not? Not once since her father had walked away had he ever tried to speak with her. Why couldn't this call have been a product of the summer heat or a building fever or . . .

No. The call had come. Her father had spoken to her. And she had spoken to him. But why had she given him permission to reach out to her again? And to have the nerve to mention Tony, after all these years . . . Frieda rubbed her forehead. She would never for-get Tony Worthington's terrible death from AIDS, back in those awful dark days before the antiretroviral drugs were available and when misinformation about the disease was rampant. She had been very young, but she remembered clearly how her father had been of significant help to Phil near the end, unafraid to comfort Tony when so many people were terrified of becoming infected by his mere presence. Ruby had often reminded Frieda about her fa-ther's generosity, but over the years Frieda had chosen to ignore, even to "forget," this knowledge about her father in an effort to keep her anger alive.

"If my father could be such a saint to a friend," Frieda had once asked Phil, "why was he such a jerk to his own wife and daughter?"

"I can't explain why people do what they do, Frieda," Phil had replied. "Sometimes I can't explain my own motives and actions."

Suddenly Frieda felt a bit weak at the knees and she sank into her chair at the kitchen table. Her father wanted to talk to her. This was going to take some serious thinking about. Was she up to the effort it would take to open a dialogue? Or was her anger, so ingrained, so much a habit, simply too great to overcome? At that moment Frieda simply didn't know.

# Chapter 16

Bella stuck the tube of sunblock back into the canvas bag she had borrowed from her grandmother. This was the first time she had ever gone to the beach without her family or friends or sometimes both. Being alone when pretty much everybody else was in a group, tossing a Frisbee, eating ice-cream cones, or just hanging out, felt weird, but Bella had hoped that maybe being in a seriously beautiful place like the beach might bring her some peace of mind. At least for a little while.

As much as Ariel had enjoyed hanging out with her friends, Bella remembered, digging her toes in the warm sand, she had been just as happy being on her own. And she was never bored, not even when they were stuck in the house during a major snowstorm and the power failed and they couldn't use their computer because one of them had let the battery run out. "You have a lot more going on inside your head than I do," Bella would say to her sister. "All that stuff keeps you from getting bored. I need, I don't know, outside stimulation or something."

Although these days even outside stimulation didn't much spark her interest. And she had made such good progress before it all went wrong back in April. Colleen had helped her get to the point where she had finally been able to look at the pictures of her father and sister taken on that fateful trip. She had finally been able to talk about her father and sister in a casual context. And she had been seriously considering signing up for driving lessons.

She had even made a few small moves toward welcoming Kerri back into her life, like telling her about a pair of sneakers she had seen online she thought Kerri would love. Those gestures of friendship, small though they were, must have made her final withdrawal that much more hurtful for Kerri.

The break had occurred a few days before Bella's birthday. After homeroom Kerri had given Bella a card. On the front was a picture of two old women arm in arm; inside it said something like *Even when we're old and gray we'll be each other's BFFs*. "Let's go to the mall after school," Kerri had suggested. "Just you and me. We can get one of those giant cookies, the ones with all the colored icing. We haven't done that in ages."

But Bella was no longer ready for Kerri—for anyone—to be nice to her. The idea of celebrating her birthday, coinciding as it did with the anniversary of the accident, had brought to the fore all the guilt Bella felt about how she had failed her father and sister.

"No," Bella had told Kerri, sticking the card in the back of the binder she was carrying and looking away. "I can't."

It was the first time ever that Kerri had gotten angry with her. "Fine," she had said. "If you want to be sad go ahead. I can't stop you. I just wish . . . Never mind."

It was the last time they had spoken.

Bella adjusted her sunglasses; it was hot and they kept sliding down her nose. The situation with Kerri was bad, but maybe worse was the situation with her mother. Bella had withdrawn from her, too, the person she had relied on so totally after the accident. Weirdly, her mother now felt almost like a stranger. For one, what was up with that crazy idea of a party for Ariel's sixteenth birthday? Bella knew that to forget was impossible, but she *wanted* to forget that her sister was gone. She was *trying* to forget, even for a few minutes at a time. And she wanted to be forgotten and left alone by others.

Except maybe for Clara, the girl she had met on the Marginal Way. It might be okay to be with someone who didn't miss Aaron

and Ariel Braithwaite like Bella and her mother and her grandmother did, like so many people back home did—

Abruptly Bella got up from the blanket and hurriedly stuffed
her belongings into her bag. *This was a bad idea,* she thought. The
problem with going to a place beautiful to calm your mind was that
your mind always came with you.

# Chapter 17

Ruby found her daughter sitting in one of the two rocking chairs on the front porch, sipping a glass of iced tea. She sank into the other rocking chair and sighed. "Stupid leg," she said. "It feels as if someone is pounding on my bone with a hammer."

Frieda sighed. "I wish you didn't have to suffer. Pain takes it out of a person."

"I'm sorry, too, but it won't kill me. Mostly it's just an annoyance and I should try to keep my mouth shut when it acts up."

"You have a right to moan and groan. And I might, too. You'll never guess who I spoke to earlier."

Ruby looked closely at her daughter. She thought Frieda looked agitated and hoped it wasn't a bill collector who had tracked her down. Frieda swore she was in decent financial condition, but she might be keeping an unhappy secret. "You're right," she said. "I probably won't. Who?"

"My father."

Ruby's eyebrows rose in surprise. "How did that happen?" she asked.

"He called to speak to me. Mom, did you know he was going to get in touch with me?"

Ruby shook her head. "No. I last talked to him in early May. I told him you and Bella would be staying with me for the summer and he did sound concerned when I told him about Bella's troubled emotional state, but I didn't give him the credit for actually acting on that concern. If that's what he's doing."

"I almost hung up on him," Frieda said. "I don't really know why I didn't. You know, Mom, I've never understood what you can possibly get out of talking to Dad."

That was understandable, Ruby thought. When Steve was no longer obliged to send child support payments he had gone off the grid. The periodic phone calls stopped; birthday and Christmas cards continued to come but with no return address. It was only when Frieda had married that Steve's sporadic calls to his ex-wife began again. At first Ruby considered the calls an annoyance and yet she had allowed them to continue and before long she had come to welcome the sound of her ex-husband's voice.

"Mom?"

"Sorry," Ruby said. "I was lost in the past and you know what a labyrinth that is. What do I get out of talking to your father? It's a question I've asked myself innumerable times over the years."

"And? What's the answer?"

"The answer is actually pretty simple. I loved him once. I loved him enough to marry him and have a child with him. For me, that counts for something. I guess it overrides—if barely—the fact of his bad behavior toward us."

Frieda frowned. "You're not saying that if Dad showed up on the doorstep asking to be taken back you'd agree?"

"God no!" Ruby laughed. *Not now, anyway,* she thought. "Accepting his occasional calls is as far as it's going to go, trust me."

"What does George have to say about Dad's keeping in touch with you? Does he even know?"

"Of course he knows, and he has nothing at all to say about it. Correction. He probably has a lot to say, but he's too smart to say it."

Frieda smiled a bit. "Aaron didn't find it strange, you know. He used to say that any attempt at family harmony should be valued. With his own family being so distant—emotionally and physically—he saw Dad's relationship with you as a good thing."

"Aaron was a smart man. Still, it was easier for him to be generous about Steve than it was—than it is—for you."

Frieda sighed. "Yeah. Being generous to someone who basically abandoned you isn't the easiest thing in the world to pull off."

Ruby reached for her daughter's hand. "Look," she said, "maybe I shouldn't have gotten pregnant by a man I knew to be irresponsible. But like I told you, I was in love and I did get pregnant and have a child and I can't regret that decision. I'm sorry for giving you a parent who couldn't be a real father to you, at least not after the first eleven years, but he did help give you the gift of life. And before he left us he did his best by you, if not always by me. I'm not lying about that."

"But he hurt you, Mom," Frieda argued. "He put you through so much by walking out. And by cheating on you with half the town. He was completely disrespectful of you and your marriage vows."

"Yeah," Ruby said, releasing her daughter's hand, "he did put me through a lot. I won't deny it. But I've never been his victim, Frieda. I promise you that. I could have walked away at any time, but I chose not to."

Frieda shook her head. "You can't mean to say you got what you deserved!"

"No. But I can say I made my own choices. Some of them were bad choices, but they were mine all the same. Now, enough talk of your father and me. Let's get back to your father and you. What did he say? What did you say?"

"He said the spirit had moved him to call me." Frieda shook her head. "Can you believe such nonsense? After all these years of virtually ignoring me! I basically told him this wasn't a good time for me to have a meaningful conversation with him."

"Is there ever a good time for a meaningful or difficult conversation?" Ruby asked.

"Probably not," Frieda said. "I don't know. The weirdest part is that for some reason I agreed to talk to him again. That is, if he deigns to call."

Ruby wondered. She couldn't know what had prompted Steve to reach out to his daughter at this point, but whatever his motive, the fact that he had reached out was monumental. "Maybe," she said after a long moment, "maybe this is the right time for you and your father to come to terms. I don't see how having a second conversation can do any damage. If you feel uncomfortable you could always end the call."

"I know but . . ."

"Or," Ruby said, "you don't have to talk to him ever again. It's your choice."

Frieda smiled grimly. "I almost wish someone would make the choice for me."

"Ah, that's one of life's many ironies. When you're a kid you get angry with adults for always making decisions on your behalf. All you want is to 'do it yourself' even if you have no idea of how to 'do' whatever it is that needs to be done. And then you grow up and now the responsibility for making decisions—and good ones at that!—is squarely on your own shoulders and you think, boy, did I have it easy back then."

Frieda sighed. "That's so depressingly true. Mom, do you think I should tell Bella that my father wants to reconnect with me? She's got so much going on right now I don't want to burden her any further."

"I don't think it can hurt to tell her," Ruby said. "It would be better than sneaking around in an attempt to keep his calls a secret. Bella needs to know that she can trust us one hundred percent. If she thinks something is going on behind her back . . ."

"I suppose you're right, Mom. As always."

Ruby chuckled. "If only!"

Frieda rose. "I think I'm going to lie down for a bit. I'll be up in time to help with dinner."

"No worries," Ruby said. "I'm going to enjoy the sun for a bit longer."

When Frieda had gone inside, Ruby turned her mind to the very important question of what exactly Frieda might want to hear from her father. Clearly she wanted to hear something; otherwise she would never have agreed to a second conversation. Did she want an abject apology for the years of his absence? Did she want a reasonable explanation for his chronic neglect? Did Frieda want to hear her father say that he loved her?

Whatever happened, Ruby thought, she hoped that Steve wasn't going to cause trouble. She supposed she could talk to him the next time he called and ask him to tread carefully with Frieda; at the same time she didn't want to come between father and daughter after all the years of silence and misunderstanding. She wanted to believe that if left alone Steve and Frieda might very well reconcile.

Ruby sighed. She really had no idea what might happen this summer. How could she? The future was always unknowable until it had happened and then it was the past. And there was nothing you could do about the past but try to forget it.

And forgetting was nearly always impossible.

# Chapter 18

It was just after lunch and Bella was on her way to meet Clara at the cottage she was sharing with three other girls employed at The Flipper. Bella had immediately accepted Clara's invitation to hang out; at the very least it was a way to spend her afternoon off. In the past few months her powers of concentration, never fantastic, not like Ariel's, had become even weaker, making it that much more difficult to keep up with her favorite blogs and websites, let alone read a book or watch a movie on YouTube.

Bella turned onto Valley Road and rode up to number 26. The cottage was a one-story structure; a lot of the paint was peeling and one of the front concrete steps was broken. Otherwise, Bella thought, it looked kind of cute, in a slightly run-down sort of way. Before she could ring the doorbell the door opened.

"Hi," Clara said. "I saw you coming. You don't have a car?"

"I don't drive." There was no need for a full explanation, Bella thought. Not now, anyway. "Nice place."

Clara shrugged. "It's okay. Come in."

Bella followed Clara through a small nondescript living room and down a narrow hall to a room at the back of the house. A small sign was tacked to the door. It read: Clara Crawford. Keep Out. The room's two small windows looked out on a minuscule patch of overgrown grass on which sat a few rickety-looking lawn chairs and an overturned milk crate. But it was the room itself that caught Bella's attention. It was a virtual shrine. Literally every inch of wall was covered in pictures of a good-looking guy on his own or with Clara. Along with selfies of the couple there were shots of the guy in a baseball uniform; diving into a pool; sitting cross-legged under a decorated Christmas tree; behind the wheel of a blue convertible; in a suit for some reason or other, maybe for a family occasion.

Bella felt slightly disoriented. Clara's room was so vastly different from her own room back in Massachusetts. There was not one photo of Ariel or her father on the dresser or walls or tucked into the frame of a mirror. There were no physical reminders of them at all. Bella needed it that way.

"All these pictures," she said. "They're of Marc? The guy you told me about?"

"Yeah. And look." Clara opened the middle drawer of the narrow dresser. "These are some of the things he gave me over the years. Like this necklace. It's an amethyst. And this little plush panda. I love pandas. Don't you love pandas?"

"They're okay," Bella said. "I like koalas better."

"And here," Clara said. "This is a ticket stub from the first movie we ever saw together."

Bella almost laughed. "You kept a ticket stub? I lose those things the minute the ticket guy hands them back. Not that I go to the movies a lot."

"Of course I kept it," Clara said. "I knew it would be important to me. To us. Sometimes it's the littlest things that matter most in a romantic relationship, you know?"

Bella nodded though in fact she didn't have much to say about what was important or not in a romantic relationship, not ever having been in one. Sometimes she wondered if she would ever fall deeply in love. Then again, what was the point of being in love when anyone could be taken away in the blink of an eye like Ariel had been, or even if the person could choose to abandon you like Marc had abandoned Clara? For that matter, like her grandfather had abandoned her mother and grandmother.

Bella pointed to a photo of Marc and Clara by a lake surrounded by pine trees. "Where was this taken?" she asked.

"That's at Marc's parents' vacation house on Lake Erie. They invited me two summers ago but not last summer." Clara frowned. "Marc went with them for a week. It was the longest week of my life. I thought I'd go crazy without him."

*It was only a week,* Bella thought. *I've lived over a year without my father and my sister.* But what she said was: "You must have been happy when he got home."

"I was," Clara said earnestly. "I was never happier in my entire life. Hey. Why don't you drive? You're old enough, right?"

Bella hesitated. Clara was being open with her; maybe she could be open with Clara. "Back before the accident," she said, "I couldn't wait to get my license. But after . . . It's no big deal. I get around okay."

Clara flopped down onto the bed. "There was a kid in my high school," she said, "who was totally paralyzed in a car accident in his freshman year. I think he broke his back. Something about his spine, anyway. His cousin was driving. The cousin was drunk and he died after about a week."

Bella sat in the room's sole chair. "That's too bad," she said. And then words just began to spill out of her mouth. "I know it's crazy, but sometimes I ask myself why both my father and my sister had to die. I think, didn't they know how hard it would be for Mom and me to get along without both of them? Okay, I know dying wasn't Dad and Ariel's fault. But then I wonder, whose fault was it? And what did I do to deserve losing both of them at the same time? What did my mother do to deserve that? None of it makes sense. I'm sort of a good person and my mother's definitely a good person. So, why us? Why can't anyone answer that question?"

Clara shrugged. "I don't know. Like you said, nothing makes sense. I was totally devoted to Marc. There was no reason for him to break up with me."

"Well, he probably had a reason. What was it?"

Clara scowled. "It doesn't matter. It didn't make sense."

"That's the weird thing in life," Bella said. "More and more it feels like nothing makes any sense at all. So what's the point in even trying to figure stuff out?"

"I don't know," Clara said. "Maybe there is no point."

"I don't know who to miss most," Bella blurted. "Every time I start to think about how much I miss my father I feel guilty I'm not thinking about my sister. And when I'm missing my sister really bad I start feeling guilty that I'm not thinking about my father. I feel like I'm going crazy. I mean, I can't blame Dad and Ariel for dying when and how they did, but sometimes I feel so mad at them. It makes no sense to be mad at dead people who didn't ask to be dead, so I must be losing my mind."

Clara leaned toward Bella. "I know, right?" she said. "Sometimes I think I'm losing my mind, too. I mean, sometimes I look in the mirror and I think, who is that? It's like I'm a totally different person than I was a few months ago. Hey, what did your sister look like?"

"My sister was a bit taller than me and had this gorgeous red hair, just like Ariel in *The Little Mermaid*. She was way better looking than me. She was like a Disney princess. Most days lately I feel like The Beast."

"Can I see a picture of her?" Clara asked, ignoring Bella's last comment. "You must have pictures on your phone."

"No," Bella said abruptly. "What I mean is there are no pictures on my phone. They got . . . they got lost." It was a lie. The photos were there. It was just that she hadn't been able to look at them in a while.

Bella got up and walked over to a photograph of Clara and Marc wearing matching Yankees sweatshirts. "I've never had a boyfriend," she said. "I mean, I like guys, but after my father and sister died I kind of lost interest in going out with anyone." Bella laughed a bit embarrassedly. "I've never even been on a date."

"Really?" Clara sighed. "I was so lucky when Marc chose me. I mean, he's perfect. He's gorgeous—well, you can see that!—and he's smart and he played trombone in the jazz band and he's going to be a lawyer someday. He could have had any girl in town, but he picked me."

Bella seriously doubted anyone was ever perfect, but what she said was: "So, were you guys having sex?"

"Yeah," Clara said. "Since we were sixteen. We had to keep it from our parents and that was sometimes tough; Marc and I almost got caught once on the daybed in his parents' basement. But it was worth sneaking around. We were in love. We *are* in love, no matter what Marc says. We'll be together forever and he'll be the only guy I'll ever sleep with. We grew up together. We *have* to spend the rest of our lives together! It makes sense that we do. Marc will see that someday." And then Clara added, very quietly, "I have to believe that he will."

Bella sighed and sank back into the sole chair. "You know," she said, "I thought Ariel would be my maid of honor someday. I thought my father would walk me down the aisle. But that's not going to happen now."

"Stupid bitch," Clara muttered.

Bella felt as if she had been slapped. "What!" she cried.

Clara waved her hand. "Not you, sorry. Don't you hear that singing?"

"Oh. Yeah. One of your housemates?"

"Yeah. She never stops singing those stupid show tunes from those stupid old musicals! It drives me nuts. All of my housemates are such idiots."

Bella listened intently for a moment. "Her voice is pretty good."

Clara shrugged. "Whatever. You don't have to live with it."

Maybe not, Bella thought, but there were far worse things than listening to show tunes. Still, Bella could understand Clara's being touchy. She had been like that for a while last summer; every little thing anyone said had made her want to scream. The whole world had seemed one colossal annoyance. She had even snapped at her grief counselor. She had apologized and Colleen had accepted her apology, but Bella had felt bad about her behavior for weeks. Somehow she had moved past that stage of being angry at the world. But were the feelings of dullness and apathy that had been oppressing her since the anniversary of her father's and sister's deaths any better?

"You know," she said suddenly, "I never thought that something really bad would happen to me or my family. Tragedy was something that happened to other people. Other people got cancer or were raped or got caught in terrorist bombings or died in car wrecks." Bella shook her head. "And then my grief counselor told me that sort of thinking is typical of teenagers. Teenagers feel invulnerable, she said. They think they're going to live forever and that all their friends and family will live forever with them."

Clara frowned. "But that's not the way it happens, is it?"

"No," Bella said. "It's not. The car accident knocked those stupid ideas out of me in a big way. Now there are days when all I can think about is the fact that someday I'm going to die. Me. Dead. I'll totally cease to exist. I think: How is that possible? And it's also possible that I might die a horrible death like my sister did. She really wanted to go to Europe. One lousy trip to London or wherever. Was that too much for her to ask from her time on this planet?"

Clara sighed. "Why can't things be the way we want them to be?"

"Because life just doesn't work that way, that's why." *Like*, Bella thought, *you want to be with Marc. He wants not to be with you, no matter what you think. Someone wins and someone loses.* "Hey," she said. "You want to come over to my grandmother's house for dinner sometime? She's an awesome griller. And she makes really good tomato sauce from scratch."

"No, thanks," Clara said quickly. "I mean, meeting other people's family makes me nervous. Especially parents and grandparents."

"Well," she said, "if you change your mind."

Clara smiled a bit. "Maybe. Damn. What time is it?"

Bella checked her phone. "It's almost two o'clock."

"I've got to be at work in half an hour. Sorry, Bella. Look, can we get together again?"

"Yeah," Bella said. "Sure."

"Cool." Clara grabbed her bag off the top of the dresser and Bella followed her out of the cottage. "Thanks for coming over," Clara said as she slid behind the wheel of her car.

Bella waved as Clara drove off, and then she got on her bike. *Clara's okay*, she thought as she rode off in the direction of home. She was kind of odd—what had Clara said about them on the Marginal Way, that they were both nuts?—but that was fine. Two nutty troubled people could probably get along pretty well for a summer, Bella thought. They might even become friends. Anything could happen. Bella had learned that the hard way.

# Chapter 19

"This is my favorite clam shack," Jack said as he and Frieda took seats at a picnic table overlooking the ocean. "The food's about the same as at The Clamshell in town, but the view is unbeatable."

Frieda smiled. "Agreed. And I haven't been to The Razor Clam in years, so this was a perfect choice." In fact, Frieda thought, the last time she had been here was with Aaron, Ariel, and Bella the summer before the accident. It had been a gusty afternoon and keeping the paper plates and cups anchored on the table had been a chore. There had been, Frieda remembered, much laughter.

"So, what's been going on since we last spoke?" Jack asked.

"Well," Frieda said. "I guess the biggest news is that my father called to talk to me. It's a first since he left us. He and my mother talk on occasion, but as for me . . ."

"Wow. That is news. What did he want? If that's not being too personal."

"I'm not sure what he wanted," Frieda admitted. "He said the spirit had moved him to call. He asked if Phil was giving his annual Independence Day party and then he asked if we could speak again."

"What did you tell him?" Jack asked.

"I told him yes, but honestly, I'm not so sure." Frieda waved her hand dismissively. "Sorry. Let's talk about something else."

"Nothing to be sorry about. Listen, that's our number. I'll go."

While Jack went up to the shack to get their orders, Frieda wondered what had moved her to tell him about her father's call. *Maybe,* she thought, *it's because Jack and I go back so far. It's almost as if he's a brother. Almost,* she amended, *but not quite.*

Jack rejoined her balancing two red plastic trays laden with food and drink.

"Impressive," Frieda said as he placed the trays on the table without sloshing the waters or sending the onion rings skidding.

"I waited tables in college. I hated it, but hey, it was a job. I had a few scholarships, but my parents weren't in a position to help much with the financial stuff. In terms of their emotional support, they were great." Jack smiled. "I guess I'm one of the lucky ones. I never hated my parents."

"Probably because you never had cause to hate them."

"That doesn't stop a lot of people from turning against the mother or father who raised them," Jack pointed out.

"That's true," Frieda said. Her father had certainly given her just cause to turn against him, but to actually hate him? Hate was just too ugly and exhausting. "I guess I'm one of the lucky ones, too," she added. "I'm eternally grateful to my mother for all she's done for me. For all she's still doing by having Bella and me here this summer."

"What else are you grateful for?" Jack asked. "I'm not trying to get all spiritual or anything; it's just that since Veronica died I've become pretty focused on the idea of gratitude. On identifying and acknowledging the good stuff in life. Frankly, it helps keep me sane."

Frieda took a bite of her lobster roll before she answered. "At the risk of sounding grim," she said, "I'm thankful for the three passersby who pulled Aaron and Ariel from the wreckage before it burst into flames. I wanted so badly to thank them personally for risking their lives trying to save two complete strangers, but I was told that once the ambulance came the Good Samaritans melted away into the crowd. And by that time there really was a crowd, gawkers and ghouls all staring at my poor husband and daughter."

"It's an unfortunate human tendency to need to connect to a tragedy," Jack said. "Most people don't mean any disrespect. And I don't think most people get a kick out of witnessing someone else's misfortune."

"I know, but . . ." Frieda shook her head. "It's hard not to imagine the scene."

"I know. Hey, can I tell you my Good Samaritan story?"

"Please do."

"There was a volunteer at the hospice named Matt," Jack said. "He was young, in his early twenties I'd guess. Anyway, one day Veronica mentioned that she used to love listening to the Allman Brothers instrumental song 'Little Martha' and that she hadn't heard it for ages. So the next day Matt brought in an old boom box and a CD copy of the original album on which the song appeared. I can't tell you how happy that made Veronica, and that a virtual stranger could be so loving to my wife is something I'll never forget. Luckily, I had the chance to express my thanks."

"That's something most of us don't do often enough in life, I think," Frieda said. "Express gratitude for all the little things other people do for us. Saying thank you when someone holds a door for you, or when someone lets you go ahead of him on line because you only have a carton of milk and he has a cart full of groceries. Saying thank you when someone makes your favorite meal even though he's absolutely exhausted." Frieda smiled. "Aaron was big on gratitude. And he was very good about teaching the girls how to be thankful."

Jack grimaced. "I know this makes me sound ancient, but given my job I spend a lot of time around young people, and too many of them have this air of entitlement, like they expect special treatment as their due. There's a lack of basic politeness and appreciation for the effort other people are making on their behalf." Jack laughed. "Okay, wow, I really am becoming a grumpy old man!"

"I hope I'm not guilty of raising a rude child," Frieda said. "I don't think that I am. Aaron and I both tried to make the girls feel valued and respected and loved. At the same time we tried to instill in them a work ethic and a sense of responsibility to others."

Frieda shook her head. "It's bad enough that Bella lost her sister, but to have lost her father, too. He was such a good role model. Let's just say nothing is the way I hoped it would be."

Jack reached across the table and gently laid his hand on Frieda's for a moment. "You can't count on anything being the way you hoped it would be," he said. "You'll go crazy unless you accept that. Believe me, I almost did go crazy at times during Veronica's illness. I'd count on a procedure being successful or a drug working the way it was supposed to work and then something altogether different would happen and I'd be left practically wailing to the heavens."

Frieda smiled sympathetically. "It must have been so awful."

"It was," he replied. "But it got a little easier once I really accepted the fact of Veronica's illness. Once I let go of the almost frantic determination that things would be well in the end. Once I really let go."

"Of hope?" Frieda asked.

"Not of hope," Jack said firmly. "Of expectations of a particular outcome."

"That makes an awful lot of sense. We're asked to bear so much in this life, aren't we? We're asked to be so brave, day after day after day. How do we do it? How does anyone manage to get through? How does anyone manage to suffer the slings and arrows of outrageous fortune?"

"I don't know. I don't think anyone knows, and that makes the act of living pretty heroic and wonderful in my opinion."

Frieda smiled. "You're an optimist, Jack Tennant."

"Not so much an optimist as a realist. For every lousy thing about being alive there's a wonderful thing. Maybe two wonderful things!" Jack smiled. "Okay, maybe I am an optimist."

"I like that about you, Jack," Frieda told him. "More than ever in my life I need to be around optimistic people."

"Good. Now, if you're not going to eat that last onion ring . . ."

Frieda snatched the onion ring from its paper tray. "Oh," she said, "but I am."

Jack sighed dramatically. "That's what I get for being a gentleman."

"Being a gentleman is always a good thing. Jack? I'm curious. How did you and Veronica meet?" Frieda asked.

"I was visiting a cousin in Connecticut and we went to a karaoke place one night. I was onstage belting out a seriously awful version of 'Don't Stop Believin' and this woman in the audience caught my eye. She was smiling at me and not in a mocking sort of way, and believe me I deserved to be mocked. So after I was through embarrassing myself I went over to her and said hello. And that's all it took for me to know I'd found The One." Jack smiled. "Sounds pretty goofy, doesn't it?"

"I think it sounds lovely," Frieda said honestly.

"After we got engaged Veronica won a teaching position at the private grammar school in South Berwick and moved in with me. She loved my house and she really made it her own as well. She made it our home." Jack shook his head. "Everything was going so smoothly."

"And then?" Frieda asked gently.

"And then we got married and Veronica had trouble getting pregnant. We both really wanted a family and after almost two years of trying without success we decided to give IVF a go."

"And it wasn't successful," Frieda said quietly.

"We'll never know if it might have been. Before we could get started Veronica was diagnosed with cancer and we turned all of our time and energy to getting her well. But in the end, we failed."

"Don't say 'failed.'" Frieda shook her head. "Sorry. It's just that when you say you failed to keep someone alive it means that you're guilty of negligence, of not caring enough. And I know that can't be true of you."

"Or of you, Frieda."

"I'm almost ready to believe that," Frieda told him.

"So, how did you and Aaron meet?"

Frieda smiled. "It was the first day of freshman orientation at college. I guess it was also one of those moments of recognition where you say to yourself, 'There he is' or 'There she is.' I loved him so much right from the start and yet . . ."

"And yet what?" Jack asked gently.

Frieda hesitated. This was a difficult admission to make and it surprised her that she wanted to share these thoughts with Jack. "And yet sometimes," she went on, "usually in the middle of the night after a particularly trying day when what I most need is a deep and dreamless sleep, I find myself blaming Aaron for the accident even though I've been assured by every authority involved that he wasn't at fault."

"I'm sorry, Frieda. What actually happened?"

"Well," Frieda said, "we decided to rent a car for the last full day of the vacation. The resort regularly used a local family-owned rental agency and they arranged everything for us. As promised, a car arrived the following morning; it was clean, the gas tank was filled, and Aaron could find nothing wrong with it. The car performed perfectly. In the morning we took a tour of a coffee plantation and in the afternoon we visited some spectacular waterfalls. It was a lovely day." Frieda swallowed hard against a lump in her throat. "It was only the next morning when Aaron and Ariel were on their way home from a museum that . . . That things went wrong."

Jack shook his head. "I'm sorry, Frieda. I know I've said it before, but I think it bears repeating over and over again."

"Thank you. Those sleepless nights . . . I start to think, why didn't Aaron detect something wrong with the car? How could he not have been aware of the danger? I hate that I doubt Aaron's competency. I really hate it. And when the first signs of dawn filter through the curtains of my bedroom I find myself in tears, apologizing to Aaron. If there had been anything he could have done to save Ariel's life he would have. Anything. It was the sort of man he was, always putting the needs of others before his own." Frieda attempted a smile. "Well, now you know what sort of a monster I am."

"You're not a monster," Jack said. "Just human."

"I wish being human meant not being so irrational."

"There's not a chance of that! Look, not long after Veronica's diagnosis I felt so scared about what would happen next that I blamed Veronica for the cancer. I couldn't stop thinking that if only she'd eaten better or exercised more often she wouldn't have gotten sick." Jack shook his head. "Of course it was ridiculous and unfair as it always is to blame the victim, and thank God I didn't actually give voice to those thoughts. Can you imagine what harm I would have done? But the thoughts were there and I was ashamed of them until I got a handle on why I was thinking the way I was. The cancer made no sense, so I had to find a responsible party to blame, when all along it was chance that was to blame. Chance, pure and simple."

"Yes, chance." Frieda glanced at her watch. "Look at the time! We've been here for almost two hours."

Jack smiled. "Time flies when you're having fun. Though the content of our conversation wasn't always fun, was it?"

"No, but the experience of the conversation has been a good thing; at least it has for me. Thanks, Jack." *He gets it*, she thought. *He really gets what it's like.*

"Thank you, too, Frieda. Though next time you might share more of the onion rings."

"It's every man, woman, or child on his or her own when it comes to onion rings and cupcakes."

Jack grinned. "Forewarned," he said, "is forearmed."

# Chapter 20

"I can't believe we're actually having a drink somewhere other than one of our homes." Phil shook his head. "We almost never go out during tourist season. Whose idea was this again?"

"Mine," Ruby said. "And since it's my treat you're not allowed to complain." Ruby lowered her voice and added, "Though if they let one more person in this bar I think they'll be breaking a law."

Ruby and Phil were sipping glasses of Prosecco at the bar in one of downtown Yorktide's most popular eateries, The Atlantic. In atmosphere it was the opposite of The Friendly Lobsterman, the cozy, unpretentious, kid-welcoming restaurant owned by the Gascoyne family for over twenty years.

"So why did you want to meet here?" Phil asked. "And I'm not complaining. It's just that an upscale place like this usually isn't your cup of tea."

Ruby shrugged. "A whim? A change of scenery? A chance to see how the other half lives? Hey, guess who reached out to Frieda the other day? Steve."

Phil's eyes widened. "Steve as in Steve Hitchens? Her father?"

"The very one. He called the house hoping to find her and she happened to pick up the phone."

"Wow. Not much astonishes me these days, but I have to say

this rates as an astonishing event. So, did she talk to him? Or did she slam the phone down?"

"She told me she was tempted to hang up, but she didn't. And she even agreed to talk with him again, though she's not sure why she did."

Phil shook his head. "I suppose there's always mere curiosity, but . . . No, I don't think curiosity would be enough of a motivation for Frieda. Not after all she's been through. As for Steve, what in the world made him reach out to his daughter now?"

"I have no idea," Ruby admitted. "I don't know what he hopes to achieve. All I can think is that he wants to make amends. I mean, why contact her after all this time if he doesn't care? What would be the point?"

"Like you," Phil said, "I have no idea. I've never pretended to understand Steve. Don't get me wrong. I don't hate the guy. Hate isn't an emotion with which I'm familiar. I just don't trust him. What if he succeeds in gaining Frieda's confidence or even her affection—and we know he can be charming—and then he just walks, like he did all those years ago?"

"I think Frieda knows what she's getting into," Ruby said. "At least, she knows her father has severe limitations when it comes to accepting responsibility of any sort."

"Still," Phil argued, "Frieda is vulnerable. She's worried about Bella. She doesn't need something else troubling her."

"True. But there's not much I can do, is there? I did consider giving Steve a warning to tread carefully, but honestly, Phil, I don't want to interfere. Maybe it's time Frieda and her father negotiate a peace without my influence."

"You might be right about that. I just don't know. What does George have to say about this development?" Phil asked, finishing his glass of Prosecco.

"I haven't told him yet," Ruby said. "I suspect he'll feel as you and I do—apprehensive. Protective of Frieda's feelings. But Phil, we have to have faith in Frieda to know what's best for her."

Phil frowned. "Since we can't have faith in Steve. Okay, I'll be nice. Steve's not evil. He's just really good at causing collateral damage."

Ruby couldn't argue with that. "There's another thing I haven't told you," she said. "Let's have another glass."

"Keeping secrets from your old friend?" Phil smiled. "Sure, one more round."

When the bartender had brought two fresh glasses of Prosecco, Ruby said, "Frieda wants to give a little party to mark what would have been Ariel's sixteenth birthday. Just the three of us, with a cake and our sharing memories and all that."

"And?" Phil asked.

"And Bella seems deeply against it," Ruby told him. "I'm not entirely sure why other than the fact that she says it's macabre to have a party for a dead person."

"Wow. She really said macabre?"

"Yup. But Phil, what I also don't understand is why I have a bad feeling about the idea. After all it's not outrageous. A memorial to a child who's gone ahead is encouraged, at least from all I've learned about mourning."

Phil shook his head. "You've got me there. I can't see much of a downside to having a small party."

"You're probably right," Ruby said, "and I'm probably making too big a deal of it all. So much these days seems . . ."

"Seems what?"

"Seems uncertain. But then again," Ruby said, raising her glass to her lips, "that's just life."

Ruby tossed restlessly in her bed. All that talk with Phil earlier about Steve and the collateral damage he had caused had thrust her mind back to the days of her marriage, the days when it was more likely than not that Ruby was busy making do when Steve lost jobs, making excuses when he failed to deliver on a promise, and turning a blind eye when he engaged in yet another affair.

There was the time, Ruby remembered now, when they had been compelled to return the substantial initial payment on a commission for a dining room table. Steve just couldn't seem to finish the job. The trip Ruby had organized to Acadia National Park had to be canceled and making rent for the next two months had been a close thing.

Ruby sighed. How many times had she caught Steve forgetting to buckle Frieda into her car seat? How many times had he brought home unannounced a fly-by-night buddy in need of a meal and a place to crash? And what about the time Ruby had gone to visit her ailing mother for four days and returned to find Frieda in dirty clothes, unwashed, and her hair knotted? No three-year-old ever protested the lack of a bath and indeed Frieda had seemed perfectly content, but Ruby had been angry. "Why is the sink full of dirty dishes?" she had demanded. "The dishwasher broke," Steve had told her. She asked if he had called the repair service. He said it had slipped his mind. He apologized with a smile and Ruby had wondered if she were being too fastidious and critical. And when Steve drew her into his arms and kissed her, her anger melted away. She cleaned the kitchen, called the repair service, and gave her daughter a bath. Getting the knots out of Frieda's hair had been a bit more difficult.

And Ruby had routinely excused these episodes of irresponsibility. After all, she believed there was no bad intent behind them, just carelessness. An inability on her husband's part to focus on someone other than himself for more than a few moments at a time. A failure to think about the consequences of his actions. After a while Ruby had begun to wonder if by keeping the extent of Steve's misconduct a secret she had really been protecting Frieda and Phil and Tony from the full truth of his faulty character, or if she had simply been acting as Steve's enabler.

In the years since his defection Ruby had often wondered if there had been other enablers in Steve's life. He had never mentioned a friend or a colleague or a lover, not even in passing. It was as if after he left Yorktide he became alienated from the human race. But he wasn't alienated from the human race because he stayed in touch with *her*, Ruby Hitchens, the woman who had been his wife. The woman who was the mother of his child.

His only child? Ruby smiled ruefully into the dark. Lothario. Don Juan. Philanderer. Rake. Cheat. *Your judgment was seriously off when you married Steve Hitchens*, she told herself. *Seriously off.*

# Chapter 21

Bella lay on her bed. She had been thinking about Clara and the shrine she had erected to her former boyfriend. Even though a part of her thought that Clara's devotion was romantic, another part of her found something about it odd. Now, on this muggy afternoon, Bella thought she might finally have identified what it was about Clara's devotion that gave her a slight case of the creeps.

In history class sophomore year they had learned how some ancient cultures had worshipped the relics of a dead person; they believed the remnant of the person or the presence of something he had owned held some special power and could protect or even grant the wishes of the living. It was an interesting idea except when it came to people collecting gross things like bits of a dead person's bones or fingernail clippings or hair.

Of course, worshipping relics wasn't really what Clara was doing—Marc was alive after all—but Clara's behavior had also gotten Bella thinking about the importance mere things had taken on in the first weeks after the crash. She and Ariel had bought matching shell necklaces in Jamaica. Ariel had been wearing hers that fateful last morning, but it hadn't been among the effects their mother had brought home from the morgue. Mad with grief, Bella had vowed never to take off her own necklace. It would be a gesture of devotion and remembrance.

But when she got home to Massachusetts the sight of the string of shells around her neck had for some reason made Bella feel sick to her stomach. Roughly she had pulled off the necklace and stuffed it deep into the garbage waiting at the curb to be taken away by the sanitation people the next morning. After a restless night Bella had woken with a feeling of intense regret and still in her pajamas she had raced out to the curb and torn open the lid of the garbage can, only to find it empty. She had spent the next several days despondent. The loss of the shell necklace was the loss of her sister all over again.

After that she had stripped her room of all photos and other reminders of her father and her sister. Even when she had begun to heal, to consider taking driving lessons, to consider spending time with Kerri, it had still been tough to bear the sight of her father's and her sister's personal possessions. *Like Dad's dress watch and Ariel's blue topaz ring,* Bella remembered now on this muggy summer afternoon. *Like Dad's running shoes and Ariel's favorite wool sweater.*

Objects, possessions, relics—call them what you liked, but things meant something; things had the value you gave to them, even if only for a short period of time. Bella glanced at the squat oak dresser that stood against the wall opposite the beds. She had no idea what might be inside the drawer that had been Ariel's. Suddenly she sat up and swung her legs off the bed. *I'm going to be brave,* she thought. *I'm going to see what Ariel left behind.*

Gently, almost reverently, Bella slid open the bottom of the two wide drawers. The first thing to catch her eye was a crystal point on a leather cord. Ariel had loved collecting crystals. Carefully Bella moved the crystal aside and focused on the other items in the drawer. There was a pair of khaki shorts and two T-shirts, one white and one blue. Ariel had hated wearing clothing with logos or pictures of celebrities printed on it. Looking at those plain, neatly folded T-shirts, Bella almost smiled. Practically every one of her own T-shirts announced its corporate origin—Abercrombie & Fitch, PINK, Adidas—or advertised a band Bella was momentarily obsessed with.

In addition to the clothing there was a black headband, the wide stretchy kind, and an unopened package of elastic hair ties. Ariel had always been getting compliments on her hair—"It's like you're a model for a Pre-Raphaelite painting!"—but she had never really understood why. "It's just hair," she would say to Bella. "What's inside a person is way more important."

The last item in the drawer was a small hardcover book bound with a metal lock. A diary? Bella had never seen it before. She lifted the book out of the drawer and stared at the picture of a white unicorn on its cover. Her sister had always been scribbling, but she had never seemed concerned with privacy. None of the notebooks Ariel had routinely left scattered throughout the house were locked and she had never asked her family not to read what she had written. Still, after the funeral, Bella's mother had gathered the notebooks, put them in a cardboard box, and sealed it with packing tape. The notebooks remained unread and, for all Bella knew, they might remain unread forever.

But this book was obviously different. What had Ariel written that was so important that she had felt compelled to hide the content from her family? Bella searched the rest of the drawer but found no key. It might be hidden somewhere else in the room or Ariel might have kept it back home in Massachusetts. It might even have been in her luggage the morning she got into that rental car.

Bella got to her feet and, holding the little book in both hands, she perched on the edge of her bed. Everyone knew that when someone committed suicide her family and friends were frantic to understand why, especially if the person hadn't left a note that made much sense to them. But this was different, Bella thought. There was no good reason for her to violate her sister's privacy just because she was dead. Ariel hadn't killed herself. She hadn't *wanted* to die. What more did Bella need to know about the sister she had lost so suddenly beyond the fact that Ariel had loved being alive?

Still, the temptation to open the little book was great, as was the fear. What if Ariel had written about how annoying her sister could be or how angry Bella made her when she wore something of Ariel's and it wound up torn or stained? What if by opening the book Bella learned that Ariel really did think her sister was dumb?

*No*, Bella thought. *I can't open this.* She wanted—she needed—Ariel's good estimation of her, maybe now more than ever. *If Ariel knew I'd broken into this book she'd be disappointed in me*, Bella thought. *But would she also understand why I did it, why I needed to read her own words, to hear her voice even if only in my head?*

Bella just didn't know the answer to that question. With a sigh she got off her bed, carefully replaced the little locked book in the dresser drawer, and slid it shut.

*Maybe*, she thought, *I'll call Clara.*

# Chapter 22

Frieda took a sip from the cup of tea she had just brewed. It was strong black tea, without the addition of milk or sugar, and if her dentist suggested one more time that she might need fewer cleanings if she gave it up she would find another dentist.

Bella was at the table, staring at her phone. She had been sitting there since before Frieda had come into the kitchen and she hadn't yet said a word. Frieda didn't think Bella was trying to be rude. Rather, it felt as if her daughter just didn't much care that there was another person with her in the room.

*Well*, Frieda thought, *I care.* "My father called me the other day," she said. "I thought you might want to know."

Frieda waited for a reply, and when none was forthcoming she repeated her words. "My father called me the other day."

Bella looked up from her phone, her expression fairly blank. "I heard you," she said.

"It was totally unexpected. I hadn't heard his voice in years, but I recognized it right away."

"This doesn't have anything to do with me, does it?" Bella asked.

"Well, no," Frieda admitted. "I guess it doesn't. Unless your grandfather calls again and asks to speak with you."

"But he hasn't yet, right?"

"No."

"So it doesn't matter." Bella got up from the table. "I'm going out for a ride."

"How long will you be?" Frieda asked.

"I don't know."

"Be careful."

Bella nodded and left the kitchen.

Frieda took another sip of tea and then another; the drink usually had a soothing effect, but not at that moment. She had hoped that Bella's spending time with the girl she had met on the Marginal Way might help lift her spirits, but so far Frieda hadn't seen any improvement in her daughter's mood. Bella's friendships, once so many and robust, had suffered as a result of the accident that had taken Aaron's and Ariel's lives. Bella's closest friend, Kerri Woods, had tried her best to reach Bella in her state of self-imposed isolation. And Frieda had encouraged her daughter to accept Kerri's overtures. But in the end Bella's grief had proved too heavy a burden for the relationship to bear. "She just misses Bella so much," Mrs. Woods had told Frieda one day not long after Bella's birthday in April. "And I don't know how to explain to her what Bella is going through."

*Sometimes,* Frieda thought now, *I can't explain it to myself, either.* And she wondered if her own process of grieving was getting in the way of her being a proper support to Bella this summer. There was Ariel's birthday for one. Frieda had promised her mother that she would reconsider the idea of marking Ariel's birthday with a party and she *had* reconsidered it, but her own need to celebrate the occasion was great and she had decided to go ahead with her plan. After all, why did Bella's needs always have to take precedence over hers?

Frieda was duly appalled by these feelings. To be resentful of your own child's pain made you a freak of sorts, didn't it?

"What's wrong? You look downright distraught."

Frieda hadn't heard her mother entering the room, so absorbed had she been in her musings. "I am distraught," she admitted. "I've been thinking the most horrible thoughts. I've been resenting Bella for distracting me these past few months. I've been resenting her for withdrawing and causing me to worry all over again with the intensity I felt in the first weeks after the accident. And I feel terrible about being resentful of my child's needs."

Ruby sighed and sat at the table. "Just because a parent feels anger or annoyance with her child doesn't mean she's evil. You know that, Frieda. I'm sure Bella has been a burden before now and at times even Ariel must have required more than you felt you had to give, more than you really wanted to give." Ruby smiled. "Come sit and I'll tell you about the times when you were, how should I say this, an inconvenience."

"Me?" Frieda said, joining her mother. "An inconvenience? When?"

Ruby looked to the heavens. "Ah, where to begin?"

"Mom."

"Okay," Ruby said, lowering her eyes. "There was that time you were into that dreadful boy band, who were they, The Wrong Direction or The Front Room Boys. Something silly like that. You'd play that infernal so-called music at full volume until I prayed I'd go deaf before I did something I'd regret."

"You could have asked me to turn down the volume," Frieda pointed out. "And 'dreadful.' 'Infernal.' Really?"

"Yes," Ruby said, "really, and I did ask you to turn down the volume, repeatedly, and you would and then a few minutes later the volume would mysteriously be at full blast again."

Frieda smiled sheepishly. "Sorry. But when did I really stand in your way of accomplishing something important?"

"When did you stand in my way or when did I think you were?" Ruby said. "When I was studying for exams in nursing school and you needed help with your homework. When I needed to be alone with my memories of your father and your dinner needed to be made and your laundry done for school the following day. When you first met Aaron and were so blissfully happy and so gosh darn vocal about it. Don't get me wrong," Ruby added hurriedly. "I was happy for you and you had every right to gush about how beautifully Aaron treated you. But there were times when your happiness only served to highlight my own aloneness and I just wished you would stop sharing. Shameful of me, right?"

Frieda shook her head. "No. No, I can understand. Parents are flesh and blood. Flawed. Weak."

"Also strong when we need to be," Ruby pointed out. "I never asked you to stop talking about Aaron, did I? I never refused to help you with long division when I had an end-of-term exam the next day, did I?"

"No. Of course you didn't."

"So be annoyed with Bella. Feelings are fine, as long as you act carefully on some feelings and not at all on others."

"I'll try to keep that in mind," Frieda promised.

"Good," her mother said briskly, rising from the table. "Now, I'm off to the hospital. Do yourself a favor and get some fresh air. It will do wonders for you."

Frieda smiled gratefully. "Thanks, Mom," she said. "I mean it."

# Chapter 23

"Happy Fourth of July, everyone!" Phil raised his glass in a toast to his guests, who responded with a great cheer.

As promised, Phil really had outdone himself this year. Even Bella, in her deeply antisocial mood, had to acknowledge that the party was pretty awesome. First, there was the food. In addition to the ubiquitous lobster rolls, corn on the cob, potato and macaroni salads, coleslaw and fruit salad, there were hamburgers and hot dogs, platters of cold shrimp with three varieties of dipping sauce, and everyone's favorite, pigs in a blanket. To drink there was beer, wine, water, and a nonalcoholic fruit punch. From a bakery up in Portland Phil had bought dozens of mini cheesecakes of all differ- ent flavors, from chocolate mint to pomegranate. And in a nod to the theme of the holiday, there were three apple pies keeping warm on electric warming trays set up in the kitchen.

There were probably about fifty or sixty people milling around the backyard or seated at the redwood picnic tables Phil had rented for the occasion. Bella recognized most of the guests, people she had known, if from afar, all of her life. One person was notably ab- sent and that was her mother's old schoolmate Jack; her mother had told her he had accepted a prior invitation. Bella was glad. She supposed he was okay on his own—not that she had ever met him—but he was not okay when he was hanging around Frieda Braithwaite.

Clara wasn't at the party, either, though Bella had invited her. She knew Phil wouldn't mind—he was one of those the more the merrier people—but Clara had said that she wasn't in the mood for parties. "Neither am I," Bella told her. "But I sort of have to go." Clara had grimaced. "Good luck. Better you than me." Bella had thought that was a bit of an odd thing to say, even kind of cold, but Clara was sometimes—what was the word? Surprising. Like that time she had called her housemate a bitch just because she was singing.

A loud burst of laughter from a far corner of the yard where a few guests—including her mother—were playing badminton caused Bella to wince. It was probably wrong of her, but she resented the laughter and the obvious good spirits of the other guests. Misery loves company, she thought. It was pretty pathetic to want other people—including your mother—to feel bad just because you felt bad. Still, it was how she felt; so Bella decided to get away from the festivities. She was sure she wouldn't be missed; she wasn't exactly giving off happy party vibes.

Bella passed through the patio doors, murmuring greetings to those guests who had come in to use the bathroom or to snag a piece of apple pie from the kitchen. She made her way to the library and quietly closed the door behind her. The room had been Ariel's favorite and even Bella thought it was amazing. Phil had spent most of his life collecting books on all sorts of subjects, from art to politics, from gardening to science. The golden-colored wood bookcases reached from floor to ceiling and there were two sliding ladders to help you reach the books on the top shelves. Years earlier Phil had given Ariel a key to the house so that even when he wasn't there she could spend time alone in his library while Bella went to the beach with her boogie board or just lazed around her grand-mother's backyard doing absolutely nothing.

Bella sighed and sank gratefully into one of the big brown leather armchairs. The room was cool and quiet and it wasn't long before she began to feel—better. Not great but better. Sure, she would have to go back outside at some point, and sure, she dreaded the party or celebration or whatever it was her mother was planning in Ariel's honor two days from now, but for these few minutes she could exist only in the present. At least she could try. Colleen had talked about learning how to live fully in the moment; she had said that if you could learn how to focus on the here and now and not on what had gone or what was to come you could achieve real peace of mind.

Whether that was true or not Bella didn't know. What she did know was that her eyes were beginning to close and her body to settle more deeply into the chair.

"You might at least pretend to be having a good time, for Phil's sake."

Bella's eyes flew open; she hadn't heard the door to the library open. It was her grandmother. "That's why I came in here," Bella said. "I didn't want to be a drag on everyone's fun."

Her grandmother put her hand on the back of the chair and smiled down at her. "Well, that was thoughtful, I suppose. Did you get anything to eat?"

"Yeah," Bella said. "I'm okay."

"Your mother seems to be enjoying herself. I'm glad."

Bella shrugged.

"People deserve what small moments of happiness they can snatch," her grandmother went on. "Misery comes to everyone, Bella. I know you've been through hell, but so have lots of other people. And if they haven't been through hell yet, they'll be going through it one day."

"Sorry," Bella said. And she remembered the quote Phil had tacked up in his office at the shop. *If you're going through hell, keep going.*

"Now, come on. Come back to the party." Her grandmother held out her hand, and after a moment Bella rose from the chair and took it.

*If it makes Grandma happy for me to pretend*, she thought, *I'll do it.*

# Chapter 24

At Ruby's urging Bella had gone off to talk with Matilda Gascoyne, current matriarch of one of Yorktide's oldest families. Matilda was a tactful woman. Ruby was sure she would never bring up painful subjects in a painful way. She might even be able to bring a smile to Bella's face.

"You need a break, Ruby." She turned to find Phil at her side. Though the temperature was pushing eighty-five, he looked cool and collected as always in an open-necked white shirt and pressed chinos. "You've been at the grills all afternoon with hardly a rest. Let me get George. Or let me take over."

"I'm okay," Ruby said. "Really. You know me. I'm most happy when I'm most busy." She wiped her brow with the back of her hand. "And sweating."

Phil sighed. "You're a workaholic, Ruby."

"Guilty as charged."

Phil walked on to chat with another of his guests and Ruby continued to lightly grill hamburger buns. What she hadn't admitted to Phil was that she was glad to have something to do other than chat with her neighbors, lovely though they were. This year's party—the first since Ariel's death—was serving to bring back the past in vivid detail. And that past, peopled as it was with her former husband, was bittersweet. How in love she had been; how much fun she and Steve had shared; how destroyed she had felt when he left.

Ruby was not unaware of the irony of the situation. A few moments ago she had urged Bella to pretend she was enjoying the festivities when she might as well have urged herself as well. Maybe she should have left Bella alone in the library, content with her own thoughts. Lately it seemed so hard to know the right thing to do or to say.

Ruby glanced in the direction of the long table piled high with food. George was there, plate in hand, talking with another member of the Gascoyne clan. She hoped he was enjoying the party. He had been so wise and reassuring when she told him that Steve had suddenly reached out to his daughter. Yes, Ruby thought. You couldn't get much of a better man than George Hastings. But why did he have to propose? Why couldn't they simply go on as they had been?

But life was never neat and orderly and the way you expected it to be. And certainly what George had offered, a formal acknowledgment of their commitment, was something potentially wonderful, not anything odd or out of the ordinary. So then why—

"Hey, Ruby!" It was Dan Stueben, looking tan and fit, no mean feat after the decidedly not neat or orderly turn his life had taken a few years back. Now he was thriving, having taken over Freddie Ross's law practice when Sheila, her partner of well over fifty years, had demanded she retire. "How about a couple of hot dogs?"

Ruby smiled. "Sure thing, Dan. I haven't had the chance to congratulate you and Allie on your wedding. I'm really happy for you."

"Thanks, Ruby. I have to admit there was a time not too long ago when I never thought I'd have my daughter back in my life and a wonderful woman as my wife. When Evelyn died and I got addicted to the painkillers . . . I'm so grateful I can't . . ." Dan shook his head. "If I go on I'll start to cry and this is supposed to be a happy occasion."

"Tears often go hand in hand with happy occasions," Ruby remarked, handing Dan a paper plate with two hot dogs in buns. "Enjoy," she said. And as Dan Stueben went to join his family she thought, *And so often, happy occasions only serve to remind us of all that we've lost. They only serve to—*

"Hey, Ruby." It was one of Phil's neighbors, a single woman in her thirties who owned a very successful full-service hair salon in town. "Can I get a hamburger?"

Ruby nodded briskly, grateful for the interruption to her thoughts. "You like yours medium rare, right?"

Katie Joyce smiled. "What a memory! Thanks, Ruby. I do."

# Chapter 25

Frieda placed a cotton napkin next to each of the three plates set out on the kitchen table. It was July 6. Sixteen years ago at seven thirty in the morning Ariel Alice Braithwaite had been born.

In the dollar store in Wells Frieda had found a small plastic replica of the Eiffel Tower to set atop the iced cake she had bought at Bread and Roses. From Pretty Blossoms, Yorktide's best florist, she had bought a bouquet of pink peonies, Ariel's favorite flower. They sat at the top of the table in a clear glass vase.

Frieda rearranged one of the flowers and glanced at the kitchen clock. Neither Bella nor Ruby had mentioned this evening's celebration when they had been together at breakfast and dinner. But that was all right. This anniversary of Ariel's birth was difficult for them all, more difficult than the anniversary of Aaron's birthday the previous October. The death of a child was the prime example of nature out of order. The death of a child felt so fundamentally *wrong*. But that didn't mean the memories of the child's life should be shunned.

"Where's Bella?"

Frieda looked up to see her mother in the doorway. "In her room, I suppose," she said. "I asked her to be here at eight."

"The table looks pretty." Ruby came into the kitchen and glanced at the clock on the wall next to the fridge. "She's got two minutes."

"You don't think she'd actually refuse to join us?" Frieda asked. Before her mother could answer, Bella appeared in the doorway. "Good," Frieda said with a smile. "Let's take our seats."

Without comment Bella and Ruby sat in their usual places at the table. Frieda noted that her daughter's expression was guarded and that her mother's expression was wary. *No matter*, she thought. *This will be a healing moment for us. I know it will.* Frieda poured three glasses of sparkling cider and lifted her glass. "To Ariel."

"To Ariel," her mother said quietly.

Bella did not lift her glass. "What are we supposed to do now?" she asked belligerently. "Just sit here?"

Frieda held back a sigh of frustration. "I thought that each of us could share our favorite memory of Ariel. Mom? Why don't you go first?"

Her mother cleared her throat. "My favorite memory of Ariel?" she said. "That's a tough one. In fact, I'm not sure I can pick just one."

"Then I'll go first," Frieda said. "There are so many wonderful memories, of course. But I'd say one of my all-time favorites is when Ariel played the baby bear in her fifth-grade play. The girl who played Goldilocks had nothing on her. Ariel absolutely stole the show."

"Yes," her mother said. "She was awfully good. The costume was adorable."

"Bella?" Frieda looked to her daughter. "Would you like to share a favorite memory of your sister?"

"No!" Bella cried. "This is stupid! Pretending won't bring Ariel back, Mom! It just won't!"

Frieda felt the blood rush to her face. She suddenly felt very angry. "I'm not pretending," she argued, her voice rising against her will. "Do you think I don't know that Ariel is gone? Do you think I don't know I'll never see her again or hold her hand or brush her hair? Do you think I'm unaware of the fact that she'll never go to college or get married or have children?" Frieda pointed at the Eiffel Tower atop the cake. "Do you think I'm not haunted by the fact that she'll never get to Europe like she wanted to do? Why can't you just—"

"Why can't you just stop talking!" Bella shouted.

Frieda gripped the edge of the table with both hands. "If Ariel were here she'd—"

"But she's *not* here! This is pathetic!" Bella shoved her plate and fork aside and roughly pushed her chair back from the table. Her glass tipped over and the sparkling cider made a widening pool. "I'm out of here!" she shouted, and ran from the room.

"Bella!" Frieda got up to follow.

Ruby put a hand on her arm. "Let her go. Sit. I'll clean up this spill."

Frieda winced as the front door slammed shut.

"But Mom—"

"Give her space, Frieda," her mother replied quietly but firmly as she mopped the table with paper towels. "She's in no condition to talk right now."

Frieda rubbed her eyes and sighed. All anger had drained from her and she was left feeling utterly defeated. "You were right, Mom. How could I have been so stupid as to think this was a good idea?"

"Not stupid," her mother corrected. "Just hopeful. Frieda, what were you going to say when Bella cut you off? That if Ariel were here she would . . ."

"I have absolutely no idea," Frieda admitted. "I didn't mean to lose my temper. All I wanted to do was to help Bella, to help all of us, move on in the healing process. I just wanted . . ."

Frieda felt her mother's hand on her shoulder. "Healing is never straightforward or predictable, Frieda, and that goes for healing after a physical trauma as well as after an emotional trauma. Trust me, I know, and not just because I work in a hospital."

Her mother returned to her seat and the two women sat in silence, the cake untouched, the sparkling cider going flat. *What would Aaron have advised me to do?* Frieda wondered. *Would he have suggested I not mark my daughter's birthday? Would he be angry with me for being so selfish and ignoring Bella's feelings?* Frieda glanced once again at the kitchen clock and her heart leaped in her chest. "Maybe we should go look for her, Mom," she said. "It's been almost twenty minutes."

"All right. But let's not just go chasing in all directions. Think where she might have headed."

"I don't know!" Frieda felt panic rising within her, like the panic she had felt in the lobby of the Jamaican resort when it began to dawn on her that something terrible might have happened to her husband and child. At least Bella didn't have her driver's license. At least she wasn't behind the wheel of a car right now, feeling distressed and making reckless decisions. "If she took her bike," Frieda said, her voice shaking, "she might have ridden into town. Or maybe she went to The Flipper to see her friend—"

Just then the front door opened, and a moment later footsteps pounded up the stairs.

"Wait for it," Ruby murmured. "And there it is. The slamming door. Well, at least she's home safe and sound."

"Thank God." Frieda took a few steadying breaths. "Maybe this party wasn't entirely a disaster after all," she said after a moment. "Bella showed more emotion tonight than I've seen her show in months. Maybe that's something for which to be grateful. Or maybe I'm just refusing to face the full extent of the mess I made."

"Well," her mother said robustly, "I don't know the answer to that, but I do know I've never been one to let a perfectly good cake go to waste. I'm having a piece and I suggest you do the same."

"After I ditch the Eiffel Tower." Frieda yanked the little monument from the cake and tossed it across the room and into the sink.

# Chapter 26

Bella lay curled on her side, her hands under her cheek. The room was dark. *What a disaster*, she thought, closing her eyes against the shame. She had gotten as far as Mr. Mathis's house three blocks away when she realized with the force of a physical slap that running off had been an incredibly foolish thing to do. She had never done anything so dramatic. Okay, once when she was about ten she had gotten really angry about something that had happened in school and she had thrown a plate across the kitchen. Ariel had burst into tears and Bella had immediately felt terrible for having caused such chaos.

Chaos like she had caused this evening. Suddenly Bella heard her mother's and grandmother's voices drawing near. They were probably coming up to bed. She hoped neither would knock on her door. She was not in the mood to talk. But neither did. Bella breathed a sigh of relief. And she wondered if one of the reasons she had been so upset earlier had anything to do with how she had felt at Phil's party, so resentful of the other guests who were clearly having a good time. Even when a customer in the shop laughed or exclaimed over a beautiful vase or set of candlesticks Bella tensed with annoyance. She didn't like feeling so negative all the time, so bitter and agitated, but she couldn't seem to help it. When her mother had gone on about Ariel playing the baby bear in Goldilocks, a big smile on her face, it was all Bella could do not to scream, "Stop smiling! This is not a fun moment! Things are awful!"

Bella flipped onto her back and frowned into the dark. What was up with her mother these days? What was her mother thinking? It was no secret that she had gone to lunch with that guy she knew from school, but she hadn't said anything about it afterward, which was weird. When things weren't a big deal you talked about them. But maybe, Bella thought guiltily, remembering the stricken look on her mother's face when she had turned and run from the kitchen, maybe she was being unfair in thinking her mother would be so disrespectful of Aaron Braithwaite's memory as to consider dating so soon after the accident.

As for the celebration . . . Bella sighed. Clearly it had been important for her mother to mark Ariel's birthday by having a cake and flowers. How many times had Colleen told her that everyone grieved in her own way, that there was no right or wrong way to mourn a loss, that it was a unique and highly personal experience? *I've been a jerk*, Bella thought. *And I'm sorry for it.* She would apologize to both her mother and her grandmother for running off like she had. They had probably been worried and worrying them had not been her intention—in fact, there had been no intention of any kind behind her tearing out of the house.

Bella suddenly got up and went over to what had been Ariel's bed. She leaned close to the pillows and thought she could smell the light lemony scent Ariel used to wear. God, she missed her sister so badly! With a sob Bella fell onto the bed and buried her face in Ariel's pillow. It was the first time in months she had been able to find relief in tears.

# Chapter 27

"Knock knock."

George looked up from his computer and smiled. "It's the lunch lady," he said. "Come in."

"I snagged the last two spinach salads from the cafeteria," Ruby told him, placing the clear plastic containers on his desk.

"Thousand Island dressing?"

"Of course." Ruby pulled two packages of dressing from her pocket and tossed one to George. From another pocket she extracted two white plastic forks, and then she sat gratefully in the guest chair. Her stupid leg was acting up again; she had already taken three ibuprofen tablets that morning and was determined to take no more.

"I'm starved," she said. "That new nursing assistant is going to be the death of me. Either that or I'll wind up killing her. How do they let some of these people graduate? I swear, George, she's as dumb as a post. Nice enough, just dumb."

"Eat. And then tell me how the party or memorial or whatever Frieda intended it to be went."

Ruby took a bite of her salad, chewed, and swallowed. "Not well," she said. "I know Frieda needed to honor what would have been a milestone birthday for Ariel, but poor Bella was so upset.

There were some harsh words spoken and then Bella ran off. She was gone about twenty minutes before she came home safe and sound."

George frowned. "How is Frieda faring this morning?"

"I don't really know, by which I mean she didn't mention the party at all and she seemed her usual self. Well, her new usual self. Not quite the Frieda she used to be."

"We none of us are the people we used to be, not ten years ago, not a year ago, not even an hour ago." George smiled. "All is change."

"You know," Ruby said musingly, "when Frieda married Aaron and the girls came along I was so relieved. I finally knew I'd done a decent job as a mother. I've given my daughter the tools she needed to make good choices and to be happy. And then it was all ripped away from her. What did Frieda do to deserve this hell she's living in now? Nothing." Ruby sighed. "Then again, no one ever does anything to deserve the pain life dishes out for them. Phil's Tony didn't deserve to die the way he did, shunned by ignorant people too scared to hold his hand when he needed comfort most. Jack's Veronica didn't deserve to die the way she did, either, never having had the experience of motherhood she so wanted. But that's just life, isn't it? Maybe the people who tell us to be happy in the moment have it right. Focus on what's happening exactly at that moment, forget the past and the future, and know that nothing stays the same for forever. I suppose there's some peace of mind to be found in that."

"There certainly is," George said with a nod. "Though from my personal experience I find that staying in the moment for more than a moment isn't particularly easy."

"I know. Sometimes I still find myself thinking that I could have prevented that crash fifteen months ago."

George shook his head. "That's magical thinking, Ruby."

"I know it is. But sometimes magical thinking is all I have."

"Sometimes it's all any of us have," George remarked.

Ruby sighed and snapped shut the lid on the empty plastic container. "I've got to get back to work. Thanks, George. I didn't mean to be so gloomy. I hope I haven't spoiled your day."

George got up from his chair and came around the desk. Ruby rose to meet him and he kissed her gently.

"You know I love you," he said.

"I know," she told him. "And I love you."

And she meant it. Then why, she wondered as she left George's office, was she still unable to take another chance on marriage?

# Chapter 28

Ruby's cell phone alerted her to an e-mail. It was from one of the members of The Page Turners. *I've got a great book for us to read this fall*, Maggie wrote. *I can't remember the title or who wrote it, but I heard about it on the radio. It's set in Australia. I think. Maybe New Zealand. Anyway, it sounds fantastic!*

Maggie meant well, but she was a bona fide airhead. Ruby wasn't sure how Maggie ever managed to make it through an entire book without forgetting what it was she was reading. Maybe she never did.

Ruby got up from the kitchen table and poured herself a glass of water. Any mention of The Land Down Under brought thoughts of Aaron's parents, who had moved to Australia shortly after Aaron and Frieda's wedding to live near their son Ben, who was nearly twenty years older than his surprise baby brother. Albert and Janet had never met Bella and Ariel, but they were dutiful grandparents from afar, sending birthday and Christmas greetings without fail; it was more than Grandpa Hitchens had ever managed. Still, it was a sore point with Ruby that Aaron's parents and brother hadn't bothered to return to the United States for the funeral. True, it was approximately a ten-thousand-mile journey and they had sent sincere condolences in the form of flowers and letters, but . . .

Ruby finished her water and put the glass into the dishwasher. It was just that she had taken to Aaron right from the start and by the time he died she had long come to regard him as her son. How many mothers-in-law were so lucky?

"Hi, Grandma."

"Hi to you," Ruby said as Bella came into the kitchen and headed for the fridge. "How was work?"

Bella shrugged. "It was all right."

Ruby hadn't seen Bella since breakfast, at which she had been largely silent. Directly after breakfast she had gone off to Phil's shop. When Ruby had gotten home from the hospital that afternoon, Bella was shut up in her room.

"Well," Ruby said, raising an eyebrow, "I hope you show a little more enthusiasm with the customers. At least fake it, like I suggested you do at Phil's party."

Bella managed a smile.

"Hi."

Frieda stood at the doorway.

"And how was your day?" Ruby asked. The awkwardness between her daughter and granddaughter was as palpable as it had been that morning and for some reason it annoyed Ruby more than it worried her.

"Fine, thanks," Frieda said.

A silence that further tested Ruby's patience descended on the room. "One of you had better say something," she announced. "Or—"

"Sorry I ran off last night, Grandma," Bella said abruptly. "Sorry, Mom."

"We were worried," Ruby said simply. This was not the time for scolding or moralizing.

"I know." Bella looked at the floor. "Sorry I got so upset."

"Please don't run off again, Bella," Frieda said. "Please. I . . . Just promise."

Bella nodded. "I promise."

Chirrup! Chirrup!

"That's me." Frieda pulled her cell phone from her pocket. "Hi," she said. "You did? . . . That's fantastic, Jack. . . . Thanks. I'll meet you there at a quarter to seven. Bye."

"What was that about?" Bella asked with a frown. "What's fantastic?"

"Jack just got tickets for third-row seats at tonight's performance of *The King and I* at The Ogunquit Playhouse. You don't mind, Mom, do you?"

"Why should I mind?" Ruby said. "Go and have a good time."

"It's my favorite musical. I'd been thinking about splurging on tickets." Frieda looked at her watch. "Yikes. I'd better go get dressed."

"I've been meaning to ask you something, Bella," Ruby said when Frieda had gone. "There's a patient on my floor, a sixteen-year-old girl who's in for surgery to help correct a pretty severe case of scoliosis."

Bella shrugged. "So? I mean that's too bad about the scoliosis, but . . ."

"Yes, it is too bad. She's in a lot of pain. Anyway, she lost her little brother about a month ago to a very aggressive cancer. She's very depressed about that and scared about the operation. I thought you might be able to help her."

"Why me?" Bella asked, and Ruby thought she looked genuinely perplexed. "What could I do?"

"You could talk to her because you lost your only sibling, too. You understand what she's going through, at least the grieving part if not the medical issue. You might be able to help her deal with her unhappiness."

Bella laughed a bit wildly. "How can I help someone else when I can't even help myself?" She turned then and stalked out of the kitchen; Ruby heard her feet pounding up the stairs and then the door of her room shut loudly. *This is getting to be a habit*, Ruby thought. But at least Bella had kept her promise and not run out of the house.

A moment later Frieda reappeared in the kitchen, wearing a mint-green linen sheath; her hair was pulled back in a chignon and Ruby noted that she was wearing earrings for the first time that summer. "What was that noise?" Frieda asked.

"That was Bella being dramatic again," Ruby told her, "not that she doesn't have cause to be. Still, I wish she'd be gentle with the doors. They are over a hundred years old."

"At least she apologized for running out last night."

"I know," Ruby said, "and apologizing was the right thing for her to do. Still, I'd like her to really mean it. I'd like her to learn that storming off isn't a solution to anything. She has to learn again how to use her words."

Frieda sighed. "Do you think I should stay home this evening? Try to talk to her? She was so upset last night. I'm sure Jack would understand if I canceled."

"No," Ruby said firmly. "I think you should go to the theater with him and enjoy yourself. I'll man the fort and deal with any further dramatic gestures."

"Thanks, Mom. Jack said the show is over at ten. I suppose we might stop for a bite to eat afterward, but I'm sure I'll be home well before midnight. Call me on my cell if—"

"There will be no ifs," Ruby said firmly. "Now go."

Frieda kissed her mother's cheek and left the room. Alone, Ruby felt suddenly exhausted. She sank gratefully into a chair at the table. At that moment she wasn't sure anything good was being accomplished this summer by having Frieda and Bella at home. Well, Frieda seemed well enough in spite of the debacle of the commemoration party, unless of course she was hiding her distress. But Bella . . .

Ruby's cell phone rang with George's familiar tone, but she let the call go to voice mail. She would call him back later. She got up from the table and winced as her right leg took her weight. Slowly she made her way upstairs. A brief nap before she made dinner was in order.

# Chapter 29

Ruby and Frieda were in the kitchen around eleven o'clock the following morning. Bella had left for work at eight, grumbling about the early hour. "Phil wants me to be at the shop to accept a delivery," she had told her mother, who had been awake since six and working on a job since seven. "He trusts you to open up," Frieda had replied. "That's a good thing." Bella had ignored her mother's remark and gone off on her bike.

"Why didn't I have a second cup of coffee this morning?" Frieda wondered aloud. "I could use one now. Do you want a cup, Mom?"

"No thanks," Ruby told her. "I'm caffeinated enough at the moment. So, you haven't told me about the play. And where did you go afterward?"

Frieda turned from the coffee maker. "The production was fantastic," she said. "The actor who played the king was—well, he was kingly. We ran into one of Jack's colleagues in the lobby and chatted for a while. Then we went to the Pine Hill Tavern and I saw people there I remember from when I was a girl, like the guy who gave guitar lessons to pretty much every kid in town for generations. He must be closing in on ninety by now. And Jack seems to be popular, just like he was back in school."

"He's popular with you these days, isn't he?" her mother asked.

Frieda chose her words carefully. "If you mean do I like spending time with him, yes. I do. He's nice." *And,* Frieda thought, *he understands what it's like.*

The phone rang. "I'll get it," Ruby said, going to the landline on the wall by the fridge. "Hello? . . . Oh, hello, Steve. . . . Fine, thanks. . . . Sure. I'll see if she's here."

Ruby put her hand over the mouthpiece and lowered her voice. "It's your father. Do you want to talk to him?"

Frieda thought for a second before saying, "Yeah, okay." She crossed the room and took the receiver from her mother. *Like Mom said,* she told herself, *I can always hang up.*

"I'll make myself scarce," Ruby whispered, and rather dramatically, Frieda thought, she tiptoed out of the room.

"Hi, Dad," Frieda said. She felt her hand grip the receiver a bit more tightly.

"Thanks for taking the call," he replied.

"Sure. What's up?"

"Not much on this end. I've been wondering how Bella's been faring since I last talked to you."

What could she tell her father? More to the point, Frieda thought, what did she want to tell him? "She's all right," she said finally.

"I know. I'm a terrible grandfather," Steve admitted.

"You're not any kind of grandfather," Frieda snapped. She wondered if he would hang up on her. She wondered if he would try to argue the point.

But what he said was: "You're right, if not technically speaking. But that doesn't mean I don't want Bella to feel better. I'm not coldhearted, Frieda, in spite of what you might think, and I admit I didn't give you much reason to think otherwise. I thought a lot about Ariel on what would have been her sixteenth birthday. I spent a long time looking at the pictures your mother sent when she was born. You see, I'd given Ruby a post office box so she could let me know that each of the births had gone well."

*What is he looking for?* Frieda thought. *A medal?* "What do you want from me, Dad?"

"What I want is to apologize for not having shown more concern for you and Bella when Aaron and Ariel died. I should have called you and not just your mother. I suppose I assumed you wouldn't want to hear from me at such a difficult time. I shouldn't have made that assumption, even if it turned out to be true. I should have just made the call."

"Yes, Dad," Frieda said. "You should have." *You should*, she thought, *have given me the choice of hanging up on you.*

"And now, well, I'd like—and I'm not saying I deserve it—I'd like at least a small acknowledgment from you that I exist. Not that you love me," he added quickly. "Just that you know I'm alive and in the world. Just that you know I'm here."

*Wherever here was*, Frieda thought. And why after all these years should her father care what she thought of him? "And then?" she asked. "Then what? What comes after that?"

"Then . . ." Steve laughed. "I don't know what to say."

Neither did Frieda.

"How is your mother?" Steve asked when the silence had gone on too long for comfort. "She was fine when we talked back in May, but things change. Well, you know that better than most."

"She's great," Frieda said robustly. "Fantastic. She's in great health and she has a wonderful man in her life."

"Yes, she told me about him a while ago. George, isn't it?"

"Right. He's smart and he's got a big job at the hospital and he's handsome and he'll do anything for her. The other day he replaced the washers in all the sinks and then he rehung a window in the living room."

Steve laughed again. "Are you trying to make me jealous?"

Frieda winced with embarrassment. To make her father regret his decision to leave her mother had indeed been her childish intention. "You know," she blurted, "kids made fun of me after you left."

"Why would they make fun of you?" her father asked.

"Because my father had walked out on me. Because he had cheated on my mother with half the town. One girl in middle school called me trailer trash." Frieda laughed bitterly. "I remember being confused because Mom and I didn't live in a trailer. The trash part I got."

Steve sighed. "I'm sorry, Frieda. Kids can be cruel; there's no doubt about that."

"And vulnerable."

"Yeah, vulnerable. You know, I had a tough time of it before I hit a growth spurt when I was about fourteen. I was a skinny little thing. I wore thick glasses that made me look like a deer in the headlights. I had 'kick me' written all over me. So, the bullies did. Broke a rib or two one time."

Frieda almost felt as if she had been slapped. This was the last thing she expected to hear from her father, a story from his childhood, a story about his being victimized. It confused her. She didn't want to feel sympathy for Steve Hitchens, but she was a mother who had once had to confront a boy who had teased her younger daughter to the point of tears. How could she not feel sympathy for the innocent child her father had been? "I'm sorry, Dad," she said after a moment. "What happened then?"

"My father taped me up and sent me back to school the next day."

"Didn't your mother do anything?" Frieda asked. "Talk to the teacher or the bully's parents? Confront the kids who hurt you? Didn't she take you to a doctor? Broken ribs can puncture organs."

Her father laughed. "Are you kidding me? Take me to a doctor? She thought I'd said or done something to provoke the other kids. She told me I'd better learn to keep my mouth shut. She told me I'd better learn how to get out of my own scrapes. She wasn't long on nurturing, my mother."

*Maybe that's why you aren't capable of . . . No*, Frieda thought. Her father was capable of nurturing. Look what he had done for Phil and Tony. Then why—

"Sorry," she said abruptly. "I've got to go now."

"Okay. Thanks for talking with me again, Frieda."

Frieda hesitated. She couldn't say "my pleasure" and really mean it. "Okay," she said. "Bye."

When she had hung up Frieda suddenly felt the need for fresh air. She went out to the front porch and sank into one of her mother's rocking chairs. Could her father have been lying about being bullied? Had he been looking for her pity, hoping to be let off the hook for his bad behavior by claiming an unhappy childhood? But Frieda didn't really think that was the case. No, she suspected her father was telling the truth about his past. The question was, why tell her now? Why tell her ever?

Frieda put her head back against the chair and sighed. It was all such a puzzle and it had been since the day Steve Hitchens had walked out on his wife and child. Since then Frieda had spent a good many hours of her life wondering where her father was living, if he had remarried, and, most important, if he had had other children. Now she had access to the one person who could give her the answers to those questions, but she knew she would never ask. What would be the point? She certainly didn't have any interest in building a relationship with her half siblings, should they exist. And she certainly didn't need to learn that her father might have stuck around for his other children longer than he had stuck around for his firstborn.

And as for the possibility that her father had other grandchildren, grandchildren he might know well and see on a regular basis . . . Well, Frieda could accept—if not with good grace—that her father had virtually abandoned *her*, but that he had ignored his granddaughters right from the start was something she still could not forgive him for. *Put aside pity for the child he was*, Frieda told herself firmly. *Think only of the man he is, selfish and unkind.*

But that was not an easy thing to do, Frieda realized. Her father had kept Ariel's baby pictures, and maybe Bella's, too. Her father had called her, twice. Didn't that mean something good? Didn't it?

# Chapter 30

"It's got to be, like, ninety degrees." Clara waved her hand in front of her face. "I wish the cottage had air-conditioning."

Bella shifted on the folding lawn chair, one of several in the small, messy yard behind the cottage. She was sweating profusely, but it was better to be in the sun rather than in Clara's cramped and airless bedroom. Still, she could use something cold to drink, but Clara hadn't offered her anything.

Someone had left a copy of the latest issue of *InStyle* on the up-turned milk crate and Bella picked it up. "I think my mother's involved with this guy who works at the college," she said, flipping idly through the pages of the magazine. "They used to go to school together."

"So?" Clara asked. She was wearing a T-shirt with the words EDOOCATION ROONED MY LIFE emblazoned across it.

"So it bothers me."

"Why? Is he married or something?"

"No," Bella said. "His wife died a few years ago. She had cancer."

Clara nodded as if something important had been decided. "Good," she said. "Then your mother and this guy have something in common. Marc and I have so much in common. We never have trouble finding something to talk about."

*You never* had *any trouble finding things to talk about,* Bella thought.

*Past tense.* "That's not the point," she protested. "The point is that I don't want her to . . ." Bella shook her head. "Never mind."

"Tear out a page of that magazine, will you?"

Bella frowned. "But it's not mine."

"Whatever. Tear out one of those back pages with all the ads. I need a fan."

Bella hesitated a moment and then did what Clara asked. "I found my sister's locked diary at my grandmother's house," she said, handing Clara the page.

"Cool. Are you going to open it?"

"I don't know. I don't think so. I mean, it's locked for a reason."

"But Ariel is gone," Clara pointed out, madly fanning her face. "What does it matter if someone reads her diary?"

"It's still hers," Bella argued, "not mine. Besides, what if she said something really critical about me? Or what if she thought something bad about me was true, but it wasn't true and now it's too late for me to tell her she was wrong? I'll know she died thinking I'd cheated on a test or stolen something or worse."

"I still say you should open it. If you can't find the key you can probably use the end of a paper clip or something. I did that once."

"You mean you picked a lock?" Bella asked.

"Yeah. It was easy."

When nothing more of Clara's lock-picking story was forthcoming, Bella said, "Look, I'm dying of thirst. Is it okay if I get some water or something?"

Clara leaped from her seat. "Oh. Yeah. I'll grab something from the fridge. Right back." She dashed into the house and returned a few minutes later with two cans of Diet Pepsi. "My housemate Julie bought these, but I'm sure she won't mind."

Bella hesitated. She felt a little weird taking someone else's soda—and tearing a page from someone else's magazine—but she really was thirsty, so she squashed her scruples and snapped open the can. Diet Pepsi was her favorite. Ariel had hated all soda but orange, which Bella thought was disgusting. The stuff didn't taste at all like real oranges.

"I hated the—the celebrity my father's and sister's deaths brought me at school," she said suddenly. "I mean, people I barely knew started acting all overly sympathetic, like they really, really cared. I felt people watching me all the time, like they were waiting for me to do something dramatic like fall to the floor kicking and screaming or something."

"So what did you do about it?" Clara asked.

"Mostly I just walked away, but sometimes I'd tell someone to leave me alone. I'd say things like, 'You don't even know me. How can you say you feel bad for me?' That usually shut them up. At least it made them too embarrassed to approach me again."

"No one told me they were sorry for me when Marc left me."

"I just wanted to be left alone," Bella went on, almost as if she were talking to herself. "I had this best friend, Kerri. I told you about her. She kept trying to make me share my feelings, but she wouldn't understand I didn't want to talk about my feelings. I wanted to forget, but nobody would allow me to forget. Everyone wanted me to remember out loud."

"I never want to forget," Clara said softly.

"Right after the accident," Bella went on, "my school set up counseling groups to help Ariel's classmates process her death. People put up these little shrines in her memory. Every time I turned a corner I was confronted by a reminder of all I had lost. It was horrible. Every time I left the building I had to pass a heap of flowers and stuffed animals and messages written on poster board. 'Rest in peace, Ariel.' 'We love you, Ariel.' 'We'll never forget you, Ariel.' I felt like I was going mad. There was never any escape from the reality that Dad and Ariel were gone."

"I don't want to forget Marc." Clara's voice was loud now and her tone insistent.

"But you want to forget the bad thing that happened, don't you?" Bella asked urgently. "You want to forget even for a moment that he rejected you, right?"

Clara didn't reply.

"I had this dream about the accident again last night," Bella said, tossing the magazine onto the milk crate. "Actually, there are a few different versions of it. Sometimes there's a happy ending and it's Ariel and my father who are walking through the doors of the hotel, not the police. Sometimes I'm at the scene of the accident, watching it all happen. I try to call out a warning or to wave my arms to get my father's and sister's attention, but I can't speak or move. And then suddenly I wake up and it's like the accident happened all over again and I feel sad for hours."

"That sounds seriously screwed," Clara said.

"Yeah. Do you dream about Marc?" Bella asked.

Clara sighed. "It's weird, but I don't. When I'm awake he's all I can think about, but when I go to sleep he's not there. My mind is just a blank."

"That must be a relief. Like what I said about forgetting."

Clara shook her head. "It's not a relief. I want to dream about him. I want to keep as much of him as I can."

"But . . ." Bella shrugged. "I don't know, maybe letting go a little is the right thing to do. I mean, he did end things, right? He's probably moving on, so . . ."

"He'll be back," Clara said firmly. "I'm sure of it."

Bella didn't argue. She knew all about wanting so badly something that wasn't going to happen that you started to convince yourself that the impossible could happen if only you believed strongly enough. If only you kept your fingers crossed. If only . . . But maybe Marc would come back to Clara. He was alive. Anything, however unlikely, was possible when you were alive. She was about to say something to this effect when Clara began to speak again.

"My parents were relieved when Marc left me," she said. "I know they were. From the beginning of our relationship they'd been worried I was going to throw my life away—that was their term—by marrying young and not experiencing the world." Clara laughed bitterly. "What's there to experience when you've lost the person you loved most?"

Bella thought about that for a moment and realized she didn't know how to answer the question. "Even if your parents are relieved that you and Marc aren't seeing each other anymore," she said, "I'm sure they don't want you to be sad. I mean, they'd have to be sick to want that."

Clara ignored Bella's comment. "Marc left for California the day after graduation," she said. "It was like he couldn't bear to be in the same town as me. Why? What did I ever do to him that was so bad he couldn't look me in the face? I didn't get to say good-bye. By the time I got to his house the next morning he was gone."

Bella put her empty soda can next to the magazine on the milk crate. "Maybe it was better that you didn't see him before he left. Maybe it would have been too painful."

"No. I needed to see him. I told you that my parents practically forced me to come to Ogunquit, right? They said that meeting new people and seeing new sights would help take my mind off Marc."

Bella looked closely at Clara for the first time that day. The strained look of grief she had seen on Clara's face when they first met on the Marginal Way was more pronounced now. "And it isn't working, is it?" she asked. "Being in a new place and meeting new people."

"No," Clara said dully. "Sometimes I think it's having the opposite effect. Sometimes . . . Sometimes, Bella, I just can't see the future."

"You mean, the future without Marc?" Bella asked.

Clara shook her head and didn't reply.

It probably wasn't helping, Bella thought, that Clara's room was a virtual shrine to her ex-boyfriend. Clara would never get past her sadness if everywhere she looked there was a vivid reminder of what she had lost. Bella thought of her own room back in Massachusetts, purposely bare of any images of her father and sister. Was the absence of visual reminders of what she had lost helping her to embrace her own future? Was it? *No*, Bella thought. *Not really.*

"Look," she said abruptly, "let me pay you for the soda. You can give the money to your housemate."

"That's okay," Clara said. "Like I told you, she won't mind."

"Are you sure?" Bella asked.

"Yeah."

Bella wasn't in the mood to argue; sweat was still pouring from her and she felt almost dizzy from the heat. "I have to go," she said, getting up from the old lawn chair.

Clara remained in her chair and shrugged. "Okay. Call me?"

Bella nodded and walked around to the front of the cottage where she had left her bike. And as she began to pedal in the direction of Kinders Lane, she realized that she felt slightly unsettled.

The conversation with Clara that afternoon had been a strange one. It was almost as if they had been talking in parallel lines. Only days ago Bella had thought that revealing her thoughts and feelings to a virtual stranger was a good thing, but now . . . It would be nice if Clara actually heard some of what she said. But had *she* really heard what Clara was saying? Yes, Bella thought, she had. Sort of.

It was an odd sort of relationship, Bella thought, turning onto her grandmother's street, not at all like what she had shared with Kerri. Or like what she had shared with Ariel. But that was okay.

Things changed. It was okay.

# Chapter 31

When Jack had suggested they spend the afternoon at the annual Bay Town Fair Frieda had said yes immediately. There was something so basically pleasing about a summer fair. Young and old and everyone in between gathered to eat fried dough and take their chances at winning oversized stuffed animals and shop for homemade crafts and foods. Frieda would have treated herself to the hand-dyed silk scarf that had caught her eye at one of the craft booths if she could have afforded it, but she did have enough money to buy a jar of blackberry preserves for her mother and a small box of maple sugar candy for Bella.

"You're sure you don't want me to win you a toy?" Jack asked. "I'm thinking a giant purple gorilla might look nice in your mother's living room."

Frieda laughed. "You sound pretty sure of yourself. Don't you mean try to win me a stuffed animal?"

"I hate to brag, but my aim is pretty good," Jack told her. "I was on the archery team in college and I guess whatever I learned about hitting a target stayed with me."

"Thanks anyway. My stuffed animal days are over." *But if Ariel were alive*, Frieda thought. Ariel had loved stuffed animals. At the time of her death she had amassed thirty-two, including a zebra, a sloth, and a fawn. All were in a storage unit not far from the house in Warden. Frieda hadn't been able to part with the toys, but neither had she been able to live with them.

As Frieda and Jack strolled past booths selling hamburgers and cotton candy, past jugglers and musicians performing for a delighted audience, past parents herding their overly excited children before them, Frieda couldn't help but feel a deep pang of nostalgia for the days when she and Aaron and the girls would take daily excursions to fairs, museums, concerts, and, of course, amusement parks. Ariel had preferred the carousel to the other rides while Bella could never get enough of the biggest roller coaster and those awful rides that turned you upside down and shook you like a can of beans.

"Penny for your thoughts?" Jack asked.

"Sorry," Frieda said. "Just reminiscing. It's so hard not to."

"There's nothing wrong with reminiscing," Jack said gently. "Visiting the past is fine and a lot of times it's healthy. The trick is not to live in the past."

"Easier said than done. Hey, speaking of the past, I talked to my father again the other day. He wanted to know how Bella was getting on. And he told me something about his childhood. He told me he was bullied for a time and that his mother wasn't exactly sympathetic. In fact, he made her sound downright cold."

"How did it feel to hear that?" Jack asked.

"It made me uncomfortable," Frieda admitted. "It . . . It humanized him a bit for me. Personalized him. I have to admit I've considered my father almost a cliché for most of my life. If that's unfair I think I can be excused."

"I agree."

Frieda smiled. "About my father Aaron would say that we shouldn't judge someone until we'd walked a mile in his shoes. All well and good in theory, but . . ."

"What about Aaron's own father," Jack asked, "and his mother for that matter? Was he close to them? Sometimes when people are very close to their birth families they have a difficult time understanding what it's like for those who have a legitimate complaint against their own."

"It's interesting you should ask that," Frieda told him. "Aaron wasn't close to his parents. He was a surprise baby; his brother was almost twenty when he was born. Aaron believed his parents loved him. They took good care of him. He was never without plenty of food and clothing. They sent him to good schools and they went on family vacations every summer. But . . ."

"But what?" Jack asked.

Frieda shook her head. "But he said he always felt that something was missing. He never complained about his parents, but he would have appreciated a more warm and fuzzy home. Aaron used to wonder if his mother and father had used up all their warm and fuzzy emotions with his brother."

"Sounds rough," Jack noted. "But it also sounds as if Aaron was emotionally resilient."

"He was," Frieda agreed, "far more so than me."

"Really? From where I stand it looks as if you've done a fine job of dealing with your father's walking away. It didn't put you off marrying and having children. It didn't damage your relationship with your mother. And now," Jack went on more softly, "it looks to me as if you're truly dealing with losing your husband and daughter. That you haven't let their deaths destroy you."

Frieda pondered that. It was true. She hadn't let Aaron's and Ariel's deaths destroy her. But there had to be a point at which a person simply couldn't survive more pain and loss without going mad. She fervently hoped she would never find herself at that point.

"Thank you, Jack," she said after a moment. "Whew, it's hot. Let's get into the shade for a bit."

They left the main thoroughfare and settled on the grass under a leafy oak tree. "Here," Jack said. "Have some water. I never leave the house without a few water bottles."

"Were you a Boy Scout?" Frieda asked, accepting the water.

"No. I'm just too cheap to pay five dollars for something I can get from my sink for a lot less." Jack paused. "It's funny how people's behavior toward you can change when someone close to you dies. See that guy over by the booth with the green sign?" he asked. "He's one of my neighbors. It's been four years since Veronica passed and he still isn't able to look me in the eye. I don't know if he feels embarrassed for some reason—he came to the funeral, so

I don't know what he could possibly be embarrassed about—or if he thinks that he'll catch something nasty from me, like my grief or my loneliness. It's disconcerting."

Frieda smiled. "'Disconcerting' is right. Want to hear my tale in the same vein?"

"Sure."

"Ariel had two very close friends since kindergarten," Frieda explained. "Jessica and Juliana. Their mothers—Maddie and Eva—and I were friends, too. The six of us were a pretty tightly knit group through the years. I can't tell you how many birthday parties and sleepovers we moms hosted, how many school plays we attended, how many Girl Scout meetings we led. But then—"

"But then Ariel died," Jack said into the sudden silence.

"Yeah." Frieda cleared her throat before going on. "Then Ariel died and everything changed. Suddenly all Maddie wanted to talk about was the accident. It was as if she thought that by endlessly talking about the accident it would eventually make sense to her and become something she could tuck away in a scrapbook and forget about. It was exhausting for me to be with her."

"And the other woman?" Jack asked.

Frieda rolled her eyes. "Eva was the complete opposite. She avoided any reference to the accident, and whenever I mentioned Aaron or Ariel's name, even in the context of a pleasant memory, she would change the subject. I'd say something like 'I was thinking of donating some of Ariel's books to the library,' and she'd say, 'I found this fantastic recipe for mushroom risotto.'"

"Ouch. I don't know which behavior sounds more upsetting."

"It became impossible for me to be with them at the same time, one wanting only to talk about the accident and the other wanting at all costs not to talk about it. After a while it became so strange it was almost amusing. I had to stifle more than one inappropriate giggle."

"A giggle sounds a lot less inappropriate than a scream," Jack pointed out. "Don't waste your precious time trying to figure out those two. They're the ones with the problem."

"Oh, I don't," Frieda assured him, "not really. Anyway, the point is I realized I'd become defined by the car crash that killed my husband and younger daughter. I made other people uncomfortable; I suppose I still do. Like you might be for your neighbor, I'm a nasty reminder to those who haven't yet been visited by tragedy of what they, too, might lose, suddenly and brutally."

"So what happened?" Jack asked. "What did you finally do about those women?"

Frieda shrugged. "I simply began to fade out of their lives. Neither of them ever protested when I canceled a lunch date or turned down an invitation to a Saturday barbeque. I'd pretty much known they wouldn't encourage me to keep up the friendship, but still, when the invitations slowly died off and months passed before I got the next text or e-mail I felt hurt. I had to keep reminding myself—I still have to—that this life I have now is the 'new normal.' I'll go mad if I keep comparing it to what went before and pining for things to go back to what they once were." Frieda smiled. "You know, some wise person once said something like: 'Forgiveness means letting go of all hope for a better past.' I've taken the liberty of changing that bit of wisdom to: 'Sanity means letting go of all hope for a different past.'"

"I'll have to keep that in mind," Jack said with a smile. "Ask my mother to embroider it on a pillow or something. Hey, I suddenly feel an urgent need for sausage and peppers. Good old-fashioned Italian street food. At least, southern Maine's version of Italian."

"You know, that sounds like a plan. I haven't had sausage and peppers since—" *Since Aaron and I went to a Red Sox game two summers ago.* But Jack didn't need to know that. "Since forever," she said.

"Then let's go." Jack rose easily to his feet and held out his hand. Frieda took it gratefully. It was a nice hand.

# Chapter 32

"To what do I owe this lovely invitation?" Ruby asked as she took a seat at one of the surprisingly comfortable wrought-iron chairs at the round granite-topped table on Phil's flagstone patio.

Phil shrugged. "I didn't want to drink alone?"

"Ha. Well, all that matters is that I'm here." And that, Ruby thought, was always a nice thing.

Phil's house had been built to his specifications ten years earlier. If Ruby were pressed to describe it she would venture to say it could pass for something that a devotee of Frank Lloyd Wright had designed. It was nothing at all like her old farmhouse but every bit as beautiful. The back lawn spread out before them was rich and green. The hydrangeas were in bloom and there was a lovely smell of lavender in the air.

"Here," Phil said. "Try this. It's my own concoction. I'm still trying to come up with a catchy name for it."

Ruby accepted the delicate wide-rimmed glass and took a sip. "Mmmm," she said. "Lovely. I'm a sucker for fresh mint. What else is in this? I can't quite identify the other flavors."

"The ingredients are a deep, dark secret. Here, have a jalapeño cheddar cracker. I made them this morning."

"Phil," Ruby said, reaching for a cracker, "you spoil me."

"Only as much as you spoil me." Phil took the seat next to Ruby. "So, what's Frieda up to today?"

"She and Jack went to the Bay Town Fair," Ruby told him.

"I'm glad she's found someone to have fun with," Phil said. "All work and worry doesn't do anyone any good."

"I know. And Steve called again to talk to her. That's two calls in the space of as many weeks."

"How did it go?" Phil asked.

"All right, I suppose. She didn't tell me much other than that he wanted to know how Bella was doing this summer. So, how is our Bella doing?" Ruby asked. "She must be fairly competent if you trust her to man the shop on her own this afternoon."

Phil shook his head. "She still doesn't know chintz from brocade and she's still trying to get her head around the concept of French doors, but she works hard enough. I just wish she'd smile more at the customers, but hopefully that will come in time. I miss the old Bella, the girl who always had such an interest in what was going on around her."

"They were alike in that way, Bella and Ariel, both so curious about the world." Ruby smiled. "The only difference was that Ariel was interested in things that bored Bella and Bella was interested in things that left Ariel shaking her head in puzzlement!"

"Isn't that the truth? Ariel with her love of history and Bella with no use for anything older than the number of years she can count on her fingers. Ariel cringing at the mere mention of soccer and Bella known for her ferocious head butts or whatever they're called. And yet they were so close. It's hard to think of one without the other. And if it's hard for me—for all of us—how much harder must it be for Bella to think of herself as . . . I don't quite know how to put it. Alone? Lost? Singular?"

"All of those. They weren't twins, but they might as well have been." Ruby sighed. "In some ways I'm sorry I didn't give Frieda a sibling. But I guess not long after Frieda was born I knew that it wouldn't be a good idea to bring another one of Steve's children into the world. Still . . ."

"The past is the past," Phil said briskly. "Leave it alone and have another cracker."

"By the way," she said, "I suggested to Bella that we try my old ice-cream maker again, but she said she had no interest."

"I wouldn't push her on it. Well, what do I know? You're her grandmother, not me."

"And," Ruby said, taking the last sip of her drink, "grandmothers can't have a second cocktail and expect to drive home safely. Goodbye, Phil. Thanks again for the snacks and conversation. Both were greatly appreciated."

Phil raised his hand in farewell and Ruby walked around the side of the house to the street where she had parked her car. The ride back to Kinders Lane was a short one and Ruby knew it like she knew the back of her hand. This allowed her mind to focus on other matters in addition to squirrels darting under her wheels and pedestrians wandering off the narrow rough shoulder and into the road. Other matters like the evening that stretched ahead. It would probably be just Ruby and Bella for dinner. Ruby didn't expect Frieda home early from the fair and George was attending a meeting of his choir. Though the choir typically disbanded for the summer, the director had been approached with a request for a special performance at a private party Labor Day weekend and rehearsals were to begin immediately. George had apologized to Ruby for a schedule that might keep him from being readily available for the next few weeks. It was so like George, Ruby thought as she drove along watching for chipmunks as well as for squirrels and humans. He was always so thoughtful of her.

Frankly, Ruby was glad that George had something other than work to keep him occupied this summer given the fact that she was not exactly the steady companion she should be. It wasn't that George was friendless. He got along famously with Phil, but Phil was her best friend and that put him out of the running as George's confidant. George was popular with his colleagues and with the other members of his choir, but what dear friends he had from childhood were far-flung. He had been very close with his father, but Walter was no longer and Ruby knew George was still grieving. In so many ways George and Walter's relationship had reminded Ruby of her own relationship with Frieda—warm, honest, and unshakable. To think of life without that relationship . . .

Ruby turned onto Kinders Lane with an unhappy feeling of guilt. By not engaging with George this summer, by virtually ignoring his proposal because she was letting her distaste for the state of marriage drown out the voice of love, she was effectively isolating the man who meant so very much to her. *Ruby,* she scolded as she pulled into her driveway. *Remember what Phil said. The past is the past. Now leave it alone and get your act together. Fast.*

# Chapter 33

With supreme patience Frieda inched her car along Shore Road. Bumper-to-bumper traffic in downtown Ogunquit was normal in summer and there was no point in letting it get to you. Besides, something as inconsequential as traffic couldn't spoil Frieda's good mood. Though she had been with Jack only two days earlier, she was looking forward to this evening as if she hadn't seen him in weeks.

Still, it wasn't as if Jack Tennant were occupying every moment of Frieda's waking hours. There were other, more important matters claiming her attention. Like Bella. Like finding more writing and copyediting work. Like her father. All that day Frieda had found herself hoping her father would call. Hoping the phone would remain silent. Hoping her father would just go away again like he had all those years ago, so she wouldn't have to deal with the very complicated feelings she had about him.

"Daddy's a free spirit," Frieda's mother would tell her in the weeks after her father's defection. "Some people just can't stay in any one place for long. It doesn't make them bad people."

For a long time Frieda had accepted (if she hadn't entirely believed) her mother's interpretation of Steve Hitchens's actions. But one day, when Frieda was a sophomore in high school, she could bear her mother's equanimity no longer. They were living in a small apartment over a hardware store at the time. Frieda had come home from school to discover that a check her father had promised had failed to arrive. The jean jacket Frieda wanted, on sale only for another day, was now out of the question.

"Did he call to say why the check hasn't come?" Frieda had asked, her voice rising. "Did he give you a reason?"

"He hasn't called," her mother had answered evenly. "Maybe he forgot he promised we'd have the check by the twentieth. Maybe the check got lost in the mail. I'm sure there's a good reason for—"

"Why do you always make excuses for him, Mom?" Frieda had demanded.

"Not excuses, Frieda," her mother corrected. "I'm just trying to explain him to you as best I can."

"It sounds like a bunch of excuses to me! Look, I never told you this, but back in middle school a girl called me trailer trash because my dad walked out on us and had had affairs with half of the women in town."

"I'm so sorry, Frieda," her mother had said, reaching out for Frieda, who had stepped farther away. "I wish you had told me. I would have talked to the girl's mother or to your teacher."

"Dad probably had affairs with them, too, and you just let him humiliate us! I hate you for that!"

Frieda had stormed off to her room, slamming the door behind her. Hours later she emerged, suffering pangs of embarrassment and regret, to find her mother sitting in the darkened kitchen with a cup of tea untouched before her. Frieda had thrown her arms around her. "I'm so sorry, Mom," she said through her tears. "I don't hate you. I could never hate you. Please forgive me."

Of course her mother had forgiven her, and, maybe more important, she had admitted to making excuses for Steve Hitchens's bad behavior. "It's just that I don't believe in feeding negative feelings," she explained. "Sure, I could bad-mouth him at every chance. But I can't see how that would be of any benefit to you. And frankly, it would cause me to be bitter and I don't want to be bitter."

"Okay," Frieda said. "But maybe from now on you could acknowledge even a little that what Dad did—what he does—isn't cool. Just be honest about him. Don't make excuses for him and don't trash him. Just be honest."

With deliberation Frieda put the memory of that momentous evening aside as she pulled into the parking lot at Main Beach. She had agreed to meet Jack outside the souvenir shop at the top of the beach, and as she approached it, cooler bag of food and drinks over her shoulder, she saw him waiting for her.

"Hello!" she called. Jack waved. Under his left arm he held a bright blue beach blanket; at his feet sat a large canvas bag. He was wearing a worn jean shirt over tan shorts; his sunglasses were classic aviators. Frieda thought he could be a model for what was best about summer in New England. Not that she would tell him that.

"If you thought you were going to get a gourmet meal you were wrong," Frieda said with a smile as she joined him. "I've got egg salad sandwiches, potato salad, and brownies. Oh, and genuine Maine root beer."

Jack put a hand to his heart. "You've made me a happy man. I've never really been big on Brie, French bread, and grapes when I could get my hands on a meal that's largely mayonnaise."

Frieda laughed. "I'm glad my instincts were right. Too many faculty parties?"

"Maybe. There are only so many times you can nibble on chunks of runny cheese and raw celery sticks before you go running for the Velveeta and potato chips."

"Keep your feelings about Velveeta and potato chips from Bella," Frieda told him as they walked down to the sand. "She thinks they're two of the official food groups."

"Well, since I haven't officially met her—seeing her a few times over the years from a distance hardly counts—I think my opinions on junk food won't do her any harm."

Frieda felt a twinge of discomfort. She probably should have introduced the two by now but . . . "Look," she said. "Let's sit here."

They settled at the spot Frieda had chosen, about a quarter of the way down the beach in the direction of Wells. "Now this is heaven," Jack said as Frieda laid out the food.

Frieda smiled. "I know. This is my favorite time to come to the beach. Just before sunset when most everyone has gone home."

"Even when you were a kid?" Jack asked.

"Yeah. I mean, I loved hanging out on the beach during the day, too. But evening was always my favorite time." Frieda laughed. "How spoiled am I? And you, too, for that matter. Growing up with access to a beautiful beach."

"Tell me one of your most vivid memories of your childhood in Yorktide," Jack asked, opening two bottles of root beer and passing one to Frieda.

"Actually," she told him, "one of my most vivid memories doesn't really have anything to do with Yorktide itself. When I was about thirteen my mother founded The Page Turners. In the beginning there were only three other women and they used to meet at one another's homes in turn. I remember when they would meet at our house; at the time Mom and I were living in a cottage on Hamilton Lane. I'd sit in this small passage outside the living room and listen to the women talk about whatever book they had chosen to read. Sometimes the discussions got really heated. One time a member actually stormed off because she was the only one who thought *Wuthering Heights* was boring. I found it all so thrilling." Frieda smiled. "I suppose the fact that I probably wasn't supposed to be spying on the grown-ups was part of the thrill."

"Were you already an avid reader?" Jack asked.

"Oh yes. The apple didn't fall far from the tree. By that time I was reading at least a book a week that had nothing to do with what we had been assigned in school. Usually it was a big, fat novel. Okay, your turn. What's one of your most vivid memories of growing up in Yorktide?"

"Do you remember that big old crumbling barn in one of the fields just past the Gascoynes' farm?" Jack asked.

Frieda nodded. "Of course. The Haunted Barn. Everyone knew it was chock-full of ghosts, but no one could agree on who the ghosts had once been. Some people said a passing tramp had died there and it was his ghost who haunted the place. Others said the ghost was that of a little milkmaid who'd gotten kicked in the head by a cow."

"That's the one. Well, the summer I was thirteen another kid dared me to spend the night alone in the barn. His name was Bobby something or other. His family used to rent a house close to the Cove for the month of July."

"Did you accept the dare?"

Jack shrugged. "Of course. What else could I do, look like a weenie in front of my buddies? So I snuck out of the house, which wasn't hard to do—my parents always went to bed before nine and were heavy sleepers—made my way to the barn, and waited."

"For ghosts?" Frieda asked.

"For morning! I kept a flashlight on the entire night and sat there like a stone, scared out of my mind. I'd never given any credence to the whole supernatural thing before, but once I was alone in that old barn, boy, was I a believer. Of course nothing happened, and the minute the sun came up I left. When I got home my mother had discovered my absence and was beside herself with worry and Dad was beside himself with anger. I got off pretty lightly, though. No video games for a week."

"How did you prove to the other kids that you'd done it?" Frieda asked. "This was way before the days of selfies. Did you bring a video camera?"

"I didn't own a video camera. I couldn't actually prove that I'd made it through the night," Jack admitted, "but I guess I told a good enough story, because no one doubted me."

"Whatever happened to that old barn?"

"It fell down long ago," Jack told her. "Luckily, no silly kids were inside at the time. Or ghosts, as far as I know. Frieda, this egg salad is killer."

"Good ole mayonnaise," she told him.

They ate in silence for a few minutes and during these few minutes Frieda worked up the nerve to ask a question that had been on her mind. It was normal to be curious, she told herself. And if the question was too personal Jack could always choose not to answer.

"Jack?" she said. "Have you dated since Veronica's death?"

Jack wiped his hands on his napkin and took a swig of root beer before answering. "Yeah," he said. "I went on a few first dates, but they came to nothing. And then I saw one woman for a few months before things ended."

*Well,* Frieda thought uneasily, *you did want to know.* "What happened?" she asked.

Jack answered promptly. "She—her name was Margo—she said she couldn't shake the feeling that I was thinking about my wife when we were together and not about her."

"And were you thinking about Veronica when you were with this woman?" Frieda asked.

Jack smiled ruefully. "Yes, sometimes. I guess she could sense that my mind was occasionally elsewhere."

The conversation had taken on a depth Frieda hadn't quite anticipated, but she didn't want to back away now. "And when we're together do you think of Veronica?" she asked. "I mean, when we're not talking about her?"

"Not often," Jack said, "but sometimes. And you think about Aaron, don't you?"

Frieda nodded. "Yes, of course. Not often but sometimes."

"I know this sounds goofy, but time really does help prevent the memories from coming up at inopportune times. It helps prevent the tendency to contrast and compare."

"I believe that. But do you think the memories ever entirely stop popping up when they shouldn't? Do you think you'll ever look at another woman and not see or hear Veronica at your shoulder?"

Jack shrugged. "I wish I had the definitive answer to that, but I don't. Remembering isn't a crime or a sin, Frieda. It's how you handle the remembering that matters."

"Yes," she said. "I guess that's true. Jack? Would you ever consider marrying again?"

Jack laughed. "I'm not decrepit yet! I like the company of a woman. I like being in love. I liked being a husband. So yeah, if the possibility of a good marriage to the right person comes along, you bet I'll be open to it. And you?"

"I can't say," Frieda admitted. It was too soon to be thinking about marrying. Too soon.

"Fair enough. Mind if I finish off this potato salad?"

"Not at all. Jack, this might be getting way too personal, so feel free to tell me to mind my own business."

"Thanks for the warning," Jack said, scraping the last of the potato salad from the plastic container.

"Did you and Veronica ever talk about your remarrying after she was gone?"

"Yes," Jack said. "When it was clear Veronica had only a few weeks at best she told me the thought of my being alone made her sad. She wanted me to promise I would never refuse love if it came my way."

Frieda felt tears come to her eyes.

"Sometimes," Jack went on, "I think that was the worst moment of my life, worse even than the moment I knew Veronica had died. I badly wanted to make her happy by promising I'd move on, but at the same time I wanted just as badly to tell her that I could never love anyone ever again. In the end, I was crying so hard all I could do was nod. I don't know if she believed I'd made the promise or not, but neither of us mentioned it again. And ten days later she was gone."

"How sad, Jack," Frieda said. "I'm so very sorry."

"The fact that we'd known for a while that it was unlikely Veronica would beat the cancer gave her time to think about my future," Jack said. "After a while I came to believe she had really meant what she said about my not being alone. She was a very generous person in life. An honest person. Why would she be any different in death?"

Yes, Frieda thought. For Veronica death was more than a moment. It was a conscious process, allowing her to think and to act under its influence. For Aaron . . . "Aaron and I never talked about death," she told Jack, "with the exception of the time we bought life insurance, and that was enough of an upsetting experience for me. It made the idea of one of us dying far too real." Frieda shook her head. "As if I could avoid the inevitable by ignoring it."

"Welcome to the human race," Jack said. "Where denial is not just a river in Egypt. Man, this egg salad is killer. What's your secret?"

Frieda laughed. "No secret. You're just an easy audience."

While Jack finished the food Frieda admired the evening sky, a palette of deepening pastels. They were virtually alone now and suddenly Frieda thought, *I want Jack to kiss me. I want to kiss him. But it's too soon. Too soon.* "Maybe we should get going," she said, reaching for the cooler bag.

"Sure." Jack got to his feet and brushed sand off his legs. "Did I mention that I loved the egg salad?"

"Several times," Frieda said. "But I'm always susceptible to flattery."

# Chapter 34

"Do you remember meeting my friend Connie?" Bella's grandmother asked as she passed the plate of chicken breasts. "She manages the hospital's gift shop."

Bella took the plate and nodded. "Yeah. She's the one with ten grandchildren or something."

"That's the one. Guess what she did? She dyed her hair green! I almost fell over when I saw her. It's actually kind of pretty, once you get over the shock."

Bella managed a smile, not that she cared one way or the other about Connie's hair. She was thinking about the little locked book she had found, the book she suspected was Ariel's diary. She was tempted to ask her grandmother's advice about opening it. Ruby Hitchens was pretty smart about things and right now Bella wasn't in the mood to talk to her mother about anything important. Not since she had met up with that old school friend.

*No,* Bella thought, mindlessly cutting into the chicken breast on her plate. *I won't say anything to Grandma about the diary.* Because if she thought that opening the little book was wrong she might judge Bella harshly for even considering such an action. That would not be good. *I need Grandma on my side,* Bella decided. *Especially now.*

"How is that girl you met on the Marginal Way? Clara, isn't it?" her grandmother asked, passing the basket of bread.

Bella took a piece of the bread and unconsciously tore it in half. "She's okay," she said. "Is Mom with that guy again tonight?"

"If by 'that guy' you mean Jack, yes. They went to the beach for a picnic dinner."

A picnic dinner on the beach was a date, Bella thought. It was something you did with someone you felt romantic about. "Why haven't I met him?"

Her grandmother shrugged. "I don't know. Do you want to meet him?"

"No," Bella lied. "Why should I?"

"Bella? Are you going to eat that bread or utterly destroy it?"

Bella looked down at her plate. The piece of bread she had taken from the basket was in shreds. "Sorry," she said.

"There's plenty more. Eat some snap peas, please. They're as sweet as candy."

Bella did as she was told, but she barely tasted the peas. "Mom told me that my grandfather called her again," she said after a moment.

"Yes. He did."

"Why do you think he wants to talk to her all of a sudden?"

"Maybe it's not all of a sudden," her grandmother pointed out. "Maybe he's been thinking about reaching out for a long time."

"It's strange I've never met him, isn't it?" Bella said. "I mean, it's not so strange that I've never met Dad's parents because they live so far away. Not that we really know where Mom's father lives."

"I suppose it is strange that you've never met your maternal grandfather, yes."

"Do you miss him?" Bella asked.

"No," her grandmother replied promptly. "I did for a while. But that was a long time ago."

Bella reached for another piece of bread from the basket and put it on her plate. "Do you hate him for what he did to you and my mother?"

"Again, no. I was upset of course. Angry, sad, even embarrassed." Her grandmother smiled a bit. "Nobody likes to be made a fool of. And for a while I could hardly believe that he had actually gone. I kept expecting him to show up for dinner as usual with that happy-go-lucky grin on his face. But he never did show up and I never did come to hate him."

"Do you think Mom hates him?" Bella asked.

Her grandmother sighed. "I think that maybe at times she thought she hated him. But I don't like to attribute such an ugly emotion to someone I love. And what do you feel about your grandfather, Bella? We've never talked about him much, have we?"

Bella shrugged. "I don't feel anything really. I mean, he doesn't sound like a great guy. Not like Dad. But he never did anything to me, so . . ."

"You could argue that he neglected you. That he failed in his duty as a grandparent."

"Maybe. But you don't miss what you never had, right? Besides . . ." Bella swallowed hard. She really didn't want to start crying. If she did she might never stop. "Ariel and I had you."

"You'll *always* have me," her grandmother said firmly.

*Until you die*, Bella added silently. *Everyone dies.* "Will you go to my grandfather's funeral?" she asked. "I mean, whenever he dies."

Her grandmother put her glass down abruptly and wiped at the water that had spilled on her chin. "Bella, what a question."

"Sorry."

"No, don't be. It's just . . . The question took me by surprise and, honestly, I don't have an answer for it."

Bella toyed with the rest of the chicken breast on her plate and managed to eat a few more snap peas before putting down her fork. "I remember the last time Dad and I went camping," she said, staring down at the table. "It was a month before he died. It was still pretty cold, but we didn't mind, even when it snowed for a while one day. It was an adventure. One night for dinner we had black beans with Monterey Jack cheese melted on top. It was the best. I remember Dad telling me about the Boy Scout camp he had gone to for a few weeks one summer, how this one leader had actually baked bread in a hole in the ground. He told me how he used to sneak out of his tent in the middle of the night and lie on his back so he could look up at the stars."

"I guess he wasn't afraid of bears and nighttime creepy-crawlies."

Bella looked up from her plate. "I asked him that. He said he never even thought about the dangers because the sky was so pretty it filled him with a sense of awe. Those were his exact words. 'A sense of awe.' He said when he looked at the night sky he could almost believe in God." Suddenly Bella pushed her chair away from the table and stood. She needed to be alone. She thought she would start screaming if she couldn't be alone. "I'm sorry," she mumbled, and half ran out of the kitchen, up the stairs, and into the room she had shared with Ariel.

And there she cried hot, bitter tears for her father.

# Chapter 35

Ruby had spent a good part of the morning thinking about that startling question Bella had asked the previous night at dinner. Bella was no longer a child, but she wasn't yet an adult. Like all teenagers, even the most emotionally astute, she lacked a full understanding of how asking a certain question of a certain person might hit a nerve—in this case, asking Ruby Hitchens if she would attend her ex-husband's funeral.

She had thought about Steve's death before, of course, and had wondered how she would learn of his passing. If the phone calls stopped coming was she to assume that he was dead? There could be other reasons for Steve to cease communication, but with no access to him how would Ruby know the truth? The fact that he had denied her the opportunity—the privilege—of contacting him when she wanted or needed to had driven her to distraction in the early years. But over time Ruby had come to accept Steve's oddities and the strange structure of their relationship, if not always to like it.

Now, Ruby thought, pouring herself a second cup of coffee, with Steve's being in touch with Frieda, with his asking after his remaining grandchild, maybe she and Frieda and Bella would be allowed to share in his end. Only time would tell.

Ruby heard a car pull into the driveway. A few moments later her daughter joined her in the kitchen.

"Hey, Mom," she said, placing a large leather tote on the table.

"Hey. I've hardly had a glimpse of you today."

"I went to the library in York. This bag is stuffed with books, not my computer."

Ruby smiled. "Your secret is safe with me. So, how was your evening with Jack? I'm sorry I didn't get to ask you before now."

Frieda sank into a chair at the table. "It was really nice," she said. "It was . . . lovely, actually."

"Do you want something romantic to happen between you two?" Ruby asked. "Sorry if that was blunt."

"Honestly, Mom, I don't know. He took my hand at the fair the other day—just to help me get up from where we were sitting under a tree—and it felt . . ." Frieda shook her head. "I just don't know."

"All right. So, what did you two talk about last night?" Ruby asked.

Frieda laughed. "What didn't we talk about? We talked about memories of our childhood. We talked about Veronica's final days. We talked about dating again. We seem to be able to talk about everything. There's never an awkward break in the conversation."

Ruby felt a stab of conscience. She and George hadn't had a conversation that didn't revolve around Frieda or Bella in what seemed like an age. *And whose fault is that?* she thought. *Mine.*

"How was your evening with Bella?" Frieda asked. "I didn't see her when I got home last night and this morning she was gone before I came down for breakfast."

"For one," Ruby told her, "Bella wanted to know why her grandfather was reaching out to you now. I told her what little I know."

Freda sighed. "And what you know isn't much more than what I know. Dad apologized again for not having been more of a presence when Aaron and Ariel died. And then he said something strange. He said that even though he doesn't deserve it he'd like if I acknowledged that he existed for me. He said he wasn't asking to hear me say that I loved him, just that I acknowledged him." Frieda shook her head. "I don't really know what he means."

"I can't pretend to know, either," Ruby told her. "Maybe over time the message will become clear."

"Maybe. So, what else did you and Bella talk about?"

"We talked about Jack," Ruby told her. "Bella wanted to know why you haven't introduced her to him. It's a valid question, Frieda. Is there a particular reason why you haven't?"

Frieda toyed with one of the handles of her tote. "No," she said. "Not really. There hasn't seemed a good time."

"Frieda," Ruby said firmly, "no time is a good time to introduce a possible romantic interest to your child, especially in a situation like yours. If you think you might want them to get to know each other at some point you're just going to have to bite the bullet and make the introduction. You don't have to make a big deal of it. 'Bella, this is my old friend Jack. Jack, this is my daughter, Bella.'"

"Do you think Bella wants to meet Jack?" Frieda asked.

Ruby hesitated. "It doesn't matter what Bella wants," she said carefully. "She's the kid. You're the adult. You're the one in charge."

"It's different being in charge when it's only you. It's so hard. When Aaron was alive . . ." Frieda shook her head. "But he's not alive."

*No*, Ruby thought. *He's not. And that's something we're all still get-ting used to.* "There was one other interesting note to the evening," Ruby told her daughter. "Bella talked about the last time she and Aaron went camping. It was a lovely memory, but I think her tell-ing me made her too sad for company. She left the kitchen abruptly. She had barely eaten half of her dinner."

"Oh." Frieda rubbed her forehead. "Maybe I shouldn't have gone out last night."

"I hope you're not going to start wallowing in guilt again for at-tempting to move on."

Frieda smiled wanly. "Start wallowing in guilt? I wasn't aware I had ever stopped wallowing."

"Bella's memory of that last camping trip with her father has nothing to do with you or with me," Ruby pointed out. "You're not responsible for her remembering or forgetting."

"But I am responsible for her otherwise." Frieda sighed, rose, and hefted her leather tote. "Well, I'd better get to work. The sooner I'm done for the day the sooner I can get to these books."

Life, Ruby thought when Frieda had left the kitchen, never stopped throwing you curveballs. When she had invited Frieda and Bella to spend the summer with her in Yorktide she hadn't anticipated the reemergence of Steve Hitchens or the possibly romantic attentions of Jack Tennant. The men were complicating the lives of her daughter and granddaughter. Ruby could only hope that what seemed to be complications now would prove in the end to be benefits.

She could only hope.

# Chapter 36

"Oh my God," Clara said with a dramatic moan. "Do you hear that? I hate when she talks on her phone in the backyard. She's so loud! All of my housemates are stupid, but Leah's the stupidest."

Bella, who could barely hear the voice that seemed to be annoying Clara, realized that she felt slightly claustrophobic in Clara's crowded bedroom. She had never felt claustrophobic before, not even when she was seven and had gotten locked in that icky old outhouse at a school picnic, but something about the small room with its tiny windows, a room stuffed with relics of a dead relationship, made her want to run.

Before Bella could suggest they go somewhere, Clara suddenly got up from the bed and went to the dresser. There was a small metal box sitting there; Bella hadn't noticed it before. Clara removed the lid and took out what looked like a fattish cigarette. Bella's eyes widened. You didn't have to be a rocket scientist to know that the fattish cigarette was a joint.

"You don't mind, do you?" Clara asked, turning to Bella.

Bella shrugged, but she was taken by surprise. She had never actually been in the presence of someone smoking pot. Sure, she could recognize the smell; Kerri had pointed it out to her once when they were at an open-air festival along the Charles River in

Boston, but that wasn't the same as being face-to-face with someone smoking. Someone you considered a friend.

"I didn't know you smoked," Bella said, watching as Clara lit a match and held it to the joint between her lips.

"I haven't been smoking for long," Clara said, waving at the smoke spiraling before her face. "It helps me feel better. Less, I don't know, unhappy and anxious. Want a hit?"

"It's not for me," Bella said, putting up her hand. "But thanks."

"I mean, why?" Clara blurted.

"Why what? Why don't I smoke pot?"

"No, why won't Marc talk to me? I was so good to him. I never argued with him. I did everything he wanted. I gave him gifts all the time. I baked cookies for him every Saturday." Clara laughed bitterly. "He wouldn't come near me at graduation. And when I tried to talk to him after the ceremony his parents and sister practically carried him away. He wouldn't even look at me!"

"That must have been awful," Bella said with sympathy.

"It was humiliating," Clara declared. "I'm the laughingstock of my hometown. Too bad I didn't have a pot source back in Whimsey Corner. I mean, I knew it was around; I just didn't know how to get it."

"By the way," Bella asked, "where did you get it?"

Clara laughed. "It's all over the place here! Marc would be furious with me if he knew I was smoking dope. He's totally anti–drugs and alcohol. He doesn't even drink beer." Clara took another hit, held in the smoke for a bit, then swallowed. "I just don't know why he had to humiliate me at graduation!"

An odd thought occurred to Bella. Could it be that Clara wasn't telling the whole truth? Why *hadn't* anyone rallied around her? Usually it was the person who was left people felt sorry for after a breakup, so why did Clara think she was a laughingstock? And why exactly had Marc ended the relationship? Clara hadn't been clear on that. Maybe Marc had found out that Clara had cheated on him. If that was the case then Clara was lying about being madly in love with her boyfriend. Or had someone (who?) with a motive (what?) told Marc a lie about Clara? Or . . .

"Bella, are you listening to me?" Clara's tone was demanding.

Bella coughed. The smoke from the joint was acrid. "What?" she said. "Oh yeah. I'm listening."

"Good, because I was saying I wish you had a car."

"Oh. I mean, why?"

"Duh, because then you could drive us around sometimes. Do you know how expensive gas is?"

"But we haven't been anywhere together," Bella said, confused and a little taken aback.

"I went to get gas yesterday after my shift and I could only afford a few gallons. It's not fair."

*Maybe,* Bella thought, *if you hadn't spent your money on pot you'd have had money for more gas. But she said nothing.*

"And why do you wear that stupid bike helmet?" Clara suddenly asked with a harsh laugh. "It makes your head look huge. You look like a bug or something. You'd better watch out that someone doesn't try to squash you."

Bella felt slightly sick. She had no reply. Could you even reply to an insult?

Clara put the rest of the joint back into the little metal box, picked up her iPhone, and began to tap away with her thumbs.

"I guess I should go now," Bella said, aware that her hands were shaking a bit.

Clara looked up from her phone for about a nanosecond. "What?" she said. "Okay."

Bella left the cottage and fought back tears as she rode to her grandmother's house. It wasn't as if she were seriously bothered by Clara's smoking. It was just . . . It was just that odd remark Clara had made about Bella's not having a car. She had told Clara why she didn't drive. Why she *couldn't* drive. Had Clara forgotten? And why had Clara made that hurtful remark about her wearing a bike helmet? And it was just that things about Clara's past didn't seem to add up the way Bella thought they should. But who said that what she thought should be clear about Clara's past actually would *be* clear? No one's life made sense, not really.

Still, as Bella pedaled in the direction of Kinders Lane she couldn't shake off a funny feeling that something, somewhere, just wasn't right. Maybe it was the secondhand smoke.

# Chapter 37

"Jack, that's too funny!" Frieda laughed. "He really called you a whippersnapper? And a scoundrel?"

As Jack continued to regale her with the tale of his good intentions gone wrong with relation to an ancient and cantankerous man he had tried to assist at the grocery store, Frieda heard the front door open. A moment later Bella came into the kitchen. Her expression was hard to read, but it certainly wasn't happy.

"I've got to go," Frieda said hurriedly. "Fine. Bye."

"That was Jack, wasn't it?" Bella asked.

"Yes." Frieda stuck the cell phone into her pocket. "As a matter of fact it was. Where were you just now?"

"Out. With Clara. You've been spending a lot of time with him."

Bella's accusatory tone was not lost on Frieda and she answered carefully. "Have I? I wouldn't say it's been a lot of time."

Bella walked over to the table and gripped the back of one of the chairs. "You know you have," she said.

"Well," Frieda admitted, "maybe it has been a lot of time. We're old schoolmates, Bella. Jack lost his wife and I lost my husband. We have a lot in common."

"Not more than you had in common with Dad."

"Maybe not," Frieda said honestly. "I can't answer that yet."

"Yet?" Bella laughed and shook her head. "So you plan on seeing even more of him? I can't believe I'm hearing this!"

"Maybe I'll see more of him. I can't say for sure."

"You don't tell me anything about what you two do together or what you talk about. Why have you kept him from me?"

Frieda recalled her mother asking her the same question and her own inadequate response. "I haven't kept him from you," she began. "It's just that . . ." Why was this such a difficult question to answer? Was it that introducing Jack to Bella would make things more real than she wanted them to be at the moment? Was she just too frightened of taking a measurable step toward a new life?

"I know what's going to happen," Bella suddenly cried. "You're going to get married to this guy and have another baby to make up for losing Ariel. Isn't that what people do when they lose a kid, have another one to replace it? And where will that leave me?"

Frieda's stomach clenched. She took a step forward, but Bella unleashed her grip on the chair and retreated closer to the door. "Bella," she said, "stop it. You're being totally unfair. I'm not going to have another baby for any reason, and certainly not to replace Ariel. Nobody can replace your father or your sister. We both know that."

"But what about getting married again?" Bella demanded. "Are you going to run off with Jack? For God's sake, Mom, Dad's only been gone a year!"

"I don't know what exactly I'm going to do in the future, Bella, but I can guarantee I'm not going to run off anywhere or with anyone. I would never leave you; you have to believe that." Again Frieda moved forward and again Bella backed away.

"How can I believe that when . . ." Bella shook her head. "If you keep seeing that guy I'll . . ."

Frieda's heart leaped with fear. "You'll what, Bella?"

"I don't know what I'll do," Bella said, her tone now strangely calm, "but it won't be pretty, and believe me, you'll regret it."

"Bella, wait!" Frieda cried, but her daughter had already turned and stalked from the kitchen.

Frieda sank into a chair at the table. Her breath was coming fast. She was frightened. Kids committed suicide for far less than a mother moving on after the death of her husband. It hadn't been smart keeping Jack from meeting Bella. If she had just introduced them as her mother had advised, plain and simple, none of this might be happening.

*Why did Aaron have to die?* Frieda thought, putting her hand to her forehead. *Why did he have to leave me to live life all alone, making such stupid mistakes—*

Suddenly her mother was in the doorway.

"I saw Bella just now in the upstairs hall," Ruby said. "Her face looked like the proverbial storm cloud. Did something happen between you two?"

"It was nothing," Frieda lied. She knew her mother didn't believe her; she could only hope her mother wouldn't press for a more honest answer.

Ruby went to the fridge and opened it. "I thought I'd make pasta with vegetables for dinner," she said, removing a carton of assorted mushrooms.

"Okay," Frieda said. "Mom? When I last talked to Dad he told me his mother was short on maternal feeling. Did he ever talk about his childhood with you?"

"Not much," Ruby admitted, gently applying a damp sponge to the mushrooms. "I gathered it wasn't a very happy childhood, but then again, so many childhoods aren't. I do know he was closer to his father than to his mother, though that isn't saying much. Steve left home at seventeen and in his own words he never looked back." Ruby shook her head. "Not even when his father was dying. So who knows what went on in that household? I wouldn't want to point the finger of blame, not at this distance and being sure of so little."

"No," Frieda said. "Of course not." But Frieda could point a finger of blame at herself. Her behavior regarding Jack was fueling at least part of Bella's current unhappiness. A parent owed a child so much. Care. Protection. Warmth.

"Frieda?"

"Yes?"

"Are you sure there's nothing else you want to tell me?"

Frieda managed a smile; at least she hoped it hadn't come out as a grimace. "No," she said, rising from her seat. "There's nothing else. I'll make a salad, okay?"

# Chapter 38

Ruby yawned. I look awful, she thought, staring at her face in the mirror over the vintage 1940s vanity table she had found while out scouting with Phil a few years back. It had been a bit of a mad purchase; she had never been the sort to fuss over her appearance and besides ensuring that she was neat and clean she had no use for dabbling with blush and eyeliner. Still, Ruby was glad she had splurged—even when the vanity's mirror reflected back to her a face worn with lack of sleep.

In the past Ariel's nightly appearances had never caused disruption to Ruby's rest, but for some reason last night her appearance had. Ruby had been unable to fall back to sleep until nearly five o'clock.

"Cucumber slices," Ruby murmured. "I need two cold cucumber slices to get rid of these bags under my eyes." With a sigh she got up from the vanity table and went to her closet for a light linen blouse and a fresh pair of chinos. And as Ruby dressed she thought about the first time Ariel had come to her, a mere month after the accident. To say that she had been disconcerted was an understatement, but the following morning, with the sun shining into the room and the sleep wiped from her eyes, Ruby had wondered if Ariel's appearance had really been just a product of her own imaginative desire. Maybe, she thought, she had willed the vision of Ariel into being. The human brain was capable of all sorts of trickery and feats of self-deception.

So shortly after breakfast she had gone online in the hopes of finding information that might help her to understand what had happened in the middle of the night. And she learned that she had experienced a popularly recognized phenomenon known as After Death Contact. The message the departed person brought to his loved ones was always the same: Life and love are eternal. "Don't grieve for me," he might say. "Please let me go; I'm all right." Ruby remembered what Ariel had told her. "I'm happy, Grandma. Dad and I are together and we're fine. We love you."

It had comforted Ruby more than a little to know that she wasn't losing her mind. And if Ariel's nocturnal visits couldn't be considered everyone's norm, they had become Ruby's norm. Ruby picked up her brush and tried to bring some order to her hair. Maybe, she thought, it was time she told Frieda and Bella about her contact with Ariel. She wasn't entirely sure why she had kept her experiences from them so far; maybe she was afraid of not being taken seriously. But now might be the time. The knowledge that Ariel's spirit was at rest could only help. Couldn't it?

With a sense of determination Ruby tossed her brush onto the vanity table and left her bedroom. The moment she entered the kitchen she felt the tension between her daughter and granddaughter. "Good morning," Ruby said, taking her seat at the table.

Frieda smiled, but the smile didn't quite reach her eyes. Bella made no reply, verbal or otherwise, but continued to chew her cold cereal. Ruby helped herself to a cup of coffee and a piece of toast. Her determination wavered. Maybe it was best not to say anything. Emotions were already riding high. But no. She had to hope that sharing Ariel's words of comfort might help heal whatever unhappiness was forcing a wedge between her daughter and granddaughter.

"I hope everyone slept well," Ruby said brightly. "I had an interesting night myself. Ariel came to me. It wasn't the first time."

Bella stopped chewing and looked at her grandmother with an expression of surprise.

Frieda frowned. "What do you mean Ariel came to you?"

"I mean," Ruby explained, "that she comes to me at night. Not every night but sometimes. She stands at the foot of the bed and we talk."

Bella put her spoon next to her bowl.

"She always has the same message," Ruby went on. "She says that she loves you both very much. She says that she and Aaron are together and happy and that neither of you should worry." Ruby paused before going on. "She said that you should turn to each other for support." Ariel had said no such thing, but Ruby thought that she certainly might have. In any case, the advice was sound.

"I'm confused, Grandma," Bella said. "How do you know you're not just dreaming?"

"That's a good question," Ruby admitted. "I'll try to explain. When Ariel appears to me there are no weird or confusing symbols like there are in a typical dream. Everything is lucid and straight-forward. There are no riddles. There's no sense of fear or frustration."

Bella leaned toward Ruby. "I want to know everything," she said. "What is she wearing? Is her hair loose or is it braided? Does she stay for long? Does she answer questions? Because if she does maybe you could ask her if she . . . If she forgives me."

"Bella, I don't—"

Ruby put a reassuring hand on her daughter's arm. "It's all right, Frieda. I usually just listen to Ariel," she told her granddaughter. "What I hear assures me that your father and sister are safe and that they love you and your mother without question." Ruby smiled. "As for what Ariel is wearing, well, I can't tell exactly, but I can tell that her hair is loose, almost like a halo around her head."

"You'll tell me when it happens again?" Bella asked urgently. "When Ariel comes to you and if she has anything to say to me about . . . about anything?"

"I will," Ruby promised. "But in the meantime, remember what she told me last night. Everything is all right." Then she turned to her daughter. "What are you up to today?" she asked.

Frieda shook her head. "After this conversation whatever I say is bound to be boring. I'm working on a new job. My deadline is right around the corner, so there's no time to waste."

Ruby nodded. "And you'll be late for work, Bella, if you don't get a move on."

Bella looked at her phone and then pushed her chair away from the table. "Bye," she said, dashing out of the kitchen.

When she had gone Ruby braced herself for the questions she knew Frieda was going to ask. Sure enough, as soon as the front door had closed Frieda said, "Mom? Are you really serious about communicating with Ariel?"

"Of course I am," she said. "I would never lie about something so profound. What I experience is popularly known as After Death Contact. It's not uncommon and it can take place in a variety of ways. In my case, Ariel comes to me at night." Ruby shrugged. "Maybe it's because I'm more receptive and relaxed than I am in the day. I don't pretend to understand it. I just choose to believe it."

Frieda shook her head. "I've never experienced any kind of contact with either Aaron or Ariel. I wonder if I lack some, I don't know, some essential quality that makes contact possible. Although I have to admit that I find the notion of a spirit making contact with a living person upsetting. Who else knows about this, Mom?"

"Don't worry," Ruby said with a small smile. "I don't go announcing it around town. I know that most people would say I'd lost my mind. Only George and Phil know. Look, Frieda, I'm sorry if I upset you; really I am. I only decided to tell you and Bella because I thought that knowing Ariel and Aaron are okay might help."

Frieda got up from the table. "I don't know if it helps or not," she admitted. "All I know is that I should get to work."

"I'll clear up the breakfast things," Ruby said quietly. But she didn't get up from her chair immediately. Instead she sat alone at the kitchen table and wondered if she had just done more harm than good; she wondered if her sharing was the disastrous equivalent of Frieda's little party in Ariel's honor, a well-intentioned attempt at healing gone wrong. Maybe she should have discussed things with George first, but even after three years of their being together she couldn't entirely shake the habit of making every decision, however big or small, on her own. Independence was a good thing; no one could argue that it wasn't. But when you had the opportunity to turn to someone you loved and trusted for an opinion or a word of advice or a differing perspective, why not take that opportunity?

*Old habits die hard; that's why,* Ruby thought, finally rising. And she had been in the habit of trusting no one but herself—and, on occasion, Phil—for a very long time.

# Chapter 39

Frieda had worked on the new copyediting project until her eyes were sore, so when Jack called and asked if she could spare half an hour for a coffee she had readily agreed. It was only when she had ended the call did she remember all too clearly Bella's threat. It was with some effort that Frieda convinced herself that having a cup of coffee with a former schoolmate in a public setting couldn't possibly be seen as objectionable. Well, she half convinced herself.

The old-fashioned diner in downtown Yorktide was almost empty at three in the afternoon. Aside from the two of them there was only a young couple sitting at the counter, eating burgers and fries.

"You seem a little, I don't know, distracted. Everything okay?" Jack asked when they had settled at the booth farthest from the young couple and ordered their coffees.

"Yeah," Frieda lied, hoping that Bella wouldn't choose this moment to take her afternoon break and stroll past the diner. I'm not doing anything wrong, she told herself, but she didn't believe a word of it, not really. "Well, my mother told me something this morning that's been bothering me. She said that Ariel comes to her at night. She says it's genuine After Death Contact." Frieda shook her head. "I don't know what to make of it all."

The waitress delivered their coffees, and when she had gone off, Jack asked, "These episodes don't upset your mother, do they?"

"They don't seem to," Frieda said. "She says the encounters are thoroughly pleasant. Assuming they're real."

"You think she's imagining them?"

"I can't help but wonder if she might be manufacturing the visitations or whatever they are in some misguided attempt to make Bella and me feel better. The messages Ariel brings are meant to comfort us."

Jack shook his head. "You really think your mother would stoop to trickery?"

"No." Frieda sighed. "You're right; she herself said she would never lie about something so profound. It's just that . . . The whole idea makes me uncomfortable. It seems so—so dark, and I can't bear for my husband or my child to be associated with anything ugly."

"But according to Ruby the episodes aren't gloomy or frightening."

"I know," Frieda admitted. "Bella seemed fascinated by the whole thing. I suspect she wishes Ariel would come to her. I just hope she doesn't start dwelling on the hereafter."

"I've heard a bit about Ruby Hitchens's older granddaughter over the years and I never got the impression she was one of those young people who glamorize death and Satan and all that black magic nonsense."

Frieda smiled a bit. "No," she said. "Bella has always been firmly on the bright side of things. Until now."

"I don't think you have to start worrying until she shows up for dinner wearing black lipstick and sporting tattoos of skulls and vampires."

"Can you imagine what my mother would say to that?" Frieda paused. "Jack," she said, "do you remember my father?"

"Not well, no," Jack admitted. "But I do know that my parents liked him. Not the fact that he left Yorktide in the way he did but who he was before that. They said he was always ready with a smile and a helping hand. They remember that he raked leaves and shoveled snow for an elderly neighbor when your parents lived out on North Hill Road, which was the back of beyond in those days. I think it was a shock to my parents when Steve left town the way he did. From what I heard he didn't say good-bye to anyone other than your mother. One day he was just gone."

*Yes*, Frieda thought. *Just gone.* "How are your parents, Jack?" she asked. "I'm sorry I haven't asked before now."

"Thriving," Jack told her. "They moved to Florida not long after Veronica passed away. They were a godsend to me at the end. I try to see them at least twice a year, which means my going to Florida. My mother says that after sixty-some years in Maine she's had enough of the cold."

"But what about our lovely summers and gorgeous autumns? Doesn't she miss those?"

Jack laughed. "I don't argue with my mother. I never win."

"I know the feeling."

The waitress returned and asked if they wanted a refill. Frieda looked at her watch and shook her head. "I should be getting home," she said. "I'm on dinner duty tonight."

Jack paid their check and together they walked out of the diner. Frieda glanced quickly in the direction of Phil's shop. "Thanks, Jack," she said.

"For the coffee?" Jack smiled.

"For listening."

"My pleasure," he assured her. "Look, there's a really fantastic jazz group playing tomorrow night at Jonathan's. Any interest in joining me?"

"I'll . . . I'll let you know. I'm hoping a marketing gig I applied for will come through, and if it does it will keep me pretty busy for a while." It was the truth, Frieda reminded herself. Part of it.

"Okay," Jack said. "I hope you can come. I never miss this group when they're in town."

Jack walked off, and as he did Frieda felt a wave of regret. She shouldn't have agreed to see Jack today. The risk had been too great and by meeting with him and sharing the story of Ariel's visitations she had in effect been leading him on. She had treated him as a friend and he couldn't be a friend.

He just couldn't be.

# Chapter 40

"Can you believe what this woman said to me today?" Bella was pacing Clara's room. "I was in the convenience store on my lunch break getting a bottle of water and this woman came up to me and said she knew who I was. I didn't recognize her, but before I could tell her that I didn't know her she was going on about how God had called my father and sister to him and about how God has his reasons for all the stuff he does even when we can't understand the reasons. It was insane!"

Clara, sitting on the edge of the bed, continued to tap away at her phone. "Maybe she was only trying to be nice."

"Nice?" Bella laughed. "That's a funny sort of way to be nice! I don't believe in God, not really. So now what? I'm supposed to think that my father's and sister's deaths were random and meaningless? And what if I did believe in God? Then suddenly their dying would make perfect sense?" Bella shook her head. "What possible sense could it make for two good people to die so horribly? Why would God want that? And if he did want to kill two good people for some reason that made sense to him if not to anyone else, why would I want to believe in that sort of God?"

"I don't believe in God anymore," Clara said, tossing her phone onto her pillow. "I used to, when I was a kid. But then . . ." Clara shrugged. "Marc is Catholic. He was an altar boy for a while. His family still goes to church on Sundays. I wonder if I'll have to become a Catholic when we get married. I'll do it, of course. I'd do anything for Marc. I'd probably even kill for him."

Bella rolled her eyes. She had been hoping for a few sympathetic words from Clara, not more about her devotion to Saint Marc. "Don't you even want to know what I said to her?" she asked.

Clara frowned. "Who?"

"The woman in the convenience store!"

"Oh. Yeah. Sure."

"I said thank you! Can you believe I thanked her? For what? I was so confused the words just came popping out of my mouth. I should have told her to mind her own business. That probably would have been rude, but isn't it rude to assume another person shares your beliefs or whatever?"

"Forget about her, Bella," Clara said, jumping up from her bed. "Come on, let's take some hits."

Bella opened her mouth to say no, but the word didn't come out. Instead she remembered the time her grief counselor had suggested she get a prescription from her GP for an antidepressant. "Something mild," Colleen had said. "Just something to help lower the noise in your head so that you can focus on getting better." But Bella had refused in spite of Colleen's reassurance that an antidepressant wouldn't fundamentally change who she was. Bella hadn't wanted anything messing with her feelings, even for the better.

But smoking marijuana was different, Bella thought, watching Clara open the metal box atop her dresser and take out a joint. Smoking pot was supposed to be fun. And she could use some fun after running into that woman in the convenience store. And after that ugly scene with her mother the other day when they had argued about Jack Tennant. Fun. It seemed like a thing of the long-distant past. It seemed like something she deserved.

"You know what?" Bella said. "Yeah, I'll do it."

Clara laughed. "This is so cool. It's much more fun to get high with someone than on your own."

"You've been smoking with other people?" Bella asked.

"A lot of people at The Flipper smoke dope, but don't tell anyone."

"Who would I tell? Look," Bella said, reaching into her cross-body bag. "Let me give you some money. I don't have a lot, but . . ."

"Don't worry about it," Clara told her. "The woman I buy it from gives me a discount."

For about half a second Bella wondered why someone dealing drugs would give a customer a discount. Weren't drug dealers all about making as much money as they could? Maybe Clara was lying. But why would she lie?

Clara lit the joint with a disposable lighter and handed it to Bella. "Inhale," she instructed, "and then hold the smoke in for a few seconds. Then exhale."

With some trepidation Bella did as she had been instructed. When she exhaled she thought she felt a bit loopy but not in a scary way, like when you had a fever. Or maybe she was just making it up. Was one hit enough to make you feel anything different? Could you talk yourself into feeling high? She didn't want to sound stupid or naïve by asking Clara those questions.

"My grandmother sees my sister at night," she blurted, passing the joint back to Clara. "I mean, Ariel shows up like she's alive and she tells my grandmother stuff."

"Freaky," Clara said. "What does she say?"

"She says that she and my father are happy."

"Do you believe they're happy?" Clara asked, taking another hit.

"My sister isn't a liar. I mean, she wasn't a liar. When she was alive. Can you lie when you're dead?" Bella laughed and accepted the joint back from Clara. "I don't know what I mean!"

Clara grinned. "Don't worry; you'll get used to it."

Bella took another hit and coughed before she could hold in much of the smoke. "Oops," she said, handing the joint back to Clara, who extinguished it and put it back into the metal box on top of the dresser. "Anyway," Bella went on, "you should have seen the look on my mother's face when my grandmother told us about Ariel. She probably thinks my grandmother is nuts."

"Well, it is pretty strange. Ghosts and all." Clara shivered dramatically.

"I wish Ariel would come to me some night," Bella went on. "I want . . . I want to apologize."

"For what?" Clara asked.

Bella shrugged. "Nothing. Forget it."

"Talking about dead people is too depressing. I want to feel good, not bummed out."

"Sorry," Bella said.

Clara didn't reply. She picked up her phone again and began to type. Bella felt a little let down by Clara's lack of attention but not as much as she had earlier. "I guess I should go," she said.

"Yeah, okay." Clara looked up briefly before turning back to her phone.

Bella left the cottage without seeing any of Clara's housemates. *My life has just taken another totally unexpected turn,* she thought as she got on her bike. In spite of swearing she would never take drugs other than maybe an aspirin when she got her period she had just shared a few puffs of a joint with Clara. And she didn't know what all the fuss was about. She felt fine. Better than fine, she felt mellow. And a bit like she was going to burst out giggling. And she felt hungry. A box of those little powdered sugar doughnuts they sold by the checkout at the convenience store would be awesome. Or chips. Barbeque-flavored potato chips.

Bella dug into her cross-body bag and pulled out a few crumpled singles. It was enough for a snack. Her mother would probably have dinner on the table by the time she got home, but she was hungry now. Bella stuffed the bills back into her bag and started off. And, she thought, pedaling down Valley Road toward the heart of town, if that woman who had babbled on about God was at the convenience store again she would totally tell her to keep her opinions to herself.

# Chapter 41

Frieda opened the toaster oven to check on the potatoes. The fork went through the skin and into the flesh easily, so she closed the door and turned off the machine. Tonight's dinner couldn't be more classic—steaks, baked potatoes, and snap peas. The snap peas had already been briefly boiled, blanched in ice water, and drained. The steaks would take only moments; they all liked their steaks rare. A classic meal and, more important, an easy one, which was good, because there was so much on Frieda's mind she felt she would fail at any more complex kitchen task.

Interestingly, the confrontation with Bella over Jack Tennant had brought back memories of those years after Steve Hitchens's defection and before Frieda had gone off to college, the years when with both Tony and Steve gone, her mother and Phil had grown even closer. In some very important ways Phil had taken her father's place. It was Phil who went with Ruby to Frieda's school plays. It was Phil who taught her to drive when Ruby gave up in frustration. At the sophomore Father-Daughter Dance, it was Phil who proudly led Frieda onto the dance floor. And at her high school graduation, it was Phil who clapped the loudest when she won top honors in English.

A girl in Frieda's junior year French class, Patti something or other, had once asked Frieda why her mother and Phil weren't married. "Because Phil is gay," Frieda had told her. Patti had shrugged. "Yeah, I know, but they're like, best friends and all, right? So it could work. I'm sure people do that sort of thing all the time."

Maybe, Frieda had thought, a marriage between Phil and her mother could work—if they both wanted it to—and then Phil would be her official stepfather. And as appealing as that sounded to Frieda, who truly loved and trusted Phil, the idea of someone moving into the house she shared with her mother and forever altering their new family had caused her something akin to panic. There had been too much alteration already. Just as there had been too much alteration in Bella's world. Of *course* Bella feared another radical change in the new life she and her mother were building, and though that new life wasn't perfect and never would be, it was *theirs* and that meant so very much.

Frieda turned on the gas under her mother's big cast-iron frying pan. No. She was sticking to the resolution she had made earlier outside the diner. She simply could not continue to see Jack Tennant, not at the risk of injuring or, worse, losing another child. Bella's threat, however vague, had to be taken seriously. Aaron would understand. He would think she was doing the right thing in choosing to put her child's happiness ahead of her own.

"Hey." It was her mother, come into the kitchen. "What's on your mind?" Ruby asked. "I could smell the wood burning. Or was it just the pan heating up?"

Frieda managed a smile. "I was just thinking about the new marketing project I landed, the one for that landscaping center in Wells. Writing brochures and catalogue copy for an owner with very specific requirements isn't as easy as it sounds."

"Nothing wrong with a challenge," her mother pointed out.

"Your indomitable spirit is showing." Frieda carefully placed the steaks into the heated frying pan. "Would you take the potatoes out of the toaster oven, Mom?"

"Gladly."

A moment later the front door slammed, causing Frieda to flinch.

"It's our delicate little Bella," her mother said.

"Hey. Is dinner ready?" Bella asked, loping into the kitchen. "I'm starving."

"Is Phil working you too hard?" Frieda asked worriedly, glancing over her shoulder. She noted with pleasure that Bella's cheeks had a healthy flush to them.

"He wouldn't do that," Ruby scolded, setting the plate of baked potatoes on the table. "He would never take advantage of an employee, let alone the granddaughter of his dearest friend."

"I know but..." Frieda turned off the heat under the pan, placed the steaks on a platter, and brought it and the bowl of snap peas to the table.

"I'm fine, Mom. Just hungry." Bella took her usual seat. "Oh, good," she said brightly. "Baked potatoes. I *love* baked potatoes. Do we have any sour cream?"

Frieda paused for a moment before answering. This was a surprising change for the better. It seemed like ages since Bella had exhibited enthusiasm for anything, and enthusiasm for baked potatoes was better than enthusiasm for nothing. "Afraid not," she said. "But I'll pick some up tomorrow, okay?"

Bella smiled, sliced open her potato, and reached for the butter. "Cool," she said. "Awesome. Grandma, that shade of green looks totally great on you."

"You've seen me in this blouse a million times," Ruby remarked as she took her own seat.

Bella shrugged. "I guess I never really noticed it until now. But green is definitely your color. Mom, the steak is amazing."

"Thanks," Frieda said as she joined her mother and daughter at the table. She was grateful for whatever miracle had occurred in the last twenty-four hours resulting in Bella's sudden high spirits. Confused—a teenager's mood swings could baffle even the most learned psychiatrist—but grateful.

"This was like the perfect summer day," Bella suddenly announced.

"You're in a good mood," Ruby remarked, and Bella laughed.

Frieda smiled at her mother and daughter. And in that moment of welcome peace and harmony she knew without the shadow of a doubt that she was doing the right thing in ending her nascent relationship with Jack Tennant. Without the shadow of a doubt.

# Chapter 42

Sweat was trickling from under Bella's helmet and she blinked rapidly, hoping the sweat wouldn't get into her eyes. The afternoon was beyond sultry and, stupidly, she had forgotten her water bottle at Clara's cottage. Now she felt totally dehydrated and . . . *Whatever*, she thought. She would be home soon enough.

Bella heard the short beep of a horn and a moment later a pickup truck passed her; the passenger waved as the truck drove slowly by, and Bella waved back. She didn't recognize the truck or the people in it, but that was one of the cool things about Yorktide. Most people were genuinely nice. You could pretty easily make friends if you wanted to. Not that Clara wanted to. Not once had Bella heard Clara say a positive word about her housemates or her colleagues at The Flipper, even the ones she smoked pot with.

Then again, Bella thought, glancing at a few cows grazing in a field to her left, Clara's housemates and colleagues might not have a positive word to say about Clara, either. They might very well find her boring, because as far as Bella could tell Clara never talked about anything but Marc. Take that afternoon, for instance. The entire time they had been together at the cottage Clara had gone on about how great Marc was and how much she loved him and how she totally couldn't understand why he had ended their relationship. Bella, who had been smoking pot and feeling mellow enough not to care about Clara and her problems for the moment, had pretty much been able to block out Clara's voice and had found that if she said things like "oh" and "wow" and "seriously" every minute or two Clara seemed to be satisfied.

The only really annoying thing about the afternoon was that the pot smoke was kind of hard to get used to; she had had a bad coughing fit after one hit. And she would have to watch the munchies after or she would blimp out. And for about a split second before leaving Clara's cottage she had wondered if maybe riding her bike when she was probably still high was such a good idea; maybe her reaction time would be impaired or something, but so far everything had been okay. She hadn't ridden off the road into a ditch or been spooked by the passing pickup truck—

"Shit!" A deep pothole had suddenly appeared a yard or two in front of her bike. Bella swerved and as she did so her tires hit a patch of loose gravel and the bike started to slide sideways out from under her. Somehow, miraculously, she managed to put one foot on the ground and let the bike drop to the pavement. She stepped away, tripping on one of the pedals and stumbling several feet before she could stop herself.

"Shit," Bella said again as she took off her helmet to wipe the sweat from her forehead and then put a hand to her pounding heart. She had come way too close to being thrown off the bike. Yeah, she had seen the pothole in time to avoid it, but she hadn't seen the patch of loose gravel. Usually she was super careful when she rode along roads like the one she was on now with long stretches of rough shoulder.

When Bella felt calm enough to continue her journey home she picked up the bike, checked it for damage—there was none that she could see—and rode the rest of the way with extra deliberation. When she reached her grandmother's house she breathed a sigh of relief. Next time she smoked with Clara she would wait awhile before getting on her bike. Maybe get a cup of coffee or tea (even though she didn't usually drink either) or a soda, something with caffeine. She didn't know if caffeine helped straighten you out after smoking pot, but it was supposed to help if you had been drinking alcohol, so . . .

After checking the bike again for any damage she might have missed, Bella went inside and found her grandmother in the kitchen, sitting at the table with one of those professional nursing journals she was always reading opened before her.

"Where were you?" her grandmother asked with a smile.

Bella went to the sink and ran the water until it was icy cold. "I stopped by to see Clara after work," she said. She reached for a glass from the drainer, filled it to the brim, and gulped the entire contents.

"How is she?"

"Fine," Bella said.

"Why don't you ever bring her around? You know she's welcome."

"I told you," Bella said, rinsing the glass and putting it back in the drainer by the side of the sink. "She's shy." And, Bella thought, *I don't really want her here.* The idea surprised her. Why didn't she want Clara in her family's home? The possible answers to that question seemed too upsetting to contemplate and Bella pushed them aside.

"Where's Mom?" she asked her grandmother.

"I don't know. She was gone when I got up from my nap. Usually she leaves a note. Maybe she went down to the beach for a break. She's been working on this latest project nonstop for the past few days."

"Oh," Bella said. "Right." *Of course Mom would be working,* Bella thought, *especially now that it's her sole responsibility to support me. To support us.* She felt a pang of guilt and tried to push that aside, too, but it refused to budge.

Her grandmother closed the journal and got to her feet with a groan. "Well," she said, "I'm off. I'm getting too old for these night shifts. It takes me days to recover a normal sleep pattern. But at least I have a job, and so many these days don't."

Bella managed a smile. "Bye, Grandma," she said.

When she was alone in the kitchen Bella sank into a chair, folded her arms on the table, and rested her head on them. Her grandmother worked so hard and was so generous. *And Mom is so much the same,* Bella thought. She was always available when Bella needed her to be. It had been seriously wrong of her to make that threat of doing something terrible if her mother continued to spend time with Jack Tennant, but she had been so upset and she just hadn't been thinking right. The threat was another unusually dramatic gesture like running off the night of Ariel's sixteenth birthday. And slamming doors. And smoking pot with Clara?

Bella lifted her head and sighed. She wondered what her grandmother would say if she knew her granddaughter had been smoking pot; maybe, being a nurse, she could tell that someone was high just by looking at her eyes or something. That was a frightening thought, but if her grandmother was able to tell if someone was using drugs, why hadn't she noticed anything just now? Because she had been too tired to pay close attention? Because her family's being with her this summer was a drain on her energy?

Bella got up from the chair and began to pace the kitchen. The worst thing about smoking dope was the lying about it. And the worrying about getting caught wasn't so great, either. But as long as she only smoked in Clara's room she was probably safe. Unless one of Clara's housemates decided to rat them out. Unless her grandmother, Nurse Ruby Hitchens, decided to pay closer attention to her granddaughter and gleaned the truth. And then her mother would also know the truth and . . . It would be one big disaster.

Bella stopped pacing and felt a wave of confusion sweep over her. *What did I get myself into?* she wondered. The lying. The deceit. Still, there was a way out. She could decide right then and there never to smoke again, but . . . But the thing was she enjoyed smoking, at least the part of it that didn't involve coughing. It wasn't exactly fun, like she had thought it might be, but it was as close as she had come to fun in what seemed like forever.

Suddenly Bella remembered the little locked book in Ariel's dresser drawer. Maybe Ariel had written something meaningful that might help her figure out the mess she was in. Some people believed that if you were in trouble and needed advice you could open the Bible or some other book of received wisdom at random, poke your finger at a line of text, and the message of the line would be just what you needed to hear.

Bella went up to her room, where she opened the bottom drawer of the dresser. The diary was where it had always been, under the plain blue and white T-shirts. Bella picked it up and stared at the image of the unicorn on its cover. *No,* she thought. It didn't feel right, the idea of violating something so personal of Ariel's, and that's what it would be, a violation, breaking the lock just to satisfy her own selfish needs. And all because she couldn't figure out how to handle the mess she seemed to be creating of her life this summer.

Bella tucked the diary back under the T-shirts and closed the drawer. Suddenly she felt very, very tired. She lay down on her bed and stared up at the ceiling. The house felt very empty. She hoped her mother would be home soon.

# Chapter 43

Frieda had been sitting on a wooden bench at the top of the beach for close to half an hour. Jack wasn't late. It was just that she needed to breathe and to gather the courage for what she was about to do. Sometimes the sight of the magnificent blue Atlantic rolling before her brought a sense of strength and purpose. Sometimes, but not so much today.

"Hey."

A smile came automatically to Frieda's face when she looked up to see Jack standing there. *Gosh, he's so handsome,* she thought. What she said was: "Hi. Thanks for coming."

"No problem," Jack said, sitting next to her. "You said on the phone you had something important to talk about."

The urge to make small talk first was powerful, but Frieda knew that it was kinder to get straight to the point. "Yes," she said, looking down at her hands crossed on her lap. "I can't spend time with you, Jack, not like we have been. It upsets Bella."

After a moment Jack said, "I see. Did she talk to you about us?"

"Yes." Frieda turned to look at Jack. "She . . . She was very agitated. She said that I was betraying her father. She said that I was abandoning her. I tried to convince her otherwise, but . . . I'm sorry, Jack. I feel I don't have a choice about this."

"You always have a choice, Frieda," Jack said quietly.

"No. Not always." *Not*, she thought, *when it comes to your child*.

"Maybe it would help if Bella met me," Jack suggested. "She could see for herself that I'm not a creep."

*Maybe*, Frieda thought. *But it's too late now.* "I'm sorry, Jack," she said. "Really."

Jack sighed. "Well, I can't say that I'm not disappointed. Tell me, Frieda, did you enjoy the time we've spent together this summer?"

"Yes," she said honestly. "Very much."

"As did I. I felt—I feel—that we connect pretty well. Things seem so easy between us. Natural."

"Yes," Frieda said. "I know."

"Being really comfortable with someone is rare. It should be treasured."

Frieda felt a trickle of annoyance. If Jack thought he could wear down her resistance by pointing out the truth about them he was simply wrong. Because there was another truth; there was the truth about mother and daughter. "I know," she said a bit testily. "But this is something I have to do, for Bella's sake."

Jack shook his head. "Frieda, you can't sacrifice your own happiness for that of your daughter and expect to be of much help to her in the end."

"What do you know about being a parent?" Frieda replied angrily. "Losing my daughter, my own flesh and blood, is the worst thing that ever happened to me. The worst. I can't, I won't, risk losing another child. Nothing matters more than the mother-child bond. Nothing!"

Suddenly all energy drained from Frieda and she became terribly aware that she and Jack were not alone. An elderly woman on the bench to the left was frowning at her. A young mother holding her baby against her chest was openly staring. Frieda heard a giggle from behind and was sure it was meant at her expense. Even the seagull strutting nearby seemed to turn its beady critical eye in her direction. She had never felt so embarrassed.

And when she saw the look of anguish on Jack's face her heart contracted. "God, Jack," she said quietly, "I'm so sorry. I should never have said what I did about your not knowing what's it like to be a parent. I should never have raised my voice, made a scene. I don't know what came over me. I'm sorry."

"I believe that you're sorry," Jack said after a moment. "I know you're not a cruel person. And I'm sorry, too. I shouldn't have said what I did. Your relationship with your daughter is none of my business. I guess hearing words I had hoped never to hear from you got to me."

Frieda put her hand to her forehead. "It's all right. It's all right."

"I should be going." Jack rose from the bench and gently, for just a moment, put his hand on her shoulder. "Take care of yourself, Frieda."

Frieda did not look up at Jack; she did not watch him walk back to his car. The young woman with the baby suddenly sat next to her. "You okay?" she asked.

Frieda shook her head. "Not really," she said hoarsely, wiping a tear from her cheek. "But I will be." Frieda rose from the bench and headed toward where she had parked her own car. When she had first come home to Yorktide for the summer she had told her mother she felt responsible for Bella's recent emotional withdrawal. Maybe now, Frieda thought, unlocking the door of her car, she could really begin to make amends. Maybe now she could really let Bella know that her mother was available for her whenever and wherever and however Bella needed her to be. Maybe it wasn't too late.

# Chapter 44

"Thanks so much for your help, Ruby." Michael shuddered. "That wound was looking pretty nasty. Wound care has never been my strong point."

"No worries," Ruby told her colleague. "I've never been able to handle vomiting. I mean, I don't let the patient see that I'm weak at the knees, but . . ."

Michael laughed. "Next time you have a patient who feels there's a Technicolor yawn coming on, call me."

"I will," Ruby promised. She continued on her rounds, and though her patients were terribly important, there was one even more important matter on her mind at the moment—the conversation she had had with George over a midmorning coffee. Well, it hadn't really been a conversation. George had talked and Ruby had listened.

"I was thinking," he had said, "that we should take a trip to Quebec City next year or the one after that, depending on our schedules and how the dollar is performing. I can't imagine why I've never been. It's like Europe without the airfare."

And while George went on enthusiastically about all they might do and see in Quebec—"we could visit the Parc Jeanne D'Arc"; "we could catch a play or a concert at the Grand Theatre"; "I doubt we could afford to stay at the Château Frontenac, but we could certainly pay it a visit"—Ruby had nodded politely and made vague sounds of interest, all the while wondering if George was really talking about a honeymoon. By imagining their future was he presuming that she would accept his proposal? Or was she being unfair in thinking that George respected her so little that he would suppose he knew her thoughts before she did? *Yes*, Ruby thought, now as she walked along the third-floor corridor. *I was probably being unfair, unfair and unkind.*

In the end Ruby had managed to avoid committing to the idea of Quebec, much as she had managed to avoid giving George an answer to his proposal. But there was a tricky thing about avoidance. Most often it couldn't go on forever. At some point you had to face the troubling situation or have the awkward conversation or give an important answer to an important question asked of you by the person you loved. And then you had to accept the consequences.

Ruby turned into Room 314, in which a seven-year-old boy named Terence was currently the sole occupant. He was sitting up in bed, surrounded by a few books, a plush dog, and a big metal dump truck.

"Hello, Terrence," Ruby said brightly as she went about checking his IV lines.

"Hi." The boy's voice was thin and Ruby thought she saw his lower lip quiver.

"How are you feeling today?" she asked.

"I'm afraid."

"Of what?" Ruby asked gently. "What are you afraid of?"

"Of something bad happening to me."

"Nothing bad is going to happen," Ruby said robustly. "The doctor who is going to perform your operation is a very, very good doctor and an even better surgeon. Plus," she added with a smile, "she's a super nice lady with two kids of her own. She'll fix you up right as rain and before you know it you'll be back home asking for all your favorite treats."

"I like mac 'n' cheese," the little boy said, eyes wide. "The kind my mom makes."

"Then she'll make you mac 'n' cheese," Ruby said. "I'm sure of it."

Terence's face grew brighter. "And I like chocolate chip cookies."

"I'm sure your mom will let you have all the cookies you need to help you get better."

Terence smiled, put the plush dog in the back of the dump truck, and began to push it around the bed. Ruby finished her chores on his behalf and left him feeling, she hoped, a bit more cheerful than she had found him. She hated falsehoods as a rule and, as everyone who knew her was aware, she was a terrible liar, but sometimes, when she thought it was important that someone in a difficult situation hear something he needed to hear, she could pull off a comforting deception. Like, Ruby thought, stepping aside to let an aide guiding a bed move past her, all those times she had lied to or kept things from her daughter in an effort to shield her from a full knowledge of her father's less than sterling character.

*And now,* Ruby thought as she continued on down the hall, *I'm deceiving Frieda again by keeping George's proposal a secret from her. But why? The knowledge can't hurt her, so is it because I'm afraid she's going to push me to accept?*

"Ruby. I'm glad I ran into you." It was one of the younger nurses on staff and, if not one of the best, definitely one of the most dedicated.

"Hello, Daria," Ruby said with a smile. "What can I do for you?"

"I just want to thank you for catching my mistake the other day," she said with a bit of a nervous laugh.

"But you already thanked me."

"I know, but . . . Well, you could have been all . . ." Daria blushed. "But you weren't. You were nice. You didn't humiliate me. You made me feel like I'm part of the team."

"You are part of the team," Ruby assured her. "A smart and enthusiastic member. And we all make mistakes, even old hands like me."

Daria laughed. "I doubt you ever make a mistake! But thanks again."

The young woman moved off and Ruby continued in the direction of the nurses' station. The thanks from Michael and Daria embarrassed her, not because she felt she didn't deserve the recognition—everyone deserved recognition for a job well done—but because it highlighted the marked contrast between her professional and personal character.

Ruby took a seat at one of the computers. *If my colleagues only knew what a coward and a weakling I really am,* she thought, *they might think twice before offering me their thanks and appreciation.*

# Chapter 45

*That's Dad,* Frieda thought. She didn't know how she knew who was at the other end of the line, but she did. "Hi, Dad," she said into the receiver.

"How did you know it was me?" Steve Hitchens asked with a bit of a laugh.

"I just did. What's up?"

"Is this an okay time to talk?"

"As good a time as any."

"You sound upset. Did something happen?"

"No," Frieda lied. Her father didn't need to know what she had done for Bella's sake. No one did. "Everything's fine. But Dad? I'd like some answers. What really prompted you to call me now, fifteen months after the accident? And please don't tell me again that the spirit moved you."

"All right," her father said after a moment. "I owe you the truth. I had a heart attack a few months back. Nothing too serious, but it shook me up. I guess I've started to realize the importance of making amends, because life's not going to go on forever. Yeah," he added quickly, "it's still all about me. I admit that. I'm reaching out to you now because I need something. But I'm also reaching out because I'm genuinely sorry for being a jerk. I'm not an evil guy,

Frieda. I'm just a highly inadequate guy and I'm genuinely sorry for that."

*The results are the same,* Frieda thought. But no. That was being unfair. He had said that he was sorry. "Have you told Mom?" she asked. "About the heart attack?"

"No," her father replied promptly. "I didn't want to worry her."

Frieda frowned. Did he really think her mother still cared enough about her ex-husband to worry about his health? What arrogance! But that was a knee-jerk reaction. Maybe she did still care enough about Steve Hitchens to be worried about his health. Either way, it wasn't for Frieda to assume.

"Do me a favor," her father went on, "and don't tell your mother I was sick."

"I'm not sure I can do that," Frieda told him. "I'm not really comfortable with keeping secrets from Mom." *Although,* she thought, *I do it often enough.*

Steve sighed. "Say what you need to say. Just don't let her get the idea I'm at death's door. I've put her through enough trouble already."

"All right," Frieda agreed.

"Hey, I was thinking about something the other day. Do you remember the time you and I went canoeing on Great Pond in Cape Elizabeth? You were eight, I think, or maybe nine."

Frieda suddenly did remember, if vaguely, but she could have sworn it had been Phil who had been with her. The past was so malleable; it simply couldn't be trusted to live on into the present in any reliable form. "Yes," she told her father. "Sort of."

"That storm came up out of nowhere. I was terrified we were going to capsize."

"Weren't we wearing life jackets?" Frieda asked. Would it be like her father, she wondered, to forget about something so important to his child's safety? She didn't know the answer to that.

"Of course," he told her, "but they're not foolproof. And while I was a wreck you were as calm as the proverbial cucumber."

"Really?"

"Really. Either you had faith in my ability to get us safely to shore or, more likely, you were too young to realize the possible dangers we faced."

"All children have faith in their parents," Frieda said automatically. *Until,* she added silently, *they don't.*

Her father laughed. "Be that as it may, I was very happy I managed to bring us back to your mother in one piece."

"Why didn't Mom go with us?" Frieda asked.

It was a moment before her father replied. "It was meant to be a father and daughter excursion," he said. "Just the two of us."

Frieda swallowed hard. *Just the two of us.* "I'd better go," she said. "I'm a bit behind on a project and—"

"Of course," Steve said promptly. "And Frieda? Thanks again for talking."

"Bye, Dad."

Frieda replaced the receiver. Something had suddenly become crystal clear. The second time she had spoken with her father this summer he had said he hoped she could acknowledge that he existed. The words and the meaning behind them had puzzled her until now. The truth was that her father had come close to death and had realized the sanctity of this wonderful but temporary life. He had realized that he had made some bad decisions, decisions that had hurt the two people he loved most. Decisions that might have hurt him as well, because it was rare that a wrongdoer wasn't as damaged by his actions as were his victims.

Frieda walked over to the sink and looked through the window at the yard beyond. Her mother's roses were in full bloom and for a brief moment Frieda imagined her father bending over them to inhale their sweet scent. Steve Hitchens had told her that his reaching out to her this summer was all about his own needs, but that wasn't the truth. It wasn't selfish of him to want to make peace, even if absolving himself of guilt was part of his motive. It was deeply human. And that, Frieda decided, was something she could respect.

# Chapter 46

"Look at the amazing detail on this silver pie server. I wonder how many people in this day and age appreciate workmanship like this."

"Mmm," Ruby said. She and Phil were browsing through their favorite antique mall on Route 1, but her mind was miles away.

"Out with it."

"Out with what?" Ruby asked, looking up at her friend.

"Something's up," Phil said, "and don't lie and say everything's fine. I can tell when you're lying. Heck, anyone can; you're a terrible liar. And don't say you're worried about Frieda and Bella, because I know you are, but this is something else. You didn't even notice the gorgeous milk glass vase back there, the one with the fluted edges."

Ruby managed a smile. "How well you know me, Phil. Okay, a few weeks back, before Frieda and Bella came to stay with me for the summer, George asked me to marry him. And I haven't yet given him an answer."

Phil's eyes widened. "This is huge," he said. "Why didn't you tell me before now?"

"Because I've been so . . . so conflicted."

"That's exactly when you should talk to an old friend," Phil pointed out, "someone who can bring some perspective to bear on a difficult situation. Friendship One-Oh-One."

"I know," Ruby admitted. "I do know."

"I'll tell you what this is about," Phil said. "You're being sexist. George is not Steve, Ruby. Don't paint every man with the same brush. You do my sex a disservice if you consider us all just a bunch of jerks out for what we can get for free."

"I'm not being sexist, Phil," Ruby protested. "That's not what's going on."

"Then what is going on?" Phil asked.

Ruby absentmindedly picked up a truly awful china statuette of a poodle with a pale-blue bow around its neck. "Fear," she said. "I'm afraid."

"Of what?" Phil demanded. "Of what the future will bring? Because a lot of other things might happen aside from George's leaving you. Like, he could stay with you and make you a very happy woman. It's no good being afraid of the future, Ruby. It's no way to live. Trust me on this one. I spent a good few months after Tony's passing convinced I was going to find out that I, too, was sick and dying. You remember how frozen with fear I was. You were there. It wasn't easy to let go of that fear and accept that what was going to happen—good or bad—was going to happen no matter how I felt about it."

"You're a stronger person than I am, Phil," Ruby said, returning the poodle to its place on the shelf. "You always were."

"That's nonsense, Ruby. Come on, let's get out of here. You haven't been able to pay proper attention to anything, not even that hilariously bad portrait of George Washington."

Obediently Ruby followed Phil out to the parking lot. Before she slid into the front passenger seat of his car, she looked at her friend over the roof and said, "Was it a mistake asking Frieda and Bella here for the summer?"

"I thought we were talking about you and George."

*We still are, in a way*, Ruby thought. "Just tell me what you think. I mean, things seemed to be going well for Frieda, at least as far as her friendship with Jack was concerned, but I'm pretty sure they haven't seen each other in days. I know something must have happened between them, but Frieda won't say anything. I suspect it had to do with Bella. I know Bella's not happy about her mother's friendship with Jack and, honestly, I can understand why. But I don't want my daughter to miss out on a chance of happiness. Not after all she's been through."

"Of course you don't." Phil smiled. "Just step back a bit, Ruby. Give Frieda some space. She's a big girl. She'll figure it all out. As you'll figure out your own romantic life."

"Promise?" Ruby asked, remembering the look of relief that had come over her young patient's face when she had promised him a bright future she had no right to promise.

Phil sighed. "Though I have absolutely no authority over you or the future, and therefore my promise means nothing, I promise. And Ruby?"

"Yes?"

"Don't keep George waiting for much longer."

Ruby managed a smile. "I won't," she said. "By the way, how much did that milk glass vase cost?"

# Chapter 47

The idea of cleaning every facet of every individual piece of crystal on the massive chandelier Phil had recently brought to the shop ordinarily would have sent Bella into deep shock. But this morning she had readily accepted the assignment and in wiping each pear-, marquise- and kite-shaped crystal drop with a clean, damp cloth Bella was finding a strange sense of peace. She realized the sense of peace probably wouldn't last much longer, but she was grateful for what she could get.

"How's Jack doing?" Phil asked.

*And there goes the peace*, Bella thought, noting Phil's suspiciously casual tone. "I don't know," she said. It wasn't a lie. She didn't know.

"I thought he and your mother were friends."

"No," she said, staring hard at a crystal drop. "They're not friends."

"Oh," Phil replied. "That's too bad. I thought they were getting along pretty well. Such nice people, your mother and Jack Tennant. Both have been through so much."

Phil walked toward the office at the back of the shop and Bella stood there, damp cloth in hand, feeling more than slightly guilty, which was probably what Phil had intended. The fact was that her mother had looked kind of sad in the past few days, something anyone who knew her well would have noticed. Bella suspected she knew why; she suspected that her mother had ended things with Jack.

Bella had thought it would make her happy, but it hadn't. And Phil must know what had happened; why else would he have mentioned Jack? And if Phil knew then her grandmother knew, too. *Everyone must think I'm a total creep,* Bella thought. If it had been the other way around, if she had been the one to die and Ariel the one to live, would Ariel have stopped their mother from doing something that made her happy? *No,* Bella thought. *Ariel was just a better person than I am, plain and simple.*

"How is that chandelier coming along?" Phil called from the back of the shop.

Bella startled at the sound of his voice. "Okay," she called. "It's coming along okay." And she got back to wiping dust off crystal drops.

At four forty-five Clara showed up at Wainscoting and Window-seats. But this was the first time she actually came inside rather than waiting for Bella on the sidewalk.

"Phil," Bella said, leading Clara forward, "this is my friend Clara. Clara, this is Phil."

Phil inclined his head politely. "Hello, Clara. It's nice to meet you."

Clara murmured what might have been something like "hi" and Bella wondered why she had bothered to come into the shop if she was going to be all shy about saying hello.

"Is it okay if I go now, Phil?" she asked. "I know it's only ten minutes to five, but there haven't been any customers in almost an hour."

"Which doesn't mean there won't be any in the next ten minutes," Phil pointed out, "but sure, go ahead. You did an excellent job cleaning that crystal chandelier. Frankly, I was dreading the task."

Bella grinned. "Thanks, Phil. See you tomorrow."

The girls left the shop and Bella unlocked her bike from the old-fashioned hitching post.

"He seems a lot nicer than my boss," Clara said as they began to walk away from Wainscoting and Windowseats, Bella pushing her bike along.

"Phil's a lot nicer than most people," Bella told her. "Sometimes I don't know how he does it. You should see some of the customers we get. If they're not whining about not being able to find exactly the fabric they want they're demanding he meet with their interior designer and 'set him straight,' whatever that means. And yet Phil never loses his temper."

"Let's go back to my house," Clara suggested suddenly.

Bella, wondering if Clara had heard anything she had just said, hesitated. She wasn't in the mood to smoke pot and she assumed that was what Clara would want to do. Smoking pot was, well, it was actually kind of boring. It wasn't like actually doing something, like playing soccer or reading a book.

"It's such a nice afternoon," she said. "Why don't we walk over to that little park in the center of town instead? There's a guy who sells Italian ices from one of those old-fashioned pushcarts. Phil said the coconut is awesome."

Clara stuck her hands in the back pockets of her jeans. "I'm not in the mood for Italian ice. Look, my car is in the lot behind that gift shop, Buttons and Bows. We can stick your bike in the trunk."

Bella considered. There was no reason she couldn't say no if Clara offered her a hit of a joint. No reason whatsoever. But she had a feeling she wouldn't be able to say no to Clara. There was something about Clara that made it hard for Bella to resist her suggestions. She wished she knew what it was.

"All right," she said reluctantly. "We'll go back to your place."

Clara beamed. "Great. You're the best, Bella."

*No,* Bella thought, following Clara to her car. *I'm not the best. I think I'm responsible for my mother doing something that's making her miserable. And I think the people I love the best know about it.*

# Chapter 48

"I've got some big news, Ruby, so hold on to your hat."

Ruby and George were in her kitchen; while Ruby prepared a bunch of green beans for cooking, George leaned against the sink, watching the process.

"If I was wearing a hat I'd be gripping it," Ruby said. "What's going on?" Had he gotten that raise he was hoping for and deserved? Scored tickets to a concert by his favorite chamber music quartet? George loved chamber music.

"You know that guy in Accounting, the one I play golf with occasionally?"

Ruby smiled. "Of course. Ted, the guy who's been wearing the same old tweed jacket for the past ten years."

"That's the one. Well, seems a friend offered Ted his family's cottage on Monhegan Island for next Thursday and Friday nights. Ted already has plans, so he offered the cottage to us. After checking with the owner, of course. Isn't that fantastic? We can head out early Thursday morning, catch the ten thirty boat from Port Clyde or even the seven o'clock boat if we get up before dawn, and be on the island before noon. Or earlier if we take the first boat, but maybe that's being unrealistic. It will take about two and a half hours to get to Port Clyde from here. Anyway, we don't have to head back to the mainland until Saturday afternoon. There's a boat at twelve thirty and one at four thirty. Round-trip tickets are only thirty-five dollars and I can book them ahead online. I'm sure you can get someone to cover your shifts, Ruby. You've come to people's rescue often enough. Well, what do you think?"

All the while George had been talking, his excitement patently obvious, Ruby's stomach had been sinking. If only George hadn't proposed, she thought, they could go away for a quiet romantic holiday without her fearing she would be pressed to give him an answer.

"Ruby?" George asked. "You in there?"

"It was very generous of Ted to offer us the cottage," she said carefully. "But I'm not sure it's a good thing that I leave Frieda and Bella just now." The moment the words were out of her mouth Ruby knew how absolutely lame they sounded.

"It's only for two nights, Ruby," George said reasonably. "We could leave the island early Saturday if you wanted."

Ruby put down the small knife she had been using to top and tail the beans. "Still," she said, "Frieda seems troubled and Bella . . ."

George sighed. He went over to the table and took a seat. "Ruby," he said, "have you given any further thought to our future? It didn't escape me that when I was talking about a vacation in Quebec next year you were pretty much checked out."

Ruby lowered her eyes to the cutting board. "How can I think about making a decision to marry or even to travel," she said, "when I've got to focus on my family?"

George was silent for a moment before going on. "Speaking of family," he said, "have you told Frieda I asked you to marry me?"

"No." Ruby shook her head. "She has so much on her mind."

"Come and sit down, Ruby," George said quietly. "Sit close to me."

Ruby hesitated for a moment and then went over to the table and sat in the chair next to George's. He reached for her hand.

"I feel like you've put our relationship on the back burner this summer," he said. "I'm not saying I need all of your attention, but I don't like feeling as if I'm being ignored."

"I'm not ignoring you!" Ruby said, aware she was speaking a bit too loudly. *The lady doth protest too much, methinks.* "You come over for dinner with us. We have lunch together at the hospital when we can. I know spending the night together has become a bit tricky this summer, but we talked about that before Frieda and Bella came to stay with me."

George squeezed her hand. "I'm not complaining about a lack of sex, Ruby. What kind of guy do you think I am? Although I'd be lying if I said I wasn't looking forward to our spending two nights alone on Monhegan. And sharing meals is all well and good, but when was the last time we really talked, just you and me, and not about what's going on with Frieda or Bella? When was the last time we watched a movie together or read aloud from our favorite funny bits of Dickens? When was the last time we went for an early-morning walk on the beach?"

Ruby couldn't answer those questions. It had been too long; that much she knew.

"It's just that I feel frustrated by the distance that seems to have opened up between us," George went on, his voice soft but urgent. "It's not a huge distance, but people can drift apart so terribly easily. If you want to know the truth, Ruby, I'm a bit scared right now. I'm scared of losing you and not really understanding why or how it happened."

Ruby returned the warm pressure of George's hand. "I'm sorry, George," she said. "I really am. Please, just give me more time."

"I'll never be the one to walk away from us, Ruby, so I guess I have no choice. Take all the time you need, but please don't ignore the question." George released her hand and got up from his chair. "Are you absolutely sure about getting away together? Because I'll need to tell Ted one way or the other."

Ruby swallowed. "I'm sure," she said. "Please give him my gratitude."

"I've got to get back to the hospital. Good-bye, Ruby."

And then he was gone from the kitchen, leaving Ruby alone and feeling as much like a craven coward as she had ever felt.

"Hi."

Ruby startled. "I didn't hear you come in," she said to her daughter.

"I just saw George on his way out. Are things okay between you guys, Mom? He seemed, I don't know, tense or something."

"It's nothing," she said. "We had a spat. It was my fault. Sometimes I can be a pill."

"Hmm. Well," Frieda said, going to the fridge, "I can't force you to tell me what's up. But if you do want to talk, I'm here."

*I'm keeping a secret,* Ruby thought, watching her daughter pour a glass of iced tea. *Frieda is keeping a secret. For all I know Bella is keeping a secret, too.* Ruby got up and went back to the cutting board. The problem with keeping secrets as well as with avoiding important issues, she thought as she picked up the knife, was that it was very hard work. And it made you feel lousy.

# Chapter 49

Ruby opened the front door the following day to find Phil holding out a white cardboard box.

"I saw these strawberry muffins at the bakery," he said, "and I thought of you. I know how you love muffins."

Ruby smiled and beckoned him inside. "The way to a woman's heart is through her stomach. Thank you, Phil. Can I send one home with you?"

"I bought a few for myself, too. No, these are for my three favorite gals."

"Thank you, again. Have a cup of coffee?" Ruby offered.

"Sure. I don't think I've said no to a cup of coffee more than two or three times in my life."

Ruby led them to the kitchen, where she put the box of muffins on the counter and switched on the coffee maker, already primed to brew a fresh pot. Phil took a seat at the table, and as he did Ruby noted a look of concern on his face.

"What's up?" she asked. "Thinking deep thoughts?"

"Deep, no," Phil said. "Serious, maybe."

"Spill," Ruby commanded.

"Well," Phil began, "I've been thinking about Bella and that girl she's been spending so much time with, the one who works at The Flipper."

Ruby frowned. "And?"

"Well," Phil went on, "some of Bella's natural enthusiasm has returned, which is a good thing, and it might be because she feels that in Clara she has someone she can talk to, but . . ." Phil shrugged. "I have a strange feeling about the girl, but it's based on nothing more than meeting her for about a minute when she came by the store the other day. Bella introduced us and Clara was virtually tongue-tied. It can't be me. I'm not intimidating."

"Have you heard anything around town?" Ruby asked, bringing two hot coffees to the table and remembering that only the day before she had been wondering what secrets Bella might be keeping from her family. "Any rumors about Clara coming out of The Flipper?"

"Not a word. That doesn't mean nothing's being said, just that I'm not aware of it. The people who frequent the nightclubs around here aren't really my crowd. They're all no older than thirty."

Ruby sat next to her friend. "Maybe I should ask George if he's heard anything. Or one of the members of my reading group might be of help. Cassie's always got her ear to the ground."

"I wouldn't launch a formal investigation, Ruby," Phil said, "not based on my random hunch."

"Phil, your so-called random hunches are always right on the money."

Phil smiled. "I do what I can. Seriously though, Ruby, don't worry. We're all keeping an eye on Bella. Nothing bad will happen."

"From your mouth to God's ears. You know, I've told Bella she can bring Clara around anytime, but she said Clara is shy—which might be why she was tongue-tied meeting you. I don't know how she handles being a waitress at one of the most popular joints in town if she's shy. But why would Bella lie?"

"She'd lie if there was something about Clara she didn't want you to find out," Phil said. "Or Bella might just want to keep Clara all to herself. Maybe she's got a girl crush, though personally I can't see Clara's appeal. She has no real affect. Is that a terrible thing to say?"

"Not if it's true." Ruby shook her head. "Bella was never drawn to retiring or self-effacing people before. The friends of hers I've met over the years have all been the life of the party, especially that girl Kerri. Total sunshine. But things are different now, aren't they?

Bella is different. None of us are who we were before the accident. I'm still reminding myself that this family is a new family and we're living in a new world now, one where we don't yet know all the rules. I'm not even sure we know the language in which the rules are written!"

"I will say that Bella looks much better than she did when she first arrived."

"I think so, too," Ruby agreed. "At least her appetite seems to have returned. She finishes her dinner and I'm sure she'll devour one of those strawberry muffins the moment she gets home."

Phil raised an eyebrow. "That Clara whatever her name is could use some fattening up."

"Phil, be nice," Ruby scolded. "Maybe she's just naturally thin."

"Maybe," Phil admitted. "But she looks unhealthy to me, you know that sort of attenuated look people who are on extreme diets get. They don't look fit; they look—strained. The veins on her arms stick out. The skin around her eyes looks papery and thin, at least, in my opinion."

"Hmm. She could be ill. I wonder if she's seeing a doctor."

"I have no idea and even if she isn't under a doctor's care and should be there's nothing either of us can do about it. Not only is she eighteen—according to Bella—but we barely know her."

"Still, I wonder if I should ask Bella if her friend is okay."

Phil raised an eloquent eyebrow. "Why do I think you wouldn't get a straight or a true answer to that question?"

"You're probably right," Ruby admitted. "Well, I'll try to keep a closer eye on Bella from now on."

"So," Phil asked, "have you given George an answer to his question?"

Ruby's conscience squirmed. She couldn't admit to Phil that she had turned down a romantic vacation with George. He would call her on the lame excuse she had given and she didn't think she could bear the shame. "Not yet," she said. "But I will. Soon."

"Swear it, Ruby," Phil said, reaching for her hand.

"I swear," she said, giving it to him. "Really."

# Chapter 50

The girls were in Clara's small bedroom at the back of the cottage on Valley Road. Clara was half lying on the bed, her shoulders against the wall. She hadn't suggested they smoke pot and for that Bella was grateful. The smoke hurt her throat too much and the last time—the day Clara had come into the shop and met Phil—she had felt a little bit nauseous after two hits. Not much was worth the risk of throwing up. Correction. Nothing was worth the risk of throwing up.

Bella waved a hand in front of her face. "Can I open a window?" she asked. "It's so stuffy in here."

"They're jammed."

"Don't you even have a fan?"

"No," Clara said. "One of my housemates has one. But she's at work and her door is locked."

Bella frowned. She wondered if the girl had locked her door because Clara was in the habit of "borrowing" her stuff, like she had borrowed her housemate Julie's Diet Pepsi. "You should tell your landlord about the windows," she said. "What if there was a fire in the hall? You'd need a way to get out."

Although, Bella thought, the windows were so small only the skinniest person could squeeze her way through. Even Clara, who had clearly lost weight in the last weeks, wasn't that thin. Bella wondered if this bedroom was legal; she remembered her father talking about rooms needing to meet certain safety requirements if they were to be used as bedrooms. But Clara's landlord wasn't her problem.

"Let's at least go outside," Bella said. "I'm suffocating."

"What?" Clara looked at Bella directly for the first time since Bella had entered the room. Her eyes looked a little unfocused.

"What's wrong?" Bella asked. "You seem kind of out of it."

"I took a pill," Clara said.

"Oh." Bella nodded. "When my sinuses act up I have to take a Benadryl. I hate how loopy it makes me feel."

Clara smiled. "It wasn't a Benadryl."

"Then what was it?" Bella asked. "Are you sick?"

"Not at the moment!" Clara laughed.

"What's going on, Clara?" Bella demanded.

"What's going on is that I feel pretty good right now. You know, if you want I could probably . . ."

Bella's heart began to beat loudly and she felt her stomach knot. "You took something way stronger than a Benadryl, didn't you?" she said. "I mean, something illegal."

Clara shook her finger at Bella. "Now, now, prescription painkillers aren't illegal, Bella."

"Are you saying a doctor prescribed something for you?" Bella asked. "Why? Did you have an accident at work or something?" It was possible, she thought. You could pull a muscle carrying heavy trays of food and drinks. You could trip over someone's foot and fall. You could cut yourself on a kitchen knife.

Clara laughed again. "I didn't have an accident or go to a doctor. I got it from this guy who hangs out at The Flipper."

"What guy? Who is he? Is he a local?"

"Jeez, you sound like my parents! Anyway, I don't really know anything about him."

"Wait, let me get this straight. You don't know anything about this guy and you bought drugs from him?"

Clara shrugged and her shoulders slipped a little down the wall. "I know the name he goes by. Hades. Anyway, he's cool. Everyone thinks so."

"Hades? Really?" Bella shook her head in disbelief. "You bought drugs from a guy whose nickname is basically Hell? What did it cost? How much did he make you pay?"

"He didn't make me pay," Clara argued. "He told me what it cost and I paid him."

"How much?"

Clara shrugged. "Fifty dollars."

Bella's eyes widened. "For one pill?"

"He said it was a fair price. Something about market competition, I don't know."

"I can't believe I'm hearing this." Bella put her hands to her head. "Clara, what that guy is doing is illegal. He's a criminal. He could be violent! You could get into serious trouble with the law—if this idiot doesn't hurt you first!"

"You won't tell anyone, will you?" Clara asked. "It's just that I've been so unhappy. This is the only thing that makes me feel okay. And I deserve to feel okay after what Marc did to me."

Bella took a deep breath. "What happens when the effects wear off?" she said. "You'll want another pill and then another. That's how it works, Clara. We learned about it in school. One pill leads to another. It's called addiction. And the longer it goes on the harder it is to stop."

"Why are you being such a pain about this?" Clara cried. "You smoke pot. You're not anti-drugs. You're being a total hypocrite."

"I—" Bella couldn't argue with Clara on that point, but she could argue with herself. *I am against drugs*, she thought. *I always have been. I wouldn't even take an antidepressant when Colleen advised it. I was too scared of no longer feeling like me. Then what was I doing smoking dope?*

"All right," she said finally. "I won't tell you to stop and I won't tell anyone. Just . . . Just be careful, Clara. I mean it."

"Yeah." Clara yawned hugely. "Oh . . . my . . . God," she said, rubbing at her eyes, "I'm so tired!"

"I'm going now," Bella said suddenly. "You're not going to drive or anything, are you?"

Clara huffed. "I'm not stupid!"

Bella didn't know about that. "Bye," she said, turning to the door. She couldn't get out of that stifling room soon enough.

# Chapter 51

Bella rode straight home, barely noticing the profusion of colorful wild flowers along the roadside basking in the summer sun. The house was empty and she went immediately to her bedroom, closing the door behind her. She lay on her bed and stared at the ceiling.

Pills. It had never occurred to Bella that Clara would get involved with anything stronger or potentially more dangerous than pot. And if smoking pot wasn't all that dangerous in the scheme of things it also wasn't glamorous or exciting. In fact, it was kind of pathetic. *At least,* she thought, *I didn't bring anything illegal into Grandma's house.* That would have been seriously wrong and seriously disrespectful.

Bella sighed. But why had she smoked in the first place? A thought occurred to her. Could her decision to indulge in self-destructive behavior have anything to do with Survivor Guilt? Colleen had explained that Survivor Guilt was a defense against pain; by overwhelming yourself with shame, you could avoid having to deal with the more complicated emotion of grief. Grief was hard work, but you could wallow in shame like a pig in a puddle of mud. You could sink into shame and not have to do anything but feel bad, and that required very little effort. After a while feeling bad became normal and it was that much more difficult to choose to crawl out of the mud and to shake off the shame that had comforted you in such a bizarre and perverse way.

*Too bad I stopped seeing Colleen,* Bella thought. *I wish I could call her now.* Slowly she got up from her bed and opened Ariel's dresser drawer. She took her sister's diary gently in her hand. She remembered the time she had been tempted to open the diary in the hopes of finding words of consolation. "I'm sorry, Ariel," she whispered to the room. "I'm sorry for taking such a risk with my life when you taught me just how wonderful it is to be alive."

Bella heard the front door open, followed by the slightly uneven footsteps that indicated it was her grandmother who had come home. She slipped the diary back under the T-shirts and ran downstairs, where she found her grandmother in the kitchen unpacking a bag of groceries.

"I'll help you put stuff away," she said.

Her grandmother smiled. "Thanks, Bella. How's your day off coming along?" she asked.

"Okay." Bella opened the fridge and put a head of lettuce in the crisper. "I was out riding around for a while." It wasn't a lie; it just wasn't the whole truth.

Ruby handed her a bunch of carrots. "Better you than me. It's pretty sticky out there. Oh, I meant to tell you earlier, but I missed you. Ariel came to me again last night."

"She did?" Bella asked, placing a bunch of bananas in a bowl on the counter. "What did she say?"

"What she usually says. That she's happy and safe and that your father is, too."

"I wonder why Dad doesn't come to one of us," Bella said. "You or me or Mom."

Ruby shrugged. "I don't know. I don't think anyone can know how or why this sort of thing happens. Maybe we're not meant to know."

Bella continued to stow boxes of cereal in the cupboard over the microwave and a plastic container of dishwasher liquid in the cupboard under the sink, and all the while her mind was busy. She had told Clara once that she didn't believe in God. But she believed that her grandmother talked to Ariel. Didn't that mean that God was real? Could an afterlife exist without God? And if you believed something you didn't have to prove it, right? Belief was supposed to be enough to make something real. Bella almost laughed. It was all too complicated for her poor brain. Ariel had been the intellectual of the family. What would Ariel think of her decidedly *not* intellectual sister struggling to figure out stuff way beyond most people's ability to comprehend? *Wait,* Bella thought. *If Ariel is still around, coming to Grandma, maybe she does know what I'm going through, trying to figure out these big and important things. And maybe if I believe hard enough she'll be able to help me.*

"Grandma?" Bella said suddenly. "I was thinking. Maybe we could try to make ice cream again."

Ruby smiled. "I think that's a great idea. Blueberry? Or are you sick of blueberries? We've been eating an awful lot of them this summer."

"No, blueberry is cool. Mom says they're good for you. Antioxidants or something."

"I think I know where we might have gone wrong the first time."

Bella laughed. "You think? You mistook the salt for sugar."

"Hey," her grandmother said with a shrug. "It happens."

# Chapter 52

"Out, damned weed!" Ruby yanked a dandelion from the soil and tossed it onto a pile of its mates.

Frieda laughed. "Feeling particularly like Lady Macbeth today, Mom?"

Ruby thought about that for a moment. "I guess not," she admitted. "It just felt like the right thing to say."

It was a beautiful day, sunny and hot but not humid, and Ruby, digging in the dirt of her garden, felt a sense of relative peace and optimism—at least regarding her granddaughter. Bella had gone off to work that morning with a fairly cheery good-bye. These days she was less likely to complain about morning hours or even the occasional overtime at the shop, and that had to be a good sign, an indication of a returning interest in the world around her.

"I'm glad George does most of the heavy lifting for you," Frieda said, on her knees about a yard from Ruby, spade in hand. "You don't want to be putting unnecessary strain on that leg."

Ruby was glad, too. Sort of. Considering the situation she had put George in this summer, she felt more than slightly guilty accepting his significant amount of help with the garden and, for that matter, with the house. She felt more than slightly guilty about the state of her judgment, too. For one brief moment she had considered suggesting to George that he go to Monhegan on his own or with a colleague—why should he miss out on a few days away from the hospital? Ruby shuddered now at the memory. Talk about insulting; she was shocked she could even think about being so careless of George's feelings.

What had Phil said to her recently? That the time to turn to a friend was when you were feeling conflicted about an important issue. Well, Ruby thought, glancing to where her daughter was working, if Frieda didn't count as a friend, who did?

Ruby got off her knees and eased herself to a relatively comfortable sitting position on the freshly mowed grass. "Frieda?" she said. "The other day you asked me if something was wrong between George and me and I said we'd had a spat. I was lying, as you know. The situation is more . . . It's more delicate."

"What is it, Mom?" Frieda asked, sticking her spade into the ground and wiping her hands on her shorts.

"Before you and Bella came to stay for the summer, George asked me to marry him."

"Mom," Frieda cried, "that's wonderful news! Why didn't you tell me before? You accepted his proposal of course."

Ruby plucked a blade of grass and began to roll it between her fingers. "The thing is I haven't accepted. Not yet."

"Why not?" Frieda asked. "You can't think I'd be upset by your getting married again, and especially to someone as wonderful as George. What am I missing?"

Ruby pushed her hair behind her ear. "What you're missing," she said, "is the fact that I'm scared stiff."

"Of what?" Frieda asked. "George is a great guy. You love him. We all do."

"I know. I do know. But I'm also insanely scared of having my heart broken again. More specifically, I'm afraid of a *husband* breaking my heart again." Ruby smiled ruefully. "Phil told me I'm being sexist by assuming that all men are rats and that George will inevitably do what Steve did and leave me high and dry."

"Phil has a point, Mom," Frieda said.

"I know. And the very fact that I'm in a relationship with George should prove that I've got the courage to risk having my heart stomped on. It's just . . . It's just that the idea of having a second marriage end in disaster, well, I'm not sure I have it in me to go through another divorce."

"Oh, Mom. You poor thing." With the ease of relative youth, Frieda got up from her knees and came to sit close enough to Ruby to give her a one-armed hug.

"I'd be grateful if you kept this to yourself," Ruby said. "Besides you only Phil knows."

"Sure. And as long as we're being honest . . . I told Jack I couldn't spend time with him anymore."

"I figured something had happened between you two," Ruby admitted. "It was because of Bella, wasn't it?"

"She threatened that if I didn't stop seeing Jack she would do something horrible, something that I would regret. I was scared. And I also felt that by spending time with Jack I was betraying Aaron. So it wasn't entirely because of Bella that I ended our friendship before it really even began."

Ruby took her daughter's hand. "I'm sorry, Frieda. I really am."

"The worst part is I can't tell if my cutting Jack off has resulted in anything beneficial for Bella. It certainly hasn't for me."

"Did you tell Bella what you did for her sake?" Ruby asked. "Did you tell her what you sacrificed?"

Frieda shook her head. "No. I'm afraid of sounding like a martyr. I don't want to make her feel guilty. But I'm sure she knows what happened, just like you did. Very little gets past teenaged girls. They have a sixth sense when it comes to emotional matters."

"Do you want my opinion?" Ruby asked.

Frieda winced. "I'm not sure that I do, but go ahead."

"I know I have no right to preach," Ruby said, "not when I'm behaving like such a coward. But I believe it's wrong to allow someone to get away with an ultimatum. Bella acted like a spoiled child demanding you behave a certain way. I understand that she probably feels scared of losing you. And I understand your fearing she might go through with her threat, however vague. But coddling her hasn't gotten her anywhere. My advice would be to remind her that you love her, assure her you're not going to abandon her, and continue to live your life."

Frieda laughed. "Easier said than done, Mom."

"Don't I know it?" Ruby sighed. "You love her so much, as I love you so much. All we ever want for our children is for them to be happy. But sometimes in trying to ensure their happiness we do us and them a disservice."

"Look at us, two frightened souls sitting in the grass bemoaning our lack of backbone!"

"That may be," Ruby said, climbing once again to her knees, "but this bed won't get weeded by itself, so let's take our minds off our troubles and get back to work."

"That's Ruby Hitchens for you," Frieda said, moving with far more grace than Ruby had managed. "Never a slacker!"

*Except,* Ruby thought ruefully, *when it comes to accepting a proposal of marriage.*

# Chapter 53

Frieda smoothed the top sheet on her bed and then laid the cotton coverlet over it. She was one of those people who felt that an unmade bed led inevitably to chaos in the larger world. Ariel had been the same. As for Aaron and Bella . . . Frieda considered checking her daughter's room to assess its current state and then decided against it. If Bella didn't mind occasional messiness . . .

The house was empty but for Frieda. Bella was out on her bike and Ruby had gone to see Phil. Frieda so hoped that Phil could persuade her mother to accept George's proposal. Only weeks ago she had remarked on how sure of herself her mother always seemed; now she had proof that even Ruby Hitchens was vulnerable to fear and doubt. For a brief moment Frieda had even considered speaking to George about the situation, but just as quickly as the idea had come it fled. It wasn't Frieda's place to take on the role of go-between. In matters of the heart it was better to let the lovers communicate directly. Lovers might need guidance at times, but they never needed interference.

Frieda looked around her bedroom and realized she felt at a bit of a loss as to what to do next. Sure, there were other household chores she could tackle or work she could finish, but she just didn't feel like doing either. A thunderstorm was brewing; maybe it was the change in the atmospheric pressure that was making her feel distracted and indecisive.

And then it occurred to her. In the smallest bedroom her mother kept the photos of the eleven years the Hitchens family had lived under one roof, sharing meals, celebrating the holidays, falling asleep together in front of the television, making pancakes on Saturday mornings. Frieda hadn't looked at the photos since her sophomore year in college when she had showed them to Aaron.

Now seemed as good a time as any to revisit the past. After all, there wasn't much point in trying to avoid it, not when the past in the form of her father had sought her out this summer. Frieda walked down the hall to the spare bedroom, selected an album from the small bookcase, and brought it over to the couch. She opened the album to find that the photos inside had been taken before she was born. Ruby and Steve holding hands at the beach; Steve with his arm around Ruby's shoulders in a restaurant; Ruby and Steve dressed to the nines on their wedding day. Frieda felt a great tenderness for the couple in those photos. How young her parents had once been, how young and, if pictures didn't lie, how in love.

Frieda continued to page through the album until she came across a photograph of Ruby in a hospital bed, cradling her newborn child; Steve was perched next to her, gazing down at his infant daughter. The look of love and awe on the faces of her parents was unmistakable. Frieda wasn't sure she had ever recognized that look as clearly as she did now.

Yes, Frieda thought as she closed the album. Her early childhood had been a happy one, which was probably why when it ended the day her father left Yorktide she had felt so entirely devastated. Even though Frieda had sensed that her father was unhappy, the thought of his walking away from her and her mother had never, ever crossed her mind.

A crash of thunder made Frieda jump. She looked to the window to see that the sky was an ominous steely gray. A moment later sheets of rain came lashing toward the earth. Frieda had always been fascinated by how a rainstorm could break so suddenly—*Rainstorm*.

Frieda got off the couch and selected another album from the bookcase; a quick flip through showed that the photos it contained dated from later years. She took out another album and about halfway through it she found what she had been hoping to find. Under the first of three photos on the page was a line in her mother's distinctive handwriting, confirming that the pictures had been taken at Great Pond in Cape Elizabeth the summer Frieda was eight. The first photo showed Frieda and her father before they started out onto the water. They had indeed been wearing life vests over their shorts and T-shirts. They were holding hands. Frieda realized that she must have taken the second photo, as it showed her father seated at the back of the canoe, his paddle in the water. He was smiling. The third picture clearly had been taken after the rainstorm had subsided and they had reached dry land. Frieda stood onshore holding her paddle, the expanse of Great Pond behind her. She was grinning in spite of the fact that she was decidedly soaked.

Frieda looked back to the first photo. She believed that her father had been happy to be with her at Great Pond that long-ago summer day. She believed that her father had wanted to be with her. That counted for something. Bad times that followed upon good times simply should not be allowed to taint those earlier happy experiences.

Carefully Frieda closed the album and returned it to the bookcase. She would return at another time to look more closely and to remember more carefully. At the moment her heart felt as full as it could feel without breaking.

# Chapter 54

The promised thunderstorm broke out only minutes after Ruby arrived at Phil's house. She was now comfortably seated in the kitchen's breakfast nook. Phil had switched on every light in the room; spectacular displays of forked lightning across a spooky gray sky were not enough to dispel the gloom that had settled over Yorktide that afternoon.

"I do love a thunderstorm," Ruby said. "Funny, I hate human drama, but I love when Nature plays the diva."

"Within reason, of course," Phil said, setting down a plate of small brioche buns and a pot of tea. "Let's not forget earthquakes and tsunamis. They're not exactly fun."

"Of course," Ruby said as Phil took a seat across the table from her. "Speaking of human drama, I finally told Frieda about George's proposal. And she told me that she did indeed break things off with Jack at Bella's request. Wait, 'request' isn't quite right. Bella threatened to do something awful and unspecified if Frieda didn't comply."

Phil frowned. "They'd barely gotten to know each other. It's a shame they weren't left alone to grow close. Have a bun. They're decadent."

"It is a shame," Ruby said, putting a brioche on her plate. "I told Frieda she was wrong to let Bella dictate her choices. I'm surprised she didn't walk away. Telling a parent she's doing something wrong in relation to her child is risky business, but I just couldn't keep my mouth shut."

"I suspect she didn't walk away because she knows you're right. I hope she'll be able to gather up the courage to follow her heart."

"And speaking of matters of the heart, I ran into one of Steve's old flames this morning in the post office." Ruby grinned. "Emily Bainbridge. It's been over thirty years since her affair with my ex-husband and she still can barely meet my eye."

"At least she has enough class to feel embarrassed by her past sins."

"And she's certainly paid the price for them!" Ruby shook her head. "That husband of hers filed for divorce the second he found out she'd cheated on him. Well, he was no prize, but since then nothing much has gone her way. Remember what happened with her second husband? Died leaving her with massive debts. And her son from her first marriage landed in prison for grand theft auto. It's too bad, really. She's a nice person."

Phil poured more tea into Ruby's cup. "How you can be so generous with the people who hurt you I'll never know."

"Emily wasn't the one who hurt me," Ruby argued. "Steve was the one who hurt us both. Besides, look who's talking! I've never heard you say one bad word against Tony's parents or any of the people who cut you two off when you needed them most. We're both old softies when it comes to forgiveness."

"Guilty as charged, I suppose. So, what are you going to do about George?" Phil asked. "He deserves an answer, and sooner rather than later. And yes, I know I'm hounding you, but old friends are allowed to hound."

Ruby sighed. "Phil, why can't things just stay the same? Well, good things at least. I know that's a stupid question that has no possible answer, but sometimes lately I feel stupid. I feel as if I've forgotten all of the life lessons I'd learned over the years, at least the most important ones."

"Don't be silly, Ruby," Phil chided. "You've forgotten nothing."

Ruby shrugged. "Maybe I'm just tired." She took another bite of the brioche and felt her animal spirits lift. "These buns really are delicious. Did you make them?"

"No," Phil said. "I picked them up at a little bakery on my way back from Kittery this morning. Do you remember Tony's brioche?"

"I certainly do. I loved when he used it to make French toast. Those brunches you two gave in your little house at the end of Patrick's Lane were legendary. The best mimosas ever. And Tony's Eggs Florentine! I've never been able to order Eggs Florentine at a restaurant after being spoiled by Tony's."

"The good old days, eh?"

*Tony and Phil. Steve and me.* "Yes," Ruby said. "But these days aren't so bad, are they?"

Phil reached across the table and took Ruby's hand. "No," he said. "These days are just fine."

*And it's important,* Ruby thought, *to remember that.*

# Chapter 55

It was a long shot but a shot worth taking. Seated at the kitchen table, Frieda opened her laptop, selected a search engine, and typed in her father's full name—*Steven Jacob Hitchens*. After his name she typed the words furniture maker.

Nothing. She amended her father's name—*Steve Hitchens*—tried the word *craftsman* and waited. Nothing. Twice again Frieda attempted to discover some mention of her father as artist but to no avail. *Well*, she thought, *I knew I'd probably come up empty-handed*. It was just that while flipping through the second album in search of pictures taken on Great Pond Frieda had come across a photo of her father standing proudly next to one of the beautiful pieces of furniture he had designed and built; under the photo her mother had written: *Bespoke desk in oak for the office of Arthur Jameson, Esq.*

Frieda had always known that people—not only her mother and Phil—considered Steve Hitchens gifted. But for a very long time she had succeeded in blocking out the fact of her father's talents, favoring instead only negative thoughts and impressions about the man who had virtually abandoned her on the cusp of adolescence.

But now . . . Frieda shook her head and remembered the photo of her and her father holding hands on the shore of Great Pond.

She highly doubted it was possible to treasure memories of earlier good times without first forgiving the sins of later, trying times. And as understandable as a negation or a "forgetting" of happy memories might be, it didn't feel right. Not now. Not since Steve Hitchens was becoming an individual, a person in addition to the famously neglectful father.

A person who might have been alone in the hospital after his heart attack, with no friend to visit with flowers or his favorite magazines. A person who might not have had anyone to shop for his groceries and keep his place clean and tidy when he was released and sent home to recover. Assuming her father had a place to live; it had never occurred to Frieda before that he might be essentially homeless. The thought made her feel slightly ill.

She supposed there were people—self-righteous ones—who would say that if Steve had been on his own during his convalescence he had gotten what he deserved; she supposed there were people who would say that he was only reaping what he had sown. But Frieda felt that was too harsh a judgment. She sincerely hoped her father had someone special in his life, a lover or a best friend, even a good neighbor. She remembered how wonderful he had been to Phil and Tony all those years ago when Tony was sick and dying. No one deserved to suffer alone. No one.

The landline rang then, startling Frieda from her reverie. It was her father.

"I was just thinking about you," she said when she had greeted him.

"You were?" he asked.

"Yes. I was remembering how good you were at designing and building furniture. Dad? What are you doing now? I mean, for work. For that matter, what are you doing for fun?"

"Same as I've always done," her father said promptly. "This and that."

"Not making furniture?" Frieda ventured.

"No."

"According to Mom," Frieda said, "you were really talented. It's Phil's opinion, too, and he should know."

"I was okay," Steve said. "Nothing more."

"But—"

"Look, Frieda," her father interrupted. "I don't have the right to brag. I haven't earned it."

Frieda wasn't sure she could argue that. "Okay," she said. "Dad? Is there anyone special in your life now? I mean . . ."

Steve cleared his throat. "I know what you mean, and no. But thank you for asking. I suppose it's normal that you have a lot of questions."

"Yeah," she said. But how many of those questions would her father be willing to answer? And how many of the answers was she really prepared to hear?

"And you, Frieda?" her father asked. "Has your heart been touched again?"

For a moment Frieda didn't know how to answer truthfully. Finally, she said, "I thought that there might be something between me and an old friend from school, but it didn't work out."

"I'm sorry. At least you were courageous enough to hope."

*Was I?* Frieda wondered. Had she been truly courageous? Or had she seen the struggle that lay ahead and chosen to back away from the challenge, using Bella's fears and her own feelings of guilt as her excuse?

"Frieda? Are you there?"

"Yes," she said. "I'm here."

"Do you know what I was thinking about the other day?" Steve asked. "I was thinking about how your mother and I argued over what to name you. Of course I was going to let her have her way in the end. She was the one doing all the hard work. But I still thought I had a right to voice my opinion."

This was news to Frieda. "And what did you want to name me?" she asked.

"Mary. It was my paternal grandmother's name. I never met her, but my father had a photograph and I thought she had such a kind and gentle face." Steve laughed. "Maybe not the best reason for choosing a baby's name but . . ."

Frieda smiled. "I think it's a very good reason, Dad."

"Maybe. But Ruby's favorite painter won out. I remember hoping that you would live a far less difficult and fraught life than

Frida Kahlo lived. I was the one who insisted that we at least spell your name differently, but I guess it wasn't enough to ward off tragedy. And my walking out the way I did certainly didn't help make things easy for you."

Frieda felt tears pricking at her eyes. "I'm all right, Dad," she said a bit gruffly. "How are you feeling? I mean, physically."

"Not bad considering. I'm not what I used to be, but none of us are."

"Have you had chest pains again?" she asked. "Do you see a doctor regularly?"

"My health is not for you to worry about, Frieda. I wouldn't have told you about the heart attack if I thought it would upset you."

Frieda pondered that for a moment. Had her father really thought that she wouldn't care he had been ill? Well, why wouldn't he have thought so?

"I went through a few of the old photo albums the other day," she said. "I hadn't looked at them since college."

It was a moment before her father replied. "Strolling down memory lane can be dangerous, Frieda," he said. "Comforting, too, I suppose, but it's a journey that should be approached with caution. I've learned that the hard way."

"I know. But it was okay actually," she told him. "I remembered so many things I thought I'd completely forgotten."

"Like what?" he asked.

*Like the obvious fact that you and Mom were in love,* she replied silently. "Like that old couch with the awful orange slipcovers."

Her father laughed. "That was a third-generation hand-me-down," he said. "My aunt had passed it on to her son, my cousin, who then passed it on to your mother and me when we married. Money was tight, so we were grateful for the couch, no matter how hideous."

"And there were photos of the three of us at what looked like an animal petting zoo. You know, sheep and goats in a pen and you, me, and Mom in the midst of the herd."

"That wasn't a petting zoo," her father corrected. "That was a local fair, one where farmers brought their livestock and vegetables for display and competition. I remember this one very aggressive goat sticking his nose into the pocket of your jacket. I guess he was looking for food. You were a little freaked for a moment and then you started to laugh. Maybe his nose tickled."

Frieda smiled. "What else do you remember about that day, Dad?"

"There were rabbits," her father said. "Bunnies. And boy, did you want a bunny after that. Neither your mother nor I was all that keen on keeping a rabbit. It was quite the struggle to get you to accept no for an answer. Phil and Tony were with us that day, too, by the way. It was probably one of them who took the pictures of the three of us."

*The three of us.* "Good times, right, Dad?"

"Yes," her father said. "They were good times."

"Dad?" Frieda said, gathering her courage. She knew that bringing up such a potentially explosive topic was a risk; she had no idea just how far her father was willing or able to go with this renewed relationship. "When you would call Mom when I was a kid, why didn't you ever ask to talk to me?"

"Because of those good times," he said without hesitation.

"I missed you."

"And I missed you, so much that I knew all it would take to bring me back to you and your mother was the sound of your voice. And that would have been a mistake, Frieda. I knew I could never settle into the role of husband and father again and be good at it. I knew I'd only wind up hurting you both far worse than I'd already hurt you." Her father sighed. "I'm sorry if that sounds stupid or if it makes me sound weak, which I fully admit that I am. But it's the truth."

"If only you could have visited once in a while . . ." Frieda wiped a tear from her cheek.

"Same problem. I had to stay away. I did it for my own sake, I'll admit that, but also for your sake, Frieda."

"I think your staying away was a mistake, Dad," Frieda said earnestly but not angrily. "I can't bring myself to believe it was good for either of us, or for Mom."

"I won't try to convince you that it wasn't. And honestly, I've never been able to convince myself that because of my decision I didn't lose out on a slew of wonderful experiences with you. I *did* miss out. But that's the past. It can't be changed. Look, Frieda, I should be going."

"I'm sorry, Dad," Frieda said. "I didn't mean to—"

Her father cut her off. "Don't apologize, Frieda. Ever. You have nothing for which to be sorry."

Frieda wiped another tear from her cheek. "All right, Dad. Take care, okay?"

"You, too, Frieda."

Carefully Frieda replaced the receiver. She wondered if she had gone too far by asking her father difficult questions. She wondered if he would call her again or if he would retreat from her curiosity, however natural it was. But what was done was done. What was said was said. Her father was right. The past—even the immediate past—couldn't be changed. But the future could be modeled on a brighter plan. Couldn't it?

# Chapter 56

Dingding!

"Whose phone is that?"

"Mine," Bella told her grandmother. "It's nothing." Just another text from Clara. *Where r u?* It was the fourth text she had sent that day.

Bella, her mother, and her grandmother were in the kitchen, trading off turning the crank of the old-fashioned ice-cream maker. When it was Bella's turn, Ruby and Frieda worked on a crossword puzzle. When it was someone else's turn, like it was now, Bella flipped through the latest copy of *InStyle* (not stolen from Clara's housemate) and tried to ignore the phone. She had never felt the tyranny of communications technology before this summer. Did a person really have an obligation to be always and immediately available to other people? Ariel hadn't thought so. She had hated Facebook and Instagram and Snapchat and the culture of over-sharing. Ariel had thought that privacy was a very precious thing.

But privacy wasn't something Clara seemed to understand. The earlier three texts had come while Bella was at work: *What r u doing?* And: *Have to tell u something.* The third text had sounded downright desperate: *Where r u? Please, call me!*

So Bella had called during her lunch break. What if Clara was in trouble with that guy who had sold her the pill? The last thing

Bella wanted was to get involved even in the remotest possible way with a drug dealer, but at the same time, if Clara was in trouble, didn't she owe Clara her help and support? They were supposed to be friends.

"Why didn't you text me back?" Clara had demanded immediately.

"Because I'm at work," Bella explained. "Phil doesn't allow me to be on my phone when I'm supposed to be helping customers. I told you that."

"That's totally not fair," Clara had stated.

"What do you need me for?"

"What? Oh. Nothing."

Bella had managed to get off the phone before too much of her lunch break had slipped by, but she had been left feeling annoyed. None of her friends from the past had ever been the clingy sort. There probably were some people who didn't mind or who even liked other people being dependent on them for everything, but Bella wasn't one of them. *Look at me. I'm miserable. You have to pay attention to me.* As she sat alone in the back room of Phil's shop, hurriedly eating the lunch her grandmother had prepared for her, it had occurred to Bella that maybe Clara liked being sad; maybe being needy gave her a sense of control over other people. She had certainly succeeded in gaining Bella's attention—

"Okay," Ruby said, interrupting Bella's wonderings. "This should be done by now. Let me just take the lid off."

Bella got up and stood next to her mother and grandmother. Together they peered into the metal cylinder inside the wooden tub.

"It's still liquid," her grandmother said. "Why didn't it freeze? I could have sworn we did everything right this time. The ice, the rock salt. Maybe we just didn't wait long enough, but we followed the recipe."

Bella dipped a spoon into the metal cylinder. "It tastes okay," she said. "It's actually delicious. We could pour it over stuff."

"Maybe the machine is the problem," her mother suggested. "It is pretty old. Maybe we should buy a new one."

"No," Bella said firmly. "We'll get this right."

"Third time is often the charm," her grandmother pointed out.

"Do we have any pound cake or biscuits or something?" Bella asked.

Dingding!

"Is that your phone again, Bella?"

Bella restrained a sigh. "Yeah," she said, reaching into her pocket to turn off the phone's ringer. "But it can wait."

"Look what I just found in the freezer," her mother announced. "A Sara Lee pound cake!"

"Awesome, Mom," Bella said. "I'll get some plates."

# Chapter 57

Frieda had dressed with some care for this evening. Phil was always so perfectly turned out; it wouldn't do to embarrass her date by showing up in jeans and sneakers when he would be wearing one of his custom-fitted navy blazers over a bespoke shirt. So she had ironed her at-the-knee blush-pink linen skirt and her crisp white blouse with the wide collar and she had slid into her pearlized silver sling-backs. The shoes might be a bit much for the opening at The Barn Gallery, where two of Phil's friends, Verity Peterson and Julia Einstein, were showing their work, but there was always the possibility that they would run into Jack Tennant. Why she should want to look attractive for someone she had turned away was a question Frieda preferred not to answer.

"Aaron used to love The Barn Gallery," Frieda said as they sipped wine from plastic glasses and nodded greetings to people in passing. "He loved all art galleries and museums, really. I guess it was no surprise that he became an architect. He was so interested in the process of making art, so fascinated by the design experience."

Phil raised an eyebrow. "And I know exactly what Aaron would say about the 'design' that informs this—this *thing* before us."

Frieda leaned closer to the object to which Phil was referring, a conglomeration of rope, chunks of metal, and what looked like an old-fashioned TV antenna. The sign on the base of the piece said DREAMSCAPE BY NICO. "Who's Nico?" she asked Phil.

"A local mixed-media sculptor who, though a nice enough fellow, is, in my admittedly amateur opinion, entirely without talent."

Frieda laughed. "Well, I have to agree with you there, but beauty is in the eye of the beholder, right?"

"And I hear he makes a fortune. People from The Big Cities actually collect his work." Phil shook his head. "Life is just full of mysteries."

They wandered on through the gallery, noting several works that evinced real beauty and that testified to real skill. "I was thinking recently about my father's talent with designing furniture," Frieda told Phil. "Do you have anything of his?"

"I do," Phil said. "There's a storage chest in the guest bedroom that your father built for Tony and me not long after we four met. You must have seen it; it used to be in the dining room when Tony and I lived on Patrick's Lane." Phil shook his head. "Your father could have made a name for himself as a true craftsman. But he could never stick to anything. It's a shame really, wasting all that talent."

As they wandered on through the gallery Frieda couldn't help but wonder if there was any joy in her father's life or if he constantly dwelt on the fact that he had made a series of bad decisions, that he had neglected the feelings of others, that he had ignored his talents. Living with relentless disappointment could drive a person mad. It could make him want to end it all. Frieda shivered. *No*, she thought. *Don't think such dark thoughts. Not about Dad.*

"It's getting a bit too crowded for my taste," Phil said, interrupting Frieda's thoughts. "Let's step outside for a bit and let this sudden influx of people see what they've come to see."

"Good idea," Frieda agreed. "I just got my toe stepped on." Frieda followed Phil out into the parking lot, where several other people were gathered in small groups, chatting and sipping wine.

"Ruby told me what happened between you and Jack," Phil said. "I'm sorry."

Frieda sighed. "I'm sorry, too. Actually, I'm a bit nervous about

running into him for the first time since . . . since our talk. I half expected to see him here tonight."

"He might well be part of the throng. And if you do run into him
don't worry. Jack is a good man. He'll be gracious."

"It's not Jack's behavior I'm worried about," Frieda told him.
"It's mine. I have a horrid feeling I'll burst out crying."

"You miss him."

"Yes," Frieda said. "I hardly know him, but I do. Maybe it's because growing up together created a sort of bond. There's something very grounding about the relationships you form in those
early years, even the ones that are more tangential than primary."
*Like the relationship with my father,* Frieda added silently. *And that was
certainly primary.*

Phil put his hand on Frieda's shoulder for a moment. "I want to
explain something to you, Frieda," he said. "Maybe it will help you
figure out your future in terms of a relationship with Jack. Maybe
not. For me, falling in love with someone else after the loss of Tony
was simply not something I could allow myself. My aloneness was
my gift to Tony. It was the sacrifice I offered to him. It was the only
way I could survive the terrible weight of the guilt. Why did Tony
get sick and not me? How could life be so random and expect us to
accept its randomness without going mad? Why was this plague at-
tacking my community? What had we done to deserve this mass
destruction?"

Frieda shook her head. "I've always wondered why someone as
wonderful as you hadn't fallen in love again. It's been so many
years."

"Now you know why. But I want you to know that I wouldn't
recommend my path of a solitary life as the healthiest way to
achieve healing. For me it was necessary, but I can be an odd duck,
Frieda."

Frieda smiled. "If you're odd then what are the rest of us?"

"Seriously, Frieda, you're not doing Bella any favors by setting
an example of stagnation or stasis. And you're certainly not showing yourself the proper respect by consciously rejecting the possibility of happiness. But that's just my opinion as someone who's
known and loved you since you were a little girl. Now come on.

Let's go back inside. Maybe the crowd has thinned a bit. Besides, I can't leave without saying hello to Verity and Julia."

Phil took Frieda's elbow and guided her back inside the building, where the crowd had indeed thinned. Two elderly men immediately approached Phil; they wanted to talk to him about purchasing fabric for a settee that needed upholstering. While Phil excused himself for a moment to advise the men, Frieda got herself another glass of wine and gazed around the gallery. There was no sign of Jack in the main room or coming out of either of the two smaller rooms or from the tiny garden out back. A part of her felt relieved; another part of her felt disappointed. She thought about what Jack had said when they had last met. *Take care of yourself,* Frieda. Was that what she was doing by rejecting a romance, "taking care of herself"? Or was she instead depriving herself of something that might actually be good for her?

Before she could tackle that difficult question, Phil rejoined her.

"Problem solved?" she asked.

Phil nodded. "Rob and Kurt will come to the shop tomorrow to take a look at a few fabrics I think might suit. And if they can't find something they love, I'll place a special order. They've been great customers for years."

"Service with a smile?" Frieda said.

"You bet. There's Verity over by one of her works; she's the woman wearing that amazing silver arm cuff. Come on," Phil said, taking her hand. "I'll introduce you."

As Frieda accompanied Phil through the gallery space, the question she had been pondering earlier came back to her. Had ending her nascent relationship with Jack Tennant been the right thing to do after all? It was still a good question to which there was still no easy answer.

*At least Bella is safe,* Frieda thought as they approached Phil's friend Verity. *At least she doesn't seem angry with me anymore. And that's all that really matters.*

# Chapter 58

Bella peered through one of the small and now rather dirty windows in Clara's room. "Are you sure you don't want to go to the beach or something?" she said. "It's a beautiful day. We shouldn't be cooped up in here. Hey, I have an idea. We could go to one of those miniature golf places in Wells. I haven't played miniature golf since . . ." *Since Ariel was alive,* she thought. "I'll help pay for gas."

"No, I'm good." Clara was slumped in the room's one chair, her legs splayed. The jeans she was wearing were dirty around the bottoms, as if she had walked through a muddy puddle and failed to notice the results.

Bella sighed and flopped down on the edge of Clara's single bed. She noticed that there was a stain on the sheet; it looked like mustard and vaguely she wondered when Clara had last done laundry. She knew there was a small washing machine and dryer off the kitchen. How hard could it be to toss a sheet and a pair of jeans into the machine?

"How are your parents?" Bella asked suddenly.

Clara frowned. "Fine."

"When was the last time you talked to them?"

"I don't know," Clara said with a shrug. "The other day, I guess."

"Do they know that you're . . ." Bella wasn't quite sure what to say. *Do they know that you're depressed? Sad? Lonely?*

"Do they know that I'm what?" Clara snapped. "We're not close. We never were."

"Oh."

"That's why when I met Marc . . . Here, I want to show you something." Clara got up from the chair, came across the room, and sat next to Bella on the bed. She reached into the small front pocket of her jeans and pulled out a silver-colored coin. Clara handed the object to Bella. The piece bore the image of a wolf's head.

"I don't understand," she said. "What is it?"

"It belongs to Marc," Clara explained. "His last name is Wolf and his favorite animal is the wolf. He's seriously into the preservation of their habitats."

"So," Bella asked, returning the coin to Clara, "if it's Marc's, why do you have it? Did he give it to you?"

"No. A few days before he left for California I took it from the glove compartment of his car."

Bella's eyes widened. "You mean you broke into his car?"

"Of course not. I had a key made for myself a long time ago."

"Did Marc know that?"

Clara shrugged. "I don't know, but I'm sure he wouldn't have minded."

*You stole the coin,* Bella thought. *That's not right. That's a crime. It's a violation of trust.* "It looks pretty old," she said. "It might be valuable."

"It *is* old," Clara said. "It once belonged to Marc's great-grandfather. I keep it under my pillow at night. And during the day I keep it in my pocket. If it's close to me always and I think hard enough about Marc, I just know he'll come back to me."

For a moment Bella didn't know what to say. She recognized this type of magical thinking from her own experience immediately after the accident. *Maybe I can reverse time if only I . . . Maybe I can bring them back if only I . . .*

"But clearly the coin means something to Marc," she finally pointed out. "It's a family heirloom. He must be upset that it's gone. His parents might even be angry with him for losing it. Except that he didn't lose it."

Clara looked down at the coin in her hand and then she twisted on the bed to face Bella. "I've been thinking," she said, "and something finally became clear. It was Marc's parents who made him break up with me. They never liked me, right from the beginning. I could tell by the way they treated me when I'd come by the house. His mother used to give me this nasty look. His sister, too. His sister hates me. She would barely say hello to me even though we were on the lacrosse team together." Clara's foot started to tap against the floor. "If I could just talk to Marc without their interfering," she went on. "But Marc changed his phone number, so I can't reach him."

Bella had no idea how to respond. Clara might be at least partially right—maybe Marc's family really didn't like her—but Bella thought she heard a strong note of paranoia in Clara's voice. And the look of almost manic determination in her eyes disturbed Bella.

Suddenly Clara jumped up from the bed and went over to the dresser. "Here," she said, lifting the lid on the small metal box. "I have something for you." She came back to Bella and told her to open her hand. Into the hand she dropped a small white pill. "Take it," she said. "It's a gift."

Bella felt her stomach flutter unpleasantly. "That's okay," she said, extending her hand toward Clara. "I don't want it."

"You can't refuse a gift," Clara said. "It's rude."

"But—"

Clara's expression darkened. "Bella, I mean it. I want you to take it."

For a moment Bella said nothing. She had had enough of Clara and her obsession with Marc. *All I want*, she thought, *is to get out of here. And the easiest way to do that would probably be to go along with Clara.* "Fine," she said. She opened her small leather cross-body bag and dropped the pill into it. "I've got to go. I promised my grandmother I'd pick up a book she put on hold at the library."

"Oh." Clara's expression changed from anger to sadness. For a second Bella thought she was going to cry. "Too bad. When will I see you again?"

Bella shrugged. "We'll talk," she said, hurrying toward the door. "Bye."

Bella stood in the middle of her room on Kinders Lane. She was glad no one else was at home. She stared down at the little white pill Clara had given her and felt afraid, as if the pill had the power to hurt her just by sitting in the palm of her hand. For the entire ride back from the cottage she had felt as if there were a big red arrow over her head, an indication that she, Bella Marie Braithwaite, was in possession of something she shouldn't be.

Suddenly Bella strode over to the dresser and pulled open the top drawer. She would hide the pill. She would forget about it. She would . . . And then she came to her senses. What in the world was she doing? Quickly she hurried to the bathroom in the hall, where without another moment's hesitation she flushed the pill into oblivion.

Once back in her room, the door closed behind her, Bella lay on her bed. Her mind was awhirl. She thought about how Clara had urged her to pick the lock of Ariel's diary. She thought about how Clara had admitted she had once picked a lock and how she had admitted to stealing Marc's heirloom coin. She thought about how Clara had almost bragged about sitting in her car outside Marc's house all night after he had dumped her; about leaving pleading notes in Marc's mailbox; about following him around town, ducking into doorways if she thought he had detected her; about spending hours in the big-box hardware store where Marc worked after school and on weekends, hoping for a glimpse of him as he wheeled a hand truck loaded with boxes or restocked shelves of lightbulbs.

Theft. Stalking. Bella wondered if Marc had ever confronted Clara, warned her he would get a restraining order if she didn't back off. She wondered if he had told his parents about what was happening. She wondered if he had ever been afraid of his ex-girlfriend. For all Bella knew, Marc's decision to go to a college on the West Coast was a desperate effort to escape from what had become a suffocating relationship. Or maybe Clara's obsession had only started after Marc broke up with her.

Bella sighed deeply. There was so much of the story she just didn't know; what she did know was that she wasn't going to get the truth from Clara. And that was all right because at that moment, secure in her grandmother's home on Kinders Lane, Bella almost didn't care if she ever saw Clara Crawford again.

Almost.

# Chapter 59

Frieda frowned at the screen of her laptop, on which appeared a long list of colleagues she was planning to contact yet again in the ongoing search for work. That was the downside of a freelance writing and copyediting career; no matter how good your reputation, the process of selling yourself never quite ended. But as important as the task was, her mind continued to wander to thoughts of Jack and of how she missed him. To thoughts of Aaron and of how she missed him, too. To thoughts of Bella.

Since breaking things off with Jack Frieda had made a concerted effort to spend more time with her daughter. She had met Bella at Wainscoting and Windowseats one afternoon, suggesting they catch the next showing of *Beetlejuice*, one of Bella's favorite movies, at the old Leavitt Theatre in Ogunquit. She had suggested they visit the outlets in Kittery. She had suggested they go to the Funky Bow Beer Company one evening to eat pizza and hear a band called The Windmills.

Frankly, Frieda wasn't sure her attentions were making a positive difference in Bella's life—Bella hadn't rejected any of her mother's efforts, but neither had she showered Frieda with thanks—but her own conscience was partly assuaged and maybe that counted as "taking care of herself." People said it so casually. "Bye. Take care of yourself." Or they might say it meaningfully, as Frieda thought

Jack had done when they had parted. Either way, the idea of taking care of oneself was a tricky one to figure out. She remembered what Phil had said to her at The Barn Gallery. *You're certainly not showing yourself the proper respect by consciously rejecting the possibility of happiness.*

But what did happiness mean to her? Above all, Frieda thought, happiness meant knowing that her sole surviving child was safe and secure in her mother's love. That came above all else; it had to. And yet . . . She remembered what her father had said to her when they had last spoken, that at least she had had the courage to hope for happiness.

It could drive you mad, Frieda thought, shaking her head. Everyone had an opinion on how she should be living her life. She knew these people, Ruby, Phil, Jack, and yes, even her father, cared for her, but—

"Am I interrupting?" It was her mother, come into the kitchen wearing a crisp linen blouse over a pair of capri pants.

Frieda closed her laptop. "No. Well, yes, but I could use an interruption from begging colleagues for job leads."

"You're not begging," Ruby said. "You're networking."

"Sometimes it feels like the same thing." Frieda sighed. "Sorry. I'm feeling a swamp of self-pity opening at my feet."

"Things can't be all bad. You were humming just now."

"I was? I wasn't aware."

"Your father used to sing that song to you at bedtime when you were about three or four."

"What song?" Frieda asked.

"The one you were humming. It's called 'The Tale of the Tadpole.' I can't remember which children's singer-songwriter made it famous and I can't recall all the lyrics, but I'm pretty sure there was a line having to do with water drops and wavelets."

Memory, Frieda thought, was a strange thing. The tune had remained with her but not the lyrics or its source. "Mom?" she asked. "Do you still have anything Dad built?"

"You mean his woodworking?" Ruby asked.

"Yeah. I mean, I know you don't have any of his furniture." Of course she didn't. She had sold it long ago out of sheer necessity.

"My jewelry box," she said. "Your father made it for my birthday the first year we were together."

"I love that box. I never knew Dad made it."

"Well, he did, and now I'm off. The Page Turners are meeting to talk about the fall reading schedule. We're having dinner out, so don't expect me back before nine."

Ruby grabbed her bag and with a wave she left the kitchen.

Frieda got up from the table to make a cup of tea. So, her father used to sing to her. It was a sweet thing for him to have done. Aaron, too, had sung to the girls at bedtime. And as she turned the gas on under the teakettle, Frieda vowed she would make a point of not letting Bella forget anything about her father, not one little thing, not what stories Aaron had read to her or how when she was a roly-poly baby he had called her Baby Belly Button, or how many times he had bandaged her scraped knees, or how he had talked to anyone who would listen about how proud he was of his children.

Frieda went to the cupboard for a tea bag. There was a long evening ahead. She would suggest that after dinner she and Bella make popcorn and watch a movie on Netflix. Or maybe they could play Monopoly, unless memories of the fun times the four Braithwaites had enjoyed over board games would upset Bella. You just never knew what seemingly mundane activity might release a flood of painfully sweet memories. Still, Frieda thought, she and her daughter would be together, which was the important thing.

The most important thing.

# Chapter 60

Bella had gotten out of bed that morning with the fixed idea of catching some sun and shortly after breakfast she had set out on her bike for the beach. It was a good thing she had left the house before ten. The tide was high and there was barely enough sand to accommodate the beachgoers who continued to arrive under burdens of chairs and umbrellas, coolers and boogie boards.

And it felt okay being at the beach alone this time. Bella actually felt kind of happy, and maybe it was because she and her mother had spent a really nice evening together. They had played Monopoly after dinner (which was an awesome chicken pot pie from one of the local farms), and while it was true that as they sat at the kitchen table buying and selling properties, landing in jail, and winning beauty contests Bella had wondered if her mother was thinking of Jack Tennant, it had been fun all the same.

In fact, in the past days she had spent more time with her mother than she had in months. And everything they had done—the movie at the Leavitt, shopping at the stores in Kittery, hearing The Windmills play at that brewery in Lyman—had been her mother's idea. It was almost as if she was courting her, trying to get her to—what? Forgive her?

Bella, who had been lying on her back, sat up and put her arms around her knees. She and her mother had clung to each other after the accident; they had been each other's most vital support through those long, trying days and those endless sleepless nights. And then, as the anniversary of the accident approached, something . . . Bella didn't know how to put it unless to say that something switched off inside her. Almost against her will she began to retreat from everyone, especially her mother, to hold her feelings of guilt closer, to feel her loss as acutely as she had felt it in the moments after being told that her father and sister had been killed.

But now . . . Bella turned her face to the sun. Now, she thought, it would be good to feel connected again, to believe that she knew her place in the world, to believe that she had a place she deserved.

A high-pitched squeal of laughter brought Bella's attention to three little boys playing in the sand not far from her. If building a sand castle was their goal they didn't seem to be making any real progress, but they sure were having a lot of fun with their plastic shovels and pails. Bella remembered building sand castles with Ariel and their father, elaborate structures, using bits of shell and stones and seaweed for decoration. There were pictures of those sand castles somewhere back in Warden.

Beyond the little boys and their hovering parents Bella noted a group of four girls about her own age settling down with blankets and overflowing beach bags. She could hear their laughter, the kind of lighthearted laughter that was evidence of real friendship. She and Clara rarely laughed together. In fact, now that Bella had begun to give their relationship some thought, she realized there were other odd things about it, like the fact that Clara never actually offered advice or sympathy when Bella talked about her father and sister. Bella would say, "I miss Ariel," and instead of saying, "What is it about her you miss most?" or "When do you miss her the most?" or even "Poor you," Clara would say something like, "I know. I miss Marc so much you wouldn't believe it." When Bella would say, "I dreamed again about the accident," Clara would say something like, "I couldn't sleep at all last night because I kept thinking about Marc."

Bella dug her hands into the warm sand. It was almost as if Clara thought they were in a competition to determine who could be more miserable. Why couldn't she be sympathetic, even sometimes? But maybe Clara couldn't care or even pretend to care about someone else's sadness because her own sadness was so big and . . . So obsessive. Bella winced. Here was a disturbing thought. Was she ignoring Clara's troubles and promoting her own troubles as more important? She hoped not. She didn't want to be a selfish person. She *did* ask Clara about her feelings. At least, sometimes she did.

Bella pulled her hands from the sand and watched as the tiny grains spilled from her fingers. She might be confused about her conduct with Clara, but there was no doubt she had ignored Kerri's pain in the wake of Ariel's death. That had been selfish. She had hurt her old friend and there were consequences for behavior, whether the behavior was conscious or unconscious, whether the motives behind the behavior were pure or self-serving. Sometimes you didn't get forgiven for something you had said or done and there was nothing you could do about it.

And it was also selfish to try to keep her mother away from a friendship with Jack Tennant. Bella frowned. Being so absorbed in your own misery made you feel kind of stupid and pathetic. *The next time Mom suggests we do something together,* she determined, *I'm going to thank her. I'm going to let her know I appreciate her paying attention to me. Isn't that what I wanted? Her attention?*

And as for Clara, Bella thought, she would try to listen the next time they met. Whenever that was. Oddly, Clara hadn't been in contact for almost two days. *Maybe,* Bella thought, *I should contact her. Maybe I should see if she's okay. But she didn't reach for her phone.*

Almost as one the four teenaged girls Bella had been watching leaped to their feet and, linking arms, ran down toward the shoreline. *I told my family that I didn't miss Kerri,* Bella thought as she reached for the water bottle in her canvas beach bag. *But I do miss her. I really do.*

# Chapter 61

"Good morning, Ms. Hitchens."

Ruby smiled at the young man who had just come out of the convenience store on Main Street. "Good morning to you, Calvin," she said. Calvin Rogers had made a bit of a name for himself several years back when he successfully petitioned the town fathers and mothers to spend what money was available in their budget on fixing up the old community playground rather than on a cosmetic project. His motto had been: *What's more important than kids' safety?* And really, Ruby thought, what was more important? "How's your summer going?"

"Awesome," Calvin said. "I'm working at the news station up in Portland. Well, I'm interning. I'm not making any money, but I'm learning tons of stuff. I want to study media and broadcasting. It's such an exciting field and so much is changing so quickly. The internship is a great experience."

"That's wonderful," Ruby told him. "Money is good, but experience can be better."

"That's what my dad told my mom when she wanted me to turn down the internship and get a job at Hannaford. Well, gotta run. Nice to see you Ms. Hitchens."

Calvin loped off and was soon lost in the crowds of summer visitors. Ruby, intending to continue on her way as well, suddenly spotted George across the street. He was chatting with Peggy Smith-son, the woman who ran the food bank in nearby Oceanside. Peggy was in her mid-forties, divorced, and one of the most beautiful women Ruby had ever seen. Rumor had it that when Peggy was in her teens her mother had urged her to try her hand at modeling but that Peggy had turned her back on the profession with disgust after one too many people made one too many inappropriate offers. She had gone on to earn a master's degree in social work and to solidify a reputation among the community for being a truly caring and compassionate person.

As Ruby watched Peggy's animated gestures, as she watched George nod and smile, she felt a wave of something she hadn't felt in a very long time. Jealousy. Ugly, green-eyed, and unreasonable. She took a deep breath and called her mind to order. George wasn't the one betraying their relationship by chatting with a neighbor. She was the one betraying their relationship by not giving George an answer to his proposal. What right did she have to feel jealous? Absolutely none.

As if in punishment for her unworthy thoughts, a dull wave of pain attacked Ruby's leg. All the care George continued to give her and she couldn't even grant him his dearest wish. Of course you shouldn't marry someone only out of gratitude for the nice things he did for you, but gratitude definitely counted for something. And caregiving should not be repaid by ignoring the caregiver. There was no denying that the last three years had been tough on George, what with settling into a new job in a new town, caring for his aging and then dying father, and taking on such an important role in the life of Ruby's family. He had done it all willingly, but that didn't mean any of it had been without hardship.

Peggy Smithson put a hand on George's arm. Ruby bit her lip. What would the good people of Yorktide say if she and George were to break up? She remembered as if it were yesterday how she had felt in the wake of Steve's defection. She had sworn she wasn't bothered by the pitying looks cast her way by the matrons of York-tide, those solidly respectable women long married to solidly re-spectable men. She had sworn she wasn't bothered by the smirks and the snide comments of the younger women, some married and some not, who saw in Ruby's situation their own unspoken fears come to life. But of course Ruby had been bothered.

*Stop it,* Ruby told herself firmly. *Stop allowing the past to intrude on the present. Send it back to where it belongs.* It was stupid to fear the opinions of her neighbors, no matter what they might be. She was not a child. She was a grown woman. But Yorktide was a small town and people would talk—

With a start Ruby realized she had been standing in the middle of the sidewalk for a full two or three minutes; at least a handful of Yorktide residents would be commenting on her odd behavior over dinner that evening. With determination Ruby turned from sight of George and Peggy Smithson and walked on toward Clove Street and her destination, The Bookworm. Being in the presence of books was one of the few things that could soothe Ruby's soul when it had been rattled. And it had been rattled.

# Chapter 62

"So, what have you been up to?"

Clara had finally contacted Bella but had offered no explanation for her brief period of silence. Bella hadn't asked for an explanation.

Clara, sitting cross-legged on the bed, shrugged. "Nothing," she said.

"I went to the beach yesterday. The weather was gorgeous."

Clara didn't comment.

Bella restrained a sigh. The little room at the back of the cottage looked even messier and dirtier than it had been on Bella's last visit, and that was saying something. Her eyes roamed over piles of clothes on the floor to the small trash pail stuffed with empty paper coffee cups, brown paper bags, and what looked like a pair of dirty white socks. And the top of the dresser was more cluttered than it had ever been, scattered with tubes of lip balm and crumpled tissues and hair ties and—Bella froze. Slowly she turned to face Clara.

"What are you doing with a hypodermic needle?" she asked. She could hear the fear in her voice.

Clara smiled. "Don't freak."

"I'm not freaking," Bella lied. "I'm just asking a question. What's a hypodermic needle doing sitting on your dresser?"

"If you must know," Clara said with an exaggerated sigh, "it's for my pain."

"What are you saying?"

"For God's sake, Bella, grow up! Don't you get it?"

Bella swallowed hard. "Yeah," she said. "I get it. Is it heroin?"

"It's no different than the pills doctors prescribe," Clara said quickly, "like oxycodone or fentanyl, except that it's way cheaper and you can get it pretty much anywhere."

"But . . ." Bella struggled to get a grip on her panic and distress. "But it's not controlled," she said. "I mean, no one is making sure each batch or whatever you call it is safe. Uncontaminated."

Clara didn't reply. She stared down at her hand and began to pick at a cuticle.

"Where did you get it?" Bella asked. "From the same guy who sold you the pill, the one with the ridiculous name?"

"No," Clara said without looking up. "Someone else."

"You're not going to tell me who?"

"No." Clara abandoned the cuticle and looked up at Bella. "Why?" she asked. "Do you want to buy some?"

"No!" Bella cried. "Clara, you'll get addicted. It happens all the time."

Clara waved her hand dismissively. "No, I won't. I'm totally on it; don't worry."

"Is the needle clean? Did he sell you the needle, too?"

"What does it matter where I got it? It's none of your business, Bella."

"Uh, yeah, it is!" Bella argued. "We're supposed to be friends. You invited me over to your place. You have drug stuff just sitting out in the open. You made it my business!"

Again, Clara had no response.

"You told me," Bella went on, "that Marc is totally against drugs of any kind. What would he think of you shooting heroin?"

With a rapidity that surprised Bella Clara leaped off the bed and crossed the room to her dresser. "He won't know," she said as she picked up the needle. Her tone was oddly cold. "He doesn't ever have to know."

There was no way Bella was going to watch what might happen

next. "I've got to go," she blurted. "I'm late for—" She didn't bother to finish the sentence but hurried out into the hall.

"Close the door!" Clara called, but Bella pretended not to have heard and kept going. When she was out the front door of the cottage she suddenly bent over and retched. She was afraid. She was disgusted. She wanted to be home. Bella wiped her mouth with the back of her hand and ran toward her bike.

The laptop was a hand-me-down from her mother; it wasn't the fastest machine, but it was fine for idling through Facebook or her favorite blogs—or, like now, for doing research. If for some reason her mother or grandmother checked the laptop's online search history Bella could quite honestly say that she had been curious to know more about the heroin crisis; the news sources had been reporting on it for the past few years. And the news sources had also been claiming an alarmingly high percentage of accidental heroin overdoses.

Bella glanced again at the door of her room to be certain she had firmly shut it behind her. She wasn't quite sure where to start her research but quickly found that information was aplenty, like the fact that heroin was sometimes cut with seriously harmful substances such as talcum powder and strychnine. There were so many dangers, not the least of which was the risk of contracting HIV from using a dirty needle. One in four people who used heroin would become addicted. Addiction could come on suddenly or over a prolonged period of time. An overdose could easily kill a person.

The facts were scary enough, but it was the "Before" and "After" photos of people addicted to heroin that really shook Bella. Sometimes the radical change in their appearance—and health—had taken place in mere months. One "After" picture in particular, that of a young man, elicited in Bella a feeling of disgust. Immediately she felt ashamed. It wasn't this guy's fault that he looked so ravaged and frail. It was the fault of the drug. It was the fault of whoever had sold it to him. It was the fault of whoever was at the top of the whole mess, manufacturing the drug for illegal sale.

Suddenly Bella couldn't take any more. She shut the laptop and looked around the beautiful room her grandmother had created for her granddaughters. The contrast between this room, with its rosy pink walls and pretty lace curtains, and Clara's room at the cottage could not be more powerful. Here was safety and peace; there was danger and threat. Here was order and cleanliness; there was chaos and dirt. *I have it so good,* Bella thought. *I have so very much.*

And she didn't want to risk losing all she had by spending time with someone who was using illegal drugs. She was glad she had flushed that pill down the toilet. She would never smoke pot again. She would never see Clara again.

But Bella's conscience pricked at her. Didn't she owe Clara a degree of loyalty and friendship? She had decided yesterday at the beach that she would try to listen and to help, but maybe it was too late for the kind of help she could offer. Still, except for her Clara was on her own in Yorktide.

Bella got up from the desk and walked to the window. She looked out at the perfectly mowed lawn and the beds of well-tended flowers. A blue jay flew onto the rim of the stone birdbath and dipped its beak into the water her grandmother refreshed daily. It was an idyllic scene for sure, but not idyllic enough to calm Bella's troubled spirit. She wished she knew how to get in touch with Clara's parents. Maybe the guy who owned The Flipper, Clara's boss, had their contact information. But he would ask why Bella wanted Clara's personal information, and what could she say without betraying Clara? And would it be right to rat on Clara to her parents? They had, after all, sent their daughter away from home this summer. Maybe they were glad she was gone.

A strange thought suddenly occurred to Bella as she watched the blue jay fly off. What had prompted Clara to approach her that rainy afternoon on the Marginal Way? What if Clara had known or sensed that Bella was someone she could . . . Someone she could use? What if a local had mentioned Bella's story to Clara in passing, pointing her out as the girl who had lost both her father and sister in one fell swoop? Had Clara ever cared for her at all, or was Bella just someone she had targeted for her usefulness, someone to support her in her downward spiral of misery? Someone who would be an enabler.

Bella turned away from the view of her grandmother's pleasant backyard. *No,* she thought. That seemed a bit far-fetched. Clara didn't seem to be thinking clearly about anything and it would take some clarity of mind to seek out someone vulnerable enough to unwittingly aid you in your journey of self-destruction.

"What a mess," Bella said aloud; she thought she had never felt so frustrated by a situation in her life. "What a stupid mess!"

# Chapter 63

"Her behavior could have put someone at risk, so I had no choice but to report her misconduct to her boss." George sighed. "Even though she needed to be reprimanded I felt like a heel, like one of those obnoxious, teacher's pet type kids in middle school who were always ratting on their classmates."

"Listen to this." Ruby looked up from the local paper opened on the kitchen table before her. "There's a Blue Grass Festival next week in Saco. How did I miss that? I bet Frieda and Bella would enjoy it."

"Did you hear any of what I just said?" George asked.

Ruby felt her stomach drop as a vivid memory of George chatting with the beautiful and animated Peggy Smithson flashed across her mind. "No," she admitted. "I'm sorry, George. It's just . . ."

"It's just that you were thinking about Frieda and Bella. I know."

"I'm sorry," Ruby repeated. "Really. Tell me what you were saying. I promise I'll listen."

George sighed and took a seat across from Ruby at the table. "It wasn't important," he said. "Look, maybe I'm speaking out of turn, but I feel I have to say this. Don't hide behind your duty to your family, Ruby. Caring for them shouldn't prevent you from caring for me—or for yourself. There's always enough love to go around."

Ruby couldn't manage a response. She felt tears prick her eyes, tears of fear and shame.

"For the three years I took care of my father," George went on, "I still had plenty of time for our relationship. If you don't want to grow old with me, I understand. I won't be happy about it, but I can accept it. But please, Ruby, be honest with me."

"I'm scared, George," Ruby admitted, wiping her cheeks with the back of her hand. "I'm scared of getting married."

George leaned across the table and put his hand on hers. "Don't you trust me? Don't you believe that I love you?"

"I do, I really do, but—"

"But what?" George took his hand off hers. "You do or you don't, Ruby."

"I do trust you," she insisted. "And I do believe in your love for me."

"Then what's stopping you from saying yes, you'll marry me? Please, Ruby, explain it to me. We've been over this before and I still don't understand. Okay, I know that Steve hurt you badly, but that was a long time ago and I'm not Steve Hitchens."

Ruby sighed. "Just give me a bit more time, please, George."

There was a long moment of silence during which Ruby wondered if she had pushed her luck too far. And then George said, "Of course you can have more time. I'm invested in this, Ruby. I'm invested in us. I've said this before—I'm not walking away unless you tell me to go. I'm a stubborn old goat; I think you know that."

Ruby managed a smile, as did George, but his smile didn't quite reach his eyes. She got up from her chair and went to him. She put her arms around him tightly. "I love you, George Hastings," she said, "and that's a fact." *And why,* she thought, *can't that be enough?*

"I love you, too, Ruby." George stood, kissed the top of her head, and took his leave without another word.

When he had gone Ruby sank back into her chair and pushed the newspaper aside. *This is getting ridiculous,* she thought. If she was honest with herself she could admit to seeing no obvious downside to marrying George. In fact, marriage might very well strengthen the union they had already built. Until George, Ruby had never been part of a team; in her marriage to Steve she had been the undisputed leader, if by default. But to formalize that union, to give official blessing to that team, would make its potential demise that much more horrible to bear.

Ruby took a deep breath. She wondered what would happen if she suggested to George that they simply live together without what in the old days was referred to as "the benefit of marriage." She suspected the idea would not be welcome. If living together were what George wanted he would not have proposed marriage. There was a difference; a choice could be made. So, what then? In spite of George's protestations of devotion, Ruby felt there was a strong possibility that he would end the relationship if she said no to marriage, and that was not what she wanted. And if George was somehow able to carry on seeing her, maybe even to move in with her, would she be comfortable, knowing she had denied the man she loved something so important to his happiness?

Ruby put her hand to her head. It was a big stupid muddle and Ruby didn't like muddles, especially ones she had created. She didn't like them at all.

# Chapter 64

"Thanks again, Mom, for suggesting this."

Frieda glanced over at her daughter as she turned off the engine of the Subaru. "I thought we could use an excursion. Portland seemed as good a destination as any. Lunch first?" she suggested as they climbed out of the car.

"Yes! Do you want to go to Andie's?" Bella asked.

"If you'd like, sure." Andie's Wharf had been a Braithwaite family favorite since the girls were small. Frieda thought it was a good sign that Bella didn't feel the need to avoid revisiting the restaurant. Together they headed down to Commercial Street, that wide thoroughfare bordered on one side by the water. The traffic was heavy and slow moving as it always was in summer and the sidewalks teemed with vacationers, many of them speaking French Canadian.

"We haven't been to Portland in a long time," Bella noted.

"You're right. Not since before the accident."

"There's all this new stuff going on. Nothing ever stays the same, does it?"

"No," Frieda said. "It doesn't. Well, feelings can sometimes remain unchanged. I mean, fundamentally unchanged. Feelings like love."

"Yeah," Bella said. "I guess that's true. Look, this is the place

Phil asked me to check out. Arabesque. He said he thought it might turn out to be fierce competition. I was like, 'How can I tell if it's going to be competition when I've only just learned to tell the difference between chintz and brocade?' "

Frieda laughed. "What did he say?"

"He said, 'Do your best, Bella.' So I guess we should go in."

Frieda followed her daughter into the high-end home decorating shop, where they were greeted by an overwhelming scent of very sweet flowers.

"There's no way this place can seriously threaten Wainscoting and Windowseats," Bella whispered after she had taken a quick walk around the shop. "They've only got like three kinds of doorknobs. What's that about? Phil's got fifteen! And what's with that smell? It's too strong. It's going to put customers off."

"The selection of home decorating books is pretty nice, though," Frieda remarked.

Bella frowned. "Phil's selection is much better. It's more wideranging. Come on. I've seen enough."

Frieda held back a smile and followed her daughter out of the shop. To think that Bella, of all people, was becoming a bit of a retail snob was pretty amusing.

Andie's Wharf was located across the street on an actual wharf long since out of commercial use. Frieda and Bella found a table on the restaurant's upper deck overlooking twenty or so leisure boats at dock. They ordered and sat back to wait for their meal.

"Remember the boat tour we went on in Jamaica," Bella said, "the one that took us to that spectacular waterfall? The scenery was so different than it is here. I remember Ariel calling the landscape fecund and I thought it was a bad word until she explained."

Frieda smiled. "Yes," she said. "I remember."

Bella pointed to the water below. "The tour boat was kind of like that one there, the one with the blue awning."

"You're right," Frieda agreed. "It was. There are reminders everywhere, aren't there?"

"Yeah." Bella cleared her throat as the waitress placed their meals on the table. "Good," she said. "I'm starved. I love the fried calamari here."

"The sauce is a little too spicy for me," Frieda admitted. "But the fish-and-chips are always perfect."

They ate for a while in companionable silence. Finally, Frieda introduced a subject she had been considering for some time. "I never apologized to you for going ahead with the party to celebrate what would have been Ariel's sixteenth. Or for getting angry that night. So I'll say it now. I'm sorry."

Bella smiled a bit wryly. "That's okay. I wasn't exactly calm, cool, and collected, was I?"

"Do you remember how Colleen and Charlie talked about how anniversaries could cause trauma for survivors?" Frieda asked her daughter. "They explained that grief could come rushing to the fore again, making you feel as raw as you did at the time of the tragedy."

"Yeah," Bella said. "I remember."

"With that in mind I felt so strongly that keeping you from attending the school's memorial for Ariel back in April was the right thing to do. I really believed the event would only serve to tighten your grip on the feelings of loss and loneliness and guilt, all those feelings you had begun to release but that seemed to be torturing you again. And I think I made a good call." Frieda paused. "But then, when Ariel's birthday came around, I felt so sure that to mark the occasion was the right thing to do. I felt it was the necessary thing for us both. But I was wrong."

"It's okay, Mom," Bella said, wiping her hands on her napkin. "I was the one with the problem, not you. Colleen told me once that for some people, constantly memorializing someone's death was a way for them to keep stuck in their grief. She said that some people needed to do things to keep them feeling sad because the idea of feeling happy was too frightening. But I guess for me it was kind of the other way around. Celebrating Ariel's birthday felt like letting go of guilt I thought I still deserved to feel. Does that make sense?"

"Yes. I understand that now," Frieda assured her. "I just wish I had understood at the time."

Bella shook her head. "Back in early April I started to think, oh my God, how am I going to get through the anniversary of the day that wrecked everything without totally going crazy? I didn't plan on losing what progress I had made. It just sort of happened. The guilt was so bad . . . I kept hearing myself laughing at Ariel and calling her a dork for wanting to go to that museum. I kept remembering how I hadn't really told Dad how much I appreciated his taking us on my dream vacation. And as the anniversary got nearer and nearer I felt worse and worse." Bella laughed a bit. "Did I even get out of bed that day?"

"I heard you use the bathroom once," Frieda told her with a smile.

"How did you handle it, Mom? Was it awful?"

"It wasn't a great day, no," Frieda admitted. "But I was so worried about you that in a way my own feelings of sadness took a backseat."

"I'm sorry I scared you."

"It's nothing for which to apologize," Frieda assured her. "We feel what we feel. Bella, do you think our coming to live with Grandma in Maine this summer has been a good idea?"

"I think so, yeah," Bella said. "I wasn't sure at first, especially when she told me I had to have a job! But I actually like working at Phil's. He gets some really whacky customers, like this one woman the other day who had one of those ridiculously little dogs with her."

"What was whacky about that?"

"Uh, the dog was wearing a dress and a hat and sunglasses. She introduced the dog as her daughter, Patricia Ann. Patricia Ann is a Libra."

Frieda laughed. "I'm glad you're having fun while making money. You are putting some of it away, aren't you?"

"Of course," Bella said. "In fact, I'm hardly spending any of it. Grandma keeps making me lunches so I don't have to pay for a sandwich at some ridiculously high-priced tourist place."

"Don't you and Clara spend money when you go out?" Frieda asked. "It's pretty hard not to spend money these days."

Bella took a long sip of her soda before answering. "Mostly we just talk," she said.

"I wish we could meet her. Is she really so shy she feels she can't come over for dinner some evening?"

Again, it was a moment before Bella replied. "I'm not so sure it's that she's shy as much as she's kind of awkward sometimes. I mean, I have the feeling she doesn't really get along with her housemates."

"But you like her?" Frieda asked. Their waitress brought the check to the table and Frieda reached for her bag.

Bella shrugged. "You know me, Mom. I can get along with pretty much anyone."

"But there must be something about Clara that attracts you," Frieda went on, "something that keeps you spending time with her. I don't mean to pry, really. But I'm your mother. I'm allowed to be curious."

"OMG! Mom, look at that puppy!" Bella cried. And indeed a young woman had taken a seat at the next table accompanied by an adorable pug puppy. Frieda suspected that Bella had used the arrival of the dog as a way to avoid answering the questions about Clara. But maybe it didn't matter.

When Bella returned to her seat, Frieda said, "I'm so glad we're talking again, I mean really talking. When you began to pull away back in April I felt so scared and helpless. I probably should have given you no choice about continuing to see Colleen. I'm afraid I've made more than one bad judgment call in the past months."

Bella laughed. "Doesn't everyone make bad judgment calls at least half of the time? Well, maybe not Ariel. She always seemed to know the right thing to do."

"I'm sure she suffered her own agonies of indecision," Frieda said. "Just because she didn't talk about her interior struggles doesn't mean she didn't endure them."

"Yeah. Do you think she wrote about her thoughts in all those notebooks she kept? She must have. I mean, what else is there to write about? Unless she was writing poems and stories, and even then they had to have been about her in some way, right?"

"I don't know," Frieda admitted. "But you're probably right. Those notebooks are Ariel in a way." *And maybe*, she thought, *someday I'll find the courage to read them.*

"What's going on with you and my grandfather?" Bella asked suddenly.

"I'm learning more about him," Frieda told her. "And about the time we spent together before he left. I'm remembering some things I thought I'd forgotten, good things."

"So, you're cool with him calling?"

"Yes. I am."

"I can't imagine—"

"What?" Frieda asked.

"I was just going to say I can't imagine life without my father around. And my father isn't around." Bella shook her head. "What I meant to say was I can't imagine my father leaving me the way your father left you. It seems . . . It seems impossible somehow, though I know it probably happens a lot. The daddy you count on to make pancakes Saturday mornings, the daddy who pumps up your bike tire when it goes flat, the daddy who takes you and your friends to the movies during Christmas break—suddenly he's not there. If Dad had left me, not died, just walked away, when I was eleven I . . ."

"But he didn't," Frieda pointed out, "and he never would have."

"I know. But you can't stop yourself from thinking about things that didn't happen, can you? You can't stop imagining all sorts of scenarios about what might have been in the past or what might happen in the future. At least, it's not easy to stop imagining."

"No. It isn't easy. And imagining isn't always a bad thing." Frieda handed the check back to the hovering waitress. "Well, if we're done here we should move on. There are the stores on Exchange Street to check out and that gelato place on Fore Street is calling my name."

Bella leaped to her feet and adjusted her cross-body bag. "About that money I haven't been spending this summer," she said. "I think that might be about to change."

Frieda laughed. "Don't even tell me how much you have with you!"

# Chapter 65

Bella frowned at her phone. Clara was calling her. A third ring, then a fourth. At the tenth ring the call would go to voice mail. There was still time to decide.

The other day at Andie's Wharf her mother had asked what she found interesting about Clara. Bella hadn't been able to tell her the truth, that Clara had nothing to offer her and that the only reason she kept spending time with Clara was out of a sense of duty. She wasn't sure that her mother—or her grandmother for that matter—would agree that she was doing the right thing. Still, there was no reason she couldn't try to be helpful to someone so clearly in need of help.

Bella answered the call. "Hi," she said.

"Hey," Clara said brightly. "What took you so long to answer? It doesn't matter. I was thinking we should go to the beach. We can work on our tans. I've never been so pale in August!"

Clara sounded clearheaded, Bella thought; maybe she hadn't taken any drugs that morning and surely she wouldn't be crazy enough to walk around high in public, especially in a place crowded with little kids.

"Sure," she said. "How about I come by the cottage around one?"

"Great. We'll take my car and stop for steamers after. I love steamers, don't you?"

People addicted to drugs usually didn't want to eat. Clara's interest in food might be a good sign. Personally, Bella thought steamers were gross, but if Clara wanted to order them, fine. She would get a crab roll. She opened her mouth to respond, but Clara abruptly ended the call without waiting for Bella's reply.

A canvas beach bag slung over her shoulder, Bella rang the doorbell of the cottage, and almost immediately it was opened by one of Clara's housemates. "Sorry," she said, brushing past Bella. "I'm late for work."

Bella went inside and passed through the living room, scattered as usual with empty soda cans, water bottles, magazines, bathing suits, and damp towels. When she came to the small room at the back of the cottage she knocked on the closed door. "Clara?" she called. "It's Bella."

There was no reply and Bella leaned closer to the door. "Clara?" she called a bit more loudly. Slowly she opened the door and peered inside. There was enough natural light coming in through the small bare windows for Bella to see Clara sitting hunched on the edge of her unmade bed.

Bella closed the door behind her and switched on the lamp that stood on Clara's dresser. As she did so she noted no sign of the hypodermic needle that had been there the other day. She also noted that Clara looked awful. Her hair was obviously unwashed. Her eyes were red and swollen and she was still in the T-shirt and sweats Bella knew she slept in.

"What's wrong?" Bella asked gently. "Why aren't you dressed? What happened?"

Clara wiped her eyes with the back of her hand. "Look," she said, holding out her phone. Bella took it and read the message on the screen.

*Marc is seeing someone in CA. Thought u should know.* "Who sent this?" Bella asked. "How do you know this is true?"

"A girl from back home sent it. Her brother is Marc's best friend. She's not lying."

"Maybe not," Bella said, "but she didn't have to tell you that Marc is seeing someone and not in this way! That was cruel."

Clara shrugged and put out her hand for the phone.

"Delete the message," Bella instructed. "Stop rereading it. You're only torturing yourself."

Clara clutched the phone but made no effort to delete the message.

"You . . ." Bella hesitated. She didn't want to make an obviously bad situation worse, but she had to know. "Did you take anything today?" she asked. "Any drugs?"

Clara's reply was spoken very softly. "No."

Bella wasn't sure she believed her, but she probably couldn't prove that Clara was lying. "Good," she said. "You're vulnerable right now. You don't need—"

"Wait," Clara interrupted. Suddenly she sat up straight and her eyes took on a look of determination. "I've lost the only guy I'll ever love," she went on fervently. "You've lost your father and your sister. What do we have to live for? I can't believe I didn't think of this before. Let's make a suicide pact. We'll do it together, end all the pain. We'll make them all feel like shits. They'll know they hurt us and that it's all their fault!"

Bella automatically took several steps backward. She was appalled. She hadn't seen this coming, not at all. Drugs were bad enough, but suicide? And she didn't want to punish anyone! "Are you crazy?" she cried, not caring if Clara's housemates heard her. "I don't want to kill myself! And neither do you!"

"Yes," Clara insisted, leaning forward. "I do. I'm tired of being alive. I'm tired of being in pain."

Bella fought the urge to run. She could simply leave the cottage and disappear from Clara's life. People did it all the time. There was even a name for it on social media. Ghosting. Cutting someone out of your life simply by ignoring her. But that was a cruel thing. It was something Ariel would never do. *No,* Bella decided. *I'll stay.* She would do what she could do, even if it was very little.

Bella knelt by Clara and reached for her hands. "Look at me, Clara," she commanded, holding her hands tightly. "Look at me."

Clara did look but only for a second before lowering her eyes.

"Life is precious, Clara. Don't throw it away! You only get one chance here, only one chance to watch a beautiful sunset and listen to your favorite music and eat your favorite foods and pet a cute dog and maybe even have a baby someday. One chance!"

Clara sighed and slipped her hands from Bella's. "I don't care about any of those things, not anymore," she said, sounding weary once again. "Not without Marc."

"Look," Bella went on, "I know it doesn't feel like you have anything to live for right now because you're hurt and you're sad. But time changes things. You won't always feel as bad as you feel right now; I promise. All sorts of good things might happen and a lot of them will happen. You just have to believe that."

Bella had no idea if Clara was really hearing what she was saying, but she had to go on. "I know what loss is," she said urgently. "But I also know that it's so much better to be alive than dead. Life is so much better than oblivion."

Clara suddenly laughed wildly, causing Bella to flinch. "Don't tell me you actually believe that crap!" she cried.

"Yes," Bella replied fiercely. "I do, and it's not crap. Maybe I didn't believe it for a while, but I do now. I don't want to die, ever, but I know that someday I *am* going to die so I want to make every single day I have count. I want to *live*."

Clara was quiet for a long moment and Bella hoped it was because she was seriously thinking about what she had just heard. "Do you really believe that good things might happen for you?" Clara asked then, almost in a whisper. "That good things might happen for me?"

"Yes," Bella repeated. "I absolutely believe that one hundred percent."

Clara turned away. "All right," she said quietly. "I won't kill myself."

"Swear it, Clara," Bella demanded. "Look at me and swear it."

Slowly Clara turned back, and Bella saw a great weariness in her eyes. "I swear," she said. "Really."

Bella believed her. She had to believe her. "Let's go to the beach like we planned. You shouldn't be driving right now, so we'll walk. It's not far and the sun and fresh air will do you good."

Clara shook her head. "No. I want to stay here," she said.

To do drugs? To think dark thoughts? To indulge again in a fantasy of ending her own life? "Then I'll stay with you for a while," Bella said.

"No. I want to be alone. I'll be fine."

Bella sighed. "Look," she said, "at least take a hot shower and put on some clean clothes. You'll feel better. Okay?"

Clara nodded. "Yeah. Okay."

"And you need to eat something. I could make you a sandwich before I go. I'm sure there's something in the fridge. Everybody has peanut butter and jelly."

"No," Clara said with a small smile. "That's okay. I'll get something myself."

"All right. Look, call me later if . . . If you need to talk."

Bella hesitated another moment and then left the room. She didn't close the door entirely. Maybe one of Clara's housemates would be moved to check on her. But Bella knew that wasn't likely. Clara hadn't exactly endeared herself to the other girls.

Bella walked through the living room, down the broken steps, and out onto the front lawn. Suddenly she felt exhausted, more exhausted than she had ever felt in her life. She had never experienced a conversation like the one she had just had with Clara, if it could be called a conversation and not an encounter with naked despair. Before getting on her bike she walked over to the big pine tree at the edge of the yard, dropped her canvas bag to the ground, and sank down against the tree's trunk. The branches provided a degree of shade and, more important, a sense of safety, something Bella realized she very much needed at the moment.

She wondered what Ariel would do in this situation, faced with a friend who wanted to take her own life. She was sure that Ariel would have seen long before now what Bella hadn't seen, that Clara needed help and not from another teen but from a professional. But Bella still felt she owed Clara a degree of personal responsibility. *And what about Clara's responsibility for me?* she thought. *Clara wanted me to commit suicide. How could she possibly care one bit for me if she wanted me to die?* Bella felt a surge of anger. To try to persuade someone you called a friend to end her life just so you wouldn't be alone when you ended yours was the most unbelievably selfish act, the most outrageously awful suggestion, Bella could imagine. Yeah, it was probably unfair to be angry with someone so obviously unwell. But how could she not be?

It was some time before Bella got to her feet, picked up her bag, retrieved her bike, and rode back to the house she was very happy to call home—and to the people who truly cherished her. The people she never, ever wanted to hurt.

# Chapter 66

Frieda had brought a book outside with her—one of the Agatha Raisin stories by M. C. Beaton—but at the moment her attention was entirely focused on the neighbor's cat Stanley, who was making his way stealthily across her mother's backyard. Stanley was a distinctive fellow. His ears were enormous, massive furry white triangles set atop a white head far too small for them. His nose was the feline equivalent of a classic Roman nose, with a sort of majestic bump to it normally not found in a domestic breed, and all four paws were black, as was the tip of his tail. The sight of Stanley slinking along, stalking real or imaginary prey, always made Frieda smile. As long as she didn't have to witness the actual kill.

When Stanley was out of sight behind the azalea bushes at the far end of the yard, Frieda opened her book, but she found her mind wandering to the lovely day she and Bella had shared in Portland. A degree of real reunion had been accomplished. Real communication had taken place. And Frieda fervently hoped that she wouldn't damage that rapprochement by reintroducing what had been such a sore topic for Bella.

It had been several weeks since Frieda had broken things off with Jack, and since then she had had a lot of time to think about her future. And what she had come to accept was that she simply did not want to be alone going forward. She loved the idea of marriage as well as the daily practice of it; marriage had nurtured her and she had flourished within its bounds. A solitary life was a good and valid choice for some—it had been for Ruby for a very long time and it was for Phil as well—but not for Frieda. She had come to realize there was no shame in needing another person. She didn't have to prove to anyone—not even to herself—that she was tough enough to stand on her own. If a solitary life were forced upon her she would accept that life. But she probably wouldn't like it very much.

"Hey, Mom."

Frieda smiled. Bella had come into the backyard from around the side of the house.

"Hi. I thought you were going to the beach this afternoon."

Bella shrugged and sank into the chair next to Frieda's. "Clara had to go into work at the last minute and I didn't feel like going on my own, so I came home. I figured you might be here and we could hang out."

Frieda reached for her daughter's hand and gave it a squeeze. "I'm sorry you missed out on the beach, but I'm glad you're here."

"It's so peaceful at Grandma's," Bella said with a sigh. "It's like a sanctuary or something. I'm glad we have this house we can come to. I feel like nothing bad can happen to us here, that all negative stuff from the outside world gets stopped at the door. I know that can't really be true, but that's how being here makes me feel."

"I feel that way, too," Frieda said. "Grateful for the security Grandma's house offers us." Frieda looked more closely at her daughter. "Did anything in particular bring on those observations?" she asked.

"No," Bella said.

Frieda wasn't entirely convinced, but she didn't push for a more honest answer. "You just missed Stanley on the prowl."

Bella smiled. "He must be twelve or thirteen by now. Did he catch anything?"

Frieda shuddered. "No, thankfully. I love Stanley, but I hate watching him toy with a poor little mouse or chipmunk."

"Mother Nature isn't pretty. That's what Grandma always says."

"And she's right." Frieda considered. Now might be as good a time as any to broach the topic of the future. At least she could sound the waters. "Bella," she said. "I've been doing some serious thinking in the past few weeks."

"Yeah." Bella laughed. "Me, too. I feel like I've done more thinking this summer than I have in my whole life."

Frieda nodded. "I know exactly what you mean. Bella, I'm sure you're aware that I haven't been spending time with my old friend Jack."

"Yeah," Bella said, shifting in her chair. "I figured . . . I mean, yeah."

"Well," Frieda went on. "I've been thinking that I would like to see him again. I would like to get to know him. I would like to see if we might actually be friends. Assuming, of course, that's what Jack wants, too, and I have no idea if he does. I'm afraid I didn't handle things quite as well as I might have when I told him I couldn't see him any longer."

Bella didn't reply immediately. Finally, looking out over the yard, she asked, "Did you tell him why you couldn't see him?"

"I told him that it wasn't a good thing for you and me." It was a slight manipulation of the truth but one Frieda thought justified.

"Oh."

"How do you feel about this, Bella?" Frieda asked, watching her daughter's profile closely. "I want us to be clear with each other."

Bella turned to look at her mother. "I guess it's okay," she said. "What I mean is, I know you don't have to have my permission to do what you want to do."

"No," Frieda agreed, "but I'd like your support."

"I just wish . . . I just wish you'd been more honest with me before. Like maybe brought him around or something."

"I should have been more honest," Frieda said. "You're absolutely right. It was another mistake in judgment."

"I guess I never thought that . . ." Bella shook her head. "I never thought that things would change again. That it might not always be just you and me. I don't know why. I know that life is always changing, even when you don't want it to."

Frieda sighed. "Oh, Bella. If only life were simple and stationary, but it never was and it never will be. That's the supposed glory of it. Let me tell you something. After Tony died and my father left us Grandma became even closer to Phil than she had been. They became virtually inseparable. At one point I thought about what it would be like if they got married. I know, Phil is gay, but I thought about it all the same. And as much as I loved Phil and considered him a friend, the thought of it not being just my mother and me frightened me. I didn't want anyone else in our little world, not even someone as wonderful as Phil."

"Yeah." Bella nodded. "I can totally understand that."

Frieda reached for her daughter's hand again. "We're sacred, the two of us, Bella," she said. "Don't ever worry that it won't always be you and me even if one or both of us get married at some point. I mean no disrespect to our other meaningful relationships, now or to come. I just mean that *our* relationship can't be violated. Our love for each other is a constant."

Bella nodded. "It's like you said the other day. Love never fundamentally changes. I thought about that. You might be angry or upset with someone you love, but that doesn't mean you don't *love* him."

"And I love you, Bella, with all my heart," Frieda promised. "I would never, ever do anything to hurt you. Please believe that. And I truly don't believe that my trying to be happy again *will* hurt you. All new things feel strange at first, but it doesn't necessarily mean they're bad."

"I know, Mom." Bella smiled. "This is so weird. I never thought I'd be talking to my mother about her dating. I always assumed you and Dad would grow old together and that someday Ariel and I would be giving you guys a fiftieth-anniversary party at some nice restaurant where everybody would make a speech about how great it was that two people had been married for so long. But now . . ."

"I thought so, too," Frieda said. "That your dad and I would celebrate anniversary after anniversary . . ." Frieda realized that she couldn't go on.

"I'm sorry I tried to keep you and Jack apart, Mom."

"There's no need to apologize," Frieda assured her, wiping a tear from her cheek. "Just promise me you won't make any more threats to do something scary and unspecified. My mind was coming up with all sorts of horrid scenarios. Remember what we were saying the other day at lunch about how hard it is not to imagine?"

Bella laughed embarrassedly. "I can't believe I made a threat like that. It was ridiculous. I would never do anything . . . anything stupid. You have to believe me. I could swear on a Bible or something, like they do in court."

"There's no need for a Bible, and anyway, it's in the past. Besides," Frieda admitted, "it wasn't entirely because of your discomfort that I told Jack I couldn't spend time with him. I was feeling as if I were betraying your father by even thinking about another man. But I've had some heart-to-heart talks with your grandmother and with Phil. They've been encouraging me to respect life by embracing it."

"Funny," Bella said. "I was just saying . . . I mean, I was just thinking the same thing. That life is pretty awesome, so you should enjoy it while you can. But not everyone agrees that life is worth living. I guess you can't judge them because you don't really know what's going on inside their head and their heart. Still . . . Still you wish you could convince them otherwise."

"Yes," Frieda agreed. "You can't judge, but you can try to help. So, assuming that Jack wants to see me again, I'd like you to meet him as soon as possible."

"Good. Mom? Is Jack like Dad? I mean, does he remind you of Dad?"

"No, he doesn't remind me of your father in any specific ways. But that's not to say I don't find myself comparing and contrasting the two on occasion. I know it's normal, but it's not necessarily healthy, not if you don't pretty quickly accept the fact that no person replicates another." Frieda smiled. "I feel as if I'm not making a lot of sense."

"I think I know what you mean," Bella told her. "Still, does he have some of Dad's good qualities, like is he honorable and hardworking? Does he respect women, I mean really respect them? Not like those guys who say women are equal and then turn around and make sick jokes about their bodies or something."

"Yes," Frieda said. "I can absolutely assure you that Jack is a good man. Phil agrees, and you know how tough he can be about a person's character. And I have your grandmother's word for Jack's being honorable. Remember, Grandma was a friend of Jack's wife. She was a witness to their relationship in good times as well as when Veronica got sick."

"Okay," Bella said. "So, when are you going to call him?"

"Soon. Wish me luck?"

"I wish you luck, Mom. Honestly. Um, Mom?"

"What is it?" Frieda asked.

"Don't look to your left," Bella directed. "Seriously, don't look. Stanley's back and he's got something brown and furry in his mouth."

# Chapter 67

Frieda got to the café a few minutes before the time she and Jack had agreed to meet. She ordered an iced drink and took it to a counter along one wall where she gave herself a little pep talk while she waited.

If a romantic relationship between her and Jack was to develop it would not be one born of a "there he is!" moment as her relationship with Aaron had been, but it would be valid nonetheless. Relationships came about in all sorts of ways. What was really important was mutual love, affection, and respect, as well as mutual intention. Frieda clearly recalled what Jack had told her the evening they had gone to the beach with a picnic. He said he liked being in love; he said he liked being a husband. Well, Frieda thought, she liked being in love, too, and she liked being a wife. Surely that counted as mutual intention?

The door to the café opened and Jack walked inside. He was wearing his ubiquitous aviators. Frieda felt her heart race as he came over to her.

"Thanks for agreeing to meet me," Frieda said. "I wouldn't have blamed you if you said no."

"There was no chance of my saying no, Frieda," Jack said. He removed his sunglasses and smiled. "I like you. I've liked you since we were kids and you used to wear those braids looped up on either side of your head, like some old-time Bavarian milk-maid."

Frieda laughed. "I can't imagine why I wanted to wear my hair like that! And I can't believe you remember it."

"You stood out from the other girls, and not only because of the braids. Look, let me grab a coffee. I'll be right back."

Frieda watched him order his drink from the unsmiling heavily tattooed barista. Her heart was still racing but now with hope. When Jack rejoined her she smiled. "Since when did coffee become so serious?" she asked.

Jack took a seat on the stool next to hers. "It must have happened when I wasn't looking. So, what is it you wanted to talk about?"

"Us," Frieda said. "I wanted to say that I would like to spend time with you again."

Jack nodded. "Right to the point. I like that. And I would like to spend time with you again, too."

"Even after how badly I acted when we last spoke? Jack, I'm so sorry for what I said about your not knowing what it was like to be a parent. A person can understand other lives; of course he can. It's called sympathy and empathy. It's called imagination."

"You were scared," Jack said. "None of us act perfectly when we're scared. Forget about that conversation, Frieda. It's over."

"Still, I'm sorry for running away, which is exactly what I did. I used Bella's discomfort as an excuse to act on my own discomfort. It wasn't only Bella who felt I was betraying Aaron by getting to know you."

"Understood. And perfectly normal." Jack took a sip of his coffee. "Hmmm," he said. "Nice but not worth the four bucks. Look, have you talked to Bella about our—how should I put it?" Jack smiled. "About our picking up where we left off?"

"Yes," Frieda told him after taking a sip of her own coffee. "She said she was sorry she had tried to keep us apart and I believe her. We've spent some quality time together in the past few weeks and I think she'll be okay from now on with my attempting to rebuild my life. There will be bumps in the road, but that's to be expected."

"Time helps," Jack pointed out. "It's not a magic bullet, but as time passes we get used to the new normal. And I think that habit counts for a lot of living successfully, and by 'successfully' I mean moving purposefully through each day and on to the next with some degree of hope and satisfaction."

*Living successfully,* Frieda thought. *It's something I very much want to do.* "I need to be entirely honest with you before one more minute goes by," she said. "I want you to know what you're in for with me."

"Then tell me," Jack said quietly.

"You've had so much more time to get past the shock of Veronica's dying than I've had to get past the shock of Aaron's dying. Sometimes I feel as if he died just last week. Jack, I'm worried that if we go forward now I'll wind up disappointing you or hurting you again."

"I'll decide what I can and cannot handle," Jack said firmly. "And you'll decide what you can and cannot handle. One step at a time."

"Are you sure?" Frieda asked. "Really sure?"

"Yes, I'm really sure. Don't try to do my thinking for me, Frieda," Jack told her. "Assumption is a dishonest practice. It allows a person to find just the excuse he needs not to face the future or take a risk."

"I never really thought of it that way," Frieda admitted, "but you're right. When you assume someone is going to react a certain way you cheat him out of his freedom to surprise you."

"Shake on our renewed friendship?"

Frieda laughed and gave Jack her hand.

"Good. Now, I'd like to finally meet Bella."

"And she wants to meet you," Frieda assured him. "You know, Bella was always such a positive person until the accident flattened her spirit. But I think I see some of her old spirit coming back. I hope I'm not wrong about that."

"I doubt that you are," Jack told her. "You're her mother. Who knows her better?"

Frieda smiled. "Should we plan dinner at The Razor Clam?" she suggested.

"Why not? All human interaction proceeds more smoothly when food is involved. Plus," Jack added, "the coffee there is way less expensive."

# Chapter 68

Bella, her mother, her grandmother, and George were gathered at the kitchen table. Though Bella was psyched for the big reveal, she couldn't quite get thoughts of Clara out of her head. *I just want to enjoy this moment,* she thought, *without worrying about what crazy or frightening thing Clara is going to say or do next.*

"Okay," Ruby Hitchens announced, popping the lid off the plastic container in which she had stored their latest attempt at homemade ice cream. "This is the big moment. Ready?"

George drew himself up. "As I'll ever be." He scooped some of the ice cream into his bowl and with a dramatic gesture he put a large spoonful into his mouth.

"Well?" Bella asked. "What do you think?"

"Don't keep us in suspense, George," her mother said.

George swallowed and sighed. "Perfect. You guys did it."

"Success at last!" her grandmother cried. "Or maybe just a bit of luck."

Bella laughed. "It wasn't luck. It was my taking charge!"

"Pride goeth before a fall, Bella," her mother teased.

"So," George asked Bella, spooning out bowls for the others, "was it worth all the effort?"

"Absolutely. But I'm not giving up on Ben and Jerry's just yet."

"Come on," her mother said with a laugh. "This is way better than anything you can buy in a store. What flavor should we make next?"

"Maple walnut," George suggested. "Just saying."

"That might be a bit of a challenge, but you know how I like a challenge. Frieda, Bella, are you in?"

"Yup," Bella said. "We'll nail it."

Frieda nodded. "Consider it done, George."

Ding ding!

Bella's heart began to race. She quickly turned away from the others and pulled her phone from her pocket, half expecting a desperate cry for help. Half dreading . . .

"Who is it?" her grandmother asked.

Bella read the message on the screen and sighed with relief. "No one," she said, turning back. "Just Verizon wanting me to upgrade my service or something."

"Good. I mean, for a moment there you looked like you were going to faint."

"I'm all right, Grandma," Bella said, stuffing her phone back into her pocket. "I'm fine. Really."

Later, when the others had gone out to the front porch to enjoy the sunset, Bella set out to visit the spring Ariel had so loved. She walked along Kinders Lane and then turned onto Grove Hill Lane until she reached the Jernigans' property. It was a beautiful evening. The sky was various shades of deepening blue. The air felt soft. That Clara—that anyone—could choose to leave all this loveliness behind . . . There were so many simple pleasures in life, like eating ice cream you had made yourself and watching delicate butterflies flitting around colorful flowers and finding an awesome pair of earrings on sale and holding a cuddly baby and hearing a really cool band perform live and watching your favorite movie for the thousandth time. How could anyone want to leave all that good stuff voluntarily?

But depression was real and it could lead people to take desperate measures. But Bella didn't know if depression was what was going on with Clara. One thing she did know. No matter how seriously depressed she had been after the accident, she had never wanted anyone else to come to harm. Sure, at Phil's Independence Day party she had felt resentful of the other guests' joy, but she hadn't demanded they stop having fun. Still, Bella had realized with a pang of shame that the "misery loves company" experience was a pale version of Clara's wanting a companion in suicide. To resent the happiness of others, to presume they were or should be as miserable as you were, was simply not right. It was probably a feeling or a state of mind all human beings experienced, but it definitely wasn't something that should be indulged.

And Clara had indulged her need for others to suffer as she was suffering. An argument could easily be made for Bella's walking away from Clara entirely and for good, but . . .

Bella breathed a sigh of relief as the spring came into view. Immediately a sense of calm descended upon her and she shivered in the pleasant coolness that always seemed to permeate the air around the spring. She thought of Ariel saying how people in ancient times believed the water of sacred springs could cure illnesses; sometimes people made offerings to appease the god or the spirit associated with the water. It was a superstitious practice, but . . . *Why not?* Bella thought. She scanned the grass-covered ground for something she could offer and her eye caught sight of a gleaming white pebble, almost perfectly round. It was pretty enough to wear on a chain around your neck.

Bella crouched by the spring and let the pebble drop into the gently gurgling water. "To the spirit of the spring," she whispered. "This is a gift for you. Look over my sister, Ariel, please. And if you can, look over my friend Clara, too."

What she had just done might result in nothing tangible at all, but Bella felt no embarrassment or remorse. In fact, offering the pebble to the spirit of the spring could probably be seen as an act of prayer. And people who knew about such things said that prayer never hurt anyone. Bella got to her feet and turned in the direction of home, where her loved ones were waiting.

# Chapter 69

Sitting in a rocking chair on the shaded front porch of your home on a beautiful summer day, all alone and reading a book by one of your favorite writers, was as close to heaven as one might hope to get on this earth. Close, Ruby thought, but not for long, for there was Frieda's car turning onto Kinders Lane and, a few moments later, pulling into the driveway.

"What, ho, Frieda!" she called.

"Watching British television again?" Frieda asked as she climbed the porch steps and dropped into the chair next to Ruby.

"No." Ruby indicated the book on her lap. "Rereading some P. G. Wodehouse. Where were you just now?"

"With Jack. There's an exhibit of old local maps at the historical society in Wells. It's a lovely old building. I'd never been inside it before; can you imagine?"

Ruby looked closely at her daughter. "You look like you've got something on your mind other than old maps."

Frieda smiled. "There's never any use in trying to hide things from your mother. I don't know why I even try. It's just that now Jack and I are spending time together again I'm a bit worried I'll start using him as a crutch. How can I tell if I'm really falling in love or if I'm just grateful to have someone I can depend on to 'fix' things like Aaron used to?"

"Might I point out," Ruby said, "that you and Aaron were a team? You were partners. You 'fixed' things for him, too."

"But that was then," Frieda argued. "Things are different now."

Ruby nodded. "I know."

"Right before I asked Jack if he was interested in resuming our friendship I told myself that I didn't have to prove to anyone that I was tough enough to stand on my own. I told myself that wanting a marriage was not a sign of weakness."

"And it's not," Ruby said. "It can be a sign of maturity." *So what does that say about me?* she added silently. *Running from it like it's the plague.*

"I know, but what if I'm latching onto Jack out of fear or cowardice?"

"You won't."

"Won't I?" Frieda shook her head. "This morning when I was driving to the store I noticed that the air-conditioning wasn't working. I called Jack to ask if he could recommend a good mechanic and he immediately volunteered to take my car to his mechanic tomorrow afternoon. It's been so long since I've heard the words 'let me take care of it' I'm afraid I was seduced. Why didn't I just ask you or Phil or George for the name of your mechanics? Why did I turn to Jack?"

Ruby patted her daughter's hand. "At the risk of sounding as if I'm dismissing your concerns, I think you might be making too big a thing out of this."

"Am I? The last thing I want is to find myself using Jack as a handy escape from having to be on my own. Being on your own takes serious courage. You know that better than most. I'm just not sure I have it in me to carry the weight of my days all alone. But that doubt isn't a good enough excuse for orchestrating a marriage."

"First of all," Ruby said, "you're right. It's not. Second of all, you're so much stronger than you realize, Frieda. And I'm not talking about superhuman strength and courage, the stuff of a Marvel comic character. I'm talking about the really heroic stuff, the day-to-day chores and duties and responsibilities that keep life livable. Answer me honestly. Do you keep a comfortable home for Bella?"

"Yes," Frieda said promptly. "If by 'comfortable' you mean I make sure that we keep to a regular schedule and that I don't allow random strangers into the house, I do."

"Good. Do you cook healthy meals and clean the bathroom on a regular basis? Do you pay the bills in a timely manner and save or invest what money is left over?"

"Yes to all of that."

"And what else?" Ruby asked. "Brag a little."

"Well, I've taken steps to upgrade my professional skills. I took a refresher course in copyediting technical documents and one in writing marketing copy for fifteen- to twenty-five-year-olds. There's been no appreciable payoff yet," Frieda added, "but there might be."

"Good," Ruby said. "And?"

"I've consciously worked on the healing practices my grief counselor advised," Frieda said. "I haven't always gotten the results I hoped for, but I do try."

"That's the point, Frieda. You try. You don't sit around moaning and wringing your hands. Which is not to say that a tiny bit of moaning and hand-wringing is always a bad thing. But it should never occupy too much of your time."

"I know, Mom. It's just that living on your own takes a special kind of courage. When Bella leaves home, which she probably will not long from now, I wonder if I'll be able to face yet another reduced reality."

"Not reduced," Ruby corrected. "Don't think in those terms. It will be a different reality. It will be a challenge. You'll make changes. You'll adopt a dog or a cat or even a bird. Animals make excellent companions, sometimes better companions than human beings. You'll find a hobby or take courses at the local college. You'll travel. You'll survive. Besides, maybe by the time Bella leaves the nest you won't be walking through the world without a partner. Anything is possible, Frieda. Never forget that."

*Something I should keep in mind,* Ruby added silently. *Like the possibility that if George and I marry we'll live happily ever after and I'll never have to endure the horrors of another divorce.*

"I'll try. Mom, you knew Veronica Tennant pretty well, right?"

"I guess you could say that. She was a regular member of The

Page Turners, as you know. When she was hospitalized I used to visit her every day." Ruby smiled. "One year we manned the apple-bobbing booth together at the Harvest Festival. We wound up soaking wet, but we had a lot of fun."

"So what was she like? I want to know what sort of person Jack fell in love with and married."

"You can't compare yourself to Veronica," Ruby warned, "just like you can't compare Jack to Aaron. Well, you can, but you shouldn't."

"I know, but still . . ."

Ruby shrugged. "All right. Veronica was able to find humor in almost every situation, even when she was ill. She loved to read. Seriously, she put the rest of The Page Turners to shame. And she really did love teaching. It was terrible for her when she finally had to give it up entirely. Jack might have told you this already, but Veronica badly wanted a child. She would have made a fine mother."

Frieda smiled. "She sounds like a hard act to follow."

"You're up to it."

"That's so something a loving mother says to her child," Frieda pointed out. "In short, not necessarily the brutal truth."

"You know I'm a terrible liar," Ruby pointed out. "Do I sound as if I'm lying now?"

"No," Frieda admitted. "So you'd be okay if something develops between Jack and me? You loved Aaron so much."

Ruby smiled at her daughter. "It's your life, Frieda. You don't need my permission or approval to live it. That said, yes, I did love Aaron; I still do. But I very much like what I know of Jack. He was wonderful to Veronica until the bitter end. Few men could have done better. He wasn't afraid of the down and dirty chores that need to be done for a dying person, and that beats cards and flowers any day." *Jack was just like Steve was at Tony's end*, Ruby thought. *A godsend.*

"That's so true," Frieda said. "It's the small, personal gestures that count most of all. Like what a mother routinely does for her child. Thank you, Mom, for everything. For the yummy meals and the sound advice. For providing me with an education. For making me laugh. I don't say thank you often enough."

"Yes, you do," Ruby corrected. "Your wanting to be here with me this summer proves more than words could ever prove that you love and respect me, as I do you."

Frieda got up from her chair, leaned down, and kissed Ruby's cheek. "Well," she said, "it's back to work for me. Thanks for the pep talk, Mom."

When Frieda had gone inside Ruby returned to her book—but not before thanking whoever or whatever was out there for the gift of her daughter.

*The ceiling fan could use a little adjustment*, Ruby thought as she lay on her bed, half mesmerized by its creaky motion. But only half mesmerized. She was wondering if Frieda realized how much she looked like her father. The same wide-set eyes. The same high cheekbones. The same generous mouth. The similarities had been pointed out to Frieda as a child, but maybe she had chosen to forget or to ignore her resemblance to Steve Hitchens.

Ruby sighed and crossed her hands on her stomach. This summer memories of life with her former husband were rarely far off. If only she weren't reminded of the bad times as well as the good, like the day only weeks before Steve's defection when Phil had confronted her with his suspicions. "I think Steve's going to run, Ruby," Phil had said. "It's something I see in his eyes. Call me crazy, and I hope that I am, but . . ."

So Ruby had called him crazy, and wrong. Phil's suspicions were not something she had been prepared to hear, in spite of the fact that she was harboring her own worries. In some ways her marriage hadn't been solid from the start, but the summer Frieda was eleven things had taken a turn for the worse. Steve had become withdrawn and moody; there were nights he didn't come home for dinner and when pressed for a reason he would reply angrily. "You're not my keeper, Ruby," he would say. "I have my own life!" And the other women. There were always the other women.

Later, when Steve had been gone close to a month, Ruby had apologized to Phil for having in effect shot the messenger. "Thank you," she had added, "for having the grace not to say, 'I told you so.'"

"Believe me," Phil had said. "I take no pleasure in being right. None whatsoever."

"At least he didn't leave in the middle of the night with only a note to explain his absence. At least he had the guts to face me before he left."

"With some nonsensical reason for abandoning his family."

"It wasn't nonsensical, not to him," Ruby had argued. "I know Steve, Phil. At least I know him now."

That night . . . That dreadful night when Steve walked away. Ruby remembered every detail, from the tan shirt Steve was wearing, to the small tear in the screen door that led from the kitchen into the minuscule backyard, to the sound of the old analog clock over the stove, ticking away the final minutes of her marriage.

"I can't do this anymore," Steve had said to her. "I should never have gotten married."

They were alone in the house; Steve had arranged a sleepover for Frieda at a friend's house. Now Ruby knew why.

"You should never have gotten married to me?" she demanded. "Is that what you're saying, that you don't love me, you've never loved me?"

"Oh, I love you, Ruby," Steve said. "That's what makes this so damn hard. I love you, but I made a big mistake by marrying you, by marrying anyone. I should have had the courage to walk away long before now, before I got myself into this mess. Before I got you into this mess." He had started to cry. "I'm so sorry, but I can't stay here. I just can't, not with you, not in Yorktide."

"How can you leave Frieda?" Ruby had demanded. "How can you do such a thing?"

Steve had put his hands over his face for a moment. When he lowered them the look of anguish on his face tore at Ruby's heart. "Where will you go?" she asked. "How will I get in touch with you?"

"I'll call you, Ruby," Steve said finally. And then he hoisted his duffel bag onto his shoulder and without another word he left.

And that was the last time Ruby had seen Steve Hitchens, the man she had loved and married, the man she had given a child.

It was weeks before Ruby received a call from him. He had not changed his mind. He was not coming back. He hoped Frieda was all right. Ruby filed for divorce and was granted sole custody of Frieda. Steve did not demand visitation rights. He dutifully sent child support payments, though they were seldom on time. Occasionally he sent a little extra in Frieda's birthday card, maybe a five-dollar bill, accompanied by a few scrawled lines. *Hope you and your mom are doing well. Can't believe you're another year older.* Generic sentiments, never anything more. It was as if Steve Hitchens had never been a part of their lives. It was as if he had never nursed his daughter through chicken pox or danced waltzes around the living room with his wife. It was as if he had never played The Tooth Fairy and slipped coins under Frieda's pillow. It was as if he had never looked Ruby in the eye and told her he loved her beyond what words could express.

Ruby got up from her bed, turned off the creaky ceiling fan, and left the room. For a very long time she had been angry with Steve for the love of which he had deprived their child. But, Ruby reminded herself as she went downstairs to the kitchen to start dinner, all of that was in the past, in spite of the memories playing like a film through her head.

Besides, Frieda might have been marked by the circumstances of her childhood—what adult hadn't been? But she hadn't been scarred. There was a difference.

# Chapter 70

On a scale of one to ten, Frieda's anxiety rated an eleven. Introducing her daughter to the man she was dating—if that's indeed what was going on with Jack—would be trying under any circumstances, but introducing them so soon after the truce she and Bella had established . . . *It's not a truce*, Frieda told herself as she took a blue linen blouse from her closet. *We were never at war, Bella and me. What we did was reconnect. And everything will be all right this evening. Everything will be fine.*

People were adaptable. Human beings learned how to accept new circumstances. They bounced back after the worst tragedies. Frieda stepped into her jeans. Tragedies like the loss of a parent.

Eleven-year-old Frieda had known in that uncanny way adolescent girls know truths about the adults around them that her father was unhappy. His behavior had been odd for months. He would come home late for dinner, without a reason or an apology. He would sit in the living room staring into space. He would make excuses for not joining his family when they socialized with Phil or the neighbors.

Frieda remembered how she had tried to put a smile on her father's face in those final weeks. She had hugged him whenever he came into a room; she had made him a friendship bracelet using bright green and blue string (his favorite colors); she had baked him his favorite oatmeal cookies. But her father had been too distracted to appreciate her efforts, assuming they had even registered with him.

She would never forget the moment her mother broke the news of her father's defection. Frieda had had so much fun at Barbara's; they had eaten pepperoni pizza for dinner and stayed up late watching an old black-and-white version of *Dracula* and Barbara's mother had made them waffles for breakfast. Frieda had raced through the front door of her home the next morning, eager to tell her parents about how Mrs. Miller had let them put Reddi-wip on their waffles and about how she thought *Dracula* wasn't scary at all.

Frieda had found her mother in the kitchen. Her eyes were red and a bunch of crumpled soggy tissues were on the table before her. Frieda remembered her mother trying to explain the inexplicable. Even now, at the distance of all these years, Frieda could almost feel the deep bewilderment she had felt at that moment. "But why did he leave?" she had asked her mother. "I don't understand. Doesn't he love us anymore?"

"He does love us," her mother had told her, her voice hoarse from crying. "He just can't . . . He needed to go away. I wish I understood it better so that I could explain it to you in a way that might make sense. But I'm afraid that I don't."

The rest of that day had passed in a blur, and the day after that as well. Frieda remembered feeling nothing much but confusion; she remembered asking her mother question after question, some vague, some terribly specific. "Is everything going to be different now?" And: "There's a package of razors in the bathroom medicine cabinet. It was Daddy's. What do we do with it? Can we keep it for when he comes back?" And: "Can we live here anymore? Do we have to move now that Daddy's gone?" And: "Does Phil know where Daddy went? Can Phil go and find him?"

Then came the overwhelming feelings of guilt, the conviction that somehow she was to blame for her father's going away. And then came the shame in having been abandoned, the conviction that she hadn't been special enough to keep hold of her own father. Every morning she felt the mocking eyes of her classmates on her;

every time she and her mother were downtown she felt the pitying looks from the adults of Yorktide.

And then came the anger, anger first at her mother for having messed up their lives. "Why didn't you stop Daddy from going? Anyway, it's your fault Daddy left. You made him leave! You were always telling him to do stuff and bossing him around."

It was odd. Frieda could clearly remember so much of what had been said in those dark days, but she could not recall what her mother's reply to those accusations had been. Had she tried to defend herself? Had she scolded Frieda for being disrespectful? The answer was lost to time.

*Time*—Frieda checked her watch, hurried into the hall, and called for Bella. "Bella! Are you ready to go?"

Bella emerged from her room. "As I'll ever be," she said with a smile.

*Here goes nothing,* Frieda thought as she descended the stairs with Bella right behind her. And then she amended that to: *Aaron, help us, okay?*

Frieda steered the Subaru into the parking area of The Razor Clam. Her anxiety was still strong, but if Bella was nervous she was hiding it well. She had chatted all the way from the house about her day at Phil's shop and about the woman who had bought the chandelier Bella had taken such care to clean crystal by faceted crystal.

"Is that Jack?" Bella asked when Frieda turned off the engine. "Over by the fence?"

"Yes," Frieda said. "How did you know?"

Bella shrugged. "Good guess. Besides, he looks like he's waiting for someone."

Jack raised a hand in salute as Frieda and Bella joined him. "Hi," he said. "Bella, I'm Jack. It's good to meet you."

Frieda was glad Jack had taken the initiative to introduce himself. She realized she was tongue-tied.

"Hi," Bella said. "I think I've seen you around before."

Jack smiled. "You probably have. I've seen you, too. Small town after all. Nowhere to hide, supposing you wanted to."

Bella smiled back at him. "Sometimes living in a small town drives me nuts," she said. "But sometimes it's okay."

Finally, Frieda found her voice. "Let's order," she suggested.

The three walked to the shack-style restaurant and examined the menu printed on a board nailed by the order window. "I always get the fried clams," Jack said. "I mean, there are all these other things on the menu and yet every single time I come here I get the fried clams."

"Maybe you just know what you like," Bella said. "When we order pizza from this place back home I always get sausage and mushrooms. I know I'd probably like other stuff, too, but I'm definitely sure I'll like the sausage and mushrooms."

Jack nodded. "Yeah, I think that's it. Why take a risk? If you can count on something, count on it."

"But what if one time your favorite thing tastes bad for some reason?" Bella went on. "Like maybe the sausage is too chewy or the fried clams are too greasy. Then what do you do?"

"I don't know," Jack admitted. "I hadn't thought about it."

"I'd give it one more try. Or I'd stop going to that place and try the sausage and mushroom pizza at a new place."

Frieda smiled to herself. The conversation was less than stimulating, but she was very glad that Jack and Bella were talking. The topic simply didn't matter.

"Well, I'm going to try the mussels this time," she announced. "I think my goal should be to work my way through the entire menu before the summer is over."

"You'd better get cracking, Mom. This menu is huge. I'm going to have a crab roll and onion rings." Bella looked to Jack. "My mother loves onion rings."

Jack laughed. "I'm aware."

They placed their order and took a table on the expanse of green lawn overlooking the ocean. "The view here is awesome," Bella said. "I don't know why anyone who lives in Maine would ever want to go away for vacation. I mean, unless it was to some place totally different, like . . ." Bella smiled a bit. "I was going to say like Jamaica."

Frieda felt her stomach drop, but before she could say anything—what?—Jack spoke.

"Or the Arctic," he said promptly. "Or, I don't know, the jungles
of South America."

Bella laughed. "Yeah. Except I bet the Arctic isn't so different
from winters in Maine."

"I concede your point."

Two women passed by carrying trays piled high with boiled lobsters and corn on the cob. One of the women was wearing a T-shirt
on which were printed the words ARRESTED DEVELOPMENT.

"My wife used to like that show," Jack said, nodding toward the
woman. "She loved the Tobias Fünke character. I never really got
into it myself. I don't hate it or anything, but I usually found something else to do when she watched it."

"I like it, too," Bella said. "So does Ariel. So did Ariel. It was one of
the few shows we agreed on. Usually our taste in TV shows is completely different. Was completely different. It's hard to remember to
use the past tense."

"I think it's okay to use the present tense," Jack said. "I mean,
just because a person is dead doesn't mean she's different from
who she was when she was alive. Or something like that."

Bella laughed. "I'm always thinking about that sort of stuff."

Frieda refrained from adding her own thoughts. Bella and Jack
didn't seem to need her conversational assistance. It was enough if
she simply watched and listened.

"Number twenty-six please. Number twenty-six."

"That's us," Frieda said.

The three fetched their trays, returned to their table, and settled to their meals.

"So, you're going to be a senior this fall?" Jack asked.

Bella finished swallowing a bite of her crab roll. "Yeah."

"I remember senior year as being really fun," Jack said. "It
seemed there were always parties and barbeques and outings." He
shrugged. "Well, I was popular. Maybe it wasn't so much fun for
unpopular kids."

"I'm not really interested in the parties and stuff," Bella said; her tone, Frieda noted, was not belligerent or self-pitying. "I'm kind of worried about getting my grades up again. I let them slip last year. I have to think about getting some serious money from a decent college."

"Don't worry about the money," Frieda told her. "Just focus on the schoolwork."

"My wife was a teacher." Jack looked to Bella. "Maybe you knew that. She absolutely loved teaching. Even when she had a really difficult student or hundreds of papers to grade during exam week she didn't complain. Not many people are lucky enough to really love what they do."

Bella looked from her mother to Jack. "I'm sorry about your wife," she said. "I don't think I ever met her, but I know Grandma really liked her."

Jack nodded. "Thanks. And I'm sorry about your father and sister."

"Thanks. Here," Bella said, pushing the paper carton of onion rings to the middle of the table. "You guys can have some."

"Do you like working at Wainscoting and Windowseats?" Jack asked. "Here, have a French fry."

"Yeah," Bella said. "I mean, at first I thought it would be boring selling stuff like wallpaper and rolls of fabric, but I like it. Phil's great, so that helps."

"What is wainscoting, anyway?" Jack asked with a frown.

Bella laughed. "I had to ask Phil the same thing when I started. It's basically wood or some other material on the inside of a wall. Think about pictures you've seen of homes in Colonial times, with wood paneling halfway up the wall."

"I probably should have known that," Jack said. "Oh, well, the old brain isn't what it used to be."

"I think my grandmother's brain gets sharper as she gets older," Bella said. "At least, it seems that way to me."

"Maybe you've just gotten better at recognizing her intelligence. No insult to Ruby Braithwaite's brainpower," Jack added hastily.

"You might be right," Bella said after a moment. "What do you think, Mom?"

Frieda laughed. "Let's just say I've never felt I could go up against my mother in a battle of wits. Maybe it's all the reading she does."

"You do a lot of reading, too, Mom," Bella pointed out. Then she turned to Jack. "My sister was a huge reader. I like to read, but there are plenty of things I'd usually rather be doing."

"Like what?" Jack asked.

"Eating!"

Frieda felt as if her heart would burst with happiness. Even if nothing ever came of her relationship with Jack, this moment at The Razor Clam, the early-evening sun warm, the breeze cool, Bella devouring her crab roll and sharing her onion rings, Jack wolfing down his fried clams and sharing his French fries, would always stand in her memory as a success of the best sort.

"Anyone want a mussel?" she asked.

Bella frowned. "Gross."

Jack grimaced. "Ew."

Frieda smiled. "Good. All for me."

# Chapter 71

Bella steered her bike around a large puddle. And while she was paying attention to the road—especially after that close call not too long ago—she was also thinking about dinner at The Razor Clam the night before. Yeah, she had been a bit nervous—though not as nervous as her mother, who at one point had looked like she was going to faint—but the meeting had turned out okay. Jack hadn't been at all touchy-feely with her mother (something Bella had been dreading) and he had asked Bella questions as if she had a brain. She had been afraid he would be one of those guys who thought all teenaged girls were idiots or one of those creeps who were intimidated by women who were even half as smart as they were. But when her mother had corrected him when he said the fourth president of the United States was James Monroe and not James Madison he had been totally cool with it. He had even laughed at himself for not knowing such a basic fact of history, not that Bella had known it, either. Her father had been like that, not macho or boastful.

Bella turned onto Valley Road and cycled up to the cottage where Clara and her housemates were spending the summer. She had thought the cottage sort of charming when she first saw it, but now she realized it was pretty decrepit. It couldn't be good for a depressed person to live in a home with peeling paint, jammed windows, and a big tear in the shade of the living room window.

With a sigh Bella climbed the broken stairs. *I'm here for Clara's sake*, she thought as she rang the bell. When no one came to the door Bella tried the handle. The door was unlocked and she went inside. "Hello," she called. When no one answered she walked back to Clara's room. Her door stood half opened. "Clara," Bella said. "It's me."

She went into the room to find Clara lying on the bed among crumpled sheets. Her eyes were bloodshot. Even from across the room Bella could tell that Clara's breath was foul. Maybe it was the drugs that made her breath smell bad; all drugs, even ones that were good for you, could have weird side effects. Her hair was greasy and there was dirt under her fingernails, with which she was scratching her arm.

"Did you get bitten?" Bella asked. "I dodged a wasp this morning."

"No," Clara said dully. "I'm just itchy."

Or maybe, Bella thought, there were bugs in the room, bedbugs or carpet beetles or even fleas. "What have you been up to?" she asked. Maybe it was another silly question, but she didn't know what else to say.

Clara scratched at her other arm. "Hanging with my new friends," she said.

"What new friends?"

"You wouldn't know them. You probably wouldn't even like them."

*She's right*, Bella thought. *I probably wouldn't.* "Let's go do something, Clara," she said. "It's a beautiful day, and besides, it's boring always sitting around here."

"I'm tired." As if to prove it Clara yawned widely.

"Fresh air can really wake you up. We could take a walk. It's not too hot and there's a breeze."

Suddenly Clara sat up and leaned back on her hands. "I need money," she said. "Can you give me some money?"

"Why do you need money?" Bella was afraid that she knew the answer to this question, but she wanted to hear Clara's reply.

Clara snorted. "I just need it, okay? Don't be so nosy."

"I don't have any money," Bella said. It was not strictly the truth; she never left the house without a few dollars in cash. But the money was for emergencies. It was not for buying illegal substances. *Or for junk food after smoking dope,* she thought. *What an idiot I was.*

Clara's expression darkened. "Liar," she spit.

"I'm not a liar," Bella stated firmly. "And even if I did have money I wouldn't give it to you."

"I'd pay you back; I swear."

Bella shook her head. "No."

"Then give back that pill I gave you," Clara demanded, sitting up fully. "I know you didn't take it." She laughed nastily. "You wouldn't have the nerve."

"I flushed it down the toilet." *And it isn't a matter of nerve,* Bella thought. *It's a matter of self-respect.*

"No, you didn't!" Clara now rose to her feet and came toward Bella, her fists clenched. "I need that pill, Bella. I need to sell it."

Bella took a step back. She was afraid that Clara might hit her. And she wondered what Clara might do if she couldn't get the money she wanted. People did awful things for drugs, like sell themselves sexually. *No,* Bella thought, *not Clara.* Not when she claimed to be so in love with Marc. But drugs made people desperate. They made people strangers to themselves. All the experts said so. Still, Bella couldn't bring herself to hand over the few dollars in her bag. "I told you," she said, swallowing her fear, refusing to back farther away. "I flushed it down the toilet. And I have no money to give you."

Suddenly Clara seemed to lose interest. She turned, sank into the room's one chair, and leaned her head against its high back.

*What am I doing?* Bella thought, watching Clara as her eyes began to close. *I'm totally out of my depth. I should tell an adult what's going on, someone who can step in and . . .* But she felt so terribly embarrassed about her own drug use, which she would probably have to admit if she brought an adult into the situation. She remembered Colleen had told her that teens recovering from the loss of a parent only want to do what makes them feel better and most often that meant immature behavior like doing drugs or self-harming or overeating. And Bella was guilty of immature behavior, no doubt about that.

No. She didn't want to cause her mother or grandmother further worry. She would keep Clara's situation to herself, at least for now. At least until . . .

"Look, Clara," she said. "Maybe if you eat something you'll feel better."

Clara's eyes popped open for a moment. "I'm not hungry," she mumbled.

Bella sighed. "You've got to stop using heroin, Clara. And taking those pills and smoking pot. I know it won't be easy, but I can help you find treatment. There are all sorts of services out there. You won't be alone."

"Nothing wrong . . ." Clara's eyes closed again.

Bella opened her mouth to say something like *Call me if you need me*, but the words failed to come out. It probably didn't matter anyway. Clara had begun to snore. Bella shook her head and left the room. When she was almost to the front door of the cottage one of Clara's housemates emerged from the kitchen.

"Look," she said loudly. "I've seen you here before. You're Clara's friend, right?"

Bella genuinely didn't know how to reply.

"Well," the girl went on, "maybe you can get her to clean up her act. She's going to lose her job if she doesn't. She's missed two shifts this week and the boss isn't happy."

"I'm not sure . . . I'll see what I can do." Bella turned away and continued toward the door.

"And maybe you can also get her to fork over the money she owes me and the other girls. She hasn't put in her share of the grocery money for the past two weeks. And she's been using our personal stuff. She took my umbrella the other day and lost it."

Without turning around, Bella nodded and opened the front door of the cottage, grateful for the fresh air. More, she was grateful for the freedom.

# Chapter 72

Jack lived in a charming A-frame house at the very end of Addison Way. Frieda was pretty sure she had never been on Addison Way before. Funny, she thought as she rang the doorbell. You could almost always find something new in something otherwise so familiar. Yorktide, it seemed, still had its surprises.

Frieda had called Jack that morning to ask if she could stop by on her way to meet with the manager of a local community arts education center to discuss doing some promotional writing for them. She had a large jar of Ruby's famous homemade tomato sauce with his name on it.

Jack opened the door with a smile and invited her in. "Got to love a good homemade tomato sauce," he said, accepting Frieda's offering. "I'm not the world's greatest cook—okay, I'm one of the worst—but I appreciate good food. In spite of what I said earlier about Velveeta."

"Then you'll love this," Frieda promised him. "I don't know what Mom does to make it so delicious."

"I know you're on your way to a meeting, but can you stay for a cup of coffee?" Jack asked. "It will only take a few minutes to make."

Frieda nodded. "Sure, thanks."

"Feel free to wander around while I'm in the kitchen."

Jack went off to make the coffee and Frieda took him up on his suggestion. The living room, just off the front hall, was large and cozy. A fireplace with a stone surround was its dominant feature; two cushy armchairs were drawn up in front of it and Frieda couldn't help but imagine Jack and Veronica sitting there, having an after-dinner coffee. The image brought a smile to her face. She moved to the dining room, where there was a large Mission-style table, chairs, and breakfront. She wondered if Jack hosted dinner parties now that he was living on his own. Probably not, she thought. Not if he couldn't cook. She wondered if Veronica had enjoyed having their friends and family over for holiday meals, if she had carefully ironed linen napkins and chosen candles in colors that suggested the season, if she had brought the main course to the table with a flourish.

Beyond the dining room was a home office. Frieda was struck by the neatness of the one desk. Two tall bookcases held books of all sizes, CDs, DVDs, a few small watercolor paintings propped on wooden stands, and a sort of tabletop grandfather clock. Next to the clock was a formal wedding portrait in a plain silver frame.

Unconsciously Frieda twisted her wedding ring as she looked steadily at the photograph. Veronica wore a gown reminiscent of those worn in the early 1960s, but with a few contemporary touches. Her bouquet was comprised of peach and yellow flowers. She wore no veil or headdress. Her smile was almost blissful. Jack looked handsome—if a bit uncomfortable—in a dark tuxedo, his hand protectively under his new wife's elbow.

"She agonized over picking that dress."

Frieda turned around to find Jack standing at the doorway to the office, two cups of coffee in hand. "She didn't want to settle for any old run-of-the-mill thing," he went on, coming farther into the room. "She wanted to be madly in love with it."

"It's beautiful," Frieda said, accepting the cup Jack offered her. "It suits her. The ivory color looks beautiful with her peaches and cream complexion and fair hair."

Jack nodded. "It did suit her, but I wouldn't have cared if she showed up to the church in an old sweatshirt, as long as she showed up."

"I know what you mean," Frieda said, looking back to the photograph. "I think a lot of what we do when we plan a wedding isn't really for us—the bride and groom—as much as it is for family and friends. My mother was never pushy or interfering until I started to plan my wedding. Then she had some very strong opinions indeed!"

Jack laughed. "So, did you agonize over your dress?"

"Of course. And Aaron would shake his head and wonder why I didn't just wear something already in my closet."

"With a few exceptions the average male just doesn't understand anything about fashion, especially the strong emotions it stirs up and the messages it sends to the world."

Frieda laughed. "You guys should count yourselves lucky."

They stood there for a moment quietly, until Jack asked, "Do you keep your wedding portrait on display?"

"I do. It's . . ." Frieda hesitated. The portrait stood on her night table. "It's in my bedroom," she said. *Well,* she thought, *that is the truth, if not the whole truth.* Surely she could be forgiven such a small transgression.

"I used to have it in the living room," Jack told her. "But when I started to date about a year after Veronica's death I realized it would be unfair to any woman I might bring here to be, well, to be confronted with it." Jack paused before going on. "Veronica donated her dress. When she knew she was dying and would never have a daughter to pass it on to she found an organization that provides wedding gowns and prom dresses and interview attire for women in tight circumstances."

"That was a wonderful thing for her to do," Frieda said earnestly. "An admirable thing."

"I agree. Hey, on another note entirely, I think the meeting with Bella was a success. At least, I hope it was."

"Oh yes," Frieda said. "An unqualified success. I couldn't have hoped for better. Frankly, I was surprised she talked so openly about her father and sister."

"Maybe being with another person who's been through the fairly recent death of a loved one made it easy for her." Jack smiled. "Or maybe she just thought I had a nice face."

"Whatever the reason, I'm glad." Frieda looked at her watch.

"Yikes, I should get going. If I get this job it won't be much money, but it'll be something to put on my résumé."

Jack took her cup and walked her to the front door. "Break a leg," he said, "or whatever it is people say to a writer when they're auditioning for a gig."

"Thanks," Frieda said. "For the good wishes and the coffee." She walked out onto the small front porch and turned to give Jack one last smile. *And thank you,* she added silently, *for the honesty.*

The meeting with the manager of the Strawberry Lane Community Arts Education Center had gone well, and when offered the job of writing the catalogue and print ads for the upcoming fall season Frieda had happily accepted. It paid more than she had assumed it might and the scope of work was entirely reasonable. Sometimes, Frieda thought, as she drove back to her mother's house, things really did go better than you thought they would.

Now in the kitchen making a pitcher of iced tea, adding sprigs of fresh mint and slices of lemon to the tea bags steeping in cold water, Frieda considered what Jack had shared with her so far this summer. That Veronica had agonized over her wedding gown. That she had donated it to charity when she knew she was dying. That she had made her husband promise not to refuse love if it came his way again.

Jack's willingness to share information about his life with Veronica had made Frieda think. How much of her life with Aaron could she legitimately keep to herself if she and Jack—or any man—were to marry? For example, Aaron had enjoyed making rather than buying cards for her birthday. He would use whatever materials he found around the house that very morning. The results—which he called Last Minute Productions—were sometimes hilarious and always touching. Decorated with bits of kitchen twine or glitter, colored in marker or crayon, the cards were among Frieda's greatest treasures, more valuable than the diamond pendant Aaron had given her for their tenth wedding anniversary, second only in meaning to her simple gold wedding ring. If she and Jack were to marry, would she be obliged to share the cards with him? Or would she be justified in keeping these testaments of Aaron's love to herself?

Frieda realized that she was jumping ahead, but these things needed thinking about. Marriage had to be about honesty if it was to thrive, and honesty was a two-way street. To a certain extent Jack would have to share his past as well and she would have to be willing to listen.

Just as Frieda was putting the pitcher of tea into the fridge so it could brew, the front door opened and shut and a moment later Bella joined her in the kitchen.

"Hey," Frieda said. "Are you okay? You look distracted."

"I'm okay," Bella told her. "Just hot. I was out on my bike."

"The iced tea isn't ready, but there's lemonade. Want some?"

"Sure," Bella said. "Thanks. Look, Mom? You know that resale shop called Dandelion Daze? You want to stop in sometime? This woman who came into Phil's shop the other day said it was pretty cool. She was wearing these awesome hot-pink patent-leather sandals she got there for only fifteen dollars. She said they hadn't even been worn."

"I didn't think thrifters also shopped at Wainscoting and Window-seats," Frieda said, handing a glass of lemonade to Bella. "Sure. How about we go today?"

"Really?" Bella drained the glass. "That'd be great. How did your meeting with that arts place go?"

"It went well," Frieda told her. "I was offered and accepted the job. Maybe I'll celebrate by buying myself a little something."

"I always want to celebrate by buying myself something!" Bella said, her expression markedly brighter than when she had first come into the kitchen.

Frieda reached for her car keys. "Then what are we waiting for? And I'll crank the AC in the car."

"Jack got it fixed?" Bella asked, following Frieda to the front door.

"He did."

"That was nice of him."

Frieda locked the front door behind them. "Yes," she said with a smile. "It was nice of him."

# Chapter 73

"Something on your mind?"

Bella startled. "What?" she said. "Oh. Sorry. Yeah, something is on my mind." She had been thinking about Clara. She had been remembering what Clara's housemate, the one who had accosted her as she was leaving the cottage the day before, had said. *You're Clara's friend, right?* The question had been haunting her.

"Let me guess," Phil said, a finger on his chin. "The something on your mind isn't the new shipment of beeswax candles."

Bella looked down at the box of white and yellow candles she was supposed to be unpacking. "Oh," she said again. "Sorry."

"'Give sorrow words; the grief that does not speak knits up the o'er-wrought heart and bids it break.'"

"What's that?" Bella asked.

"That, my dear Bella," Phil said, walking toward the door of the shop, "is a line from Shakespeare's *Macbeth*."

"We read that in English class last semester, but I don't remember much of it. It wasn't a very good year for me school wise."

"You can always read the play again," Phil pointed out.

"I guess," Bella said, though she knew it was unlikely she ever would. "But why did you quote that line just now? And why did you turn the sign on the door to Closed? What's going on?"

"Forget about the candles for the moment, Bella. I think it's time for me to share something important with you. Nothing scary; don't look like that. It's something your grandparents and your mother know about; they were there when it all happened even though your mother was only a child. And eventually your father was told, of course."

"Phil!" Bella cried. "You're killing me. What is it?"

"Once upon a time not so very long ago there was a very special man named Tony Worthington."

"I know. Your Tony."

"Yes. And he died way before he should have."

"I know that, too," Bella said.

"But you don't know how he died."

"Yes, I do. It was cancer."

"Yes and no. Come to the office and have a seat."

Bella followed Phil to the back of the shop and sat in the chair at the small desk. Phil perched on the desk's edge.

"Bella, Tony died of complications brought about by AIDS, specifically, bronchial pneumonia. He did have cancer as well, something called Kaposi's sarcoma." Phil shook his head. "So many people afflicted with AIDS suffered that horror."

Bella felt her stomach drop. "I didn't know any of this," she said. "That's awful."

"You weren't supposed to know."

"But why tell me now?" she asked. "I don't understand."

"Like I said, I just have a feeling it's time for you to know the whole story. You're certainly old enough. You've certainly experienced enough heartbreak of your own to hear the tale of another person's heartbreak." Phil smiled. "I would have told you and Ariel at the same time if things had been different."

Bella nodded. "Okay. So, now that I'm old enough or whatever, tell me everything."

"Remember that this was before the first antiretroviral drugs became available, so it didn't take long for the disease to do its nasty work."

"AZT, right?" Bella asked. "That was the first drug. I learned about it in health class."

"Right," Phil confirmed. "But AZT wasn't introduced until 1987 and by then . . . One of the worst things about the crisis—and believe me, it was a crisis—was that the vast majority of people diagnosed with AIDS were so young. It was . . . At times it felt as if the world were coming to an end."

"Like an apocalypse," Bella murmured.

"You could say that, yes."

"You said my mother remembers Tony being sick."

"Yes. She was little, but she remembers. She'll sometimes mention the time we celebrated Tony's birthday at Chauncey Creek. He didn't look so good at the time—Kaposi's sarcoma had pretty much wrecked his appearance—and I think Frieda was a little frightened at first, but it didn't take her long to realize Tony was the same person she had always loved."

"Did he . . ." Bella hesitated a moment before going on. "Was he in the hospital when he died?" Dying anywhere was terrible, Bella thought, but dying in a place as universally frightening as the hospital sounded doubly terrible. At least it did to her.

"No," Phil said. "Tony wanted to die at home. The alternative would have been for him to be admitted to hospice. Frankly, I was scared witless to have him home—there's a reason I don't work in the medical profession—but how could I say no? So we had a nurse to handle administering his pain meds and your grandparents were amazing through it all. They stayed our loyal friends to the end. They weren't the only ones, of course, but they were the most important to me and Tony."

"Grandma I can see," Bella said. "She's all about taking care of people. But my grandfather, really?"

"Really," Phil said. "He's a strong guy—at least, he was back then—and he'd lift Tony out of bed and get him into the wheelchair. That is, until Tony was too weak to sit up. Steve would even help me bathe Tony while Ruby was in the kitchen cooking meals for us. And when I simply needed a break, a breath of fresh air or some time to myself, Ruby and Steve would take turns staying with Tony, reading to him when he was awake—he was blind at the end—or just watching over him until I got home. I couldn't have managed without friends like your grandparents. So many of my community were sick or caring for someone who was sick. It was all so overwhelming."

Bella shook her head. "It seems so long ago. I mean, I wasn't even born when things were at their worst. Everything is so different now, isn't it? HIV isn't an automatic death sentence. It doesn't automatically become full-blown AIDS."

"You're right. Thirty years ago we lived in a very different world. Want to hear the worst part, at least for me?"

Bella wasn't sure that she did, but she nodded.

"Tony's family refused to allow me to attend the funeral."

A little sob escaped Bella's throat. She jumped out of the chair and threw her arms around Phil. "But why?" she cried against his chest. "You were the one who took care of him when he was sick! You loved him!"

Bella dropped her arms and Phil grabbed a few tissues from the box on the desk and handed them to her. "Thanks," Bella murmured. Her father and sister's funeral was awful, but to be kept from it would have been even worse than the misery of attending it. *Other people have suffered, too,* Bella thought as she blew her nose. *Other people have endured far worse things than I have. And they've survived. I can't ever forget that.*

"Tony's parents blamed me for their son's illness," Phil explained when Bella had regained her composure. "They blamed me for 'making' Tony gay. Not being legally family, I had to accept their decision." Phil smiled ruefully. "By that time in my life I was already an old hand at being the excluded one."

"Did my grandparents go to the funeral?" Bella asked, sitting back in the chair.

"They did, though Frieda stayed home with me. Your grandparents felt the funeral would be too much for her." Phil smiled ruefully. "As Phil's friends, Ruby and Steve Hitchens weren't exactly welcomed with open arms. Your grandfather tried to talk to Tony's father afterward, but he just turned away. Steve knew enough not to make a scene. After all, these people were grieving the untimely loss of their only son."

"Did you forgive Tony's parents for keeping you away?" Bella asked. "I'm not sure if I could."

Phil shrugged. "I'm not sure if I have forgiven them. I just try not to think about it. In fact, before today I haven't talked about the funeral in years. I think forgiveness requires a good deal of thought and attention and energy. Maybe I've never really tried to forgive Mr. and Mrs. Worthington."

"Well, I think they should apologize to you!" Bella said stoutly. "Maybe ignorance was an excuse way back when, but it's not an excuse now. They should know that AIDS isn't anyone's fault. They should know you can't 'make' someone heterosexual or homosexual or transgender or whatever. People just are who they are."

"The Worthingtons are old people now, Bella," Phil pointed out, "if they're still alive. Even if they wanted to apologize they might not know how. They might never have stopped grieving their loss. They might feel ashamed of how they treated me."

"You're making excuses for their bad behavior."

Phil smiled. "Am I? Then maybe I have forgiven them after all. Hey, have you ever heard of the Names Project AIDS Memorial Quilt?"

"Of course," Bella told him. "We learned about it in social studies class years ago."

"Well, when Tony died your grandmother urged me to make a panel for the quilt."

"And did you?" Bella asked.

"No. Tony was a very private person, so I wasn't at all sure he'd want to be a part of such a public memorial. But sometimes I wish I had participated. I don't think he would mind, not really. Not now."

"Maybe it's not too late," Bella said. "Maybe people are still making panels for the quilt. I could find out for you if you want."

Phil smiled. "Thank you, Bella. That would be nice."

"Why didn't Mom or Grandma ever tell me any of this?"

"Because I asked them not to talk about Tony's illness to anyone," Phil explained. "As far as I know, your grandparents kept their word and your mother only told your father after asking my permission. Frankly, I'm surprised the Yorktide rumor mill hasn't let the source of Tony's illness slip in all these years, but people in a small community can be surprisingly compassionate. They can close ranks when it's the right thing to do."

"And people like you, Phil. Nobody would want to hurt you."

Phil laughed. "I don't know about that!"

"Thank you," Bella said. "Thank you for telling me your story."

"And thank you, Bella, for listening. Hey, do you want to see my favorite picture of Tony?" Phil asked. "I know you've seen photos at my house, but this one is special to me."

"Sure. If it's not too painful for you."

"Not anymore." Phil took his wallet from his back pocket and extracted a small photo encased in a protective plastic covering. "This was taken not long after we came to Yorktide, back in 1981. Before he got sick."

Bella took the photo Phil offered. "Oh, wow," she said. "I can see why this is special. His eyes look so soulful. He looks like a hero from some old-time romance."

"I know. I could never quite believe my luck, decidedly average-looking old Phil with someone so beautiful holding my hand!"

Bella lightly swatted Phil's arm. "Don't say things like that. You're a very attractive guy. You know, for someone ancient."

Phil laughed and put his hand to his lower back. "I'd argue about the ancient part if I could. That shipment of drapery rods was a bear to lift."

"You should let me do the heavy lifting, Phil," Bella said sincerely. "I'm kind of out of shape since I quit soccer, but I'm naturally pretty strong."

"Like your grandfather. You know, in some ways you remind me of Steve. Good ways."

"Really?" Bella asked. It had never occurred to her that she might in some ways be like her grandfather, but why not? DNA was powerful stuff. "Like how?"

"Like he had the habit—maybe he still does—of half closing his left eye when he was thinking seriously about something. You do the same thing. And you have a similar personality. Upbeat. Energized."

"I used to be upbeat and energized," Bella said. "But since the accident . . ."

Phil smiled. "You're coming back, Bella. I can see it."

"Really?" she asked. "You can?"

"I think we all can." Phil clapped his hands together. "Now, let's get back to work. There are still the shelves to dust and the candles to unpack."

"And the new pillows to put out. People are mad for pillows, aren't they?" Bella noted. "Especially women."

"It's the coziness pillows represent. Pillows and throws. Now, let's get busy before I talk myself into needing a nap."

Phil went off to reopen the store and Bella went back to unpacking the box of beeswax candles. And as she worked she thought about how much she really wanted to be the old Bella again. What fun she and her mother had had shopping at Dandelion Daze; her mother had bought a real silk blouse for three dollars and Bella had scored vintage sunglasses for six dollars. What fun it had been making ice cream with the old crank machine. What a gift it was to be trusted with someone's secret heartbreak. And opposed to all of the good stuff happening in her life, there was Clara, trying to pull her back down into a pit of self-pity and despair. Maybe Clara wasn't doing it consciously, but she was doing it all the same.

Candles neatly displayed, Bella picked up the empty box and headed out behind the shop where the recycling bin was kept. What Clara was doing to her wasn't right, she thought as she tossed the box into the bin. It just wasn't.

# Chapter 74

Ruby was preparing dinner for her family. Usually she found real contentment in peeling and slicing vegetables, in making classic sauces, in popping a loin of pork into the oven. But this evening, and in spite of the fact that the chicken dish she was preparing was a longtime favorite, she found no joy in concocting the savory marinade of vinegar, garlic, oregano, bay leaves, and olive oil. She had felt uneasy ever since waking that morning from a dream that had had the distinct quality of a nightmare with all the attendant feelings of fear, anxiety, and frustration. Though some of the details had faded since the morning, Ruby could still remember a good deal of it.

She had been alone in the house, standing at the window of her bedroom, contentedly watching a large white rabbit hopping across the backyard—the grass had been an exceptionally bright green and the flowers in their beds almost neon in hue—when suddenly her eyes began to cloud and a sense of dread began to come upon her. Someone close to her was in danger. This she knew more clearly as her eyesight continued to dim, but what she didn't know was the source of this danger or its specific target.

Now largely blinded to the vivid colors in the yard, Ruby turned from the window and stumbled into the hallway. The sense of menace grew stronger. Somehow she found the staircase and, clutching tightly to the banister, blinking rapidly in a vain attempt to clear her vision, she managed to reach the first floor, by which time she was totally and absolutely blind and the fear was raging inside her. She had to warn whoever it was who was in danger—Frieda? Bella? Phil? George? She had to find the front door or the door in the mudroom and get out of the house and shout with all her might for help. And then her hand was on a doorknob and she twisted it and pulled on it and nothing at all happened. She began to sob and to pound on the door and—

And then she woke. She remembered sitting up and rubbing her eyes as if to clear them, but they didn't need clearing. She could see the room around her, walls and windows and furniture and knickknacks, even her bra thrown over the back of a chair, all in perfect detail. But what she still couldn't make out was the nature of the danger the dream had been warning her of. That someone she knew was in danger there was no doubt. Or was there? As Ruby came further awake she began to question her first assumption. Dreams didn't necessarily foretell the future or predict the inevitable. Like ghosts, they might be summoned by an undigested bit of beef or a fragment of underdone potato as Dickens's infamous Scrooge had argued. Or, more likely, dreams might be caused by something you had read or seen or heard about the day before, some bit of information or sensory impression that had lingered on into the night when your subconscious brain could make of it what it would.

This dream, Ruby thought, built on the themes of blindness and fear and confusion, might simply have to do with her hesitation to accept George's proposal of marriage. Maybe her brain had been trying to tell her that the person in danger was actually her own self, in danger of missing a wonderful opportunity. Or maybe the person in danger was in fact George, at risk of having his heart broken. In either case, the dream might be telling Ruby that her home, the place she considered a warm and safe haven, had in reality become a prison of sorts, a physical structure as well as a state of mind that was standing in the way of her taking the next step in her life.

By the time Ruby had finished breakfast her head was hurting from trying to decipher the meaning behind the dream. She hated things she couldn't understand. In contrast, Ariel's coming to her as she did was so blessedly clear and comforting. By the time the breakfast dishes were done, Ruby had decided to put the dream out of her mind as best she could.

Besides, now there were other matters to consider. At the hospital that afternoon one of Ruby's colleagues had announced she had decided to retire. "I'm sixty-eight," Abby told her over coffee in the cafeteria. "I've waited too long already. I'm beyond tired and I can't help but think of all I might have done these past three years or so instead of dispensing medicines and changing sweaty bedsheets. I have too many regrets, Ruby. Too many regrets."

Abby's announcement had come as a surprise and had made Ruby realize she hadn't given her own date of retirement any real thought. Retirement of course would mean the loss of her salary; her monthly Social Security payout wouldn't be enough on which to live, but she had been saving smartly and her IRA was heftier than a lot of people might imagine. With continued frugality she would be okay going forward into old age. Insurance was insanely expensive, but as soon as she turned sixty-five she would be eligible for Medicare; she could easily continue to work until that date less than a year in the future. But a year was so little time in which to mentally prepare to feel and even to be viewed as—as redundant.

Ruby went to the cabinet in which she kept the dry goods and took out a box of rice. And, she thought, as she measured rice and water into the automatic rice cooker, there was George. If she didn't give him the answer he wanted and he did in fact end their relationship, retirement might be very lonely indeed. She had counseled Frieda not to consider a single life as a diminished or a reduced life, but she wasn't sure she could follow her own advice, not after three years spent in a relationship with a person she genuinely loved.

Ruby Hitchens did not indulge in self-delusion. She was well aware that the monthly meetings of The Page Turners could never fill the emptiness that losing George and her job would leave behind. Not even the presence of her daughter and granddaughter, whether here in Yorktide or not so far away in Massachusetts, could replace the love George offered and the mental stimulation and challenges her career afforded her. What had Abby said with a sad shake of her head? *I have too many regrets, Ruby. Too many regrets.*

Maybe, Ruby thought as she took a bunch of broccoli from the crisper, she would table the thought of leaving her job for now. And the thought of marrying George? Ruby reached for the vegetable peeler. That matter couldn't be tabled for very much longer without causing some very severe damage.

# Chapter 75

"This chicken is awesome, Grandma."

"Thanks," her grandmother said. "It's called Chicken Marbella."

Bella nodded. "It's like something you'd make for a celebration dinner, which I guess is appropriate, because something big happened today."

"And what was that?" her mother asked.

Bella looked from her mother to her grandmother. "Phil told me all about Tony having AIDS. About how Grandma and Grandpa helped them when Tony got sick and then when he died. He told me about Grandma's suggesting he have a panel made for the Names Project AIDS Memorial Quilt and his saying no. And he told me he wasn't allowed at the funeral. That really made me cry."

Her grandmother put down her fork. "Wow," she said. "I'm surprised Phil broke his silence. And I'm also very pleased that he trusted you with his story."

"I told him I'd find out if the quilt project is still going on. He said that sometimes he wishes he'd gone ahead and had a panel made for Tony. What was Tony like, Grandma?" Bella asked. "I mean, I've always known he was handsome, but that's not saying much."

"He was a fantastic cook," her grandmother told her. "He was entirely self-taught, but I swear he could have cooked in a five-star Michelin-rated restaurant and nobody would have been the wiser."

"I remember once he made me a little cake in the shape of a frog." Her mother smiled. "It had pink crème inside its mouth and glossy green icing as its skin and chocolate drops for eyes. I was so fascinated by it I didn't want to eat it. I wanted to keep it as a treasure."

"Did you?" Bella asked.

"No way! I ate it, of course. What eight-year-old doesn't scarf down a cake, especially one in the shape of a frog? Tony had flavored the green icing with mint. Yum."

"What else can you tell me about Tony, Grandma?" Bella asked.

"Well, he was a quiet sort, not shy exactly but never the one with a lampshade on his head. He went to services at a Lutheran church every Sunday. He was a regular volunteer at an animal shelter in Wells. He and Phil couldn't have a dog or a cat; you know how allergic Phil is to dander. And he loved Phil with all his being. It was a joy to see them together. To be honest, with my own relationship falling to shreds it was sometimes difficult to witness such a devoted couple. If I didn't love Phil and Tony I might have felt hugely jealous of what they shared."

Bella sighed. "Poor Phil. And all these years he's been alone? I mean, I don't remember ever seeing him with a partner."

"He's been alone except for his friends," her mother said. "Except for us and a few other people from the old days. He was close with his mother, but she died about ten years ago."

"My experience with Tony's illness and death was what inspired me to become a nurse after Steve left Yorktide for good."

"Really, Grandma?" Bella asked.

"Yes. I was so impressed by the nursing care Tony received when he was in the hospital. With one or two exceptions the nurses were courageous and kind to him as well as to Phil. And the nurse who tended to Tony at home in his final days was a saint."

"Do you remember her, Mom?" Bella asked.

"No. I wasn't allowed to see Tony in those last weeks," her mother explained. "He was in such poor physical condition I guess the adults thought I'd be too upset. They were probably right."

"He asked about you, though. Right until the end he wanted to know that you were well. I think in a more enlightened day and time Phil and Tony would have adopted a child. They would have made great daddies."

"Phil was pretty much a father figure to you, right, Mom?" Bella asked. "I mean, after my grandfather left."

"Yes, he was. And he was wonderful. Now, on a vastly lighter note, Jack and I thought we'd stop in at the Pine Hill Tavern this evening. Is that all right?"

Bella rolled her eyes. "Mom, you don't have to ask permission to do normal stuff."

"Remember, Frieda, it's your night to clean up after dinner," Ruby said.

"Your grandmother is such a stickler for discipline, isn't she, Bella?"

Bella laughed. She felt so very happy at that moment. Seriously, her life was pretty wonderful in spite of the bad stuff that had happened. "I'll clean up, Mom," she said. "You've covered for me before. Just don't stay out too late. You know how Grandma and I worry."

# Chapter 76

The Pine Hill Tavern was crowded and Jack and Frieda were lucky to get the last available table for two. Jack went to the bar to get their drinks. The moment he was gone Frieda caught the eye of a well-built man with a magnificent head of silver hair.

"Hello, Frieda," Karl Auerbach said, striding toward her. "It's nice to see you again." He reached for her hand and took it in both of his in a typically avuncular gesture.

"Hello, Mr. Auerbach," Frieda said with a smile. "It's nice to see you, too."

He released her hand and beamed at her. "You're looking very well," he said.

"Thanks. I'm feeling pretty good, too. It's probably because of my mother's healthy cooking."

"And she seems to have recovered nicely after that nasty fall she took last year. Recovery must have taken an enormous amount of patience and hard work."

"It did," Frieda agreed. "But you know my mother. She's the original can-do gal."

Karl Auerbach squinted off into the distance. "You know," he said, "I remember when your father broke his wrist. It must have been about thirty years ago now. He was working construction at the time." Karl Auerbach looked back to Frieda and smiled. "But you probably don't remember that. And now look what I've gone and done! Mentioned your father—"

"It's okay, Mr. Auerbach," Frieda assured him. "Really. In fact, my father and I have been in touch this summer."

Karl Auerbach's eyebrows rose. "Have you? I always did like Steve Hitchens, in spite of his wild and careless streak. You never know what surprises life will bring, do you? Parents and children reuniting after all these years . . . And speaking of family, I'd better get on. The missus will be waiting for me."

Frieda watched as Mr. Auerbach made his way through the crowd and toward the door of the tavern. She had enjoyed the exchange with one of the more popular locals in Yorktide. In fact—and why hadn't she considered this before?—it might be a good thing to move back once Bella was on her own. There was something very comforting and grounding about seeing familiar faces from your childhood, people who had witnessed the major events that had helped shape your life, people who could help you remember the things you didn't want to forget. Most important, Frieda thought, if she lived in Yorktide she could see her mother on a more regular basis and be right on hand for her as she aged.

And, of course, there was Jack. Frieda watched him maneuver through the crowd, a drink in each hand. She would be lying to herself if she denied that he was one of Yorktide's main attractions for her. But she was leaping ahead yet again.

"It's a mob scene in here tonight," Jack said, carefully setting the drinks on their table. "I saw old Karl Auerbach chatting with you a moment ago."

"Yes. He never seems to change. I swear I remember him looking exactly the same as he did when I was a teenager, silver hair and all."

Jack laughed. "Rumor has it that Shelly waits at the door for him to come home from the Pine Hill. If he's as much as one minute after eight o'clock he's banned from going out for his after-dinner drink for the next two nights."

"Yikes! How long have they been married?" Frieda asked. "It must be over fifty years. Something must be working for them."

"Luck? Hard work? Genuine friendship? A bit of all three, I imagine."

*Yes,* Frieda thought. *A bit of all three.* "I heard from my lawyer today," she said.

"About?" Jack asked.

"Not good news but nothing surprising, either. A while back we sued the rental company that provided the car Aaron was driving at the time of the accident. But it's a small family-owned business and it doesn't look like we'll see a settlement anytime soon. And when we do, it won't be much. Frankly," Frieda admitted, "sometimes I think I should drop the suit and let them keep the money. It won't bring Aaron and Ariel back. And then I think, no, every little bit will help Bella in the future."

"Frieda," Jack said, "please don't think I'm being impertinent. But are you and Bella financially secure?"

"You're not being impertinent," Frieda assured him. "Money is a fact of life and it's important. Yes, we're all right. Not as solid as we were back when Aaron was providing for the family. He had life insurance of course, I think I told you that before, but . . . Everything was so expensive. Bringing Aaron and Ariel home. The funerals." Frieda shook her head. "Selling the house brought in some cash and I take whatever jobs I can find, like that new gig with Strawberry Lane. Bella and I are better off than so many families and I take nothing for granted."

"Neither do I. The loss of an income can be devastating. Veronica's salary was never hefty, but it certainly helped." Jack leaned in a bit before going on. "I never shared this with anyone, but not long before Veronica died she told me she wanted me to sell her jewelry. She didn't want me to suffer in the slightest."

"What did you do?" Frieda asked gently.

"A few weeks after the funeral I brought her best pieces to a jeweler for an appraisal and the price everything would have fetched was significant, but in the end I just couldn't go through with a sale. I chose to keep a gold locket I had given her and I gave the rest to her parents. It felt like the right thing to do. Veronica's nieces will inherit eventually."

Frieda glanced at her left hand. "What happened to Veronica's wedding ring?" she asked.

"Oh, I kept that, too, along with my own. Sentimental treasures."

"I know all about those. As you can see, I'm still wearing my wedding ring. Aaron didn't wear one, but it never bothered me. I didn't need him to wear a ring to prove that he loved me."

"My father only wore his ring to church on Sundays. I suppose it only got in the way during the workweek. Plumbing and jewelry don't make for a very good match."

"You know," Frieda said. "I don't remember if my father wore a wedding ring. I suppose I could ask my mother, but I don't want to bring up a topic that might be stressful. She's fine talking with my father on occasion, but I have no idea if unhappy memories still keep her up at night."

"They must have, for a time. Hopefully, not any longer."

"Maybe now it's only Ariel who visits her when the lights are out. Though it's interesting. Mom hasn't mentioned that happening lately. Maybe her sleep is blissfully uninterrupted."

Jack raised an eyebrow. "Is an adult's sleep ever blissfully uninterrupted?"

"Probably not. Jack?" Frieda said. "When you were growing up did you ever think you'd stay on in Yorktide?"

"I don't remember giving it much thought," Jack admitted. "I went away for college and grad school and after that I worked at a school just outside of Boston and then in Connecticut for a few years. I was in my early thirties before I took the job here at YCC."

"But why did you take a job here and not somewhere else?" Frieda asked.

"I like it in Yorktide, plain and simple. When the mood for change would come upon me I traveled, but it always felt good to come home." Jack smiled. "And as I mentioned, the travel bug largely seems to have left me. Maybe that will change when I retire someday in the distant future."

"I'm afraid the idea of getting on a plane for a distant shore holds absolutely no appeal for me, not after what happened in Jamaica. Not that the accident couldn't have happened anywhere, but . . ." Frieda shrugged. "I'm being superstitious, I know. And maybe someday I will be ready again to travel."

"It would be a shame to let that one tragic incident cut off an entire avenue of experience. A shame but understandable."

"Jack, look," Frieda said suddenly. "I think we're going to get a free show." Two of Yorktide's favorite professional musicians, instruments in tow, had just come into the Pine Hill to shouts of greeting and calls for a song.

Jack smiled. "Who says life in a small town is boring? Wherever there are human beings there are surprises."

*And they're often nice surprises,* Frieda thought. *Very nice surprises.*

# Chapter 77

Bella had cleaned up after dinner at top speed, loading the dishwasher, washing the knives and pots and pans, wiping the table
and counters, and sweeping the floor. She was eager to be done because she had some serious thinking to do. And she knew where
she had to do it.

"Don't worry about my falling in," she said to her grandmother
with a smile. "I've got a flashlight on my phone. Besides, the water
is pretty shallow."

"Just don't be out too long," Ruby advised. "You've got to be up
early for work tomorrow."

"I won't. I'll be just as long as it takes me to think through
something that's been on my mind." Bella waved, grabbed a sweatshirt from one of the coat pegs in the front hall, and left the house.
She would take her usual path along Kinders Lane until the turn
for Grove Hill Lane, and then on until she reached the Jernigans'
property. There was still light in the sky and the heat of the day
had given way to evening cool, making for a pleasant journey.

As Bella walked along to the gentle sounds of a country evening,
she thought about her sister's firm belief in an afterlife. If there was
such a thing as heaven, some place or state of being magical and beautiful with all the restricting rules of life on earth suspended, maybe
Ariel was hanging out with people from across past centuries. Maybe

she was sipping tea with Jane Austen or watching Leonardo da Vinci paint one of his masterpieces or listening to Vivaldi play the violin in some concert hall. Maybe she was zipping around the world, visiting all of the places she had wanted to visit when she was alive, Paris and London and Vienna. Maybe she was communing with life-forms on other planets. Maybe she was peering into the future and seeing that one day all war and strife would be at an end and human beings would finally be happy. Yeah, maybe it was fanciful thinking, but why not? Bella thought. Who knew what came after death? Why couldn't it be something wonderful? Was it any more reasonable to assume a negative, miserable outcome?

Bella heard the gentle gurgling of the water before she saw it. Of course there was no sign of the gleaming white pebble she had offered on Ariel's behalf; it might now be buried in mud and silt. Or maybe it had drifted with the gentle stream that ran across the Jernigans' property and was by now miles away. . . .

Wherever the pebble was, it was time to make a decision. Bella knelt on the damp ground. For days now—or had it been weeks?—she had been trying to understand the notion of reciprocity in a relationship. Okay, relationships shifted through time, first one person accepting most of the burden, then the other taking charge for a while, and at other times both people accepting equal responsibilities. The thing was that Clara was such a terribly needy person, such a desperate seeker of attention, that Bella doubted she was capable, at least at this point in her life, of giving back a quarter of the time and attention she demanded.

And, Bella realized, she must have known this about Clara on a subconscious level before the truth dawned on her conscious mind. She hadn't told Clara about the ultimatum she had given her mother regarding her relationship with Jack Tennant. She hadn't told Clara about her change of heart and about how she and her mother had grown close again. And not for one minute had she felt the need to share Phil's story with Clara. Not that she would ever break Phil's trust, but the fact that she felt absolutely no urge to communicate with Clara about the important things that were currently happening in her life meant something. It meant that she didn't consider Clara a true friend, someone who would treat a confidence with respect, someone who would appreciate the gift of her story.

Bella looked up at the darkening sky. There was a pattern of stars overhead. Ariel would have been able to recognize the constellation. Ariel had been so smart about so many things. She would have been able to negotiate the line between duty to a friend and duty to one-self. "Ariel," Bella asked aloud, "is it okay if I walk away from Clara? Would it be wrong? I don't think she has anyone else. If I leave her will she be all right?"

Bella listened and, though she heard nothing with her ears, she thought she sensed something with her heart. It was Ariel, pointing her in the direction of a true friend. Kerri, someone Bella had known since fourth grade when the Woods family had moved to Warden from New Jersey. Kerri had been a bit shy on her first day at school, so Bella had invited Kerri to sit with her at lunch. By the end of the first term they were inseparable. By the time they reached seventh grade they were the nucleus of a group of eight girls who practically lived and breathed as one. In high school a few boys were gradually included in the group of friends. Bella ran her hand gently through a tall clump of grass and thought about Annie and Janet and Connie, all of whom had been her fellow soccer stars. She thought about Justin and Theo and Bryce, always forming a band, breaking up, and re-forming. She thought about the cousins, Chrissy and Tanya, who had lived next door to each other all their lives. She thought about Grace, a seriously good artist. She thought about Kerri, the most honest and kind person in the world next to Ariel. "And me?" Bella whispered. "Can I belong again?"

And right then, kneeling by the spring that her sister had loved so much, Bella decided that she would break all ties with Clara. It would be a difficult thing to do, but it would be for the best. For her best and maybe even for Clara's; either way, Clara could no longer be her top priority. Her top priority now was to show respect for Life with a capital letter by showing respect for herself.

"Thank you, Ariel," Bella whispered. "And thank you, spirit of the spring." Then she got up, brushed the dirt from her knees, and with a lighter heart headed home to her grandmother.

# Chapter 78

While Bella was paying a visit to the Jernigans' spring (they were awfully nice about letting their neighbors trespass) and while Frieda was with Jack at the Pine Hill Tavern, Ruby settled in one of the comfortable chairs before the fireplace with a copy of *The Egypt-ologist* by Arthur Phillips. A cup of tea sat next to the phone on the little round table at her side. But before she could open the cover of one of her favorite books—she had read it twice already—the phone rang. Ruby reached for the receiver. "Hello?" she said.

"It's Steve. I was hoping to reach you."

"Hi. You usually don't call in the evening."

"You're right," he said. "Am I interrupting anything?"

"No. Just my thoughts, and they could use some interrupting. I was about to try a dose of therapeutic reading when you called."

"What's wrong?" Steve asked.

"Nothing really," Ruby demurred.

"Is it that fellow George? Has he been a jerk?"

Ruby laughed. "God, no! Anything but."

"Are you trying to decide whether or not to marry him?"

"What has Frieda been telling you?" Ruby demanded.

"Nothing, but now I have my answer."

"Okay," Ruby said. "Yes, he asked me to marry him. And I haven't given him an answer."

"Ruby, you deserve to be happy and if you think that marrying this guy will make you happy, even for a little while, then you should do it. Though I suppose it's none of my business."

"But for the love you once bore me," Ruby said.

"For the love I still bear you, Ruby," her former husband corrected. "You're the mother of my only child. You were my one and only wife. You never entirely shut me out, even when I richly deserved to be shut out. How can I not love you?"

Ruby felt herself smiling. *His one and only wife.* "Are you sure it's not just gratitude you feel?"

"Both," Steve said firmly. "Love and gratitude. Anyway, you'll make the right choice about this fellow. I know you will."

*How can anyone know what kind of choice another person will make?* Ruby thought, but what she said was: "Thanks, Steve. I know Frieda wants me to accept. As does Phil. I don't know what's stopping me."

"I do," Steve said. "And I'm sorry for my part in all this. If it weren't for me you wouldn't have such a—is 'distaste' the right word?—for the state of marriage."

"Don't blame yourself, Steve," Ruby said after a moment. "I'm responsible for my feelings. No one else."

"Well . . ." Steve cleared his throat before going on. "How is Frieda? And Bella?"

"Both are out at the moment," Ruby told him. "And both are doing much better than they were a few weeks ago."

"No doubt due to your nurturing presence, Ruby."

"Now, Steve . . ."

"Well, I should let you get back to your book. Be well, Ruby."

"You, too, Steve," Ruby said sincerely, replacing the receiver.

Ruby's tea had grown cold while she had been on the phone, so she brought the cup into the kitchen to heat it up. Moments later, Bella returned. "See?" she announced, arriving in the kitchen through the mudroom. "I didn't fall in. Dry as a bone. Well, except for slightly muddy knees."

Ruby smiled. "I'm glad you're back safe and sound."

Bella opened the fridge and reached for the carton of orange juice. "That place is so beautiful at night," she said. "Magical. I half expected to see fairies or sprites dancing around. Do you ever go to the spring, Grandma?"

"Sometimes, yes," Ruby told her. "Though not at night, not since my leg got broken. I'm wary of uneven ground. So, did you get your thinking done?"

"I did. What were you up to while I was out? Anything wild and crazy?"

Ruby considered the question for a moment. Was it wild and crazy to have a warm conversational exchange with your ex-husband, the man who had virtually abandoned you and your child? Maybe. *But so what?* Ruby thought. "I was talking to your grandfather," she told Bella.

"Yeah? Grandma, why did you keep his name after he left?"

"Because it was your mother's name, too," Ruby explained. "I wanted us to be recognized as a family in whatever way we could be, especially once Steve left."

"I guess that makes sense. But I think I'll probably always keep my last name. In memory of Dad, if that makes sense."

"It only needs to make sense to you, Bella, no one else. So, are you going to tell me what was so important you had to think about it all on your own at the spring?"

Bella shook her head and put her empty glass into the sink. "Not yet," she said. "After I actually do what I decided to do, then I'll tell you. And Mom. Sorry, Grandma. It's nothing bad. It's just . . . private."

Private, Ruby wondered, or secret? There could be a big difference. She remembered the frightening dream of the other night, the sense of a loved one in danger. "Bella," she said. "You'll always be careful, won't you? I don't only mean not crossing the street against the light sort of careful. I mean . . ."

"I know what you mean, Grandma. And yes, I promise I'll always be careful. I won't fall into springs or cross against the light and I won't waste my life doing stupid things."

Ruby opened her arms and Bella came to her for a hug.

"Put those jeans in the laundry hamper," Ruby said when they had drawn apart.

Bella rolled her eyes and gave a mighty mock sigh. "Yes, Grandma."

# Chapter 79

"Phil?" Bella said. "Can I tell you something awful? I mean, something I feel awful about."

Phil looked up from the notebook in which he had been writing and nodded. "Sure."

The two were preparing to open the shop the following morning. Bella had slept more soundly than she had in weeks and she felt an energy she hadn't felt in months. She had no doubt that the decision to cut ties with Clara was behind these positive developments.

"You promise you won't hate me or anything?"

"As I've told your grandmother on many an occasion," Phil said, "hate is not in my repertoire."

"Okay. Here goes. When Dad and Ariel came back from Jamaica—their bodies, I mean—a few weeks after the accident I felt angry. I felt like Mom and I were being forced to go through the trauma all over again. I thought, Why couldn't they have been buried in Jamaica so there wouldn't have to be a funeral? I felt resentful of them." Bella shook her head. "It was horrible of me to be thinking those thoughts, wasn't it?"

"What we experience when we grieve can sometimes feel embarrassing afterward," Phil said gently. "Anger toward the victim for causing all the trouble. Anger for his messing up our plans for a nice, neat life. Your favorite Netflix shows don't have the same appeal as they once had and it's all so-and-so's fault for dying and making you sad. You can't enjoy loaded nachos anymore because you always used to share them with so-and-so and he had to go and die. You can't look at a beautiful sunset without thinking that it might be the very last sunset you see because so-and-so had died and you would die, too, and it's all her fault for reminding you of something so depressing." Phil sighed. "Ridiculous, of course, but perfectly normal. You can't beat yourself up for your feelings, good or bad. You just have to acknowledge them, try not to act on the worst ones, and move on."

"I guess," Bella said. "Did you ever feel angry at Tony for dying?"

"Not at Tony, exactly," Phil said after a moment. "I felt absolute rage toward the horrible plague that was decimating so many of my friends and colleagues. And I used to think: What are you supposed to do with anger that's fundamentally directionless? What are you supposed to do with the intense frustration when there's no easy target to absorb it? The danger is that the anger and frustration can morph into depression or reckless behavior. Or it can even take the form of aggression toward an innocent target."

"Yeah," Bella said. "I think I understand. No one likes to think of her life as out of control. No one likes to admit she had absolutely no power over a situation, like a car crash or AIDS. So instead of blaming chance for the bad thing that happened—which is the only smart thing to do even though it doesn't feel very satisfying—a person can decide to blame herself." Bella frowned. "It's weird. Blaming yourself gives you a sort of false sense of power for a while. It's like you were actually responsible for something big and terrible happening. You were powerful, like God. But in the end blaming yourself for the tragedy can't give it a meaning. Or something like that."

"Exactly like that," Phil agreed.

"Ariel comes to my grandmother in her dreams. You probably know that."

"I do," Phil told her. "The first time it happened she was a bit freaked out, not because it was scary but because the encounter was so utterly normal. There's never been anything spooky about the visitations."

"Did Tony ever come back to you?" Bella asked.

"Yes, he did. It went on for about a year."

"How?" Bella asked. "What happened? Were you frightened? How could you be sure it was Tony and not some, I don't know, some trickster spirit or something?"

Phil smiled. "One question at a time! No, I wasn't frightened, just a little startled at first."

"So, did you see him?" Bella pressed. "Did he talk to you?"

"Tony's favorite flower was hyacinth," Phil explained. "What happened was I'd smell hyacinth in the strangest places, like in a hardware store or when I was walking along the beach in the middle of winter. At first I thought I was imagining it; you know how that can happen, you think about a particular food you haven't had in a while and suddenly you can smell and taste it. But then I realized that these experiences were different. Don't ask me how I knew, but I knew it was Tony, not just my own brain toying with me."

"Wow," Bella said. "That's pretty cool. So it was a good thing that Tony made contact with you?"

Phil nodded. "Absolutely. It helped to know he wanted to be with me, that he wasn't angry with me for being alive and well. It helped me to believe that there's something good for us after we die, that Tony and every other being who has passed is safe and content somewhere, not wandering the universe cold and alone and scared."

"The person who died might be okay," Bella said, "but what about those of us left behind? We're the ones who are cold and alone and scared."

"But not forever. Trust me."

"So when Tony stopped coming to you were you sad?" Bella asked. "Did you miss him?"

"For a while, yes," Phil told her. "I felt as if I'd lost him all over again. But before long I came to believe that Tony had moved on to an even better place. I felt happy for him and I felt a sort of contentment. I still wished he hadn't died, but I was better able to accept the fact that he had. And as everyone comes to learn, acceptance of what has happened or of what is currently happening is a key to survival."

Bella shook her head. "Acceptance is a weird thing, isn't it? It can be sort of like giving up, like saying okay, even though I hate this I won't argue it anymore because I'm wiped out. Or it can be doing the mature thing and saying okay, I hate this, but you can give this to me and I'll agree to take it and, what's more, I'll try to understand it." Bella smiled. "Ariel would know how to put it better."

"You didn't do too bad a job, Bella. I hope you give yourself credit for how far you've come since the accident."

"I do," Bella assured him. "But honestly? Sometimes I wonder if I'll ever be able to look at the news without worrying I'll see a story about a car crash and have an anxiety attack or something because all the memories of that horrible day Dad and Ariel died will come storming back." Bella shrugged. "But I guess that's something I'll just have to live with, not knowing when or if or how I'll remember. And maybe I will get well enough to view bad stuff with some healthy detachment. That's one of the terms I learned in counseling. I used to think all those terms were stupid, but now not so much."

Phil laughed. "Some of the lingo is stupid, but not the ideas behind it. On a lighter note, how's that friend of yours, Clara? You haven't mentioned her in a while."

Bella shrugged. "Okay. I don't think she's really a friend, though."

"Oh."

"In fact," Bella went on, a bit surprised that she was, "I've decided not to see her anymore. She's . . . She's not at all like me. Not really."

"Sometimes opposites attract," Phil pointed out.

"Yeah, but not this time."

"Well," Phil said, "you know what's best for you. Now, it's time to open up. Can't keep the customers waiting."

"Especially not when it's Mr. Abbott," Bella whispered. "He's been pacing outside for the past five minutes."

Phil winced as he walked toward the door. "What a way to start the day," he muttered. "A visit from Arrogant Adam Abbott."

# Chapter 80

The girl who opened the door of the cottage was wearing her waitstaff uniform of white shirt and black pants. Bella hadn't seen her before; maybe this was Julie. "I'm here to see Clara," she said. "Is she in?"

The girl laughed. "I didn't know she had any friends other than those losers she's been hanging around with after her shifts."

*The druggies,* Bella thought. *Those are the people she means.*

"So, is she in?" she asked.

"Yeah." The girl stepped back to allow Bella into the cottage. "I'm off for work and Leah will be leaving soon, too, so if you and Clara go out, lock the front door, okay? Clara's not great about remembering stuff like that."

Bella nodded and walked on to Clara's room. The door wasn't quite closed and it opened a few inches with the force of her gentle knock. "It's me," she called out. "Can I come in?"

There was a dry cough, followed by a grunt that Bella chose to interpret as a yes. She pushed the door fully open and stepped inside. Clara was leaning against the window frame, staring out, arms folded across her stomach. She was wearing a short-sleeved T-shirt with a large stain down one side. Her cut-off jean shorts hung low on her bony hips. Her hair was pulled into a messy knot at the top of her head. Bella was shocked by the rapid deterioration Clara had undergone in just a few days. Shocked and dismayed. For a moment she wondered if she had the courage to do what she had come here to do. But did she really have a choice? Her being Clara's companion hadn't helped Clara at all, had it? If anything, Bella thought, she might unwittingly have encouraged Clara's decline.

Bella closed the door behind her. "What are you looking at?"

Clara didn't turn from the window. "Nothing," she said.

Bella considered sitting in the room's one chair and then thought better of it. Standing might help her feel brave enough to accomplish this act of self-preservation. "Clara," she began, "we need to talk about something."

Clara slowly turned her gaze from the window and looked at Bella. Her eyes had an awful hollow look. "What?" she asked.

Bella took a deep breath. "We need to talk about our—about our relationship."

"What about it?" Clara asked.

"I . . . I can't be your friend any longer, Clara. I mean, I can't spend time with you."

For a long moment Clara didn't move or speak. Finally, she pushed off the window frame, let her arms drop from around her stomach, and shook her head. "Why?" she asked.

"Because," Bella said carefully, "your behavior is self-destructive and it bothers me."

Clara laughed a bit wildly. "What do you mean self-destructive? I swore I wouldn't kill myself."

"Yes," Bella said, "I know, and that makes me happy, Clara; it does. But you haven't stopped using heroin, have you?"

Clara didn't answer, which was answer enough for Bella. "It makes me sad to see you using that stuff," she said. "Heroin is bad news, Clara. Nothing good ever comes of it. I can't be a party to your drug use anymore."

"I'm fine," Clara protested, again crossing her arms against her stomach. "Everything's under control."

"No," Bella argued, "you're not fine and everything is not under control. It's obvious you've lost a lot of weight. Are you even eating? When was the last time you took a shower? You're going to lose your job if you don't shape up."

"I don't care about the stupid job."

Clara took a step back and again leaned against the window frame. Bella wondered if Clara was too weak to stand unsupported. "I really think you should tell your parents how miserable you are," she said. "I think you should go back home so they can help you. I can't help you, Clara. I tried, honestly I did, but I never could succeed. I don't know how."

Suddenly Clara became agitated. She began to scratch her arms so intensely Bella could hear the rasp of dry skin under her nails. "You're abandoning me!" Clara cried.

"No! That's not it. It's . . ." Bella put her hand to her forehead. "It's not abandonment. It's that I need to really get past the grief and guilt that have been haunting me since my father and sister died. And that's not going to happen if I continue to hang out with you. I know that." Bella paused before going on in a softer voice. "I'm not saying you're a bad person or that I don't like you. Believe me."

Clara dropped her hands to her sides; Bella saw the raw red marks her nails had made on her forearms. "You can't leave me," Clara said dully. "Everybody leaves me. Go home to my parents? Really? They didn't want me around; I told you, they were the ones who sent me away. I have no one, Bella, no one but you."

*Just like she once had no one but Marc*, Bella thought. "I'm sorry about that," she said gently. "I really am."

Suddenly Clara stumbled over to the unmade bed and sank onto the mattress. She sat with shoulders hunched and her hands clasped between her bony knees. "You're right," she said, and in her voice Bella thought she heard a note of resignation—or maybe, just maybe, it was a note of realization. "I'm in trouble. I promise I'll call my parents tonight."

"Why not right now?" Bella suggested.

Clara shook her head. "They're at work."

"You're their daughter, Clara. They'll talk to you at any time, especially if you tell them it's important."

"I'll call tonight," Clara said more firmly.

Bella restrained a sigh. "All right." There didn't seem to be anything else to say but good-bye. Bella turned and walked to the door, the back of which was covered with pictures of Marc. Marc on his own. Marc with Clara. Only weeks earlier Bella had thought Clara's devotion to her former boyfriend sort of romantic. How wrong she had been. "Take care of yourself, Clara," she said without turning back.

Clara didn't reply and Bella left the room to make her way to the front door. She heard noises from the kitchen and she wondered if any of Clara's housemates knew what Clara was doing to herself. She wondered how they would feel about having a user of illegal drugs share their summer home. Then again, for all Bella knew one of Clara's housemates might be the one supplying the heroin; one might be a user herself.

Bella put her hand on the doorknob but did not immediately open the door. She felt guilty about walking away from Clara, so clearly a troubled person. But she also felt relieved. In breaking away from Clara she had given her own sanity and recovery priority. It felt like a mature thing to have done. Difficult but mature. *Dad and Ariel would have approved,* she thought. Finally, she opened the door of the cottage and with tears in her eyes she headed back to her grandmother's house. Her home for the summer.

# Chapter 81

Ruby stripped the final leaves and silk from the tenth ear of corn she had bought at her favorite farm stand. If she tended to binge on corn in the summer it was perfectly understandable. Get it while the getting was good was a motto shared by all locavores.

After filling a big pot with water and putting it on the stove to boil, Ruby went back to the sink and looked out of the window over it. There was George; he had come by to drop off a promised cutting from his garden and to mow the lawn, which he was now doing. Ruby smiled. He was wearing his goofy sun hat and those dreadful old cargo shorts he refused to toss in the trash though they were permanently stained with green paint and who knew what else and the hem of the left leg was shredded. "They're perfect for working," he argued, and of course he was right. Ruby still thought they looked awful.

She watched as George guided the mower around the Japanese maple tree. She had been thinking about the conversation with her former husband the other evening. Steve had told her she deserved to be happy. He had tried to take the blame for her fear and distrust of marriage. He had told her that he loved her still. To have Steve's blessing regarding her relationship with George felt like a gift of sorts, and the fact of her ongoing relationship with her ex-husband seemed like a bit of a miracle. Maybe, Ruby thought now, it was also a message. Maybe the message was that love was worth whatever risk it entailed and all love involved a certain amount of risk. That's just the way it was and if you didn't like it you might as well go off and be a hermit in the desert.

*What is wrong with me?* Ruby thought as she watched George shut off the mower and wipe his forehead with the back of his gloved hand. *I've been such an incredible fool!* Even though she had kept George on tenterhooks this summer, avoiding giving him an answer to a terribly important question, he still mowed her lawn and brought her cuttings from his garden and agreed to be a guinea pig in her ice-cream experiment. Even though in the past year and a half he had been witness to her daughter and granddaughter's difficult and sometimes self-absorbed passage through grief, he had never wavered in his devotion to any member of the family. *He loves me,* Ruby thought, her heart flooding with feelings of affection, *and he shows it in the most important and meaningful ways— through service. He gives of himself to me and mine. Of course I'll marry this man—if he'll still have me!*

Ruby dashed to the door of the mudroom and out into the yard. George looked quizzically at her, but before he could say a word she threw her arms around him and buried her face against his neck. "Yes," she whispered fiercely. "Yes, I will marry you. Please say you'll have me as your wife."

"Of course I will," George said, wrapping his arms around her and kissing the top of her head. "Thank you, Ruby," he said. "Thank you."

"I should be thanking you," Ruby said, pulling away a bit so she could see his face. His dear face! "You have more patience than Job. I promise I'll never take advantage of it again."

"I'll hold you to that." George laughed. "So, what made you finally come to a decision?"

Ruby smiled slyly. "You're the hottest guy I've ever known."

"Prove it. Though I am pretty sweaty at the moment."

"I don't care if you're sweaty or if you never throw those disgusting shorts in the garbage." And as Ruby kissed the man she loved she realized she was perfectly and one hundred percent happy.

# Chapter 82

Frieda had made a cold pasta salad for dinner with sliced red and green peppers, chopped hard-boiled egg, celery, and tuna, tossed with a garlicky mayonnaise dressing. On the side she served a green salad and a loaf of bread from Bread and Roses. For dessert there was blueberry pie.

Frieda watched curiously as her mother ate with more than her usual gusto. Between swallows she smiled beamingly on her daughter and granddaughter, and when Bella related a humorous anecdote about a customer who had come into Phil's shop earlier that day Ruby had practically screamed with laughter. "You look like the cat who discovered the cream, Mom," Frieda said at last. "What's going on?"

Ruby shrugged. "Nothing. I'm just happy. Life is beautiful. It's a fine summer evening and I'm sharing a lovely meal with two of my favorite people in the world."

Bella raised an eyebrow. "She's hiding something all right. Grandma, you are such a lousy liar. What's lovely about pasta salad? No offense, Mom."

"I've got to run," Ruby said, suddenly getting up from the table. "George and I are going to the Leavitt to see a screening of *Roman Holiday*. Do you know I've never seen it? How is that possible, that

I should reach this ripe old age and have never seen such an iconic movie?"

"No pie, Mom?"

"I'll have some when I get back later. There's George's car now. I can recognize that Volvo engine a mile away. Gotta dash!"

And she did, leaving the kitchen at a run.

"Well, that was interesting," Frieda noted.

"Yeah." Bella put down her glass of lemonade. "I've been thinking about something, Mom. Why do you still call your father Dad when for so many years he wasn't really around to be your dad?" Bella asked. "I mean, why not call him Steve?"

Frieda shrugged. "I don't know. Old habits die hard?"

"Or maybe you do really feel he's still your father, you know, deep down in your heart, and that's why you call him Dad."

"Maybe you're right," she admitted.

"Do you look forward to talking to him?" Bella asked. "I mean, do you think, when Dad calls again I want to tell him about X or Y?"

"I didn't look forward to his calls at first," Frieda told her daughter. "I kind of dreaded them even though I was the one to agree to them. But then something changed. Now I look forward to hearing his voice. It's . . . familiar." *It's even comforting in an odd way,* Frieda thought with some surprise. *My father's voice is one of the two most important voices of my childhood.*

"I hear Dad's voice in my head so clearly," Bella said. "And Ariel's. Sometimes it feels like my own thoughts are happening in their voices. Does that make sense?"

"Yes. Most certainly."

Bella sighed. "I lost my father and it's awful. I'd do anything to have him back. Anything. So, what does it matter how you lost yours, Mom? I mean, okay, maybe he was a jerk, but he's back now, at least for a while, so why not enjoy him while you can, right? Besides, Grandma thinks he's okay."

"You know he probably doesn't have any interest in being a real grandfather to you," Frieda pointed out.

Bella laughed. "So what? Grandma is enough of a grandparent for an army!"

"That's true." And, Frieda thought, she wouldn't be surprised if her mother's happy mood this evening meant that she had finally accepted George's proposal. If she had then Bella would be gaining another grandparent and that would be no bad thing.

"I never knew my grandfather, so I can't miss him. But for eleven years you knew him as Daddy. That has to count for something, doesn't it?"

"It does," Frieda admitted. "Eleven years together is eleven years better than nothing. Thank you, Bella."

"For what?"

"For being so smart and supportive about me and your grandfather."

Bella smiled and shrugged. "Whatevs."

"Now," Frieda said, "how about a slice of that blueberry pie?"

# Chapter 83

Bella went to the window of her room and looked out at her grandmother's well-kept yard, at the daylilies that had already tucked themselves in for the night, at the birdbath empty now of visitors, and she felt a great sense of peace come over her. She thought about what she and her mother had talked about just a little while ago. They had agreed that having someone in your life for a space of time was far better than never having had him. That space of time, however long or short, mattered.

The same principle, Bella thought, applied to her friendship with Kerri. All those years they had spent together mattered. Bella remembered as if it were yesterday the day she had asked Kerri to sit next to her at lunch so she wouldn't feel left out and alone. And she thought about all the times Kerri had returned that first gesture of friendship, like when Bella had a bad flu in sixth grade and Kerri had slipped a Get Well card under the Braithwaites' front door for the entire ten days Bella had missed school. And when they were in eighth grade Bella had broken her arm falling off a set of monkey bars and had to wear a cast that wouldn't fit into the sleeve of the dress her mother had bought her for the graduation dance. Kerri had totally saved the day by offering Bella the brand-new sleeveless dress she had bought for the dance.

*And when Dad and Ariel died,* Bella thought, *Kerri was there.* She hadn't shied away like some of her other friends and if the words she had spoken to Bella weren't always the words Bella needed to hear, well, who could blame her? How was Kerri supposed to know what to say to someone who had just lost her father and sister so tragically? The point was that Kerri had tried. She had *tried* to show Bella that she cared. And she had only given up after Bella's harsh rejection back in April.

Bella took a deep breath. She wanted Kerri back in her life and there would be no running away again if she took this step toward reconciliation. Abandoning Kerri a second time would be downright cruel and Ariel would be the first to say so. Bella turned from the window and went over to her bed where her laptop sat. She opened it and went into the e-mail program. And then she began to type.

*Hey, Kerri. It's me. Look, I know I checked out on you and I'm sorry for that. I really wish it could have been different. You've always been the best friend anyone could ever have. I want you to know that a lot has changed this summer. At least, I feel like it has. So if you want to be my friend again, I promise I'll do my absolute total best to be a friend back. Love, Bella.*

Bella read through what she had written and hit send. Leaving her laptop open, she got off the bed. She knew she couldn't expect Kerri to reply immediately. Nevertheless, she found herself pacing the room, wondering how she would handle Kerri's not responding, wondering how she would handle Kerri's responding with anger or, worse, with coldness.

*Ding!*

Bella ran to her laptop, her heart racing. It was Kerri.

*Call me when you get home. We'll go to the mall for a giant cookie. K. xx*

Bella smiled even as she felt tears flowing from her eyes. The best thing possible had happened. Kerri had given her another chance. And while Bella felt optimistic about the future of their relationship, the experiences of the past year and a half had taught her a very important lesson about living with uncertainty. Pessimism wasn't a great choice; optimism, tempered with a dash of realism, was a great choice.

Hurriedly Bella typed a reply.

*Can't wait! B. xx*

Then she went to the dresser and withdrew Ariel's diary from the bottom drawer. She held the little book against her heart for a moment and felt her sister right there with her. "Thank you, Ariel," she whispered. "Thank you for always believing in me."

Things really were going to be okay, Bella thought, returning the diary to its home. Not everything, but some things, maybe a lot of things. Amazingly, Bella believed that.

# Chapter 84

"OMG," Bella said, "I almost passed out, I swear!"

Phil shrugged. "I had no idea who this person was, but Bella knew immediately."

"That's because you don't watch reality TV," Bella told him. "If you did you would have recognized Tricia MacAdams as the winner of last season's *Dance 'Til You Drop*. She was awesome. And she was so totally nice in person! She gave me her autograph!"

"And Bella managed to sell her a very expensive occasional table," Phil added.

"It was nothing. I like selling stuff. I think I have a talent for it, right, Phil?"

"You're a natural," he affirmed.

Ruby smiled across the table at her granddaughter. She felt that a bit of a miracle had been worked these past weeks. Bella was so much more her old happy and optimistic self than she had been at the start of the summer. Ruby looked with gratitude at the others gathered this evening at the Yorktide Lobster Pound. Frieda and Jack. Phil, her oldest and dearest friend. And, most important at that moment, George.

Just then two waiters arrived and placed on the table before the group platters of cooked lobsters with plastic picks and metal crackers, two buckets of steamers, a plate of corn on the cob, little containers of coleslaw, three large orders of French fries, and enough clarified butter to satisfy even the most rabid proponent of full fat.

"Who's better than us?" Jack said, shaking his head. "Look at this bounty. I feel almost guilty sitting at this table. Almost."

"So, Mom," Frieda said. "What's the occasion? Why did you ask us all here tonight? Not that we need an excuse to eat al fresco when we have another long New England winter to look forward to."

"Isn't that the truth?" Phil said.

"Well," Ruby began, "we asked everyone to be here this evening because we have an announcement." She looked to George, who sat beside her, and he took her hand in his. "We've decided to get married. More specifically, I've accepted George's proposal."

"Hurrah!" Bella cried. "That's awesome, Grandma!"

Jack raised his beer. "To the happy couple!"

Phil wiped his eyes with his napkin, then cleared his throat. "And about time, too!"

Frieda, sitting on her mother's other side, put her arm around Ruby's shoulders and squeezed. "Oh, Mom, that's fantastic news! Congratulations to you both!"

"Thank you, Frieda," George said. "Thank you, everyone. I'm a very lucky man. And a very happy one."

"Jack!" Frieda laughed. "What are you doing?"

And there was Jack Tennant, college administrator, with a straw stuck on to each of his canine teeth. "What?" he said, the straws bouncing ridiculously. "I can't help it. When I'm around straws I have to play with them."

"That's okay," Bella said reassuringly. "My father was kind of goofy, too."

Jack removed his walrus tusks. "Yeah?" he said.

"Yeah. Ariel and I used to toss Goldfish crackers at him and he'd tried to catch them in his mouth. He'd keep his hands clasped behind his back so he wouldn't cheat. It was so funny. Remember, Mom?"

"I remember finding stray Goldfish in the most unlikely places, like at the back of one of the drawers of the credenza."

"But it was funny, wasn't it?" Bella pressed. "When Dad was dancing around with his mouth open."

"Yes," Frieda said, smiling. "It was hilarious actually."

"I have an announcement, too," Phil said. "It's not as exciting as Ruby and George's, but it's big enough. I'm finally planning a long trip to Italy, something Tony and I used to talk about doing. We wanted to wander aimlessly through narrow twisty streets, gaze at gorgeous old churches, pluck ripe figs from trees, and drink Campari while sitting by a fountain in a beautiful old piazza. I don't even like Campari, but the thought of drinking it in Italy appeals." Phil looked to Frieda and smiled. "Especially after a long winter in Maine!"

"This is huge," Ruby said. "Phil, how did you manage to keep this a secret?" And then she shuddered. "Campari tastes like medicine to me, but it is a beautiful color. Isn't it one of those herbal liqueurs first made by medieval monks?"

George pulled his iPhone out of his pocket. Ruby groaned. "You are so addicted to that phone!"

"You're worse than I am!" Bella said.

"Yes, I'm addicted, and yes, I am probably worse than you are, and nope," George said. "No medieval monks. Says here on the official website that the formula started to come about around 1860."

"Let's eat," Phil said. "I'm starved. We can talk wedding and vacation plans later."

And they did eat, until every last fry had been consumed and the table was littered with empty shells, denuded corncobs, and a few remaining shreds of coleslaw.

"I propose a toast," Ruby said when the waiters had removed the evidence of their feast. She raised her plastic cup of wine. "To those gone ahead." *To Aaron, Ariel, and Tony,* Ruby added silently.

Frieda nodded. "And to those here at this table."

"Hear, hear!" Phil boomed.

"And to those still to come!" Bella added.

Ruby looked carefully at her granddaughter. "You're not suggesting that George and I . . ."

Bella laughed. "No! I meant me. I meant that someday I might have kids."

"Someday in the distant future," Ruby corrected. "After college. Maybe after graduate school. And a few years into your career. And not before you're thirty."

Frieda nodded. "What your grandmother said."

"First of all, me in grad school? Not likely. But yeah," Bella said, "in the distant future I might have kids."

Ruby glanced lovingly at her daughter. *We give birth to our children with such hope,* she thought. *With so many dreams. We take such a risk when we choose to love. But it's all worth it.*

"Does anyone dare have dessert?" Jack asked.

"I dare," Bella said. "They have a fantastic strawberry shortcake here. I remember it from last time. They make the biscuits by hand. Yum!"

Jack grinned. "Split it with you?"

Bella smiled. "Sure."

"We're going to have to carry you two to the cars," George said. "Just saying."

"Food coma," Bella said. "The best kind!"

Ruby felt her heart swell with happiness. The moment was as near perfect as one might hope to experience. The one thing that might just make it totally perfect, she thought, was the presence of Frieda's father. But she believed that Steve was with them in spirit. And that would have to be good enough.

# Chapter 85

The next morning Bella woke in a good mood. In fact, she felt happier than she had in ages, definitely since before the accident that had turned her world upside down. She hurriedly showered and dressed and made her way to the kitchen. On the table was a note from her mother and grandmother telling her they had gone to visit one of Ruby's colleagues whose daughter had just had her first baby. *Be back by lunchtime,* her mother had written in her very upright script. *Love, us.* Bella ate a carton of yogurt and drank a glass of juice. She wasn't due at Phil's until one, so she decided to take advantage of a sunny morning and get out on her bike.

About fifteen minutes after leaving her grandmother's house Bella found herself cycling down Deering Way, thoroughly enjoying the fresh air and thinking about what she was going to have for lunch. She was hardly conscious of the fact that she was approaching The Flipper; when it suddenly came in sight she was surprised. A moment later she was even more surprised to see Clara's car sitting at an odd angle at the back of the lot reserved for employees, half on to the grass and dirt behind. Stranger still, the driver's door was open.

Bella brought her bike to a stop just outside the restaurant. Something was wrong. There might be a totally rational reason for Clara's car being parked so badly, but there was no rational reason for the door being left open. Yorktide wasn't a high-crime town, but still, people didn't go around leaving the doors of their vehicles open.

Bella got off her bike and propped it against the building. Slowly she walked to Clara's car and peered inside. Clara's handbag sat on the front passenger seat. Bella turned away from the car and scanned the parking lot. Nothing. Nobody. Until . . . Bella's heart leaped into her mouth. Sticking out from behind the giant green Dumpster was a pair of legs.

Bella ran toward the Dumpster and as she rounded its corner she saw that the prone figure was Clara. She was lying on her back in a pair of dirty jeans and a hoodie. One sneaker was missing. There was a hypodermic needle at her side. Bella pulled her phone from her pocket and pressed 911. Her heart was pounding in her ears. She cursed herself for not knowing CPR, but maybe CPR wasn't what was required in this situation. She just didn't know.

"My friend," she said when the dispatcher answered. "I think she's overdosed. She's . . . I think it's heroin. She's behind The Flipper on Deering Way. Please, hurry!"

The dispatcher spoke in a calm and matter-of-fact manner. "Listen to me," she said. "Please stay on the line. How long has she been down?"

"I don't know! I just found her."

"How old is she?"

"Eighteen," Bella replied. "Please, hurry!"

"Listen to me," the dispatcher said. "Is she breathing?"

"I don't know!"

"I want you to put your ear to her mouth, okay?"

"Okay." Bella dropped to her knees and leaned close to Clara's face. Her skin was an awful shade of grayish white.

"Do you hear or feel her breathing?" the dispatcher asked.

Bella willed her mind empty of all thoughts but that moment in time. She willed her senses to focus on nothing but Clara. And then she could feel against her cheek the faintest of breath. "Yes!" Bella cried into the phone. "Yes, I do!"

"Is she responsive?"

"Clara!" Bella cried. "Can you hear me?"

"No," she told the dispatcher. "No, she's not responding to me."

"Okay. Please stay with me, all right? EMS is on the way."

"Please hurry!" One hand gripping the phone against her ear, Bella reached with the other for Clara's. It was limp and bony; the skin was dry and flaky. Had no one else seen what was happening to Clara? Had her boss and her shift manager really been so blind to her erratic behavior; had they not investigated the times she failed to show up for work? Had her housemates been so absorbed in their own lives they hadn't noticed that the young woman in the back bedroom was becoming a ghost of her former self? Had they only cared about the money she owed them?

"Is there any change in your friend?" the dispatcher asked. "Is she still breathing?"

Again Bella placed her ear close to Clara's mouth. "Yes," she said. "She's still breathing. Can she hear me? Do you think she can hear me?"

"I can't say for sure," the dispatcher told Bella, "but why don't you talk to her."

Bella bent over again and whispered urgently in Clara's ear, "You can't die, Clara. I won't let you die!" And as Bella continued to kneel by Clara's side she remembered those three men who had pulled her father and sister from the wreck before the car had exploded, those three men who had waited with them until the ambulance arrived. Here she was watching over someone in an extremely vulnerable state, someone whose life was temporarily in her keeping. It was a duty she could perform for Clara's parents, who had to love her no matter what Clara claimed.

It seemed like hours, but of course it was only minutes before an ambulance came screeching into view. As it came to a halt a yard or so away from the Dumpster Bella finally released Clara's hand and got to her feet. "They're here!" she told the dispatcher. "Oh, thank you!"

"You did a good job," the dispatcher replied. "Now let the paramedics take over."

Bella ended the call. "It's heroin, I think," she said to the first paramedic, already on his knees at Clara's side.

"Step back please," a second paramedic asked, and Bella did, her hands clasped tightly together to stop them from shaking. She watched in awe as the team worked with astonishing speed and authority. When Clara was safely strapped to a stretcher, an oxygen mask firmly over her mouth and nose, and the rear doors of the ambulance had been closed and secured, Bella approached the third paramedic. "Will she be okay?" she asked. "She won't die, will she?"

The young woman smiled kindly. "I can't promise you anything. I'm sorry. But she looks pretty stable at this point."

"Can I ride in the ambulance with her?"

"Afraid not. But don't worry. Your friend is in good hands." The paramedic climbed into the driver's seat and Bella watched as the ambulance pulled out of the parking lot, siren blaring, lights flashing. When she could no longer see and could barely hear the vehicle she took her phone out of her pocket.

"Mom," she said, her voice trembling, tears beginning to choke her. "I'm okay, but something bad has happened to Clara. I need you to come and get me. Please, Mom. Hurry."

# Chapter 86

"When? Okay. Uh-huh."

Bella sat at the kitchen table while her grandmother was on the phone with a friend from the hospital. Her mother, sitting next to her, was stirring a cup of tea, her face a mask of worry and sympathy. Neither of them had spoken much on the way home from The Flipper.

*How quickly life can change,* Bella thought, taking a sip of the water in her glass. Only the night before she and her family and friends had been celebrating new beginnings and warmly remembering loved ones who had gone before. And then, only hours later, Bella had found herself kneeling at the side of someone in serious danger of losing her life. That life had been saved, but it would never be the same as it had been. And maybe that was a good thing. As long as the overdose had caused no lasting physical damage.

"Thanks, Joe. I owe you one."

"What's happening?" Bella asked as her grandmother hung up the receiver of the landline, sighed, and sank into a chair at the table. "Did your friend in the ER have any news?"

"Joe said that Clara is going to be fine. Her parents are on the way. It was a good thing you came upon her when you did, Bella. And it's a good thing paramedics carry those overdose kits."

"What's an overdose kit?"

"I read about it online," Bella told her mother. "It's called a 'save shot.' You give it to someone who's overdosed on heroin or Percocet or oxycodone."

"Its official name is Narcan," her grandmother added. "It's an opiate antidote and it's quite literally a lifesaver."

Bella shook her head. "I know I found her in time, but I still feel guilty. I knew Clara was in trouble. And I knew she'd started to use heroin. I didn't want to get her in trouble so I kept her secret."

"Oh, Bella." Her mother sighed.

"I know it was stupid, Mom," Bella said forcefully. "I should have come to one of you. Look, all I was doing was trying to help Clara, but I realized that I had failed. I realized that I couldn't take her neediness any longer. I couldn't take watching her wasting away and not listening to me when I tried to talk sense to her. So yesterday I told her that I couldn't spend time with her. I told her she was dragging me down with her. She was angry at first, but by the time I left the cottage she had promised she would call her parents and tell them she needed to come home. She swore. And I believed her."

"She might have half believed herself, Bella," her grandmother said gently. "That's the thing about addictive drugs. They make you a liar all around. Don't feel bad about not doing more for Clara. You did plenty."

"Thanks, Grandma. But there's something else." Bella took a deep breath before going on. "Not too long ago Clara told me she wanted to take her own life. She found out that the guy she'd been seeing for four years, the one who dumped her just before graduation, was seeing someone else. And . . ." Bella hesitated again; she knew that what she was about to say would frighten her family even more than what she had already told them. "She thought we should make a suicide pact. She said that neither of us had anything to live for."

Her mother gasped and Bella reached for her hands. "Mom, I didn't consider it for a second!" she cried. "I was horrified! I've never wanted to kill myself; you have to believe me!"

"The thought of suggesting that someone you supposedly care

for end her life . . . It's disgraceful. And yet if Clara is truly sick we can't blame her entirely. Don't worry, Bella. We believe that you wanted nothing to do with her scheme."

"Thanks, Grandma. I tried to convince her that life is wonderful even when bad things happen. I told her that I really believed there were good things to come for us both. Finally, she swore to me she wouldn't try to hurt herself. I believed her then, too, but she was lying."

"We don't know for sure the overdose was a suicide attempt," her grandmother pointed out. "We may never know if Clara doesn't want to talk. But Bella, it would have been a good idea for you to tell one of us that Clara was contemplating suicide. Generally when a person threatens such a desperate act there's something to the threat."

Bella looked from her mother to her grandmother and felt her heart swell with love and gratitude. "I'm sorry for everything," she said. "I promise things will be calmer from now on. And I'll apologize to Phil for not being able to go into work this afternoon."

Her grandmother smiled. "I'm sure he thoroughly understands that you were too upset to be dealing with fussy customers. It's not every day a person comes across the victim of an overdose. Besides, Phil had his suspicions about Clara all along. He had a hunch something wasn't right with her. As always, he was on target."

Bella's mother got up from the table and put her arm around her daughter's shoulders. "You must have been so scared when you found Clara this morning."

"I was," Bella admitted. "But I was more—well, not angry exactly, but I felt determined that she wasn't going to die. I just hope . . ."

"What?" her mother asked gently.

"I hope that I didn't help save her life for nothing." Bella shook her head. "What I mean is I hope she can get control of her life again—if she ever had control, and I guess I'll never know that. I hope she can build something good and happy for herself. I don't want to think that she'll try to commit suicide again or that she'll get totally obsessed with another guy like she was with her ex-boyfriend." Bella shook her head. "She was stalking Marc. She even stole something important from him, a keepsake coin that had been in his family for generations."

"You helped give Clara a second chance. What she does with that chance now is not your concern. Let go of the worry, Bella."

"I'll try," Bella promised her grandmother.

"You know," her grandmother went on, "a few nights ago I had a very frightening dream. In the dream I was physically blinded to an unknown danger coming for someone close to me. I knew the dream wasn't a message from Ariel. I convinced myself that it was the product of my own personal fears and concerns. I convinced myself that neither of you were in danger. And you weren't, were you, at least not directly? It was Clara who needed saving. And because Clara was close to Bella, she was also close to me. We're none of us truly alone."

"You know what," Bella said after a moment. "Clara was close to me and I was close to her, but she was never my friend and I was never hers. I don't know what we were to each other, but it wasn't friends."

"I was just thinking," her mother said suddenly. "There is one more thing Bella might be able to do to help Clara. Bella, did she tell you who sold her the heroin?"

Bella shook her head. "No. I know she got a few prescription pills from some guy who hangs out at The Flipper. She said he was called Hades, but for all I know she was making that up."

Her mother sighed. "Is there any point in going to the police with only a nickname?"

"And a ridiculous one at that! Still, would you be willing to tell the police the little you know of this guy?"

"Sure, Grandma," Bella said. "If it might help them catch the creep and keep someone else from overdosing."

"Good. The rest is up to Clara, but I wouldn't count on her talking. That's just my guess. Anyway, with heroin addiction being such a big problem these days the police probably have a long list of probable suspects. There's a chance this Hades character is known to them."

"Hades." Bella's mother shook her head. "It's almost funny. Almost."

Suddenly Bella's stomach growled loudly and she laughed. "OMG, I am suddenly so hungry! I haven't thought of food all day, but now I could totally raid the fridge."

Her grandmother got up from the table. "I'm on it. How about I grill some pork chops? There's fresh corn on the cob and bread and salad, too."

"What about our blueberry ice cream?" Bella asked.

Her mother cleared her throat. "Um," she said, "I'm afraid I ate it all last night."

"Mom!" Bella laughed. "And you teased me for ordering strawberry shortcake at the lobster pound!"

"What can I say? Around two in the morning I had a craving."

"A gal's gotta do what a gal's gotta do," Bella's grandmother added. "But don't worry. We'll go into the Cove after dinner and get ice-cream cones."

"My treat," her mother said.

Bella grinned. "You guys are awesome," she said. And oh, how she meant it.

# Chapter 87

Bella took a deep breath and knocked on her mother's bedroom door. It was almost eleven o'clock, and though the day had been one of the most trying in her life, Bella just couldn't sleep. Not when she still needed to make a very important confession.

"Come in," her mother called.

Bella opened the door and peered around its edge. "Mom, do you have a few minutes?"

"Of course." Her mother put the book she had been reading—one of those cozy mysteries she routinely gobbled—next to her and patted the mattress. "Join me."

Bella crawled into the bed and settled against the pillows. Her grandmother always had the fluffiest pillows. Maybe she had bought them from Phil.

"Look, Mom," she began. "I'm going to tell you something and I need you not to freak out. Everything's okay now, seriously."

Her mother's eyes widened. "You know I'm freaking out, right?"

"Sorry. The thing is that for a while this summer I was smoking pot."

"Oh, Bella . . ."

"Clara got me into it," Bella went on hurriedly. "I know, I know, it was seriously stupid, and I'm so over it. I swear, Mom. Never again. I just felt so . . ." Bella shook her head. "So like I just didn't care about anything. But things have changed now. I care again, Mom. I care about you and Grandma and Phil and George and even about myself." Bella scrunched up her face. "Are you angry?"

Her mother sighed and reached for Bella's hand. "Yes," she said. "I'm angry with myself for not being able to help you before things got so bad. I'm so sorry, Bella. How could I not have known? I've let you down. I was so focused on my own mourning and on mending the relationship with my father . . . And yes, with getting to know Jack."

Bella shook her head. "Mom, you didn't know because I kept it a secret. Don't blame yourself for anything. I'm okay now; I promise." Bella squeezed her mother's hand. "There's one more thing I want to tell you. Clara gave me a pill once, a prescription painkiller that Hades guy sold her. I took it from her because she kept insisting, but I flushed it down the toilet the minute I got home. I'm sorry. I can't believe I didn't stand up to her. I think I might have been a bit scared that she would hurt herself or even me if I didn't go along with her." Bella sighed. "And when I did finally work up the nerve to stand up to Clara look what happened."

"Clara's overdosing is not your fault, Bella," her mother insisted. "It's not."

"I know," Bella said. "If she really wanted to kill herself she would have found anything to use as an excuse, getting fired or someone on the street bumping into her. My walking away from our relationship just happened to be the excuse right in front of her. I think she was in a lot of pain way before I came along this summer."

Her mother looked at her closely. "Promise me you'll never, ever again go anywhere near drugs, please."

"I promise, Mom. Believe me, the whole thing made me sick, literally."

"Or cigarettes," her mother went on. "Don't go near them, either. Or alcohol. Well, except for a nice crisp Sauvignon Blanc or a good, robust Cabernet—but only after you're twenty-one!"

Bella laughed. "Okay, okay, I get it! But Mom? Can we keep the pot stuff a secret from Grandma and the others? I feel so stupid about it."

"Of course. No one else need know." Her mother smiled. "This has been an important summer for us, hasn't it? I think we've both made progress in understanding that we live in a new world. Dad and Ariel are no longer with us in the old way and there's nothing we can do about that but accept it. I think that we both finally have. It's you and me now, Bella, and we've got to stick together."

"You and me and Grandma and George and Phil," Bella amended. "We can't forget them."

Her mother smiled. "Yes. We've got a good family, don't we?"

"Yeah. I guess that sometimes you wind up with a family you never thought you'd have. People join. People leave. They die or they move on. Everything's always changing and that's not necessarily a bad thing."

"Right, and the point is to love everyone the best you can while you can."

"Even my grandfather?" Bella asked.

Her mother nodded. "Even your grandfather. When he next calls I'll tell him that I accept the apology he offered at the beginning of the summer. He told me that though he knew he didn't deserve it, he hoped I would acknowledge that he means something to me. He does mean something to me. I do love him and I'll tell him that, if only in memory of the first eleven years of my life when he was here for me. When he sang me songs and gave me piggyback rides and took me to country fairs."

"I'm glad," Bella said. "You know, Mom, all along you were doing what I wasn't able to do until now—healing. Moving on. Recovering. Letting go of the guilt for something neither of us could possibly have stopped from happening. You helped me, Mom, even if I couldn't see that at first. You set the example."

"I'm glad you feel that way, Bella. It's what parents are supposed to do, be a good example for their kids, but believe me, sometimes it feels like an impossible task. Sometimes a parent just wants to crawl into bed and pull the covers over her head and say, 'Nope. Can't do it.'"

"So what makes you not hide under the covers?"

"Love," her mother said. "Plain and simple. And a sense of duty, I suppose."

"But not every parent can do that, can they?" Bella said. "Be there for their kid. My grandfather couldn't and yet . . . Yet he has to love you. He wouldn't have reached out to you this summer if on some level he wasn't capable of loving you."

"Yes. People do the best they can do and it's unfair to ask more of them."

Bella hesitated a moment and then decided to take the risk. "About you and Jack," she said. "He's pretty nice. I think he really likes you, I mean, in the important ways."

"And I really like him, too," her mother admitted. "I didn't expect to feel . . . Well, to feel anything for anyone ever again. I think maybe I could be genuinely happy someday."

"We deserve to be happy. Didn't Grandma tell us that's what Ariel wants for us? And Ariel never lied." Bella laughed. "Do you remember the time Mrs. White from the pharmacy asked us what we thought of her new haircut and you said something like, 'It's very becoming,' and I said, 'It's nice,' and Ariel said what we were all really thinking, which was, 'Your stylist did a terrible job. You should ask for your money back.'"

Her mother put her hand to her heart. "I almost passed out on the spot! I thought we'd get thrown out of the store!"

"And Ariel had no idea she had insulted Mrs. White. She thought she was being helpful!" Bella smiled. "You know, Mom, it was the right thing to do, us being here this summer."

Her mother nodded. "Your grandmother is smart. She knew that coming home to Yorktide would help all of us heal."

"Mom? Do you think Clara will be okay?"

Her mother sighed. "I wish I could say yes and mean it, but I just don't know. If she gets the help she needs then I think she stands a good chance of becoming a healthy young woman. At least, I hope that she does."

"I'm going to send good thoughts into the universe for Clara. It can't hurt, right? You know, Clara's despair sort of helped me to see myself from the outside. It helped me to realize that since the accident I'd been devaluing my life by letting grief and guilt win. But grief and the guilt weren't getting me anywhere."

"Do you know the poem by John Donne that starts with the words 'Death, be not proud'?" her mother asked.

"Mom," Bella said, with a roll of her eyes. "Be serious. Me? Poetry?"

Her mother laughed. "Well, the opening lines go like this: 'Death, be not proud, though some have called thee /Mighty and dreadful, for thou are not so.' And the final line is really wonderful—though I should be quoting the entire poem so you'd hear the triumph in the words. Problem is I don't remember it all. Anyway, the final line goes like this: 'Death, thou shalt die.'"

Bella nodded. "That's pretty good actually. Life wins in the end. You know, I was thinking about what Colleen told me about the importance of 'self-care' while you're grieving. She said that the survivor tends to punish herself when what she should be doing is treating herself nicely. She said that grief is particularly difficult for teenagers because we're caught between two worlds—a child's world and an adult's world. Our brains switch back and forth from a child's way of thinking and an adult's. Our emotions go back and forth, too, which makes getting past grief more of a challenge than it would be for a little kid or a real adult."

"As if teenagers don't already have enough to deal with!"

"Tell me about it!" Bella gave her mother another hug and climbed off the bed. "Oh, one more thing, Mom," she said. "I found Ariel's diary. I mean, I think it's a diary. It's locked, but I couldn't find the key."

"Really? Are you tempted to open it?" her mother asked.

"I was," Bella admitted, "but I wasn't tempted very hard. Whatever it is, it's Ariel's, not mine. I just wanted you to know we have it."

"I'm glad," her mother said. "Together we'll keep it safe."

"Good night, Mom." Bella left her mother's bedroom, quietly closed the door behind her, and walked back to her own room with a light heart. It was so much better to have told her mother everything rather than to walk around burdened by secrets. So, so much better.

# Chapter 88

"So Clara is out of danger and her parents are on the way."

Jack, who was sitting across the table from Frieda at The Razor Clam, shook his head. "I read in the paper this morning about a girl being found unconscious due to an overdose, but I had no idea that Bella was the one who called for an ambulance. My God, Frieda, what an ordeal for her."

"I know," Frieda agreed. "And what an ordeal for Clara. She was troubled and alone here in Yorktide. She was vulnerable. It was sheer luck that Bella was passing The Flipper at just the right time."

"It's disgusting what's going on in this country. So much waste of life. And it's not only troubled and vulnerable youth who get snared. People of all ages and walks of life find themselves addicted to opiates."

"You know, when Bella called me to say that something bad had happened to Clara..." Frieda wiped a few tears from her eyes. "She was so brave, Jack. I feel sick about how close I came to losing another child. What if it had been Bella who had gotten started on heroin? What if it had been Bella who succumbed to a despair deep enough to tempt her to suicide?"

Jack reached across the picnic table and took her hand. "Yes," he said gently, "but it wasn't Bella. Bella is still here with you, with us all."

"I know. I will focus on that, I promise. I feel . . . I feel as if we're facing a brighter future now, me and Mom and Bella."

"I'm glad. And thank you for telling me what happened with Bella and that poor girl. Your sharing the story with me means a lot."

Frieda hesitated only a moment. She would seize the opportunity that seemed to have presented itself. "I realized something important about myself this summer," she told Jack. "I suppose I always knew it on some level, but losing Aaron really brought the truth home to me. I'm not a person who is meant to walk through this world on her own. I'm a better person when I'm with a partner. I'm happiest when I'm half of a whole. I felt so guilty admitting this to myself after Aaron died. I felt as if I were betraying him by being who I am. But that's nonsense, isn't it? Aaron knew me. He knew I was a good partner, as was he. I know he wouldn't want me to pretend I was someone other than who I am." Frieda suddenly put her hands over her face. "I'm sorry, Jack. And I don't mean to be putting any pressure on you to . . . I—" Frieda didn't quite know how to go on.

"It would help if I could see your face."

Frieda lowered her hands to see Jack smiling kindly. "I'm not feeling any pressure," he said. "In fact, I'm feeling very good at this moment. Happy. And making a person feel happy and optimistic about his future is nothing for which to apologize."

*And that's what Jack's helping me to feel,* Frieda thought. *Happy and optimistic about my future.* "I believe in my feelings for you, Jack," she told him. "I believe that they're genuine and not a product of neediness or weakness."

Jack cleared his throat. "Now that we've got that settled, I have a very important question to ask. Are we too old to be 'going steady'?"

Frieda laughed. "I'm not sure anyone uses that term anymore, so yeah, we're too old! But I'm okay with being your girl."

"My one and only girl." Jack leaned across the picnic table and kissed Frieda on the lips. "I've been waiting to do that since seventh grade."

"You have not!"

Jack shrugged. "Okay, maybe eighth grade."

"I hope it was worth the wait."

"Yes," Jack said. "Well worth the wait."

"Order number twenty-three!"

"That's us," Jack said. "I'll go."

Frieda smiled. "Just don't eat all of my onion rings before you come back."

"Rats," Jack said with a snap of his fingers. "Foiled again."

# Chapter 89

"Are you ready for this?"

Bella nodded. "Yeah," she said. "As ready as I'll ever be. I know Mom doesn't think this a good idea, but it's something I need to do."

"It's closure," her grandmother said as they stood at the door of Clara's room. "Everyone needs closure. Come see me after if you want to talk, okay? Call me on my cell and I'll let you know where I am."

"Thanks, Grandma," Bella said. "Well, here goes."

Her grandmother walked off and Bella went quietly into the room. She knew that Clara was about to be discharged, so she wouldn't be in bed hooked up to drips and monitors and wearing an awful johnny. She knew that Clara had been told how she had been found and by whom. What she didn't know was if Clara felt resentful of the person largely responsible for saving her life, a life she might not have wanted saved.

Clara was sitting in one of the two visitor chairs by the bed. She was wearing a clean pair of jeans and an oversized T-shirt. Her hair looked freshly washed, but her eyes still had a hollow look and the skin was still tight across her cheekbones. Bella supposed it would take some time for Clara to gain back the weight she had lost so rapidly this summer. She would need proper rest, good nourishment, and, above all, love.

"Hi," Bella said. She remained standing; she didn't want to sit next to Clara; it might suggest a friendship that wasn't really there.

Clara looked up at her. "My parents are here," she said without expression. "They're picking up my stuff from the cottage and when they get back to the hospital I'll be discharged."

"Good," Bella said. She wondered what Mr. and Mrs. Crawford would feel when they saw that their daughter's room was a shrine to her ex-boyfriend. Would they be shocked? Or would they have known what to expect? "What about your car?" Bella asked. "You're not driving back to New York alone, are you?"

Clara laughed. "Are you kidding? I'm being watched like a hawk watches a mouse. My parents are going to find someone to drive my car home."

"That's good. I mean, it's good you won't be alone."

"I'll be a prisoner," Clara spit.

Bella bit back a sharp reply. *Patience*, she thought. *Be patient with her.* "They just care, Clara," she said. "That's what parents do."

Clara shrugged and looked toward the window. The blinds were lowered, but the strong late-morning August sun shone through. "I'm going to send Marc's wolf head coin back to his parents," she said after a moment. "It's not mine to keep and it never was. I can't believe I took it the way I did."

"You're doing the right thing giving it back," Bella said.

"I won't put a return address on the package. They won't know where it came from."

*Yes*, Bella thought. *They'll know.*

Clara turned back to Bella. "The overdose was accidental," she said with some vehemence. "I swear. I never meant to kill myself. The doctors told me the strength of the stuff I injected was double what I was used to, but I swear I didn't know that!"

But why had Clara chosen to shoot up in a public place? Had it been a cry for attention? Or had she cared so little for her life she didn't mind doing something not only illegal but also humiliating in full view of passersby? Whatever the case, Bella wasn't sure she believed Clara's overdose was unintentional. The only thing she was sure of was that her responsibility toward Clara was at an end. "Okay," she said.

"Bella?" Clara scratched a red patch on her wrist. "Thanks for coming to see me."

"Sure."

"None of my housemates have come by."

Bella said, "Oh?" but she wasn't surprised by this news. Clara had never spent any time with her housemates; she had almost seemed proud of that; she had called them all losers. Why should any of them care?

"If you hadn't been riding your bike past The Flipper the other day . . ."

"Don't think about it, Clara," Bella said quickly. "Just think about getting better."

"Yeah. My parents want me to see a therapist. I told them I'm not crazy, just sad. Marc made me sad. It's his fault."

*No*, Bella thought. *Marc hurt you, but you made yourself sad. Maybe you couldn't help it, but it wasn't Marc's fault.* "Being sad is hard," she said carefully. "It takes a lot out of you. I think maybe you should listen to your parents." Bella smiled a bit. "It's annoying, but they usually know best."

Clara shrugged. "I wonder if Marc will find out about what happened. I wonder if . . ." Clara looked up at Bella then, a pleading expression on her face. "Do you think he'll come back to me when he hears that I almost died?"

Bella swallowed hard. "I've got to go," she said. "I hope that your future is happy."

Clara shifted in the chair and looked again toward the window with its lowered blinds. Bella left the room and made her way to the main lobby. She did not check in with her grandmother. She didn't need her support, not at the moment. But it was nice to know that it was there.

Bella walked through the front entrance/exit of the main lobby and out into the welcoming summer sunshine. She knew that she would probably never see Clara again, though she might think of her from time to time. They had needed each other for a while. And now they needed each other no longer. Bella looked over her shoulder at the hospital building for a very brief moment and then she walked purposely toward where she had locked up her bike.

# Chapter 90

"Coming, coming," Frieda called to no one in particular as she hurried from the hall into the kitchen, dust cloth in hand. As she reached for the receiver of the phone she thought, *Good. It's Dad.*

"Hello?" she said.

"Frieda, it's Dad."

Frieda smiled. This was the second time she had known it was her father on the other end of the line and for about a half a second she wondered if her father had intuited that she wanted to talk to him. But that was wishful thinking. That was hoping for too deep a connection with the man who had walked away so long ago. The fact that he had called would have to be enough.

"Hey, Dad," she said. "What's up?"

Steve laughed. "Nothing worth telling. Besides, I'm more interested in what's going on back in Yorktide."

"Well," she said, "we had some excitement here." And she told her father about Bella's having come across Clara in the nick of time. "The hospital confirmed that she had overdosed on heroin," Frieda explained. "It seems it's everywhere these days."

"Damn," her father said. "That's pretty awful. You must have been a wreck when you learned what had happened."

"'A wreck' is putting it mildly."

"How is Bella faring after such a frightening experience?" her father asked.

"Strangely," Frieda told him, "or maybe not so strangely, Bella's involvement with this troubled girl helped her to let go of the guilt and grief that was hounding her and move forward. She's definitely in a better place now than she was at the start of the summer."

"Well, I'm glad for that, but I'm sorry Bella had to experience what she did. I've come across a fair share of people in my time who use hard drugs and it almost never ends well, for anyone even remotely involved with them. But if you say Bella's all right now I believe you. Look, if you think it appropriate, please tell her I think she was brave to stay with her friend until the ambulance came."

"I will, Dad," she promised. "I'll tell her. Hey, do you remember singing a song called 'The Tale of the Tadpole' to me when I was little? I don't actually remember—Mom says I was only about three—but the tune has stuck in my head all these years."

"Yes, I do, Frieda." Her father sang a line—"Through the wavelets and under the dew/the littlest tadpole sings how do ye do"—and then laughed. "I haven't been in voice in years. Sorry."

Frieda wiped the tears from her eyes and cleared her throat before going on. "Remember how at the start of the summer you apologized for not doing more when Aaron and Ariel died. I want you to know that I accept your apology."

There was a moment of silence before her father replied; Frieda wondered if he felt as emotional as she did at that moment. "I'm grateful," he said finally. "I probably don't deserve your kindness, but I am genuinely grateful for it."

"And one more thing." Frieda took a deep breath. "You also said you hoped to learn that you existed for me. You said you weren't asking for me to tell you that I loved you, but just that . . . just that you were alive for me."

"I remember," her father said quietly.

"Well, you do exist for me, Dad. You're my father and I love you." God, Frieda thought, it felt so good to say those words after so many years of silence!

"I love you, too, Frieda," her father said promptly. "I always have, though I've been lousy at showing it. Maybe you're right. Maybe I shouldn't have gone away. Maybe . . ."

"What's done is done. What matters is what's happening now. You have to believe that."

"I try."

"Dad? Do you think you'll ever come back to Yorktide? I mean, even just for a visit?"

"I wouldn't count on it, Frieda," her father replied. "But if I should get the itch I promise I'll let you know before I just show up on your mother's doorstep. Deal?"

"Deal," Frieda agreed. *I'll take what I can get*, she thought. *And I'll be glad for it.* "Oh, and Dad? Remember when I said I thought there was something between me and an old friend from school but that it didn't work out?"

"Yeah. I do."

"We're trying again. I was the one who put a halt on our friendship. I was scared and I felt I was betraying Aaron. But Mom and Phil helped me to gather my courage and ask if he'd like to start over."

"Good for you," her father said robustly. "Do I know this guy?"

"Jack Tennant. His wife died about four years ago. His family used to live on Trainor Lane."

"Sure," Steve said. "I remember them. Nice people. I hope they're well."

"They are. Jack said his parents always liked you. He said they were surprised when you left Yorktide."

Steve laughed. "I'm sure they weren't the only ones. Well, Frieda, I've got to go. Take care and we'll talk again. I promise."

Frieda chose to believe him. "Good-bye, Dad," she said. "I love you."

There was a beat of silence before her father spoke again. "I love you, too, Frieda," he said. And then he was gone.

Slowly, Frieda replaced the receiver. Before she could begin to process the momentous fact that her father had told her he loved her, her mother came into the kitchen.

"Who was on the phone?" she asked.

"It was Dad," Frieda said.

"How is he?"

"Okay, I guess. Mostly we talked about what's been going on here. Well, with the exception of your getting engaged. I didn't think that was my business to tell."

Ruby smiled. "I'll tell your father when I next talk to him. He'll be happy for me."

"Yeah," Frieda said. "I think he will. He told me that he loved me, Mom. And I told him the same."

Frieda saw tears spring to her mother's eyes. "I can't tell you how happy that makes me, Frieda. I know it's not an ideal relationship, but I really do believe that what exists now between you and your father is better than nothing. I really do."

*The new normal,* Frieda thought. *Aaron and Ariel gone and Dad back in my life.* "Mom," she said, "do you have a photo of Dad I could take back to Massachusetts with me?"

Ruby smiled. "As a matter of fact, I have one handy. I dug it out a few weeks ago in the hopes of your asking. See? I'm an optimist at heart. And you know there are albums full of photos upstairs. Take what you want."

Her mother went over to the drawer in which she kept recent unrecorded grocery receipts and rubber bands and chip clips and from it retrieved a four-by-six-inch photograph she handed to Frieda.

Frieda looked down at the image of her father holding her in his arms. She thought she must have been about two years old. She was wearing a pink dress and a white bonnet; her father was in a short-sleeved T-shirt and jeans. Both of them were smiling. "We look happy," she said quietly. "Genuinely happy."

"Things weren't always bad," Ruby said, tucking her arm through Frieda's. "And neither was your father."

"I guess if you loved him, Mom, he can't have been a total bum."

Ruby sighed. "He was awfully good-looking in those days, wasn't he? I wonder what havoc life has wreaked on him. Time gets to us all."

Until that moment Frieda hadn't made a decision whether or not to tell her mother about Steve Hitchens's heart attack. Now, she made that decision. She would fulfill her father's request to keep his illness a secret and spare her mother the pain knowing about it might bring. Frieda didn't enjoy keeping secrets from the people she loved, but in this case she honestly felt it was for the best.

"I finally understand why you're okay with Dad's calling like he does," she said. "I really do. He's part of us and we're part of him. We're a family."

"Good," Ruby said briskly, withdrawing her arm from Frieda's. "And I hope you can also understand why I'm thinking of retiring next February when I turn sixty-five."

"You!" Frieda cried. "Mom, I thought you'd work until your very last breath!"

"So did I, but I was young and naïve then. Now I'm older and wiser. And this darn leg acts up when I've been on my feet for a few hours. I'm worried I won't be able to do my job properly if I keep on for too much longer. Better to bow out gracefully while I still can."

"What does George think of your retiring?" Frieda asked.

Ruby laughed. "He's all for it. But if he thinks I'm suddenly going to become an old-fashioned housewife and greet him at the door each evening with a martini and a three-course meal in the oven he's sorely mistaken!"

"I don't think George is that kind of man, Mom."

"I know. It's just that I'm worried about who I'll become when I stop working. I've been working since I was fourteen, babysitting, mowing lawns, bagging groceries. I took whatever jobs I could get, and though some of them were unpleasant, I never wanted not to work."

"You'll still be you, Mom," Frieda assured her mother. "You'll still be the intelligent and curious and optimistic and loving woman we all know and admire."

Ruby put her hands to her face. "If I were the type to be embarrassed easily my cheeks would be aflame!"

"It's all true, Mom," Frieda insisted. "And once George retires in a few years, assuming he's waiting until he turns sixty-five as well, you'll have a companion in crime and who knows what adventures you'll have."

"Hmm. 'A companion in crime' does sound interesting! On another note entirely, I wanted to tell you that Ariel hasn't been to visit me in weeks. I have a feeling she's done her job for us and has decided to move on, now that she knows we'll be okay, you and me and Bella."

Frieda felt an enormous sense of relief upon hearing these words; the idea of Ariel's visitations had never sat easily with her. "I'm glad," she said. "Besides, you have enough to focus on in the here and now. Like planning a wedding!"

"You will stand up for me, won't you?" Ruby asked. "George has asked Phil to be his best man."

"I'd be honored, Mom. Nothing would make me happier."

Bella chose that moment to join them in the kitchen. "So," she said. "Not that I was eavesdropping or anything, but can I be a bridesmaid?"

"Of course!" Ruby said.

"Good. As long as I don't have to wear a scratchy dress with poofy sleeves. Ugh."

"No scratchy dresses with poofy sleeves, I swear." Ruby shuddered. "And no big white gown for me, either! Once was enough for that and look where it got me!"

Bella grinned and opened the door of the fridge. "What will you wear, Grandma?"

"I have no idea. But I've got plenty of time to shop around. The wedding isn't until next fall. There's no need to rush."

"I suppose I'll need something nice to wear, too," Frieda said. "I think a trip to the shopping center at Copley Place is in order, Bella. By the way, I was just talking to your grandfather and he asked for you."

Bella turned from the fridge to face her mother. "Really?"

"Yes. He said he thought that what you did for Clara was brave."

"Yeah?" Bella grinned. "Cool."

Yeah, Frieda thought. It was cool.

"Well, next time you talk to him," Bella said, "tell him I said hi."

"I will," Frieda promised. "I know he'll be glad. He is, after all, our family."

Bella put an arm around her grandmother's shoulders. "Hey,

speaking of family. I was thinking that maybe Mom and I could spend next summer here, too. Make it a tradition. What do you guys think?"

Frieda laughed. "I don't think we should put Grandma on the spot like this, Bella."

"Nonsense," Ruby said robustly. "I think it's a fantastic idea. And I won't take no for an answer."

# Epilogue

Bella tossed the flowered midi dress she had been planning to wear onto the bed. What had she been thinking? It was way too casual, like something you would wear to a party on the beach. She wanted to show respect for Phil on this big occasion. *I'll wear the plain blue dress*, she decided, taking it from her closet. With its high neckline and at-the-knee hem it was way more appropriate for the morning's event.

Actually, Bella thought as she pulled the dress over her head, this was a big occasion for everyone in her life, not only Phil. Last fall Bella had made good on her promise and contacted the offices of the Names Project AIDS Memorial Quilt to find out how to make and submit a panel in memory of Tony Worthington. Armed with instructions and advice, Ruby and Phil had constructed the panel together. Along with Tony's name and the dates of his birth and death it was decorated with meaningful images, like a whisk constructed of thin flexible wire that stood for Tony's passion for cooking. Cutouts of a paisley dog and a calico cat represented the endless hours Tony had dedicated to the local animal shelter. A border of hyacinth flowers embroidered in silk thread paid homage to Tony's continued presence in Phil's life. In the center of the panel there was a felt outline of a heart with Phil's and Tony's names stitched on to it in bright purple thread; both Tony and Phil were mad for purple.

Over thirty years after Tony's passing the completed panel had been sent off to the organization's headquarters along with an application form, a letter from Phil about Tony, and a photograph of Tony before he got sick. Today, Tony's friends would finally see his panel as part of a completed quilt on display at the public library in Congressville, Maine.

Bella reached for a tube of mascara and, looking into the mirror over her dresser, began to swipe it on her lashes. These days when she looked into the mirror she saw a very different person from the one she had seen there the previous spring. A happier person. Bella exchanged the tube of mascara for a tube of lip gloss; after applying it she slipped the tube into her bag. *Jewelry,* she thought. She would wear the silver hoop earrings her mother had given her for her eighteenth birthday last month and the matching silver necklace that had been a gift from her grandmother and George.

*I'm a happier person,* Bella thought as she fastened the chain around her neck, *and a wiser person.* Just before Bella had walked away from counseling the previous spring, Colleen had suggested she make a list of the positive qualities she had discovered in herself as a result of the trauma. The point of this exercise, Colleen explained, was to help the survivor realize she had a necessary role in life. But Bella had come up blank. Who could possibly find her necessary, the stupid sister and ungrateful daughter of the two most wonderful people in the world?

But shortly after returning to Warden the previous August, Bella had decided to give this exercise another try. This time she decided to list the good qualities she had discovered in herself during the summer in Yorktide. For one, she believed that she had genuinely helped Clara in some small way and the experience had taught her that if she focused less on wallowing in her own pain she would find the capacity to help relieve the pain of others. In January she had joined a local support group where she co-led discussions intended to help young people who had recently lost a close family member. The experience was fulfilling in ways that only a year ago Bella never would have thought possible.

Second, she had accepted her mother's relationship with Jack Tennant—they were getting married next year—and that meant she had matured. Third, Bella's friendship with Phil had deepened; he had trusted her enough to share the story of his own journey through loss and beyond and that meant that Phil believed she had something to offer him in return. Finally, Bella had found the courage to ask forgiveness from Kerri. She hadn't hurt Kerri purposely, but she had hurt her. Having Kerri back in her life was something for which Bella was seriously grateful.

Bella was also seriously pleased that she had done well in school this year and that she would graduate with a decent GPA. She had been accepted at a small college with a good reputation in Vermont and planned to spend the summer co-managing Wainscoting and Windowseats while Phil traveled through Italy. She would live with Ruby and George in the house on Kinders Lane. That house— well, that house with her grandmother in it!—was the heart of their family.

As important as doing well in school, Bella had found the courage to get her driver's license. She wasn't terribly comfortable behind the wheel, but neither was she terrified and she figured that since everything in life changed, it was likely that one day she would be comfortable driving and maybe even come to enjoy it. It was what Ariel would have wanted for her sister.

Ariel's locked diary was tucked safely in the top drawer of Bella's desk. Sometimes when she looked at the diary she remembered the time Clara had urged her to break its lock and that memory opened the door for lots of other memories of the strange weeks she had spent with Clara Crawford.

Clara's parents had contacted Bella shortly after they brought their daughter home to Whimsey Corner. They had thanked her and let her know that Clara was getting professional help. There had been no further contact and Bella was fine with this. She and Clara had only bonded because they were grieving. There had never been any real compatibility between them. Over time they might have found more prosaic things in common, like a preference for ranch-flavored potato chips or an abhorrence of wedge shoes, but maybe not. She had learned nothing about Clara but the fact that she was in pain. And Clara had learned nothing about Bella, either, aside from the fact of her grief. Bella wondered if years from now they would even remember each other's name and if it would matter.

"Bella! Let's go. We've got a two-hour drive ahead of us."

Bella glanced one last time in the mirror and, liking what she saw, she dashed to the door of her room. "Coming, Mom!"

"I had this weird thought," Bella said when they were about twenty minutes from their destination.

Frieda glanced at her daughter in the passenger seat beside her. "Weird in what way?" she asked.

"Weird as in it probably won't happen. I thought that maybe my grandfather would show up at the exhibition today."

"You're right," Frieda said. "It probably won't happen. But I'd bet he's thinking of Phil this morning."

In fact, Frieda thought, she was sure her father was with them all in spirit, as he had been at Christmas when everyone had gathered at the house on Kinders Lane. Bella had tasted her first eggnog and hated it; George had managed to blow a fuse due to his too-enthusiastic decorating scheme; Jack had been suffering a bad cold that left him only half-aware of the festivities going on around him. Ruby had sliced her finger with a knife whose handle was slippery with goose grease and Frieda had fallen on a patch of ice and for weeks had had the bruises to prove it. In spite of these calamities, it had been a perfect few days because they had all been together. "Minor disasters don't deserve the name disasters," Ruby had announced as they gathered around the kitchen table for dinner on Christmas Eve. "Obstacles to perfection make life more interesting."

Steve had called Christmas morning to wish everyone a happy holiday.

"Are you with friends, Dad?" Frieda had asked worriedly.

"I'm not alone," he told her. "Don't worry about me, Frieda. Please. Just hug your mother for me and give Bella a kiss and be sure Phil knows I was asking for him. Tell Jack he's got the best gal ever and say hello to that George fellow, too."

When Frieda hung up there were tears in her eyes. Tears of gratitude for all the love she possessed—including the love of Aaron and Ariel. Love, after all, never died with the death of the loved one. It just transformed into something greater than it ever had been.

Frieda continued to speak to her father on a fairly regular basis and back in April, around the time of Bella's birthday and the anniversary of the accident that had taken Aaron's and Ariel's lives, Frieda and Bella had received a box—no return address—that contained a delicately beautiful wooden sculpture of a mother and child embracing. With it was a brief note: *I thought I'd try my hand again.*

It had taken a lot of courage for her father to revisit his art, just as it had taken Frieda a lot of courage to embrace love once again. She and Jack were planning to wed the following summer, after which Frieda would sell the house in Warden and buy a new home with Jack in Yorktide. Bella had accepted this development with grace and maturity, though Frieda knew there must be a part of her daughter—as there was a part of her—that still felt a bit tentative about their new reality.

*The new reality,* Frieda thought. *Life without Aaron and Ariel.* Another anniversary of their deaths had come and gone. Frieda and Bella had paid an early-morning visit to the cemetery, where they reminisced about the good times all four had shared as a family. Afterward they had gone for a long walk through the Arnold Arboretum and then on to lunch at their favorite Italian restaurant, where they had toasted the memory of their loved ones. It had been a simple, quiet day, one without trauma if not entirely free of melancholy.

Frieda glanced down at her iPhone; GPS told her they were only moments away from the library. *My new reality,* she thought. *Life with the addition of Jack, my father, and new friends.* Upon her return to Massachusetts at the end of the previous summer, Frieda had made a conscious effort to meet new people, people who hadn't labeled her as a grim reminder of mortality. When she did run into her former friends around town they met with perfect politeness but little warmth and that was fine by Frieda. Neither Maddie nor Eva had ever managed to be comfortable with being uncomfortable. People did what it was in them to do, Frieda had realized, and you could ask no more of them.

"There's Jack's car," Bella noted as Frieda brought the Subaru to a stop outside the impressive library. "And Phil's, but I don't see George's Volvo."

Frieda turned to her daughter. "I know I've said this before, but thank you for encouraging Phil to do this."

Bella shrugged. "No problem. He's my friend. Besides, he taught me everything I know about wainscoting."

"I wonder how many hours a day you spend looking at that thing."

Ruby shrugged. "Two or three tops."

George was behind the wheel of his Volvo, and Ruby, seated next to him, was paying far less attention to the passing scenery than she was to the ring on her left hand. When she had accepted George's proposal last August she had insisted she didn't want an engagement ring—"I don't want us wasting our hard-earned money on something so frivolous"—but George had finally convinced her to pay a visit to Cross Jewelers in Portland. "They've been around since 1908 and are totally reputable," he told her. "Come on. At the very least it's an excuse for a road trip." Once she was in the store Ruby Hitchens's frugal soul had dashed out the back door, allowing her to succumb at long last to the allure of precious metal and stones. After some deliberation she chose the Lady Captain's ring, one of the jeweler's most popular designs. George chose the Sea Light Wedding Ring in hammered yellow gold.

"It's fun spoiling you," George said later, when they were sipping champagne at the Top of the East, Portland's only rooftop bar. "You'd better get used to it."

Ruby had reached for his hand. "George," she said, "you've been spoiling me in the best possible ways since the day we met."

"Where are we having lunch after the viewing?" George asked now. "I know virtually nothing about Congressville."

"I found a nice little bistro not far from the library," Ruby told him. "Now that I've got all this free time on my hands I told Phil I'd handle picking a place and making a reservation."

And the reason Ruby had time on her hands was because she had retired after her sixty-fifth birthday in February. Which wasn't to say she was idle. When she wasn't volunteering or leading passionate discussions with The Page Turners or taking long walks on Ogunquit Beach, she was planning her October wedding at York Harbor Inn and enjoying every moment of it. "I could do this professionally," she told Phil one afternoon after she had successfully negotiated a deal on the flowers from Pretty Blossoms. "You're forgetting one thing," Phil pointed out. "The Bridezillas." Ruby's sudden enthusiasm had come to a crashing halt. "Oh. Right. Them."

"Is Phil all packed and ready to go?" George asked.

Ruby laughed. "He's been packed for weeks." Phil had hired a manager who, with Bella, would run Wainscoting and Windowseats while he spent the summer in Italy, soaking up the culture, basking in the heat of the Mediterranean sun, and enjoying magnificent meals. "I hope this morning won't be too much of a trial for Phil," Ruby said as they crossed the Congressville town line. "Making the panel had its difficult moments."

"It will be an emotional experience, that's for sure," George said. "But we'll be there to support him."

Ruby nodded and thought of those who would not be present on this important occasion. Phil had sent a note to Tony's parents informing them of what he had done in memory of their son and inviting them to the opening day of the exhibition. The Worthingtons had not replied. And Ruby had informed Steve of the exhibition, but she was highly doubtful she would ever come face-to-face with Steve Hitchens again.

Still, further progress had been made. Not long after Christmas Steve had asked if he might speak with Bella. Bella had readily agreed. "He's nice," she told her mother and grandmother after the first call. "And his voice sounds kind of like yours, Mom, only deeper of course. Oh, and he asked if it would be okay if he had a recent picture of the three of us. He gave me a post office box number." So they had duly sent a few of the photos taken at the Christmas holidays.

Steve had also asked Ruby if he might call Phil, who did not so readily agree. "I feel so protective of you, Ruby; you know that," Phil had told her. "I feel my talking to Steve would be a betrayal of the bond you and I share."

"Talk to him if you want to, Phil," Ruby told him. "Or don't. But I shouldn't be a factor in your decision."

In the end Phil had agreed to accept a call from Steve, if only, he told Ruby, for the care Steve had shown Tony all those years ago.

"How did it go?" Ruby had asked afterward.

"I was unexpectedly moved," Phil admitted. "Whatever emotional walls I had constructed to keep from feeling anything warm toward him just fell apart the moment I heard his voice. The memories . . ."

"Yes," Ruby had said, placing her hand on her old friend's arm. "The memories."

"It's true, isn't it?" Phil had replied. "Love is love is love."

George turned onto Foyle Boulevard and Ruby spotted Frieda, Jack, Bella, and Phil standing on the steps of the imposing library building midway down the street. "Looks like we're the last to arrive," she said. "I'm not sure why, but it's important for Phil that we all go in together."

George parked the car alongside Jack's and together he and Ruby joined the others on the library steps. Frieda and Jack were holding hands. Bella was standing close to Phil, who wore a purple flower in the lapel of his charcoal-colored suit jacket.

"The big moment has finally arrived," Ruby said after she had greeted everyone.

As Frieda, Jack, George, and Bella moved toward the library doors, Phil put a hand on Ruby's arm. "It can't be," he murmured.

"What is it, Phil?" Ruby asked. "Do you feel all right? You look like you just saw a ghost."

"Close enough." Phil nodded toward an old black Cadillac that was just pulling up along the curb. A moment later an elderly couple began to emerge. "I'd recognize that car anywhere. It's the

Worthingtons. Tony's parents. They didn't respond to my invitation. I thought . . . I didn't think they would come."

Ruby watched as the elderly couple made their way toward the library. When they were at the foot of the stairs, Mr. Worthington raised his hand in greeting and Mrs. Worthington offered a tentative smile. "Love is love is love," Ruby whispered to her dear friend. "We can't ever forget that."

Please turn the page
for a very special Q&A
with Holly Chamberlin!

Q. In *Home for the Summer* you touch on drug addiction, a topic all too often in the news. What brought you to build this issue into the story?

A. Though I have in no way delved into the heart of the topic—this is after all a novel and not a scientific study or a social treatise—I did want to glance at the current problem of prescription drug abuse and its relation to heroin use. The prescribing and the abuse of opiates is a complicated issue and one I'm not qualified to speak to other than to present in the character of Clara one particular example of a person in a weakened psychological state who is vulnerable to people more concerned with making fast cash than with the sustaining of human life. And I want to be clear that I in no way blame the victims of these dealers. Besides legislation what is needed most is compassion.

Q. You tackle another difficult topic in this novel, namely the sudden loss of a close family member. How much did you draw on your own experiences in this regard?

A. So far, in my own life I've been exceptionally lucky. While it's true that my grandparents are gone and that two dear uncles and a wonderful aunt passed away at relatively young ages, both of my parents, my stepmother, and my brother are still here with me. As always, I researched the loss of a spouse/parent/sibling to gain insight into the experience. After that it's down to empathy and a sympathetic imagination to create a story that rings at least partially true both for those who have experienced a similar tragedy as well as for those who have not. Every situation is different and grief has as many shapes as there are people on this planet, but hopefully I've managed to get it right for Ruby, Frieda, and Bella.

Q. This is not the first novel in which you present several generations of a family interacting closely. Why does this dynamic interest you?

A. I've always been drawn to relationships with people either significantly older or younger than me and I think that has a lot to do with the fact that I grew up in a family that socialized across the generations. I can't get my head around the idea of spending quality time with only people my own age. Boring! And unnatural.

**Q. An important character in *Home for the Summer* is said to have lost his life partner to AIDS over thirty years before the opening of the novel. Why did you choose to make Phil's and Tony's experience a part of this story?**

A. Because the theme of love is important to the novel and because I remember. I was still living in New York City, my hometown, when the AIDS crisis hit. I remember the sense of fear and confusion. I was an undergraduate student at New York University, in the heart of Greenwich Village, so there was no avoiding (should I have wanted to, and I didn't) an awareness of the disease as it attacked classmates, friends, and colleagues. I don't think a crisis is ever really over or in the past. My friend Deborah Freedman, a Maine storyteller and quilter, was a vital part of the Names Project AIDS Memorial Quilt back then and to this day her work with the family and friends of victims—as well as with victims themselves—lives with her. Another friend, a Licensed Massage Therapist then working in San Francisco, offered her services gratis for those dying of the disease and still shares stories of her experiences in offering physical relief and hands-on compassion. None of us should ever forget.

**Q. What's next for Holly?**
A. More novels set in Yorktide, Maine, and its surrounds! Some will be set in the summer and others around Christmas, that "most wonderful time of the year."

# HOME FOR THE SUMMER

## Holly Chamberlin

### ABOUT THIS GUIDE

The suggested questions are included
to enhance your group's reading of
Holly Chamberlin's *Home for the Summer*.

# DISCUSSION QUESTIONS

1. Discuss Frieda's decision to allow her father back into her life. Could a good argument be made for her rejecting him out of hand? Do you agree with Frieda that the first eleven years of her life spent with her father count for something good in spite of her father's later neglectful behavior? Do you think her accepting the limitations her father puts on their renewed relationship was a smart thing for her to do? Should she have insisted on setting the rules of their relationship?

2. Bella talks with Phil about acceptance. She says, "Acceptance is a weird thing, isn't it? It can be sort of like giving up, like saying okay, even though I hate this I won't argue it anymore because I'm wiped out. Or it can be doing the mature thing and saying okay, I hate this, but you can give this to me and I'll agree to take it and, what's more, I'll try to understand it." Talk about the differing notions of acceptance.

3. Ruby's ongoing relationship with her ex-husband might strike some as unusual or possibly even as destructive to Ruby and/or to Frieda. Talk about this. For example, how much does Ruby's hesitation to accept George's marriage proposal have to do with her experience of being married to Steve and how much to a reluctance to give up a hard-won degree of independence? Ruby swears to Frieda that she was never a victim in her ill-fated marriage; she swears the choice to stay with him was hers to make. Do you think this assessment of her past decisions and emotional state is accurate or the product of long years in which Ruby's anger and shame have had time to abate? How much does Ruby's willingness to keep Steve in her life affect Frieda's decision to welcome him back?

4. Frieda wonders how much of her marriage to Aaron she will feel comfortable sharing with Jack should they decide to marry. Talk about a person's right to keep details of her past to herself, assuming the withholding of those details doesn't constitute a danger to anyone in the present. Would, for example, it be morally acceptable for Frieda not to share the handmade birthday cards Aaron made for her with a new husband? Would it be a kindness to her new husband to keep those romantic gifts from him? When does privacy become secrecy? Is full disclosure something that belongs only in a court of law or a business agreement?

5. Bella struggles with the decision to stick by Clara when Clara turns to heroin and makes the outrageous suggestion of a suicide pact. Discuss the factors that lead Bella to stay with Clara and the factors that finally allow her to walk away from the troubled young woman. When is self-preservation genuinely more important than the care of another person? When does an attempt at constructive care become destructive enabling? Have there been people in your life you have felt compelled to cut loose in order to maintain/regain your own peace of mind and emotional health?

6. Has anyone in your book group or among your friends and family seen an exhibition of the Names Project AIDS Memorial Quilt? If so, please share what you can of the experience with your fellow readers. Phil's decision to reach out to Mr. and Mrs. Worthington after their harsh treatment of him at the time of Tony's death demonstrates that he has truly forgiven Tony's parents. In turn, Mr. and Mrs. Worthington's decision to attend the exhibition demonstrates courage and a new enlightenment. Compare this moment of rapprochement and healing with the coming together of Steve Hitchens and his daughter after years of silence and misunderstanding.